PRAISE FOR RICHARD MATHESON

"One of the most important writers of the twentieth century."

—Ray Bradbury

"A long time ago I read *I Am Legend,* and I started writing horror about the same time. Been at it ever since. Matheson inspires, it's as simple as that."

—Brian Lumley

"Richard Matheson is one of the great names in American terror fiction."

—*The Philadelphia Inquirer*

"Nobody can top Matheson's talent for terror."

—Robert Bloch, author of *Psycho*

I AM LEGEND

RICHARD MATHESON

A TOM DOHERTY ASSOCIATES BOOK | NEW YORK

I AM LEGEND

THIS BOOK IS PRINTED ON ACID-FREE PAPER.

AN ORB EDITION
PUBLISHED BY TOM DOHERTY ASSOCIATES, INC.
175 FIFTH AVENUE
NEW YORK, NY 10010

TOR BOOKS ON THE WORLD WIDE WEB: http://www.tor.com

LIBRARY OF CONGRESS CATALOGING-IN-PUBLICATION DATA

MATHESON, RICHARD
    I AM LEGEND / RICHARD MATHESON. —1ST ORB PBK. ED.
        P.   CM.
    "A TOM DOHERTY ASSOCIATES BOOK."
    ISBN 0-312-86504-X
    1. VAMPIRES—FICTION.   I. TITLE.
PS3563.A8355I18   1997
813'.54—DC21   97-13698
                                                              CIP

PRINTED IN THE UNITED STATES OF AMERICA

25 26 27 28 29 30

CONTENTS

I AM LEGEND

PART ONE: January 1976

🔷🔷🔷

CHAPTER ONE

On those cloudy days, Robert Neville was never sure when sunset came, and sometimes they were in the streets before he could get back.

If he had been more analytical, he might have calculated the approximate time of their arrival; but he still used the lifetime habit of judging nightfall by the sky, and on cloudy days that method didn't work. That was why he chose to stay near the house on those days.

He walked around the house in the dull gray of afternoon, a cigarette dangling from the corner of his mouth, trailing threadlike smoke over his shoulder. He checked each window to see if any of the boards had been loosened. After violent attacks, the planks were often split or partially pried off, and he had to replace them completely; a job he hated. Today only one plank was loose. Isn't that amazing? he thought.

In the back yard he checked the hothouse and the water tank. Sometimes the structure around the tank might be weakened or its rain catchers bent or broken off. Sometimes they would lob rocks over the high fence around the hothouse, and occasionally they would tear through the overhead net and he'd have to replace panes.

Both the tank and the hothouse were undamaged today.

He went to the house for a hammer and nails. As he pushed open the front door, he looked at the distorted reflection of himself in the cracked mirror he'd fastened to the door a month ago. In a few days, jagged pieces of the silver-backed glass would start to fall off. Let 'em fall, he thought. It was the last damned mirror he'd put there; it wasn't worth it. He'd put garlic there instead. Garlic always worked.

He passed slowly through the dim silence of the living room, turned left into the small hallway, and left again into his bedroom.

Once the room had been warmly decorated, but that was in another time. Now it was a room entirely functional, and since Neville's bed and bureau took up so little space, he had converted one side of the room into a shop.

A long bench covered almost an entire wall, on its hardwood top a heavy band saw, a wood lathe, an emery wheel, and a vise. Above it, on the wall, were haphazard racks of the tools that Robert Neville used.

He took a hammer from the bench and picked out a few nails from one of the disordered bins. Then he went back outside and nailed the plank fast to the shutter. The unused nails he threw into the rubble next door.

For a while he stood on the front lawn looking up and down the silent length of Cimarron Street. He was a tall man, thirty-six, born of English-German stock, his features undistinguished except for the long, determined mouth and the bright blue of his eyes, which moved now over the charred ruins of the houses on each side of his. He'd burned them down to prevent *them* from jumping on his roof from the adjacent ones.

After a few minutes he took a long, slow breath and went back into the house. He tossed the hammer on the living-room couch, then lit another cigarette and had his midmorning drink.

Later he forced himself into the kitchen to grind up the five-day accumulation of garbage in the sink. He knew he should burn up the paper plates and utensils too, and dust the furniture and wash out the sinks and the bathtub and toilet, and change the sheets and pillowcase on his bed; but he didn't feel like it.

For he was a man and he was alone and these things had no importance to him.

⊏◇⊐

It was almost noon. Robert Neville was in his hothouse collecting a basketful of garlic.

In the beginning it had made him sick to smell garlic in such quantity; his stomach had been in a state of constant turmoil. Now the smell was in his house and in his clothes, and sometimes he thought it was even in his flesh. He hardly noticed it at all.

When he had enough bulbs, he went back to the house and dumped them on the drainboard of the sink. As he flicked the wall switch, the light flickered, then flared into normal brilliance. A disgusted hiss passed his clenched teeth. The generator was at it again. He'd have to get out that damned manual again and check the wiring. And, if it were too much trouble to repair, he'd have to install a new generator.

Angrily he jerked a high-legged stool to the sink, got a knife, and sat down with an exhausted grunt.

First, he separated the bulbs into the small, sickle-shaped cloves. Then he cut each pink, leathery clove in half, exposing the fleshy center buds. The air thickened with the musky, pungent odor. When it got too oppressive, he snapped on the air-conditioning unit and suction drew away the worst of it.

Now he reached over and took an icepick from its wall rack. He punched holes in each clove half, then strung them all together with wire until he had about twenty-five necklaces.

In the beginning he had hung these necklaces over the windows. But from a distance they'd thrown rocks until he'd been forced to cover the broken panes with plywood scraps. Finally one day he'd torn off the plywood and nailed up even rows of planks instead. It had made the house a gloomy sepulcher, but it was better than having rocks come flying into his rooms in a shower of splintered glass.

And, once he had installed the three air-conditioning units, it wasn't too bad. A man could get used to anything if he had to.

When he was finished stringing the garlic cloves, he went outside and nailed them over the window boarding, taking down the old strings, which had lost most of their potent smell.

He had to go through this process twice a week. Until he found something better, it was his first line of defense.

Defense? he often thought. For what?

All afternoon he made stakes.

He lathed them out of thick doweling, band-sawed into nine-inch lengths. These he held against the whirling emery stone until they were as sharp as daggers.

It was tiresome, monotonous work, and it filled the air with hot-smelling wood dust that settled in his pores and got into his lungs and made him cough.

Yet he never seemed to get ahead. No matter how many stakes he made, they were gone in no time at all. Doweling was getting harder to find, too. Eventually he'd have to lathe down rectangular lengths of wood. Won't *that* be fun? he thought irritably.

It was all very depressing and it made him resolve to find a better method of disposal. But how could he find it when they never gave him a chance to slow down and think?

As he lathed, he listened to records over the loudspeaker he'd set up in the bedroom—Beethoven's Third, Seventh, and Ninth symphonies. He was glad he'd learned early in life, from his mother, to appreciate this kind of music. It helped to fill the terrible void of hours.

From four o'clock on, his gaze kept shifting to the clock on the wall. He worked in silence, lips pressed into a hard line, a cigarette in the corner of his mouth, his eyes staring at the bit as it gnawed away the wood and sent floury dust filtering down to the floor.

Four-fifteen. Four-thirty. It was a quarter to five.

In another hour they'd be at the house again, the filthy bastards. As soon as the light was gone.

❉

He stood before the giant freezer, selecting his supper. His jaded eyes moved over the stacks of meats down to the frozen vegetables, down to the breads and pastries, the fruits and ice cream.

He picked out two lamb chops, string beans, and a small box of orange sherbet. He picked the boxes from the freezer and pushed shut the door with his elbow.

Next he moved over to the uneven stacks of cans piled to the ceiling. He took down a can of tomato juice, then left the room that had once belonged to Kathy and now belonged to his stomach.

He moved slowly across the living room, looking at the mural that covered the back wall. It showed a cliff edge, sheering off to green-blue ocean that surged and broke over black rocks. Far up in the clear blue sky, white sea gulls floated on the wind, and over on the right a gnarled tree hung over the precipice, its dark branches etched against the sky.

Neville walked into the kitchen and dumped the groceries on the table, his eyes moving to the clock. Twenty minutes to six. Soon now.

He poured a little water into a small pan and clanked it down on a stove burner. Next he thawed out the chops and put them under the broiler. By this time the water was boiling and he dropped in the frozen string beans and covered them, thinking that it was probably the electric stove that was milking the generator.

At the table he sliced himself two pieces of bread and poured himself a glass of tomato juice. He sat down and looked at the red second hand as it swept slowly around the clock face. The bastards ought to be here soon.

After he'd finished his tomato juice, he walked to the front door and went out onto the porch. He stepped off onto the lawn and walked down to the sidewalk.

The sky was darkening and it was getting chilly. He looked up and down Cimarron Street, the cool breeze ruffling his blond hair. That's what was wrong with these cloudy days; you never knew when they were coming.

Oh, well, at least they were better than those damned dust storms. With a shrug, he moved back across the lawn and into the house, locking and bolting the door behind him, sliding the thick bar into place. Then he went back into the kitchen, turned his chops, and switched off the heat under the string beans.

He was putting the food on his plate when he stopped and his eyes moved quickly to the clock. Six-twenty-five today. Ben Cortman was shouting.

"Come out, Neville!"

Robert Neville sat down with a sigh and began to eat.

He sat in the living room, trying to read. He'd made himself a whisky and soda at his small bar and he held the cold glass as he read a physiology text. From the speaker over the hallway door, the music of Schönberg was playing loudly.

Not loudly enough, though. He still heard them outside, their murmuring and their walkings about and their cries, their snarling and fighting among themselves. Once in a while a rock or brick thudded off the house. Sometimes a dog barked.

And they were all there for the same thing.

Robert Neville closed his eyes a moment and held his lips in a tight line. Then he opened his eyes and lit another cigarette, letting the smoke go deep into his lungs.

He wished he'd had time to soundproof the house. It wouldn't be so bad if it weren't that he had to listen to them. Even after five months, it got on his nerves.

He never looked at them any more. In the beginning he'd made a peephole in the front window and watched them. But then the women had seen him and had started striking vile postures in order to entice him out of the house. He didn't want to look at that.

He put down his book and stared bleakly at the rug, hearing *Verklärte Nacht* play over the loud-speaker. He knew he could put plugs in his ears to shut off the sound of them, but that would shut off the music too, and he didn't want to feel that they were forcing him into a shell.

He closed his eyes again. It was the women who made it so difficult, he thought, the women posing like lewd puppets in the night on the possibility that he'd see them and decide to come out.

A shudder ran through him. Every night it was the same. He'd be reading and listening to music. Then he'd start to think about sound-proofing the house, then he'd think about the women.

Deep in his body, the knotting heat began again, and he pressed his lips together until they were white. He knew the feeling well and it enraged him that he couldn't combat it. It grew and grew until he couldn't sit still any more. Then he'd get up and pace the floor, fists bloodless at his sides. Maybe he'd set up the movie projector or eat something or have too much to drink or turn the music up so loud it hurt his ears. He had to do something when it got really bad.

He felt the muscles of his abdomen closing in like tightening coils. He picked up the book and tried to read, his lips forming each word slowly and painfully.

But in a moment the book was on his lap again. He looked at the bookcase across from him. All the knowledge in those books couldn't put out the fires in him; all the words of centuries couldn't end the wordless, mindless craving of his flesh.

The realization made him sick. It was an insult to a man. All right, it was a natural drive, but there was no outlet for it any more. They'd forced celibacy on him; he'd have to live with it. You have a mind, don't you? he asked himself. Well, *use* it!

He reached over and turned the music still louder, then forced himself to read a whole page without pause. He read about blood cells being forced through membranes, about pale lymph carrying the wastes through tubes blocked by lymph nodes, about lymphocytes and phagocytic cells.

". . . to empty, in the left shoulder region, near the thorax, into a large vein of the blood circulating system."

The book shut with a thud.

Why didn't they leave him alone? Did they think they could *all* have him? Were they so stupid they thought that? Why did they keep coming every night? After five months, you'd think they'd give up and try elsewhere.

He went over to the bar and made himself another drink. As he turned back to his chair he heard stones rattling down across the roof and landing with thuds in the shrubbery beside the house. Above the noises, he heard Ben Cortman shout as he always shouted.

"Come out, Neville!"

Someday I'll get that bastard, he thought as he took a big swallow of the bitter drink. Someday I'll knock a stake right through his goddamn chest. I'll make one a foot long for him, a special one with ribbons on it, the bastard.

Tomorrow. Tomorrow he'd soundproof the house. His fingers drew into white-knuckled fists. He couldn't stand thinking about those women. If he didn't hear them, maybe he wouldn't think about them. Tomorrow. Tomorrow.

The music ended and he took a stack of records off the turntable and slid them back into their cardboard envelopes. Now he could hear them even more clearly outside. He reached for the first new record he could get and put it on the turntable and twisted the volume up to its highest point.

"The Year of the Plague," by Roger Leie, filled his ears. Violins scraped and whined, tympani thudded like the beats of a dying heart, flutes played weird, atonal melodies.

With a stiffening of rage, he wrenched up the record and snapped it over his right knee. He'd meant to break it long ago. He walked on rigid legs to the kitchen and flung the pieces into the trash box. Then he stood in the dark kitchen, eyes tightly shut, teeth clenched, hands clamped over his ears. Leave me alone, leave me alone, *leave me alone!*

No use, you couldn't beat them at night. No use trying; it was their special time. He was acting very stupidly, trying to beat them. Should he watch a movie? No, he didn't feel like setting up the projector. He'd go to bed and put the plugs in his ears. It was what he ended up doing every night, anyway.

Quickly, trying not to think at all, he went to the bedroom and undressed. He put on pajama bottoms and went into the bathroom. He never wore pajama tops; it was a habit he'd acquired in Panama during the war.

As he washed, he looked into the mirror at his broad chest, at the dark hair swirling around the nipples and down the center line of his chest. He looked at the ornate cross he'd had tattooed on his chest one night in Panama when he'd been drunk. What a fool I was in those days! he thought. Well, maybe that cross had saved his life.

He brushed his teeth carefully and used dental floss. He tried to take good care of his teeth because he was his own dentist now. Some things could go to pot, but not his health, he thought. Then why don't you stop pouring alcohol into yourself? he thought. Why don't you shut the hell up? he thought.

Now he went through the house, turning out lights. For a few minutes he looked at the mural and tried to believe it was really the ocean. But how could he believe it with all the bumpings and the scrapings, the howlings and snarlings and cries in the night?

He turned off the living-room lamp and went into the bedroom.

He made a sound of disgust when he saw that sawdust covered the bed. He brushed it off with snapping hand strokes, thinking that he'd better build a partition between the shop and the sleeping portion of the room. Better do this and better do that, he thought morosely. There were so many damned things to do, he'd never get to the real problem.

He jammed in his earplugs and a great silence engulfed him. He turned off the light and crawled in between the sheets. He looked at the radium-faced clock and saw that it was only a few minutes past ten. Just as well, he thought. This way I'll get an early start.

He lay there on the bed and took deep breaths of the darkness, hoping for sleep. But the silence didn't really help. He could still see them out there, the white-faced men prowling around his house, looking ceaselessly for a way to get in at him. Some of them, probably, crouching on their haunches like dogs, eyes glittering at the house, teeth slowly grating together; back and forth, back and forth.

And the women . . .

Did he have to start thinking about *them* again? He tossed over on his stomach with a curse and pressed his face into the hot pillow. He lay there, breathing heavily, body writhing slightly on the sheet. Let the morning come. His mind spoke the words it spoke every night. Dear God, let the morning come.

He dreamed about Virginia and he cried out in his sleep and his fingers gripped the sheets like frenzied talons.

CHAPTER TWO

The alarm went off at five-thirty and Robert Neville reached out a numbed arm in the morning gloom and pushed in the stop.

He reached for his cigarettes and lit one, then sat up. After a few moments he got up and walked into the dark living room and opened the peephole door.

Outside, on the lawn, the dark figures stood like silent soldiers on duty. As he watched, some of them started moving away, and he heard them muttering discontentedly among themselves. Another night was ended.

He went back to the bedroom, switched on the light, and dressed. As he was pulling on his shirt, he heard Ben Cortman cry out, "Come out, Neville!"

And that was all. After that, they all went away weaker, he knew, than when they had come. Unless they had attacked one of their own. They did that often. There was no union among them. Their need was their only motivation.

After dressing, Neville sat down on his bed with a grunt and penciled his list for the day:

Lathe at Sears
Water
Check generator
Doweling (?)
Usual

Breakfast was hasty: a glass of orange juice, a slice of toast, and two cups of coffee. He finished it quickly, wishing he had the patience to eat slowly.

After breakfast he threw the paper plate and cup into the trash box and brushed his teeth. At least I have one good habit, he consoled himself.

The first thing he did when he went outside was look at the sky. It was clear, virtually cloudless. He could go out today. Good.

As he crossed the porch, his shoe kicked some pieces of the mirror. Well, the damn thing broke just as I thought it would, he thought. He'd clean it up later.

One of the bodies was sprawled on the sidewalk; the other one was half concealed in the shrubbery. They were both women. They were almost always women.

He unlocked the garage door and backed his Willys station wagon into the early-morning crispness. Then he got out and pulled down the back gate. He put on heavy gloves and walked over to the woman on the sidewalk.

There was certainly nothing attractive about them in the daylight, he thought, as he dragged them across the lawn and threw them up on the canvas tarpaulin. There wasn't a drop left in them; both women were the color of fish out of water. He raised the gate and fastened it.

He went around the lawn then, picking up stones and bricks and putting them into a cloth sack. He put the sack in the station wagon and then took off his gloves. He went inside the house, washed his hands, and made lunch: two sandwiches, a few cookies, and a thermos of hot coffee.

When that was done, he went into the bedroom and got his bag of stakes. He slung this across his back and buckled on the holster that held his mallet. Then he went out of the house, locking the front door behind him.

He wouldn't bother searching for Ben Cortman that morning; there were too many other things to do. For a second, he thought about the soundproofing job he'd resolved to do on the house. Well, the hell with it, he thought. I'll do it tomorrow or some cloudy day.

He got into the station wagon and checked his list. "Lathe at Sears"; that was first. After he dumped the bodies, of course.

He started the car and backed quickly into the street and headed for Compton Boulevard. There he turned right and headed east. On both sides of him the houses stood silent, and against the curbs cars were parked, empty and dead.

Robert Neville's eyes shifted down for a moment to the fuel gauge. There was still a half tank, but he might as well stop on Western Avenue and fill it. There was no point in using any of the gasoline stored in the garage until he had to.

He pulled into the silent station and braked. He got a barrel of gasoline and siphoned it into his tank until the pale amber fluid came gushing out of the tank opening and ran down onto the cement.

He checked the oil, water, battery water, and tires. Everything was in good condition. It usually was, because he took special care of the car. If it ever broke down so that he couldn't get back to the house by sunset . . .

Well, there was no point in even worrying about that. If it ever happened, that was the end.

Now he continued up Compton Boulevard past the tall oil derricks, through Compton, through all the silent streets. There was no one to be seen anywhere.

But Robert Neville knew where they were.

The fire was always burning. As the car drew closer, he pulled on his gloves and gas mask and watched through the eyepieces the sooty pall of smoke hovering above the earth. The entire field had been excavated into one gigantic pit; that was in June 1975.

Neville parked the car and jumped out, anxious to get the job over with quickly. Throwing the catch and jerking down the rear gate, he pulled out one of the bodies and dragged it to the edge of the pit. There he stood it on its feet and shoved.

The body bumped and rolled down the steep incline until it settled on the great pile of smoldering ashes at the bottom.

Robert Neville drew in harsh breaths as he hurried back to the station wagon. He always felt as though he were strangling when he was here, even though he had the gas mask on.

Now he dragged the second body to the brink of the pit and pushed it over. Then, after tossing the sack of rocks down, he hurried back to the car and sped away.

After he'd driven a half mile, he skinned off the mask and gloves and tossed them into the back. His mouth opened and he drew in deep lungfuls of fresh air. He took the flask from the glove compartment and took a long drink of burning whisky. Then he lit a cigarette and inhaled deeply. Sometimes he had to go to the burning pit every day for weeks at a time, and it always made him sick.

Somewhere down there was Kathy.

On the way to Inglewood he stopped at a market to get some bottled water.

As he entered the silent store, the smell of rotted food filled his nostrils. Quickly he pushed a metal wagon up and down the silent, dust-thick aisles, the heavy smell of decay setting his teeth on edge, making him breathe through his mouth.

He found the water bottles in back, and also found a door opening on a flight of stairs. After putting all the bottles into the wagon, he went up the stairs. The owner of the market might be up there; he might as well get started.

There were two of them. In the living room, lying on a couch, was a woman about thirty years old, wearing a red housecoat. Her chest rose and fell slowly as she lay there, eyes closed, her hands clasped over her stomach.

Robert Neville's hands fumbled on the stake and mallet. It was always hard when they were alive; especially with women. He could feel that senseless demand returning again, tightening his muscles. He forced it down. It was insane, there was no rational argument for it.

She made no sound except for a sudden, hoarse intake of breath. As he walked into the bedroom, he could hear a sound like the sound of water running. Well, what *else* can I do? he asked himself, for he still had to convince himself he was doing the right thing.

He stood in the bedroom doorway, staring at the small bed by the window, his throat moving, breath shuddering in his chest. Then, driven on, he walked to the side of the bed and looked down at her.

Why do they all look like Kathy to me? he thought, drawing out the second stake with shaking hands.

Driving slowly to Sears, he tried to forget by wondering why it was that only wooden stakes should work.

He frowned as he drove along the empty boulevard, the only sound the muted growling of the motor in his car. It seemed fantastic that it had taken him five months to start wondering about it.

Which brought another question to mind. How was it that he always managed to hit the heart? It had to be the heart; Dr. Busch had said so. Yet he, Neville, had no anatomical knowledge.

His brow furrowed. It irritated him that he should have gone through this hideous process so long without stopping once to question it.

He shook his head. No, I should think it over carefully, he thought, I should collect all the questions before I try to answer them. Things should be done the right way, the scientific way.

Yeah, yeah, yeah, he thought, shades of old Fritz. That had been his father's name. Neville had loathed his father and fought the acquisition of his father's logic and mechanical facility every inch of the way. His father had died denying the vampire violently to the last.

At Sears he got the lathe, loaded it into the station wagon, then searched the store.

There were five of them in the basement, hiding in various shadowed places. One of them Neville found inside a display freezer. When he saw the man lying there in this enamel coffin, he had to laugh; it seemed such a funny place to hide.

Later, he thought of what a humorless world it was when he could find amusement in such a thing.

About two o'clock he parked and ate his lunch. Everything seemed to taste of garlic.

And that set him wondering about the effect garlic had on them. It must have been the smell that chased them off, but why?

They were strange, the facts about them: their staying inside by day, their avoidance of garlic, their death by stake, their reputed fear of crosses, their supposed dread of mirrors.

Take that last, now. According to legend, they were invisible in mirrors, but he knew that was untrue. As untrue as the belief that they transformed themselves into bats. That was a superstition that logic plus observation had easily disposed of. It was equally foolish to believe that they could transform themselves into wolves. Without a doubt there were vampire dogs; he had seen and heard them outside his house at night. But they were only dogs.

Robert Neville compressed his lips suddenly. Forget it, he told himself; you're not ready yet. The time would come when he'd take a crack at it, detail for detail, but the time wasn't now. There were enough things to worry about now.

After lunch, he went from house to house and used up all his stakes. He had forty-seven stakes.

CHAPTER THREE

"The strength of the vampire is that no one will believe in him."

Thank *you*, Dr. Van Helsing, he thought, putting down his copy of *Dracula*. He sat staring moodily at the bookcase, listening to Brahms' second piano concerto, a whisky sour in his right hand, a cigarette between his lips.

It was true. The book was a hodgepodge of superstitions and soap-opera clichés, but that line was true; no one had believed in them, and how could they fight something they didn't even believe in?

That was what the situation had been. Something black and of the night had come crawling out of the Middle Ages. Something with no framework or credulity, something that had been consigned, fact and figure, to the pages of imaginative literature. Vampires were passé, Summers' idylls or Stoker's melodramatics or a brief inclusion in the Britannica or grist for the pulp writer's mill or raw material for the B-film factories. A tenuous legend passed from century to century.

Well, it was true.

He took a sip from his drink and closed his eyes as the cold liquid trickled down his throat and warmed his stomach. True, he thought, but no one ever got the chance to know it. Oh, they knew it was something, but it couldn't be that—not *that*. *That* was imagination, *that* was superstition, there was no such thing as *that*.

And, before science had caught up with the legend, the legend had swallowed science and everything.

He hadn't found any doweling that day. He hadn't checked the generator. He hadn't cleaned up the pieces of mirror. He hadn't eaten supper; he'd lost his appetite. That wasn't hard. He lost it most of the time. He couldn't do the things he'd done all afternoon and then come home to a hearty meal. Not even after five months.

He thought of the eleven—no, the twelve children that afternoon, and he finished his drink in two swallows.

He blinked and the room wavered a little before him. You're getting blotto, Father, he told himself. So what? he returned. Has anyone more right?

He tossed the book across the room. Begone, Van Helsing and Mina and Jonathan and blood-eyed Count and all! All figments, all driveling extrapolations on a somber theme.

A coughing chuckle emptied itself from his throat. Outside, Ben Cortman called for him to come out. Be right out, Benny, he thought. Soon as I get my tuxedo on.

He shuddered and gritted his teeth edges together. Be right out. Well, why not? Why *not* go out? It was a sure way to be free of them.

Be one of them.

He chuckled at the simplicity of it, then shoved himself up and walked crookedly to the bar. Why not? His mind plodded on. Why go through all this complexity when a flung-open door and a few steps would end it all?

For the life of him, he didn't know. There was, of course, the faint possibility that others like him existed somewhere, trying to go on, hoping that someday they would be among their own kind again. But how could he ever find them if they weren't within a day's drive of his house?

He shrugged and poured more whisky in the glass; he'd given up the use of jiggers months ago. Garlic on the windows and nets over the hothouse and burn the bodies and cart the rocks away and, fraction of an inch by fraction of an inch, reduce their unholy numbers. Why kid himself? He'd never find anyone else.

His body dropped down heavily on the chair. Here we are, kiddies, sitting like a bug in a rug, snugly, surrounded by a battalion of bloodsuckers who wish no more than to sip freely of my bonded, 100-proof hemoglobin. Have a drink, men, this one's really on me.

His face twisted into an expression of raw, unqualified hatred. *Bastards!* I'll kill every mother's son of you before I'll give in! His right hand closed like a clamp and the glass shattered in his grip.

He looked down, dull-eyed, at the fragments on the floor, at the jagged piece of glass still in his hand, at the whisky-diluted blood dripping off his palm.

Wouldn't they like to get some of it, though? he thought. He started up with a furious lurch and almost opened the door so he could wave the hand in their faces and hear them howl.

Then he closed his eyes and a shudder ran through his body. Wise up, buddy, he thought. Go bandage your goddamn hand.

He stumbled into the bathroom and washed his hand carefully, gasping as he daubed iodine into the sliced-open flesh. Then he bandaged it clumsily, his broad chest rising and falling with jerky movements, sweat dripping from his forehead. I need a cigarette, he thought.

In the living room again, he changed Brahms for Bernstein and lit a cigarette. What will I do if I ever run out of coffin nails? he wondered, looking at the cigarette's blue trailing smoke. Well, there wasn't much chance of that. He had about a thousand cartons in the closet of Kathy's—

He clenched his teeth together. In the closet of the *larder*, the *larder*, the *larder*.

Kathy's room.

He sat staring with dead eyes at the mural while "The Age of Anxiety" pulsed in his ears. Age of anxiety, he mused. You thought you had anxiety, Lenny boy. Lenny and Benny; you two should meet. Composer, meet corpse. Mamma, when I grow up I wanna be a wampir like Dada. Why, bless you, hon, of course you shall.

The whisky gurgled into the glass. He grimaced a little at the pain in his hand and shifted the bottle to his left hand.

He sat down and sipped. Let the jagged edge of sobriety be now dulled, he thought. Let the crumby balance of clear vision be expunged, but post haste. I hate 'em.

Gradually the room shifted on its gyroscopic center and wove and undulated about his chair. A pleasant haze, fuzzy at the edges, took over sight. He looked at the glass, at the record player. He let his head flop from side to side. Outside, they prowled and muttered and waited.

Pore vampires, he thought, pore little cusses, pussyfootin' round my house, so thirsty, so all forlorn.

A thought. He raised a forefinger that wavered before his eyes.

Friends, I come before you to discuss the vampire; a minority element if there ever was one, and there was one.

But to concision: I will sketch out the basis for my thesis, which thesis is this: Vampires are prejudiced against.

The keynote of minority prejudice is this: They are loathed because they are feared. Thus . . .

He made himself a drink. A long one.

At one time, the Dark and Middle Ages, to be succinct, the vampire's power was great, the fear of him tremendous. He was anathema and still remains anathema. Society hates him without ration.

But are his needs any more shocking than the needs of other animals and men? Are his deeds more outrageous than the deeds of the parent who drained the spirit from his child? The vampire may foster quickened heartbeats and levitated hair. But is he worse than the parent who gave to society a neurotic child who became a politician? Is he worse than the manufacturer who set up belated foundations with the money he made by handing bombs and guns to suicidal nationalists? Is he worse than the distiller who gave bastardized grain juice to stultify further the brains of those who, sober, were incapable of a progressive thought? (Nay, I apologize for this calumny; I nip the brew that feeds me.) Is he worse, then, than the publisher who filled ubiquitous racks with lust and death wishes? Really, now, search your soul, lovie—is the vampire so bad?

All he does is drink blood.

Why, then, this unkind prejudice, this thoughtless bias? Why cannot the vampire live where he chooses? Why must he seek out hiding places where none can find him out? Why do you wish him destroyed? Ah, see, you have turned the poor guileless innocent into a haunted animal. He has no means of support, no measures for proper education, he has not the voting franchise. No wonder he is compelled to seek out a predatory nocturnal existence.

Robert Neville grunted a surly grunt. Sure, sure, he thought, but would you let your sister marry one?

He shrugged. You got me there, buddy, you got me there.

The music ended. The needle scratched back and forth in the black grooves. He sat there, feeling a chill creeping up his legs. That's what was wrong with drinking too much. You became immune to drunken delights. There was no solace in liquor. Before you got happy, you collapsed. Already the room was straightening out, the sounds outside were starting to nibble at his eardrums.

"Come out, Neville!"

His throat moved and a shaking breath passed his lips. Come out.

The women were out there, their dresses open or taken off, their flesh waiting for his touch, their lips waiting for—

My blood, my *blood*!

As if it were someone else's hand, he watched his whitened fist rise up slowly, shuddering, to drive down on his leg. The pain made him suck in a breath of the house's stale air. Garlic. Everywhere the smell of garlic. In his clothes and in the furniture and in his food and even in his drink. Have a garlic and soda; his mind rattled out the attempted joke.

He lurched up and started pacing. What am I going to do now? Go through the routine again? I'll save you the trouble. Reading-drinking-soundproof-the-house—the women. The women, the lustful, bloodthirsty, naked women flaunting their hot bodies at him. No, not hot.

A shuddering whine wrenched up through his chest and throat. Goddamn them, what were they waiting for? Did they think he was going to come out and hand himself over?

Maybe I am, maybe I am. He actually found himself jerking off the crossbar from the door. Coming, girls, I'm coming. Wet your lips, now.

Outside, they heard the bar being lifted, and a howl of anticipation sounded in the night.

Spinning, he drove his fists one after the other into the wall until he'd cracked the plaster and broken his skin. Then he stood there trembling helplessly, his teeth chattering.

After a while it passed. He put the bar back across the door and went into the bedroom. He sank down on the bed and fell back on the pillow with a groan. His left hand beat once, feebly, on the bedspread.

Oh, *God*, he thought, how long, how long?

CHAPTER FOUR

The alarm never went off because he'd forgotten to set it. He slept soundly and motionlessly, his body like cast iron. When he finally opened his eyes, it was ten o'clock.

With a disgusted muttering, he struggled up and dropped his legs over the side of the bed. Instantly his head began throbbing as if his brains were trying to force their way through his skull. Fine, he thought, a hangover. That's all I need.

He pushed himself up with a groan and stumbled into the bathroom, threw water in his face and splashed some over his head. No good, his mind complained, no good. I still feel like hell. In the mirror his face was gaunt, bearded, and very much like the face of a man in his forties. Love, your magic spell is everywhere; inanely, the words flapped across his brain like wet sheets in a wind.

He walked slowly into the living room and opened the front door. A curse fell thickly from his lips at the sight of the woman crumpled across the sidewalk. He started to tighten angrily, but it made his head throb too much and he had to let it go. I'm sick, he thought.

The sky was gray and dead. Great! he thought. Another day stuck in this boarded-up rat hole! He slammed the door viciously, then winced, groaning, at the brain-stabbing noise. Outside, he heard the rest of the mirror fall out and shatter on the porch cement. Oh, *great!* His lips contorted back into a white twist of flesh.

Two cups of burning black coffee only made his stomach feel worse. He put down the cup and went into the living room. To hell with it, he thought, I'll get drunk again.

But the liquor tasted like turpentine, and with a rasping snarl he flung the glass against the wall and stood watching the liquor run down onto the rug. Hell, I'm runnin' out of glasses. The thought irritated him while breath struggled in through his nostrils and out again in faltering bursts.

He sank down on the couch and sat there, shaking his head slowly. It was no use; they'd beaten him, the black bastards had beaten him.

That restless feeling again; the feeling as if he were expanding and the house were contracting and any second now he'd go bursting through its frame in an explosion of wood, plaster, and brick. He got up and moved quickly to the door, his hands shaking.

On the lawn, he stood sucking in great lungfuls of the wet morning air, his face turned away from the house he hated. But he hated the other houses around there too, and he hated the pavement and the sidewalks and the lawns and everything that was on Cimarron Street.

It kept building up. And suddenly he knew he had to get out of there. Cloudy day or not, he had to get out of there.

He locked the front door, unlocked the garage, and dragged up the thick door on its overhead hinges. He didn't bother putting down the door. I'll be back soon, he thought. I'll just go away for a while.

He backed the station wagon quickly down the driveway, jerked it around, and pressed down hard on the accelerator, heading for Compton Boulevard. He didn't know where he was going.

He went around the corner doing forty and jumped that to sixty-five before he'd gone another block. The car leaped forward under his foot and he kept the accelerator on the floor, forced down by a rigid leg. His hands were like carved ice on the wheel and his face was the face of a statue. At eighty-nine miles an hour, he shot down the lifeless, empty boulevard, one roaring sound in the great stillness.

Things rank and gross in nature possess it merely, he thought as he walked slowly across the cemetery lawn.

The grass was so high that the weight of it had bent it over and it crunched under his heavy shoes as he walked. There was no sound but that of his shoes and the now senseless singing of birds. Once I thought they sang because everything was right with the world, Robert Neville thought. I know now I was wrong. They sing because they're feeble-minded.

He had raced six miles, the gas pedal pressed to the floor, before he'd realized where he was going. It was strange the way his mind and body had kept it secret from his consciousness. Consciously, he'd known only that he was sick and depressed and had to get away from the house. He didn't know he was going to visit Virginia.

But he'd driven there directly and as fast as he could. He'd parked at the curb and entered through the rusted gate, and now his shoes were pressing and crackling through the thick grass.

How long had it been since he'd come here? It must have been at least a month. He wished he'd brought flowers, but then, he hadn't realized he was coming here until he was almost at the gate.

His lips pressed together as an old sorrow held him again. Why couldn't he have Kathy there too? Why had he followed so blindly, listening to those fools who set up their stupid regulations during the plague? If only she could be there, lying across from her mother.

Don't start that again, he ordered himself.

Drawing closer to the crypt, he stiffened as he noticed that the iron door was slightly ajar. Oh, *no*, he thought. He broke into a run across the wet grass. If they've been at her, I'll burn down the city, he vowed. I swear to God, I'll burn it to the ground if they've touched her.

He flung open the door and it clanged against the marble wall with a hollow, echoing sound. His eyes moved quickly to the marble base on which the sealed casket rested.

The tension sank; he drew in breath again. It was still there, untouched.

Then, as he started in, he saw the man lying in one corner of the crypt, body curled up on the cold floor.

With a grunt of rage, Robert Neville rushed at the body, and, grabbing the man's coat in taut fingers, he dragged him across the floor and flung him violently out onto the grass. The body rolled onto its back, the white face pointing at the sky.

Robert Neville went back into the crypt, chest rising and falling with harsh movements. Then he closed his eyes and stood with his palms resting on the cover of the casket.

I'm here, he thought. I'm back. Remember me.

He threw out the flowers he'd brought the time before and cleared away the few leaves that had blown in because the door had been opened.

Then he sat down beside the casket and rested his forehead against its cold metal side.

Silence held him in its cold and gentle hands.

If I could die now, he thought; peacefully, gently, without a tremor or a crying out. If I could be with her. If I could believe I would be with her.

His fingers tightened slowly and his head sank forward on his chest.

Virginia. Take me where you are.

A tear, crystal, fell across his motionless hand. . . .

He had no idea how long he'd been there. After a while, though, even the deepest sorrow faltered, even the most penetrating despair lost its scalpel edge. The flagellant's curse, he thought, to grow inured even to the whip.

He straightened up and stood. Still alive, he thought, heart beating senselessly, veins running without point, bones and muscles and tissue all alive and functioning with no purpose at all.

A moment longer he stood looking down at the casket, then he turned away with a sigh and left, closing the door behind him quietly so as not to disturb her sleep.

He'd forgotten about the man. He almost tripped over him now, stepping aside with a muttered curse and starting past the body.

Then, abruptly, he turned back.

What's this? He looked down incredulously at the man. The man was dead; really dead. But how could that be? The change had occurred so quickly, yet already the man looked and smelled as though he'd been dead for days.

His mind began churning with a sudden excitement. Something had killed the vampire; something brutally effective. The heart had not been touched, no garlic had been present, and yet . . .

It came, seemingly, without effort. Of course—the daylight!

A bolt of self-accusation struck him. To know for five months that they remained indoors by day and never *once* to make the connection! He closed his eyes, appalled by his own stupidity.

The rays of the sun; the infrared and ultraviolet. It had to be them. But why? Damn it, why didn't he know anything about the effects of sunlight on the human system?

Another thought: That man had been one of the true vampires; the living dead. Would sunlight have the same effect on those who were still alive?

The first excitement he'd felt in months made him break into a run for the station wagon.

As the door slammed shut beside him, he wondered if he should have taken away the dead man. Would the body attract others, would they invade the crypt? No, they wouldn't go near the casket, anyway; it was sealed with garlic. Besides, the man's blood was dead now, it—

Again his thoughts broke off as he leaped to another conclusion. The sun's rays must have done something to their blood!

Was it possible, then, that all things bore relations to the blood? The garlic, the cross, the mirror, the stake, daylight, the earth some of them slept in? He didn't see how, and yet . . .

He had to do a lot of reading, a lot of research. It might be just the thing he needed. He'd been planning for a long time to do it, but lately it seemed as if he'd forgotten it altogether. Now this new idea started the desire again.

He started the car and raced up the street, turning off into a res-
idential section and pulling up before the first house he came to.

He ran up the pathway to the front door, but it was locked and he
couldn't force it in. With an impatient growl, he ran to the next
house. The door was open and he ran to the stairs through the darkened living room and jumped up the carpeted steps two at a time.

He found the woman in the bedroom. Without hesitation, he
jerked back the covers and grabbed her by the wrists. She grunted as
her body hit the floor, and he heard her making tiny sounds in her
throat as he dragged her into the hall and started down the stairs.

As he pulled her across the living room, she started to move.

Her hands closed over his wrists and her body began to twist and
flop on the rug. Her eyes were still closed, but she gasped and muttered and her body kept trying to writhe out of his grip. Her dark
nails dug into his flesh. He tore out of her grasp with a snarl and
dragged her the rest of the way by her hair. Usually he felt a twinge
when he realized that, but for some affliction he didn't understand,
these people were the same as he. But now an experimental fervor
had seized him and he could think of nothing else.

Even so, he shuddered at the strangled sound of horror she made
when he threw her on the sidewalk outside.

She lay twisting helplessly on the sidewalk, hands opening and
closing, lips drawn back from red-spotted lips. Robert Neville
watched her tensely.

His throat moved. It wouldn't last, the feeling of callous brutality.
He bit his lips as he watched her. All right, she's suffering, he argued
with himself, but she's one of them and she'd kill me gladly if she got
the chance. You've got to look at it that way, it's the only way. Teeth
clenched, he stood there and watched her die.

In a few minutes she stopped moving, stopped muttering, and her
hands uncurled slowly like white blossoms on the cement. Robert
Neville crouched down and felt for her heartbeat. There was none.
Already her flesh was growing cold.

He straightened up with a thin smile. It was true, then. He didn't need the stakes. After all this time, he'd finally found a better method.

Then his breath caught. But how did he know the woman was really dead? How could he know until sunset?

The thought filled him with a new, more restless anger. Why did each question blight the answers before it?

He thought about it as he sat drinking a can of tomato juice taken from the supermarket behind which he was parked.

How was he going to know? He couldn't very well stay with the woman until sunset came.

Take her home with you, fool.

Again his eyes closed and he felt a shudder of irritation go through him. He was missing all the obvious answers today. Now he'd have to go all the way back and find her, and he wasn't even sure where the house was.

He started the motor and pulled away from the parking lot, glancing down at his watch. Three o'clock. Plenty of time to get back before they came. He eased the gas pedal down and the station wagon pulled ahead faster.

It took him about a half hour to relocate the house. The woman was still in the same position on the sidewalk. Putting on his gloves, Neville lowered the back gate of the station wagon and walked over to the woman. As he walked, he noticed her figure. No, don't start that again, for God's sake.

He dragged the woman back to the station wagon and tossed her in. Then he closed the gate and took off his gloves. He held up the watch and looked at it. Three o'clock. Plenty of time to—

He jerked up the watch and held it against his ear, his heart suddenly jumping.

The watch had stopped.

CHAPTER FIVE

His fingers shook as he turned the ignition key. His hands gripped the wheel rigidly as he made a tight U turn and started back toward Gardena.

What a fool he'd been! It must have taken at least an hour to reach the cemetery. He must have been in the crypt for hours. Then going to get that woman. Going to the market, drinking the tomato juice, going back to get the woman again.

What time *was* it?

Fool! Cold fear poured through his veins at the thought of them all waiting for him at his house. Oh, my God, and he'd left the garage door open! The gasoline, the equipment—*the generator*!

A groan cut itself off in his throat as he jammed the gas pedal to the floor and the small station wagon leaped ahead, the speedometer needle fluttering, then moving steadily past the sixty-five mark, the seventy, the seventy-five. What if they were already waiting for him? How could he possibly get in the house?

He forced himself to be calm. He mustn't go to pieces now; he had to keep himself in check. He'd get in. Don't worry, you'll get inside, he told himself. But he didn't see how.

One hand ran nervously through his hair. This is fine, fine, commented his mind. You go to all that trouble to preserve your existence, and then one day you just don't come back in time. Shut up! his mind snapped back at itself. But he could have killed himself for forgetting to wind his watch the night before. Don't bother killing yourself, his mind reflected, they'll be glad to do it for you. Suddenly he realized he was almost weak from hunger. The small amount of canned meat he'd eaten with the tomato juice had done nothing to alleviate hunger.

The silent streets flew past and he kept looking from side to side to see if any of them were appearing in the doorways. It seemed as if it were already getting dark, but that could have been imagination. It couldn't be that late, it couldn't be.

He'd just gone hurtling past the corner of Western and Compton when he saw the man come running out of a building and shout at him. His heart was contracted in an icy hand as the man's cry fluttered in the air behind the car.

He couldn't get any more speed out of the station wagon. And now his mind began torturing him with visions of one of the tires going, the station wagon veering, leaping the curb and crashing into a house. His lips started to shake and he jammed them together to stop them. His hands on the wheel felt numb.

He had to slow down at the corner of Cimarron. Out of the corner of an eye he saw a man come rushing out of a house and start chasing the car.

Then, as he turned the corner with a screech of clinging tires, he couldn't hold back the gasp.

They were all in front of his house, waiting.

A sound of helpless terror filled his throat. He didn't want to die. He might have thought about it, even contemplated it. But he didn't want to die. Not like *this*.

Now he saw them all turn their white faces at the sound of the motor. Some more of them came running out of the open garage and his teeth ground together in impotent fury. What a stupid, brainless way to die!

Now he saw them start running straight toward the station wagon, a line of them across the street. And, suddenly, he knew he couldn't stop. He pressed down on the accelerator, and in a moment the car went plowing through them, knocking three of them aside like tenpins. He felt the car frame jolt as it struck the bodies. Their screaming white faces went flashing by his window, their cries chilling his blood.

Now they were behind and he saw in the rear-view mirror that they were all pursuing him. A sudden plan caught hold in his mind, and impulsively he slowed down, even braking, until the speed of the car fell to thirty, then twenty miles an hour.

He looked back and saw them gaining, saw their grayish-white faces approaching, their dark eyes fastened to his car, to *him*.

Suddenly he twitched with shock as a snarl sounded nearby and, jerking his head around, he saw the crazed face of Ben Cortman beside the car.

Instinctively his foot jammed down on the gas pedal, but his other foot slipped off the clutch, and with a neck-snapping jolt the station wagon jumped forward and stalled.

Sweat broke out on his forehead as he lunged forward feverishly to press the button. Ben Cortman clawed in at him.

With a snarl he shoved the cold white hand aside.

"Neville, Neville!"

Ben Cortman reached in again, his hands like claws cut from ice. Again Neville pushed aside the hand and jabbed at the starter button, his body shaking helplessly. Behind, he could hear them all screaming excitedly as they came closer to the car.

The motor coughed into life again as he felt Ben Cortman's long nails rake across his cheek.

"Neville!"

The pain made his hand jerk into a rigid fist, which he drove into Cortman's face. Cortman went flailing back onto the pavement as the gears caught and the station wagon jolted forward, picking up speed. One of the others caught up and leaped at the rear of the car. For a minute he held on, and Robert Neville could see his ashen face glaring insanely through the back window. Then he jerked the car over toward the curb, swerved sharply, and shook the man off. The man went running across a lawn, arms ahead of him, and smashed violently into the side of a house.

Robert Neville's heart was pounding so heavily now it seemed as if it would drive through his chest walls. Breath shuddered in him and his flesh felt numb and cold. He could feel the trickle of blood on his cheek, but no pain. Hastily he wiped it off with one shaking hand.

Now he spun the station wagon around the corner, turning right. He kept looking at the rear-view mirror, then looking ahead. He went the short block to Haas Street and turned right again. What if they cut through the yards and blocked his way?

He slowed down a little until they came swarming around the corner like a pack of wolves. Then he pressed down on the accelerator. He'd have to take the chance that they were all following him. Would some of them guess what he was trying?

He shoved down the gas pedal all the way and the station wagon jumped forward, racing up the block. He wheeled it around the corner at fifty miles an hour, gunned up the short block to Cimarron, and turned right again.

His breath caught. There was no one in sight on his lawn. There was still a chance, then. He'd have to let the station wagon go, though; there was no time to put it in the garage.

He jerked the car to the curb and shoved the door open. As he raced around the edge of the car he heard the billowing cry of their approach around the corner.

He'd have to take a chance on locking the garage. If he didn't, they might destroy the generator; they couldn't have had time to do it already. His footsteps pounded up the driveway to the garage.

"Neville!"

His body jerked back as Cortman came lunging out of the dark shadows of the garage.

Cortman's body drove into his and almost knocked him down. He felt the cold, powerful hands clamp on his throat and smelled the fetid breath clouding over his face. The two of them went reeling back toward the sidewalk and the white-fanged mouth went darting down at Robert Neville's throat.

Abruptly he jerked up his right fist and felt it drive into Cortman's throat. He heard the choking sound in Cortman's throat. Up the block the first of them came rushing and screaming around the corner.

With a violent movement, Robert Neville grabbed Cortman by his long, greasy hair and sent him hurtling down the driveway until he rammed head on into the side of the station wagon.

Robert Neville's eyes flashed up the street. No time for the garage! He dashed around the corner of the house and up to the porch.

He skidded to a halt. Oh, God, the keys!

With a terrified intake of breath he spun and rushed back toward the car. Cortman started up with a throaty snarl and he drove his knee into the white face and knocked Cortman back on the sidewalk. Then he lunged into the car and jerked the key chain away from the ignition slot.

As he scuttled back out of the car the first one of them came leaping at him.

He shrank back onto the car seat and the man tripped over his legs and went sprawling heavily onto the sidewalk. Robert Neville pushed himself out, dashed across the lawn, and leaped onto the porch.

He had to stop to find the right key and another man came leaping up the porch steps. Neville was slammed against the house by the impact of his body. The hot blood-thick breath was on him again, the bared mouth lunging at his throat. He drove his knee into the man's groin and then, leaning his weight against the house, he raised his foot high and shoved the doubled-over man into the other one who was rushing across the lawn.

Neville dived for the door and unlocked it. He pushed it open, slipped inside, and turned. As he slammed it shut an arm shot through the opening. He forced the door against it with all his strength until he heard bones snap, then he opened the door a little, shoved the broken arm out, and slammed the door. With trembling hands he dropped the bar into place.

Slowly he sank down onto the floor and fell on his back. He lay there in the darkness, his chest rising and falling, his legs and arms like dead limbs on the floor. Outside they howled and pummeled the door, shouting his name in a paroxysm of demented fury. They grabbed up bricks and rocks and hurled them against the house and they screamed and cursed at him. He lay there listening to the thud of the rocks and bricks against the house, listening to their howling.

After a while he struggled up to the bar. Half the whisky he poured splashed onto the rug. He threw down the contents of the glass and stood there shivering, holding onto the bar to support his wobbling legs, his throat tight and convulsed; his lips shaking without control.

Slowly the heat of the liquor expanded in his stomach and reached his body. His breath slowed down, his chest stopped shuddering.

He started as he heard the great crash outside.

He ran to the peephole and looked out. His teeth grated together and a burst of rage filled him as he saw the station wagon lying on its side and saw them smashing in the windshield with bricks and stones, tearing open the hood and smashing at the engine with insane club strokes, denting the frame with their frenzied blows. As he watched, fury poured through him like a current of hot acid and half-formed curses sounded in his throat while his hands clamped into great white fists at his sides.

Turning suddenly, he moved to the lamp and tried to light it. It didn't work. With a snarl he turned and ran into the kitchen. The refrigerator was out. He ran from one dark room to another. The freezer was off; all the food would spoil. His house was a dead house.

Fury exploded in him. Enough!

His rage-palsied hands ripped out the clothes from the bureau drawer until they closed on the loaded pistols.

Racing through the dark living room, he knocked up the bar across the door and sent it clattering to the floor. Outside, they howled as they heard him opening the door. I'm coming out, you bastards! his mind screamed out.

He jerked open the door and shot the first one in the face. The man went spinning back off the porch and two women came at him in muddy, torn dresses, their white arms spread to enfold him. He watched their bodies jerk as the bullets struck them, then he shoved them both aside and began firing his guns into their midst, a wild yell ripping back his bloodless lips.

He kept firing the pistols until they were both empty. Then he stood on the porch clubbing them with insane blows, losing his mind almost completely when the same ones he'd shot came rushing at him again. And when they tore the guns out of his hands he used his fists and elbows and he butted with his head and kicked them with his big shoes.

It wasn't until the flaring pain of having his shoulder slashed open struck him that he realized what he was doing and how hopeless his attempt was. Knocking aside two women, he backed toward the door. A man's arm locked around his neck. He lurched forward, bending at the waist, and toppled the man over his head into the others. He jumped back into the doorway, gripped both sides of the frame and kicked out his legs like pistons, sending the men crashing back into the shrubbery.

Then, before they could get at him again, he slammed the door in their faces, locked it, bolted it, and dropped the heavy bar into its slots.

Robert Neville stood in the cold blackness of his house, listening to the vampires scream.

He stood against the wall clubbing slowly and weakly at the plaster, tears streaming down his bearded cheeks, his bleeding hand pulsing with pain. Everything was gone, everything.

"Virginia," he sobbed like a lost, frightened child. "Virginia. *Virginia.*"

PART TWO: March 1976

CHAPTER SIX

The house, at last, was livable again.

Even more so than before, in fact, for he had finally taken three days and soundproofed the walls. Now they could scream and howl all they wanted and he didn't have to listen to them. He especially liked not having to listen to Ben Cortman any more.

It had all taken time and work. First of all was the matter of a new car to replace the one they'd destroyed. This had been more difficult than he'd imagined.

He had to get over to Santa Monica to the only Willys store he knew about. The Willys station wagons were the only ones he had had any experience with, and this didn't seem quite the time to start experimenting. He couldn't walk to Santa Monica, so he had to try using one of the many cars parked around the neighborhood. But most of them were inoperative for one reason or another: a dead battery, a clogged fuel pump, no gasoline, flat tires.

Finally, in a garage about a mile from the house, he found a car he could get started, and he drove quickly to Santa Monica to pick up another station wagon. He put a new battery in it, filled its tank with gasoline, put gasoline drums in the back, and drove home. He got back to the house about an hour before sunset.

He made sure of that.

Luckily the generator had not been ruined. The vampires apparently had no idea of its importance to him, for, except for a torn wire and a few cudgel blows, they had left it alone. He'd managed to fix it quickly the morning after the attack and keep his frozen foods from spoiling. He was grateful for that, because he was sure there were no places left where he could get more frozen foods now that electricity was gone from the city.

For the rest of it, he had to straighten up the garage and clean out the debris of broken bulbs, fuses, wiring, plugs, solder, spare motor parts, and a box of seeds he'd put there once; he didn't remember just when.

The washing machine they had ruined beyond repair, forcing him to replace it. But that wasn't hard. The worst part was mopping up all the gasoline they'd spilled from the drums. They'd really outdone themselves spilling gasoline, he thought irritably while he mopped it up.

Inside the house, he had repaired the cracked plaster, and as an added fillip he had put up another wall mural to give a different appearance to the room.

He'd almost enjoyed all the work once it was started. It gave him something to lose himself in, something to pour all the energy of his still pulsing fury into. It broke the monotony of his daily tasks: the carrying away of bodies, the repairing of the house's exterior, the hanging of garlic.

He drank sparingly during those days, managing to pass almost the entire day without a drink, even allowing his evening drinks to assume the function of relaxing nightcaps rather than senseless escape. His appetite increased and he gained four pounds and lost a little belly. He even slept nights, a tired sleep without the dreams.

For a day or so he had played with the idea of moving to some lavish hotel suite. But the thought of all the work he'd have to do to make it habitable changed his mind. No, he was all set in the house.

Now he sat in the living room, listening to Mozart's Jupiter Symphony and wondering how he was to begin, *where* he was to begin his investigation.

He knew a few details, but these were only landmarks above the basic earth of cause. The answer lay in something else. Probably in some fact he was aware of but did not adequately appreciate, in some apparent knowledge he had not yet connected with the over-all picture.

But what?

He sat motionless in the chair, a sweat-beaded glass in his right hand, his eyes fastened on the mural.

It was a scene from Canada: deep northern woods, mysterious with green shadows, standing aloof and motionless, heavy with the silence of manless nature. He stared into its soundless green depths and wondered.

Maybe if he went back. Maybe the answer lay in the past, in some obscure crevice of memory. Go back, then, he told his mind, go back.

It tore his heart out to go back.

❧

There had been another dust storm during the night. High, spinning winds had scoured the house with grit, driven it through the cracks, sifted it through plaster pores, and left a hair-thin layer of dust across all the furniture surfaces. Over their bed the dust filtered like fine powder, settling in their hair and on their eyelids and under their nails, clogging their pores.

Half the night he'd lain awake trying to single out the sound of Virginia's labored breathing. But he couldn't hear anything above the shrieking, grating sound of the storm. For a while, in the suspension between sleeping and waking, he had suffered the illusion that the house was being sandpapered by giant wheels that held its framework between monstrous abrasive surfaces and made it shudder.

He'd never got used to the dust storms. That hissing sound of whirlwind granulation always set his teeth on edge. The storms had never come regularly enough to allow him to adapt himself to them.

Whenever they came, he spent a restless, tossing night, and went to the plant the next day with jaded mind and body.

Now there was Virginia to worry about too.

About four o'clock he awoke from a thin depression of sleep and realized that the storm had ended. The contrast made silence a rushing noise in his ears.

As he raised his body irritably to adjust his twisted pajamas, he noticed that Virginia was awake. She was lying on her back and staring at the ceiling.

"What's the matter?" he mumbled drowsily.

She didn't answer.

"Honey?"

Her eyes moved slowly to him.

"Nothing," she said. "Go to sleep."

"How do you feel?"

"The same."

"Oh."

He lay there for a moment looking at her.

"Well," he said then and, turning on his side, closed his eyes.

The alarm went off at six-thirty. Usually Virginia pushed in the stop, but when she failed to do so, he reached over her inert body and did it himself. She was still on her back, still staring.

"What is it?" he asked worriedly.

She looked at him and shook her head on the pillow.

"I don't know," she said. "I just can't sleep."

"Why?"

She made an indecisive sound.

"Still feel weak?" he asked.

She tried to sit up but she couldn't.

"Stay there, hon," he said. "Don't move." He put his hand on her brow. "You haven't got any fever," he told her.

"I don't feel sick," she said. "Just . . . tired."

"You look pale."

"I know. I look like a ghost."

"Don't get up," he said.

She was up.

"I'm not going to pamper myself," she said. "Go ahead, get dressed. I'll be all right."

"Don't get up if you don't feel good, honey."

She patted his arm and smiled.

"I'll be all right," she said. "You get ready."

While he shaved he heard the shuffling of her slippers past the bathroom door. He opened the door and watched her crossing the living room very slowly, her wrappered body weaving a little. He went back in the bathroom shaking his head. She should have stayed in bed.

The whole top of the washbasin was grimy with dust. The damn stuff was everywhere. He'd finally been compelled to erect a tent over Kathy's bed to keep the dust from her face. He'd nailed one edge of a shelter half to the wall next to her bed and let it slope over the bed, the other edge held up by two poles lashed to the side of the bed.

He didn't get a good shave because there was grit in the shaving soap and he didn't have time for a second lathering. He washed off his face, got a clean towel from the hall closet, and dried himself.

Before going to the bedroom to get dressed he checked Kathy's room.

She was still asleep, her small blonde head motionless on the pillow, her cheeks pink with heavy sleep. He ran a finger across the top of the shelter half and drew it away gray with dust. With a disgusted shake of his head he left the room.

"I wish these damn storms would end," he said as he entered the kitchen ten minutes later. "I'm sure . . ."

He stopped talking. Usually she was at the stove turning eggs or French toast or pancakes, making coffee. Today she was sitting at the table. On the stove coffee was percolating, but nothing else was cooking.

"Sweetheart, if you don't feel well, go back to bed," he told her. "I can fix my own breakfast."

"It's all right," she said. "I was just resting. I'm sorry. I'll get up and fry you some eggs."

"Stay there," he said. "I'm not helpless."

He went to the refrigerator and opened the door.

"I'd like to know what this *is* going around," she said. "Half the people on the block have it, and you say that more than half the plant is absent."

"Maybe it's some kind of virus," he said.

She shook her head. "I don't know."

"Between the storms and the mosquitoes and everyone being sick, life is rapidly becoming a pain," he said, pouring orange juice out of the bottle. "And speak of the devil."

He drew a black speck out of the orange juice in the glass.

"How the hell they get in the refrigerator I'll never know," he said.

"None for me, Bob," she said.

"No orange juice?"

"No."

"Good for you."

"No, thank you, sweetheart," she said, trying to smile.

He put back the bottle and sat down across from her with his glass of juice.

"You don't feel any pain?" he said. "No headache, nothing?"

She shook her head slowly.

"I wish I *did* know what was wrong," she said.

"You call up Dr. Busch today."

"I will," she said, starting to get up. He put his hand over hers.

"No, no, sweetheart, stay there," he said.

"But there's no *reason* why I should be like this."

She sounded angry. That was the way she'd been as long as he'd known her. If she became ill, it irritated her. She was annoyed by sickness. She seemed to regard it as a personal affront.

"Come on," he said, starting to get up. "I'll help you back to bed."

"No, just let me sit here with you," she said. "I'll go back to bed after Kathy goes to school."

"All right. Don't you want something, though?"

"No."

"How about coffee?"

She shook her head.

"You're *really* going to get sick if you don't eat," he said.

"I'm just not hungry."

He finished his juice and got up to fry a couple of eggs. He cracked them on the side of the iron skillet and dropped the contents into the melted bacon fat. He got the bread from the drawer and went over to the table with it.

"Here, I'll put it in the toaster," Virginia said. "You watch your . . . Oh, God."

"What is it?"

She waved one hand weakly in front of her face.

"A mosquito," she said with a grimace.

He moved over and, after a moment, crushed it between his two palms.

"Mosquitoes," she said. "Flies, sand fleas."

"We are entering the age of the insect," he said.

"It's not good," she said. "They carry diseases. We ought to put a net around Kathy's bed too."

"I know, I know," he said, returning to the stove and tipping the skillet so the hot fat ran over the white egg surfaces. "I keep meaning to."

"I don't think that spray works, either," Virginia said.

"It doesn't?"

"No."

"My God, and it's supposed to be one of the best ones on the market."

He slid the eggs onto a dish.

"Sure you don't want some coffee?" he asked her.

"No, thank you."

He sat down and she handed him the buttered toast.

"I hope to hell we're not breeding a race of superbugs," he said. "You remember that strain of giant grasshoppers they found in Colorado?"

"Yes."

"Maybe the insects are . . . What's the word? Mutating."

"What's that?"

"Oh, it means they're . . . changing. Suddenly. Jumping over dozens of small evolutionary steps, maybe developing along lines they might not have followed at all if it weren't for . . ."

Silence.

"The bombings?" she said.

"Maybe," he said.

"Well, they're causing the dust storms. They're probably causing a lot of things."

She sighed wearily and shook her head.

"And they say we won the war," she said.

"Nobody won it."

"The mosquitoes won it."

He smiled a little.

"I guess they did," he said.

They sat there for a few moments without talking and the only sound in the kitchen was the clink of his fork on the plate and the cup on the saucer.

"You looked at Kathy last night?" she asked.

"I just looked at her now. She looks fine."

"Good."

She looked at him studiedly.

"I've been thinking, Bob," she said. "Maybe we should send her East to your mother's until I get better. It may be contagious."

"We could," he said dubiously, "but if it's contagious, my mother's place wouldn't be any safer than here."

"You don't think so?" she asked. She looked worried.

He shrugged. "I don't know, hon. I think probably she's just as safe here. If it starts to get bad on the block, we'll keep her out of school."

She started to say something, then stopped.

"All right," she said.

He looked at his watch.

"I'd better finish up," he said.

She nodded and he ate the rest of his breakfast quickly. While he was draining the coffee cup she asked him if he'd bought a paper the night before.

"It's in the living room," he told her.

"Anything new in it?"

"No. Same old stuff. It's all over the country, a little here, a little there. They haven't been able to find the germ yet."

She bit her lower lip.

"Nobody knows what it is?"

"I doubt it. If anybody did they'd have surely said so by now."

"But they must have *some* idea."

"Everybody's got an idea. But they aren't worth anything."

"What do they say?"

He shrugged. "Everything from germ warfare on down."

"Do you think it is?"

"Germ warfare?"

"Yes," she said.

"The war's over," he said.

"Bob," she said suddenly, "do you think you should go to work?"

He smiled helplessly.

"What else can I do?" he asked. "We have to eat."

"I know, but . . ."

He reached across the table and felt how cold her hand was.

"Honey, it'll be all right," he said.

"And you think I should send Kathy to school?"

"I think so," he said. "Unless the health authorities say schools have to shut down, I don't see why we should keep her home. She's not sick."

"But all the kids at school."

"I think we'd better, though," he said.

She made a tiny sound in her throat. Then she said, "All right. If you think so."

"Is there anything you want before I go?" he asked.

She shook her head.

"Now you stay in the house today," he told her, "and in bed."

"I will," she said. "As soon as I send Kathy off."

He patted her hand. Outside, the car horn sounded. He finished the coffee and went to the bathroom to rinse out his mouth. Then he got his jacket from the hall closet and pulled it on.

"Good-by, honey," he said, kissing her on the cheek. "Take it easy, now."

"Good-by," she said. "Be careful."

He moved across the lawn, gritting his teeth at the residue of dust in the air. He could smell it as he walked, a dry tickling sensation in his nasal passages.

"Morning," he said, getting in the car and pulling the door shut behind him.

"Good morning," said Ben Cortman.

CHAPTER SEVEN

"Distilled from *Allium sativum*, a genus of Liliaceae comprising garlic, leek, onion, shallot, and chive. Is of pale color and penetrating odor, containing several allyl sulphides. Composition: water, 64.6%; protein, 6.8%; fat, 0.1%; carbohydrates, 26.3%; fiber, 0.8%; ash, 1.4.%."

There it was. He jiggled one of the pink, leathery cloves in his right palm. For seven months now he'd strung them together into aromatic necklaces and hung them outside his house without the remotest idea of why they chased the vampires away. It was time he learned why.

He put the clove on the sink ledge. Leek, onion, shallot, and chive. Would they all work as well as garlic? He'd really feel like a fool if they did, after searching miles around for garlic when onions were everywhere.

He mashed the clove to a pulp and smelled the acrid fluid on the thick cleaver blade.

All right, what now? The past revealed nothing to help him; only talk of insect carriers and virus, and they weren't the causes. He was sure of it.

The past had brought something else, though; pain at remembering. Every recalled word had been like a knife blade twisting in him. Old wounds had been reopened with every thought of her. He'd finally had to stop, eyes closed, fists clenched, trying desperately to accept the present on its own terms and not yearn with his very flesh for the past. But only enough drinks to stultify all introspection had managed to drive away the enervating sorrow that remembering brought.

He focused his eyes. All right, damn it, he told himself, *do* something!

He looked at the text again, water—was it that? he asked himself. No, that was ridiculous; all things had water in them. Protein? No. Fat? No. Carbohydrates? No. Fiber? No. Ash? No. What then?

"The characteristic odor and flavor of garlic are due to an essential oil amounting to about 0.2% of the weight, which consists mainly of allyl sulphide and allyl isothicyanate."

Maybe the answer was there.

Again the book: "Allyl sulphide may be prepared by heating mustard oil and potassium sulphide at 100 degrees."

His body thudded down into the living-room chair and a disgusted breath shuddered his long frame. And where the hell do I get mustard oil and potassium sulphide? *And* the equipment to prepare them in?

That's great, he railed at himself. The first step, and already you've fallen flat on your face.

He pushed himself up disgustedly and headed for the bar. But halfway through pouring a drink he slammed down the bottle. No, by God, he had no intention of going on like a blind man, plodding down a path of brainless, fruitless existence until old age or accident took him. Either he found the answer or he ditched the whole mess, life included.

He checked his watch. Ten-twenty A.M.; still time. He moved to the hallway resolutely and checked through the telephone directories. There was a place in Inglewood.

Four hours later he straightened up from the workbench with a crick in his neck and the allyl sulphide inside a hypodermic syringe, and in himself the first sense of real accomplishment since his forced isolation began.

A little excited, he ran to his car and drove out past the area he'd cleared out and marked with chalked rods. He knew it was more than possible that some vampires might have wandered into the cleared area and were hiding there again. But he had no time for searching.

Parking his car, he went into a house and walked to the bedroom. A young woman lay there, a coating of blood on her mouth.

Flipping her over, Neville pulled up her skirt and injected the allyl sulphide into her soft, fleshy buttock, then turned her over again and stepped back. For a half hour he stood there watching her.

Nothing happened.

This doesn't make sense, his mind argued. I hang garlic around the house and the vampires stay away. And the characteristic of garlic is the oil I've injected in her. But nothing's happened.

Goddamn it, nothing's happened!

He flung down the syringe and, trembling with rage and frustration, went home again. Before darkness, he built a small wooden structure on the front lawn and hung strings of onions on it. He spent a listless night, only the knowledge that there was still much left to do keeping him from the liquor.

In the morning he went out and looked at the matchwood on his lawn.

—◆—

The cross. He held one in his hand, gold and shiny in the morning sun. This, too, drove the vampires away.

Why? Was there a logical answer, something he could accept without slipping on banana skins of mysticism?

There was only one way to find out.

He took the woman from her bed, pretending not to notice the question posed in his mind: Why do you always experiment on women? He didn't care to admit that the inference had any validity. She just happened to be the first one he'd come across, that was all. What about the man in the living room, though? For God's sake! he flared back. I'm not going to rape the woman!

Crossing your fingers, Neville? Knocking on wood?

He ignored that, beginning to suspect his mind of harboring an alien. Once he might have termed it conscience. Now it was only an annoyance. Morality, after all, had fallen with society. He was his own ethic.

Makes a good excuse, doesn't it, Neville? Oh, shut up.

But he wouldn't let himself pass the afternoon near her. After binding her to a chair, he secluded himself in the garage and puttered around with the car. She was wearing a torn black dress and too much was visible as she breathed. Out of sight, out of mind. . . . It was a lie, he knew, but he wouldn't admit it.

At last, mercifully, night came. He locked the garage door, went back to the house, and locked the front door, putting the heavy bar across it. Then he made a drink and sat down on the couch across from the woman.

From the ceiling, right before her face, hung the cross.

At six-thirty her eyes opened. Suddenly, like the eyes of a sleeper who has a definite job to do upon awakening; who does not move into consciousness with a vague entry, but with a single, clearcut motion, knowing just what is to be done.

Then she saw the cross and she jerked her eyes from it with a sudden rattling gasp and her body twisted in the chair.

"Why are you afraid of it?" he asked, startled at the sound of his own voice after so long.

Her eyes, suddenly on him, made him shudder. The way they glowed, the way her tongue licked across her red lips as if it were a separate life in her mouth. The way she flexed her body as if trying to move it closer to him. A guttural rumbling filled her throat like the sound of a dog defending its bone.

"The cross," he said nervously. "Why are you afraid of it?"

She strained against her bonds, her hands raking across the sides of the chair. No words from her, only a harsh, gasping succession of breaths. Her body writhed on the chair, her eyes burned into him.

"The cross!" he snapped angrily.

He was on his feet, the glass falling and splashing across the rug. He grabbed the string with tense fingers and swung the cross before her eyes. She flung her head away with a frightened snarl and re-coiled into the chair.

"*Look* at it!" he yelled at her.

A sound of terror-stricken whining came from her. Her eyes moved wildly around the room, great white eyes with pupils like specks of soot.

He grabbed at her shoulder, then jerked his hand back. It was dribbling blood from raw teeth wounds.

His stomach muscles jerked in. The hand lashed out again, this time smashing her across the cheek and snapping her head to the side.

Ten minutes later he threw her body out the front door and slammed it again in their faces. Then he stood there against the door breathing heavily. Faintly he heard through the soundproofing the sound of them fighting like jackals for the spoils.

Later he went to the bathroom and poured alcohol into the teeth gouges, enjoying fiercely the burning pain in his flesh.

CHAPTER EIGHT

Neville bent over and picked up a little soil in his right hand. He ran it between his fingers, crumbling the dark lumps into grit. How many of them, he wondered, slept in the soil, as the story went?

He shook his head. Precious few.

Where did the legend fit in, then?

He closed his eyes and let the dirt filter down slowly from his hand. Was there any answer? If only he could remember whether those who slept in soil were the ones who had returned from death. He might have theorized then.

But he couldn't remember. Another unanswerable question, then. Add it to the question that had occurred to him the night before.

What would a Mohammedan vampire do if faced with a cross?

The barking sound of his laugh in the silent morning air startled him. Good God, he thought, it's been so long since I've laughed, I've forgotten how. It sounded like the cough of a sick hound. Well, that's what I am, after all, isn't it? he decided. A very sick dog.

There had been a light dust storm about four that morning. Strange how it brought back memories. Virginia, Kathy, all those horrible days . . .

He caught himself. No, *no*, there was danger there. It was thinking of the past that drove him to the bottle. He was just going to have to accept the present.

He found himself wondering again why he chose to go on living. Probably, he thought, there's no real reason. I'm just too dumb to end it all.

Well—he clapped his hands with false decision—what now? He looked around as if there were something to see along the stillness of Cimarron Street.

All right, he decided impulsively, let's see if the running-water bit makes sense.

He buried a hose under the ground and ran it into a small trough constructed of wood. The water ran through the trough and out another hole into more hosing, which conducted the water into the earth.

When he'd finished, he went in and took a shower, shaved, and took the bandage off his hand. The wound had healed cleanly. But then, he hadn't been overly concerned about that. Time had more than proved to him that he was immune to their infection.

At six-twenty he went into the living room and stood before the peephole. He stretched a little, grunting at the ache in his muscles. Then, when nothing happened, he made himself a drink.

When he got back to the peephole, he saw Ben Cortman come walking onto the lawn.

"Come out, Neville," Robert Neville muttered, and Cortman echoed the words in a loud cry.

Neville stood there motionless, looking at Ben Cortman.

Ben hadn't changed much. His hair was still black, his body inclined to corpulence, his face still white. But there was a beard on his face now; mostly under the nose, thinner around his chin and cheeks and under his throat. That was the only real difference, though. Ben had always been immaculately shaved in the old days, smelling of cologne each morning when he picked up Neville to drive to the plant.

It was strange to stand there looking out at Ben Cortman; a Ben completely alien to him now. Once he had spoken to that man, ridden to work with him, talked about cars and baseball and politics with him, later on about the disease, about how Virginia and Kathy were getting along, about how Freda Cortman was about . . .

Neville shook his head. There was no point going into that. The past was as dead as Cortman.

Again he shook his head. The world's gone mad, he thought. The dead walk about and I think nothing of it. The return of corpses has become trivial in import. How quickly one accepts the incredible if only one sees it enough! Neville stood there, sipping his whisky and wondering who it was that Ben reminded him of. He'd felt for some time that Cortman reminded him of somebody, but for the life of him he couldn't think who.

He shrugged. What was the difference?

He put down the glass on the window sill and went into the kitchen. He turned on the water there and went back in. When he reached the peephole, he saw another man and a woman on the lawn. None of the three was speaking to either of the others. They never did. They walked and walked about on restless feet, circling each other like wolves, never looking at each other once, having hungry eyes only for the house and their prey inside the house.

Then Cortman saw the water running through the trough and went over to look at it. After a moment he lifted his white face and Neville saw him grinning.

Neville stiffened.

Cortman was jumping over the trough, then back again. Neville felt his throat tightening. The bastard knew!

With rigid legs he pistoned himself into the bedroom and, with shaking hands, pulled one of his pistols out of the bureau drawer.

Cortman was just about finishing stamping in the sides of the trough when the bullet struck him in the left shoulder.

He staggered back with a grunt and flopped onto the sidewalk with a kicking of legs. Neville fired again and the bullet whined up off the cement, inches from Cortman's twisting body.

Cortman started up with a snarl and the third bullet struck him full in the chest.

Neville stood there watching, smelling the acrid fumes of the pistol smoke. Then the woman blocked his view of Cortman and started jerking up her dress.

Neville pulled back and slammed the tiny door over the peephole. He wasn't going to let himself look at that. In the first second of it, he had felt that terrible heat dredging up from his loins like something ravenous.

Later he looked out again and saw Ben Cortman pacing around, calling for him to come out.

And, in the moonlight, he suddenly realized who Cortman reminded him of. The idea made his chest shudder with repressed laughter and he turned away as the shaking reached his shoulders.

My God—*Oliver Hardy*! Those old two-reelers he'd looked at with his projector. Cortman was almost a dead ringer for the rolypoly comedian. A little less plump, that was all. Even the mustache was there now.

Oliver Hardy flopping on his back under the driving impact of bullets. Oliver Hardy always coming back for more, no matter what happened. Ripped by bullets, punctured by knives, flattened by cars, smashed under collapsing chimneys and boats, submerged in water, flung through pipes. And always returning, patient and bruised. That was who Ben Cortman was—a hideously malignant Oliver Hardy buffeted and long-suffering.

My God, it was hilarious!

He couldn't stop laughing because it was more than laughter; it was release. Tears flooded down his cheeks. The glass in his hand shook so badly, the liquor spilled all over him and made him laugh harder. Then the glass fell thumping on the rug as his body jerked with spasms of uncontrollable amusement and the room was filled with his gasping, nerve-shattered laughter.

Later, he cried.

He drove it into the stomach, into the shoulder. Into the neck with a single mallet blow. Into the legs and the arms, and always the same result: the blood pulsing out, slick and crimson, over the white flesh.

He thought he'd found the answer. It was a matter of losing the blood they lived by; it was hemorrhage.

But then he found the woman in the small green and white house, and when he drove in the stake, the dissolution was so sudden it made him lurch away and lose his breakfast.

When he had recovered enough to look again, he saw on the bedspread what looked like a row of salt and pepper mixed; just about as long as the woman had been. It was the first time he'd ever seen such a thing.

Shaken by the sight, he went out of the house on trembling legs and sat in the car for an hour, drinking the flask empty. But even liquor couldn't drive away the vision.

It had been so *quick*. With the sound of the mallet blow still in his ears, she had virtually dissolved before his eyes.

He recalled talking once to a Negro at the plant. The man had studied mortuary science and had told Robert Neville about the mausoleums where people were stored in vacuum drawers and never changed their appearance.

"But you just let some air in," the Negro had said, "and *whoom*!—they'll look like a row of salt and pepper. Jus' like *that*!" And he snapped his fingers.

The woman had been long dead, then. Maybe, the thought occurred, she was one of the vampires who had originally started the plague. God only knew how many years she'd been cheating death.

He was too unnerved to do any more that day or for days to come. He stayed home and drank to forget and let the bodies pile up on the lawn and let the outside of the house fall into disrepair.

For days he sat in the chair with his liquor and thought about the woman. And, no matter how hard he tried not to, no matter how much he drank, he kept thinking about Virginia. He kept seeing himself entering the crypt, lifting the coffin lid.

He thought he was coming down with something, so palsied and nerveless was his shivering, so cold and ill did he feel.

Is *that* what she looked like?

CHAPTER NINE

Morning. A sun-bright hush broken only by the chorus of birds in the trees. No breeze to stir the vivid blossoms around the houses, the bushes, the dark-leaved hedges. A cloud of silent heat was suspended over everything on Cimarron Street.

Virginia Neville's heart had stopped.

He sat beside her on the bed, looking down at her white face. He held her fingers in his hand, his fingertips stroking and stroking. His body was immobile, one rigid, insensible block of flesh and bone. His eyes did not blink, his mouth was a static line, and the movement of his breathing was so slight that it seemed to have stopped altogether.

Something had happened to his brain.

In the second he had felt no heartbeat beneath his trembling fingers, the core of his brain seemed to have petrified, sending out jagged lines of calcification until his head felt like stone. Slowly, on palsied legs, he had sunk down on the bed. And now, vaguely, deep in the struggling tissues of thought, he did not understand how he could sit there, did not understand why despair did not crush him to the earth. But prostration would not come. Time was caught on hooks and could not progress. Everything stood fixed. With Virginia, life and the world had shuddered to a halt.

Thirty minutes passed; forty.

Then, slowly, as though he were discovering some objective phenomenon, he found his body trembling. Not with a localized tremble, a nerve here, a muscle there. This was complete. His body shuddered without end, one mass entire of nerves without control, bereft of will. And what operative mind was left knew that this was his reaction.

For more than an hour he sat in this palsied state, his eyes fastened dumbly to her face.

Then, abruptly, it ended, and with a choked muttering in his throat he lurched up from the bed and left the room.

Half the whisky splashed on the sink top as he poured. The liquor that managed to reach the glass he bolted down in a swallow. The thin current flared its way down to his stomach, feeling twice as intense in the polar numbness of his flesh. He stood sagged against the sink. Hands shaking, he filled the glass again to its top and gulped the burning whisky down with great convulsive swallows.

It's a dream, he argued vainly. It was as if a voice spoke the words aloud in his head.

"Virginia . . ."

He kept turning from one side to another, his eyes searching around the room as if there were something to be found, as if he had mislaid the exit from this house of horror. Tiny sounds of disbelief pulsed in his throat. He pressed his hands together, forcing the shaking palms against each other, the twitching fingers intertwining confusedly.

His hands began to shake so he couldn't make out their forms. With a gagging intake of breath he jerked them apart and pressed them against his legs.

"Virginia."

He took a step and cried aloud as the room flung itself off balance. Pain exploded in his right knee, sending hot barbs up his leg. He whined as he pushed himself up and stumbled to the living room. He stood there like a statue in an earthquake, his marble eyes frozen on the bedroom door.

In his mind he saw a scene enacted once again.

The great fire crackling, roaring yellow, sending its dense and grease-thick clouds into the sky. Kathy's tiny body in his arms. The man coming up and snatching her away as if he were taking a bundle of rags. The man lunging into the dark mist carrying his baby. Him standing there while pile driver blows of horror drove him down with their impact.

Then suddenly he had darted forward with a berserk scream.

"Kathy!"

The arms caught him, the men in canvas and masks drawing him back. His shoes gouged frenziedly at the earth, digging two ragged trenches in the earth as they dragged him away. His brain exploded, the terrified screams flooding from him.

Then the sudden bolt of numbing pain in his jaw, the daylight swept over with clouds of night. The hot trickle of liquor down his throat, the coughing, a gasping, and then he had been sitting silent and rigid in Ben Cortman's car, staring as they drove away at the gigantic pall of smoke that rose above the earth like a black wraith of all earth's despair.

Remembering, he closed his eyes suddenly and his teeth pressed together until they ached.

"No."

He wouldn't put Virginia there. Not if they killed him for it.

With a slow, stiff motion he walked to the front door and went out on the porch. Stepping off onto the yellowing lawn, he started down the block for Ben Cortman's house. The glare of the sun made his pupils shrink to points of jet. His hands swung useless and numbed at his sides.

The chimes still played "How Dry I Am." The absurdity of it made him want to break something in his hands. He remembered when Ben had put them in, thinking how funny it would be.

He stood rigidly before the door, his mind still pulsing. I don't care if it's the law, I don't care if refusal means death, I won't put her there!

His fist thudded on the door.

"Ben!"

Silence in the house of Ben Cortman. White curtains hung motionless in the front windows. He could see the red couch, the floor lamp with the fringed shade, the upright Knabe Freda used to toy with on Sunday afternoons. He blinked. What day *was* it? He had forgotten, he had lost track of the days.

He twisted his shoulders as impatient fury hosed acids through his veins.

"Ben!"

Again the side of his hard fist pummeled the door, and the flesh along his whitening jawline twitched. Damn him, where *was* he? Neville jammed in the button with a brittle finger and the chimes started the tippler's song over and over and over. "How dry I am, how dry I am, how dry I am, how dry I . . ."

With a frenzied gasp he lurched against the door and it flew open against the inside wall. It had been unlocked.

He walked into the silent living room.

"Ben," he said loudly. "Ben, I need your car."

They were in the bedroom, silent and still in their daytime comas, lying apart on the twin beds, Ben in pajamas, Freda in silk night-gown; lying on the sheets, their thick chests faltering with labored breath.

He stood there for a moment looking down at them. There were some wounds on Freda's white neck that had crusted over with dried blood. His eyes moved to Ben. There was no wound on Ben's throat. And he heard a voice in his mind that said: If only I'd wake up.

He shook his head. No, there was no waking up from this.

He found the car keys on the bureau and picked them up. He turned away and left the silent house behind. It was the last time he ever saw either of them alive.

The motor coughed into life and he let it idle a few minutes, choke out, while he sat staring out through the dusty windshield. A fly buzzed its bloated form around his head in the hot, airless inte-rior of the car. He watched the dull green glitter of it and felt the car pulsing under him.

After a moment he pushed in the choke and drove the car up the street. He parked it in the driveway before his garage and turned off the motor.

The house was cool and silent. His shoes scuffed quietly over the rug, then clicked on the floor boards in the hall.

He stood motionless in the doorway looking at her. She still lay on her back, arms at her sides, the white fingers slightly curled in. She looked as if she were sleeping.

He turned away and went back into the living room. What was he going to do? Choices seemed pointless now. What did it matter *what* he did? Life would be equally purposeless no matter what his deci-sion was.

He stood before the window looking out at the quiet, sun-drenched street, his eyes lifeless.

Why did I get the car, then? he wondered. His throat moved as he swallowed. I can't burn her, he thought. I *won't*. But what else was there? Funeral parlors were closed. What few morticians were healthy enough to practice were prevented from doing so by law. Everyone without exception had to be transported to the fires immediately upon death. It was the only way they knew now to prevent communication. Only flames could destroy the bacteria that caused the plague.

He knew that. He knew it was the law. But how many people followed it? He wondered that too. How many husbands took the women who had shared their life and love and dropped them into flames? How many parents incinerated the children they adored, how many children tossed their beloved parents on a bonfire a hundred yards square, a hundred feet deep?

No, if there was anything left in the world, it was his vow that she would not be burned in the fire.

An hour passed before he finally reached a decision.

Then he went and got her needle and thread.

He kept sewing until only her face showed. Then, fingers trembling, a tight knot in his stomach, he sewed the blanket together over her mouth. Over her nose. Her eyes.

Finished, he went in the kitchen and drank another glass of whisky. It didn't seem to affect him at all.

At last he went back to the bedroom on faltering legs. For a long minute he stood there breathing hoarsely. Then he bent over and worked his arms under her inert form.

"Come on, baby," he whispered.

The words seemed to loosen everything. He felt himself shaking, felt the tears running slowly down his cheeks as he carried her through the living room and outside.

He put her in the back seat and got in the car. He took a deep breath and reached for the starter button.

He drew back. Getting out of the car again, he went into the garage and got the shovel.

He twitched as he came out, seeing the man across the street approaching slowly. He put the shovel in the back and got in the car.

"Wait!"

The man's shout was hoarse. The man tried to run, but he wasn't strong enough.

Robert Neville sat there silently as the man came shuffling up.

"Could you . . . let me bring my . . . my mother too?" the man said stiffly.

"I . . . I . . . I . . ."

Neville's brain wouldn't function. He thought he was going to cry again, but he caught himself and stiffened his back.

"I'm not going to the . . . *there*," he said.

The man looked at him blankly.

"But your . . ."

"I'm not going to the fire, I said!" Neville blurted out, and jabbed in the starter button.

"But your wife," said the man. "You have your . . ."

Robert Neville jerked the gear shift into reverse.

"*Please,*" begged the man.

"I'm not *going* there!" Neville shouted without looking at the man.

"But it's the *law*!" the man shouted back, suddenly furious.

The car raced back quickly into the street and Neville jerked it around to face Compton Boulevard. As he sped away he saw the man standing at the curb watching him leave. Fool! his mind grated. Do you think I'm going to throw my wife into a fire?

The streets were deserted. He turned left at Compton and started west. As he drove he looked at the huge lot on the right side of the car. He couldn't use any of the cemeteries. They were locked and watched. Men had been shot trying to bury their loved ones.

He turned right at the next block and drove up one block, turned right again into a quiet street that ended in the lot. Halfway up the block he cut the motor. He rolled the rest of the way so no one would hear the car.

No one saw him carry her from the car or carry her deep into the high-weeded lot. No one saw him put her down on an open patch of ground and then disappear from view as he knelt.

Slowly he dug, pushing the shovel into the soft earth, the bright sun pouring heat into the little clearing like molten air into a dish. Sweat ran in many lines down his cheeks and forehead as he dug, and the earth swam dizzily before his eyes. Newly thrown dirt filled his nostrils with its hot, pungent smell.

At last the hole was finished. He put down the shovel and sagged down on his knees. His body shuddered and sweat trickled over his face. This was the part he dreaded.

But he knew he couldn't wait. If he was seen they would come out and get him. Being shot was nothing. But she would be burned then. His lips tightened. No.

Gently, as carefully as he could, he lowered her into the shallow grave, making sure that her head did not bump.

He straightened up and looked down at her still body sewn up in the blanket. For the last time, he thought. No more talking, no more loving. Eleven wonderful years ending in a filled-in trench. He began to tremble. No, he ordered himself, there's no time for that.

It was no use. The world shimmered through endless distorting tears while he pressed back the hot earth, patting it around her still body with nerveless fingers.

✦

He lay fully clothed on his bed, staring at the black ceiling. He was half drunk and the darkness spun with fireflies.

His right arm faltered out for the table. His hand brushed the bottle over and he jerked out clawing fingers too late. Then he relaxed and lay there in the still of night, listening to the whisky gurgle out of the bottle mouth and spread across the floor.

His unkempt hair rustled on the pillow as he looked toward the clock. Two in the morning. Two days since he'd buried her. Two eyes looking at the clock, two ears picking up the hum of its electric chronology, two lips pressed together, two hands lying on the bed.

He tried to rid himself of the concept, but everything in the world seemed suddenly to have dropped into a pit of duality, victim to a system of twos. Two people dead, two beds in the room, two windows, two bureaus, two rugs, two hearts that . . .

His chest filled with night air, held, then pushed it out and sank abruptly. Two days, two hands, two eyes, two legs, two feet . . .

He sat up and dropped his legs over the edge of the bed. His feet landed in the puddle of whisky and he felt it soaking through his socks. A cold breeze was rattling the window blinds.

He stared at the blackness. What's left? he asked himself. What's left, anyway?

Wearily he stood up and stumbled into the bathroom, leaving wet tracks behind him. He threw water into his face and fumbled for a towel.

What's left? What's . . .

He stood suddenly rigid in the cold blackness.

Someone was turning the knob on the front door.

He felt a chill move up the back of his neck and his scalp began prickling. It's Ben, he heard his mind offering. He's come for the car keys.

The towel slipped from his fingers and he heard it swish down onto the tiles. His body twitched.

A fist thudded against the door; strengthless, as if it had fallen against the wood.

He moved into the living room slowly, his heartbeat thudding heavily.

The door rattled as another fist thudded against it weakly. He felt himself twitch at the sound. What's the matter? he thought. The door is open. From the open window a cold breeze blew across his face. The darkness drew him to the door.

"Who . . ." he murmured, unable to go on.

His hand recoiled from the doorknob as it turned under his fingers. With one step, he backed into the wall and stood there breathing harshly, his widened eyes staring.

Nothing happened. He stood there holding himself rigidly.

Then his breath was snuffed. Someone was mumbling on the porch, muttering words he couldn't hear. He braced himself; then, with a lunge, he jerked open the door and let the moonlight in.

He couldn't even scream. He just stood rooted to the spot, staring dumbly at Virginia.

"Rob . . . ert," she said.

CHAPTER TEN

The Science Room was on the second floor. Robert Neville's footsteps thudded hollowly up the marble steps of the Los Angeles Public Library. It was April 7, 1976.

It had come to him, after a half week of drinking, disgust, and desultory investigation, that he was wasting his time. Isolated experiments were yielding nothing, that was clear. If there was a rational answer to the problem (and he had to believe that there was), he could only find it by careful research.

Tentatively, for want of better knowledge, he had set up a possible basis, and that was blood. It provided, at least, a starting point. Step number one, then, was reading about blood.

The silence of the library was complete save for the thudding of his shoes as he walked along the second-floor hallway. Outside, there were birds sometimes and, even lacking that, there seemed to be a sort of sound outside. Inexplicable, perhaps, but it never seemed as deathly still in the open as it did inside a building.

Especially here in this giant, gray-stoned building that housed the literature of a world's dead. Probably it was being surrounded by walls, he thought, something purely psychological. But knowing that didn't make it any easier. There were no psychiatrists left to murmur of groundless neuroses and auditory hallucinations. The last man in the world was irretrievably stuck with his delusions.

He entered the Science Room.

It was a high-ceilinged room with tall, large-paned windows. Across from the doorway was the desk where books had been checked out in days when books were still being checked out.

He stood there for a moment looking around the silent room, shaking his head slowly. All these books, he thought, the residue of a planet's intellect, the scrapings of futile minds, the leftovers, the potpourri of artifacts that had no power to save men from perishing.

His shoes clicked across the dark tiles as he walked to the beginning of the shelves on his left. His eyes moved to the cards between the shelf sections. "Astronomy," he read; books about the heavens. He moved by them. It was not the heavens he was concerned about. Man's lust for the stars had died with the others. "Physics," "Chemistry," "Engineering." He passed them by and entered the main reading section of the Science Room.

He stopped and looked up at the high ceiling. There were two banks of dead lights overhead and the ceiling was divided into great sunken squares, each square decorated with what looked like Indian mosaics. Morning sunlight filtered through the dusty windows and he saw motes floating gently on the current of its beams.

He looked down the row of long wooden tables with chairs lined up before them. Someone had put them in place very neatly. The day the library was shut down, he thought, some maiden librarian had moved down the room, pushing each chair against its table. Carefully, with a plodding precision that was the cachet of herself.

He thought about that visionary lady. To die, he thought, never knowing the fierce joy and attendant comfort of a loved one's embrace. To sink into that hideous coma, to sink then into death and, perhaps, return to sterile, awful wanderings. All without knowing what it was to love and be loved.

That was a tragedy more terrible than becoming a vampire.

He shook his head. All right, that's enough, he told himself, you haven't got the time for maudlin reveries.

He bypassed books until he came to "Medicine." That was what he wanted. He looked through the titles. Books on hygiene, on anatomy, on physiology (general and specialized), on curative practices. Farther down, on bacteriology.

He pulled out five books on general physiology and several works on blood. These he stacked on one of the dust-surfaced tables. Should he get any of the books on bacteriology? He stood a minute, looking indecisively at the buckram backs.

Finally he shrugged. Well, what's the difference? he thought. They can't do any harm. He pulled out several of them at random and added them to the pile. He now had nine books on the table. That was enough for a start. He expected he'd be coming back.

As he left the Science Room, he looked up at the clock over the door.

The red hands had stopped at four-twenty-seven. He wondered what day they had stopped. As he descended the stairs with his armful of books, he wondered at just what moment the clock had stopped. Had it been morning or night? Was it raining or shining? Was anyone there when it stopped?

He twisted his shoulders irritably. For God's sake, what's the difference? he asked himself. He was getting disgusted at this increasing nostalgic preoccupation with the past. It was a weakness, he knew, a weakness he could scarcely afford if he intended to go on. And yet he kept discovering himself drifting into extensive meditation on aspects of the past. It was almost more than he could control, and it was making him furious with himself.

He couldn't get the huge front doors open from the inside, either; they were too well locked. He had to go out through the broken window again, first dropping the books to the sidewalk one at a time, then himself. He took the books to his car and got in.

As he started the car, he saw that he was parked along a red-painted curb, facing in the wrong direction on a one-way street. He looked up and down the street.

"Policeman!" he found himself calling. "Oh, poli*ce*man!"

He laughed for a mile without stopping, wondering just what was so funny about it.

⬥

He put down the book. He'd been reading again about the lymphatic system. He vaguely remembered reading about it months before, during the time he now called his "frenzied period." But what he'd read had made no impression on him then because he'd had nothing to apply it to.

There seemed to be something there now.

The thin walls of the blood capillaries permitted blood plasma to escape into the tissue spaces along with the red and colorless cells. These escaped materials eventually returned to the blood system through the lymphatic vessels, carried back by the thin fluid called lymph.

During this return flow, the lymph trickled through lymph nodes, which interrupted the flow and filtered out the solid particles of body waste, thus preventing them from entering the blood system.

Now.

There were two things that activated the lymphatic system: (1) breathing, which caused the diaphragm to compress the abdominal contents, thus forcing blood and lymph up against gravity; (2) physical movement, which caused skeletal muscles to compress lymph vessels, thus moving the lymph. An intricate valve system prevented any backing up of the flow.

But the vampires didn't breathe; not the dead ones, anyway. That meant, roughly, that *half* of their lymph flow was cut off. This meant, further, that a considerable amount of waste products would be left in the vampire's system.

Robert Neville was thinking particularly of the fetid odor of the vampire.

He read on.

"The bacteria passes into the blood stream, where . . .

". . . the white corpuscles playing a vital part in our defense against bacterial attack.

"Strong sunlight kills many germs rapidly and . . .

"Many bacterial diseases of man can be disseminated by the mechanical agency of flies, mosquitoes . . .

". . . where, under the stimulus of bacterial attack, the phagocytic factories rush extra cells into the blood stream."

He let the book drop forward into his lap and it slipped off his legs and thumped down on the rug.

It was getting harder and harder to fight, because no matter what he read, there was always the relationship between bacteria and blood affliction. Yet, all this time, he'd been letting contempt fall freely on all those in the past who had died proclaiming the truth of the germ theory and scoffing at vampires.

He got up and made himself a drink. But it sat untouched as he stood before the bar. Slowly, rhythmically, he thudded his right fist down on the top of the bar while his eyes stared bleakly at the wall.

Germs.

He grimaced. Well, for God's sake, he snapped jadedly at himself, the word hasn't got thorns, you know.

He took a deep breath. All right, he ordered himself, is there any reason why it couldn't be germs?

He turned away from the bar as if he could leave the question there. But questions had no location; they could follow him around.

He sat in the kitchen staring into a steaming cup of coffee. Germs.

Bacteria. Viruses. Vampires. Why am I so against it? he thought. Was it just reactionary stubbornness, or was it that the task would loom as too tremendous for him if it were germs?

He didn't know. He started out on a new course, the course of compromise. Why throw out either theory? One didn't necessarily negate the other. Dual acceptance and correlation, he thought.

Bacteria could be the answer to the vampire.

Everything seemed to flood over him then.

It was as though he'd been the little Dutch boy with his finger in the dike, refusing to let the sea of reason in. There he'd been, crouching and content with his iron-bound theory. Now he'd straightened up and taken his finger out. The sea of answers was already beginning to wash in.

The plague had spread so quickly. Could it have done that if only vampires had spread it? Could their nightly maraudings have propelled it on so quickly?

He felt himself jolted by the sudden answer. Only if you accepted bacteria could you explain the fantastic rapidity of the plague, the geometrical mounting of victims.

He shoved aside the coffee cup, his brain pulsing with a dozen different ideas.

The flies and mosquitoes had been a part of it. Spreading the disease, causing it to race through the world.

Yes, bacteria explained a lot of things; the staying in by day, the coma enforced by the germ to protect itself from sun radiation.

A new idea: What if the bacteria were the strength of the true vampire?

He felt a shudder run down his back. Was it possible that the same germ that killed the living provided the energy for the dead?

He had to know! He jumped up and almost ran out of the house. Then, at the last moment, he jerked back from the door with a nervous laugh. God's *sake*, he thought, am I going out of my mind? It was nighttime.

He grinned and walked restlessly around the living room.

Could it explain the other things? The stake? His mind fell over itself trying to fit that into the framework of bacterial causation. Come on! he shouted impatiently in his mind. But all he could think of was hemorrhage, and that didn't explain that woman. And it wasn't the heart. . . .

He skipped it, afraid that his new-found theory would start to collapse before he'd established it.

The cross, then. No, bacteria couldn't explain that. The soil; no, that was no help. Running water, the mirror, garlic . . .

He felt himself trembling without control and he wanted to cry out loudly to stop the runaway horse of his brain. He had to find *something*! Goddamn it! he raged in his mind. I won't let it go!

He made himself sit down. Trembling and rigid, he sat there and blanked his mind until calm took over. Good Lord, he thought finally, what's the matter with me? I get an idea, and when it doesn't explain everything in the first minute, I panic. I must be going crazy.

He took that drink now; he needed it. He held up his hand until it stopped shaking. All right, little boy, he tried kidding himself, calm down now. Santa Claus is coming to town with all the nice answers. No longer will you be a weird Robinson Crusoe, imprisoned on an island of night surrounded by oceans of death.

He snickered at that, and it relaxed him. Colorful, he thought, tasty. The last man in the world is Edgar Guest.

All right, then, he ordered himself, you're going to bed. You're not going to go flying off in twenty different directions. You can't take that any more; you're an emotional misfit.

The first step was to get a microscope. That is the first step, he kept repeating forcefully to himself as he undressed for bed, ignoring the tight ball of indecision in his stomach, the almost painful craving to plunge directly into investigation without any priming.

He almost felt ill, lying there in the darkness and planning just one step ahead. He knew it had to be that way, though. That is the first step, that is the first step. Goddamn your bones, that is the first step.

He grinned in the darkness, feeling good about the definite work ahead.

One thought on the problem he allowed himself before sleeping. The bitings, the insects, the transmission from person to person— were even these enough to explain the horrible speed with which the plague spread?

He went to sleep with the question in his mind. And, about three in the morning, he woke up to find the house buffeted by another dust storm. And suddenly, in the flash of a second, he made the connection.

CHAPTER ELEVEN

The first one he got was worthless.

The base was so poorly leveled that any vibration at all disturbed it. The action of its moving parts was loose to the point of wobbling. The mirror kept moving out of position because its pivots weren't tight enough. Moreover, the instrument had no substage to hold condenser or polarizer. It had only one nosepiece, so that he had to remove the object lens when he wanted any variation in magnification. The lenses were impossible.

But, of course, he knew nothing about microscopes, and he'd taken the first one he'd found. Three days later he hurled it against the wall with a strangled curse and stamped it into pieces with his heels.

Then, when he'd calmed down, he went to the library and got a book on microscopes.

The next time he went out, he didn't come back until he'd found a decent instrument; triple nose stage, substage for condenser and polarizer, good base, smooth movement, iris diaphragm, good lenses.

It's just one more example, he told himself, of the stupidity of start-ing off half-cocked. Yeah, yeah, yeah, he answered disgustedly.

He forced himself to spend a good amount of time familiarizing himself with the instrument.

He fiddled with the mirror until he could direct a beam of light on the object in a matter of seconds. He acquainted himself with the lenses, varying from a three-inch power to a one-twelfth-inch power. In the case of the latter, he learned to place a drop of cedar-wood oil on the slide, then rack down until the lens touched the oil. He broke thirteen slides doing it.

Within three days of steady attention, he could manipulate the milled adjustment heads rapidly, could control the iris diaphragm and condenser to get exactly the right amount of light on the slide, and was soon getting a sharply defined clarity with the ready-made slides he'd got.

He never knew a flea looked so godawful.

Next came mounting, a process much more difficult, he soon dis-covered.

No matter how he tried, he couldn't seem to keep dust particles out of the mount. When he looked at them in the microscope, it looked as if he were examining boulders.

It was especially difficult because of the dust storms, which still occurred on an average of once every four days. He was ultimately obliged to build a shelter over the bench.

He also learned to be systematic while experimenting with the mounts. He found that continually searching for things allowed that much more time for dust to accumulate on his slides. Grudgingly, al-most amused, he soon had a place for everything. Glass slips, cover glasses, pipettes, cells, forceps, Petri dishes, needles, chemicals—all were placed in systematic locations.

He found, to his surprise, that he actually gleaned pleasure from practicing orderliness. I guess I got old Fritz's blood in me, after all, he thought once in amusement.

Then he got a specimen of blood from a woman.

It took him days to get a few drops properly mounted in a cell, the cell properly centered on the slide. For a while he thought he'd never get it right.

But then the morning came when, casually, as if it were only of minor import, he put his thirty-seventh slide of blood under the lens, turned on the spotlight, adjusted the draw tube and mirror, racked down and adjusted the diaphragm and condenser. Every second that passed seemed to increase the heaviness of his heartbeat, for somehow he knew this was the time.

The moment arrived; his breath caught.

It wasn't a virus, then. You couldn't see a virus. And there, fluttering delicately on the slide, was a germ.

I dub thee *vampiris*. The words crept across his mind as he stood looking down into the eyepiece.

By checking in one of the bacteriology texts, he'd found that the cylindrical bacterium he saw was a bacillus, a tiny rod of protoplasm that moved itself through the blood by means of tiny threads that projected from the cell envelope. These hairlike flagella lashed vigorously at the fluid medium and propelled the bacillus.

For a long time he stood looking into the microscope, unable to think or continue with the investigation.

All he could think was that here, on the slide, was the cause of the vampire. All the centuries of fearful superstition had been felled in the moment he had seen the germ.

The scientists had been right, then; there *were* bacteria involved. It had taken him, Robert Neville, thirty-six, survivor, to complete the inquest and announce the murderer—the germ *within* the vampire.

Suddenly a massive weight of despair fell over him. To have the answer now when it was too late was a crushing blow. He tried desperately to fight the depression, but it held on. He didn't know where to start, he felt utterly helpless before the problem. How could he ever hope to cure those still living? He didn't know anything about bacteria.

Well, I *will* know! he raged inside. And he forced himself to study.

❈

Certain kinds of bacilli, when conditions became unfavorable for life, were capable of creating, from themselves, bodies called spores.

What they did was condense their cell contents into an oval body with a thick wall. This body, when completed, detached itself from the bacillus and became a free spore, highly resistant to physical and chemical change.

Later, when conditions were more favorable for survival, the spore germinated again, bringing into existence all the qualities of the original bacillus.

Robert Neville stood before the sink, eyes closed, hands clasped tightly at the edge. Something there, he told himself forcefully, something there. But *what*?

Suppose, he predicated, the vampire got no blood. Conditions then for the *vampiris* bacillus would be unfavorable.

Protecting itself, the germ sporulates; the vampire sinks into a coma. Finally, when conditions become favorable again, the vampire walks again, its body still the same.

But how would the germ know if blood were available? He slammed a fist on the sink in anger. He read again. There was still something there. He felt it.

Bacteria, when not properly fed, metabolized abnormally and produced bacteriophages (inanimate, self-reproducing proteins). These bacteriophages destroyed the bacteria.

When no blood came in, the bacilli would metabolize abnormally, absorb water, and swell up, ultimately to explode and destroy all cells.

Sporulation again; it had to fit in.

All right, suppose the vampire didn't go into a coma. Suppose its body decomposed without blood. The germ still might sporulate and—

Yes! The dust storms!

The freed spores would be blown about by the storms. They could lodge in minute skin abrasions caused by the scaling dust. Once in the skin, the spore could germinate and multiply by fission. As this multiplication progressed, the surrounding tissues would be destroyed, the channels plugged with bacilli. Destruction of tissue cells and bacilli would liberate poisonous, decomposed bodies into surrounding healthy tissues. Eventually the poisons would reach the blood stream.

Process complete.

And all without blood-eyed vampires hovering over heroines' beds. All without bats fluttering against estate windows, all without the supernatural.

The vampire was real. It was only that his true story had never been told.

Considering that, Neville recounted the historical plagues.

He thought about the fall of Athens. That had been very much like the plague of 1975. Before anything could be done, the city had fallen. Historians wrote of bubonic plague. Robert Neville was inclined to believe that the vampire had caused it.

No, not the vampire. For now, it appeared, that prowling, vulpine ghost was as much a tool of the germ as the living innocents who were originally afflicted. It was the germ that was the villain. The germ that hid behind obscuring veils of legend and superstition, spreading its scourge while people cringed before their own fears.

And what of the Black Plague, that horrible blight that swept across Europe, leaving in its wake a toll of three-fourths of the population?

Vampires?

By ten that night, his head ached and his eyes felt like hot blobs of gelatin. He discovered that he was ravenous. He got a steak from the freezer, and while it was broiling he took a fast shower.

He jumped a little when a rock hit the side of the house. Then he grinned wryly. He'd been so absorbed all day that he'd forgotten about the pack of them that prowled around his house.

While he was drying himself, he suddenly realized that he didn't know what portion of the vampires who came nightly were physically alive and what portion were activated entirely by the germ. Odd, he thought, that he didn't know. There had to be both kinds, because some of them he shot without success, while others had been destroyed. He assumed that the dead ones could somehow withstand bullets.

Which brought up another point. Why did the living ones come to his house? Why just those few and not everyone in that area?

He had a glass of wine with his steak and was amazed how flavorsome everything was. Food usually tasted like wood to him. I must have worked up an appetite today, he thought.

Furthermore, he hadn't had a single drink. Even more fantastic, he hadn't wanted one. He shook his head. It was painfully obvious that liquor was an emotional solace to him.

The steak he finished to the bone, and he even chewed on that. Then he took the rest of the wine into the living room, turned on the record player, and sat down in his chair with a tired grunt.

He sat listening to Ravel's Daphnis and Chloe Suites One and Two, all the lights off except the spotlight on the woods. He managed to forget all about vampires for a while.

Later, though, he couldn't resist taking another look in the microscope.

You bastard, he thought, almost affectionately, watching the minuscule protoplasm fluttering on the slide. You dirty little bastard.

CHAPTER TWELVE

The next day stank.

The sun lamp killed the germs on the slide, but that didn't explain anything to him.

He mixed allyl sulphide with the germ-ridden blood and nothing happened. The allyl sulphide was absorbed, the germs still lived.

He paced nervously around the bedroom.

Garlic kept them away and blood was the fulcrum of their existence. Yet, mix the essence of garlic with the blood and nothing happened. His hands closed into angry fists.

Wait a minute; that blood was from one of the living ones.

An hour later he had a sample of the other kind. He mixed it with allyl sulphide and looked at it through the microscope. Nothing happened.

Lunch stuck in his throat.

What about the stake, then? All he could think of was hemorrhage, and he knew it wasn't that. That damned woman . . .

He tried half the afternoon to think of something concrete. Finally, with a snarl, he knocked the microscope over and stalked into the living room. He thudded down onto the chair and sat there, tapping impatient fingers on the arm.

Brilliant, Neville, he thought. You're uncanny. Go to the head of the class. He sat there, biting a knuckle. Let's face it, he thought miserably, I lost my mind a long time ago. I can't think two days in succession without having seams come loose. I'm useless, worthless, without value, a dud.

All right, he replied with a shrug, that settles it. Let's get back to the problem. So he did.

There are certain things established, he lectured himself. There *is* a germ, it's transmitted, sunlight kills it, garlic is effective. Some vampires sleep in soil, the stake destroys them. They don't turn into wolves or bats, but certain animals acquire the germ and become vampires.

All right.

He made a list. One column he headed "Bacilli," the other he headed with a question mark.

He began.

The cross. No, that couldn't have anything to do with the bacilli. If anything, it was psychological.

The soil. Could there be something in the soil that affected the germ? No. How would it get in the blood stream? Besides, very few of them slept in the soil.

His throat moved as he added the second item to the column headed by a question mark.

Running water. Could it be absorbed porously and . . . No, that was stupid. They came out in the rain, and they wouldn't if it harmed them. Another notation in the right-hand column. His hand shook a little as he entered it.

Sunlight. He tried vainly to glean satisfaction from putting down one item in the desired column.

The stake. No. His throat moved. Watch it, he warned.

The mirror. For God's sake, how could a mirror have anything to do with germs? His hasty scrawl in the right-hand column was hardly legible. His hand shook a little more.

Garlic. He sat there, teeth gritted. He had to add at least one more item to the bacilli column; it was almost a point of honor. He struggled over the last item. Garlic, garlic. It *must* affect the germ. But how?

He started to write in the right-hand column, but before he could finish, fury came from far down like lava shooting up to the crest of a volcano.

Damn!

He crumpled the paper into a ball in his fist and hurled it away.

He stood up, rigid and frenzied, looking around. He wanted to break things, anything. So you thought your frenzied period was over, did you! he yelled at himself, lurching forward to fling over the bar.

Then he caught himself and held back. No, no, don't get started, he begged. Two shaking hands ran through his lank blond hair. His throat moved convulsively and he shuddered with the repressed craving for violence.

The sound of the whisky gurgling into the glass angered him. He turned the bottle upside down and the whisky spurted out in great gushes, splashing up the sides of the glass and over onto the mahogany top of the bar.

He swallowed the whole glassful at once, head thrown back, whisky running out the edges of his mouth.

I'm an animal! he exulted. I'm a *dumb, stupid* animal and I'm going to drink!

He emptied the glass, then flung it across the room. It bounced off the bookcase and rolled across the rug. Oh, so you won't break, won't you! he rasped inside his head, leaping across the rug to grind the glass into splinters under his heavy shoes.

Then he spun and stumbled to the bar again. He filled another glass and poured the contents down his throat. I wish I had a pipe with whisky in it! he thought. I'd connect a goddamn hose to it and flush whisky down me until it came out my ears! Until I *floated* in it!

He flung away the glass. Too slow, too *slow*, damn it! He drank directly from the uptilted bottle, gulping furiously, hating himself, punishing himself with the whisky burning down his rapidly swallowing throat.

I'll choke myself! he stormed. I'll strangle myself, I'll *drown* myself in whisky! Like Clarence in his malmsey, I'll die, die, *die*!

He hurled the empty bottle across the room and it shattered on the wall mural. Whisky ran down the tree trunks and onto the ground. He lurched across the room and picked up a piece of the broken bottle. He slashed at the mural and the jagged edge sliced through the scene and peeled it away from the wall. There! he thought, his breath like steam escaping. That for you!

He flung the glass away, then looked down as he felt dull pain in his fingers. He'd sliced open the flesh.

Good! he exulted viciously, and pressed on each side of the slices until the blood ran out and fell in big drops on the rug. Bleed to death, you stupid, worthless bastard!

An hour later he was totally drunk, lying flat on the floor with a vacuous smile on his face.

World's gone to hell. No germs, no science. World's fallen to the supernatural, it's a supernatural world. Harper's Bizarre and Saturday Evening Ghost and Ghoul Housekeeping. "Young Dr. Jekyll" and "Dracula's Other Wife" and "Death Can Be Beautiful." "Don't be half-staked" and Smith Brothers' Coffin Drops.

He stayed drunk for two days and planned on staying drunk till the end of time or the world's whisky supply, whichever came first.

And he might have done it, too, if it hadn't been for a miracle.

It happened on the third morning, when he stumbled out onto the porch to see if the world was still there.

There was a dog roving about on the lawn.

The second it heard him open the front door, it stopped snuffling over the grass, its head jerked up in sudden fright, and it bounded off to the side with a twitch of scrawny limbs.

For a moment Robert Neville was so shocked he couldn't move. He stood petrified, staring at the dog, which was limping quickly across the street, its ropelike tail pulled between its legs.

It was *alive*! In the *daytime*! He lurched forward with a dull cry and almost pitched on his face on the lawn. His legs pistoned, his arms flailed for balance. Then he caught himself and started running after the dog.

"Hey!" he called, his hoarse voice breaking the silence of Cimarron Street. "Come back here!"

His shoes thudded across the sidewalk and off the curb, every step driving a battering ram into his head. His heart pulsed heavily.

"Hey!" he called again. "Come 'ere, boy."

Across the street, the dog scrambled unsteadily along the sidewalk, its right hind leg curled up, its dark claws clicking on the cement.

"Come 'ere, boy, I won't hurt you!" Robert Neville called out.

Already he had a stitch in his side and his head throbbed with pain as he ran. The dog stopped a moment and looked back. Then it darted in between two houses, and for a moment Neville saw it from the side. It was brown and white, breedless, its left ear hanging in shreds, its gaunt body wobbling as it ran.

"Don't run away!"

He didn't hear the shrill quiver of hysteria in his voice as he screamed out the words. His throat choked up as the dog disappeared between the houses. With a grunt of fear he hobbled on faster, ignoring the pain of hangover, everything lost in the need to catch that dog.

But when he got into the back yard the dog was gone.

He ran to the redwood fence and looked over. Nothing. He twisted back suddenly to see if the dog were going back out the way it had entered.

There was no dog.

For an hour he wandered around the neighborhood on trembling legs, searching vainly, calling out every few moments, "Come 'ere, boy, come 'ere."

At last he stumbled home, his face a mask of hopeless dejection. To come across a living being, after all this time to find a companion, and then to lose it. Even if it was only a dog. *Only* a dog? To Robert Neville that dog was the peak of a planet's evolution.

He couldn't eat or drink anything. He found himself so ill and trembling at the shock and the loss that he had to lie down. But he couldn't sleep. He lay there shaking feverishly, his head moving from side to side on the flat pillow.

"Come 'ere, boy," he kept muttering without realizing it. "Come 'ere, boy, I won't hurt you."

In the afternoon he searched again. For two blocks in each direction from his house he searched each yard, each street, each individual house. But he found nothing.

When he got home, about five, he put out a bowl of milk and a piece of hamburger. He put a ring of garlic bulbs around it, hoping the vampires wouldn't touch it.

But later it came to him that the dog must be afflicted too, and the garlic would keep it away also. He couldn't understand that. If the dog had the germ, how could it roam outdoors during the daylight hours? Unless it had such a small dosing of bacilli in its veins that it wasn't really affected yet. But, if that were true, how had it survived the nightly attacks?

Oh, my God, the thought came then, what if it comes back tonight for the meat and they kill it? What if he went out the next morning and found the dog's body on the lawn and knew that he was responsible for its death? I couldn't take that, he thought miserably. I'll blow out my brains if that happens, I swear I will.

The thought dredged up again the endless enigma of why he went on. All right, there were a few possibilities for experiment now, but life was still a barren, cheerless trial. Despite everything he had or might have (except, of course, another human being), life gave no promise of improvement or even of change. The way things shaped up, he would live out his life with no more than he already had. And how many years was that? Thirty, maybe forty if he didn't drink himself to death.

The thought of forty more years of living as he was made him shudder.

And yet he hadn't killed himself. True, he hardly treated his body welfare with reverence. He didn't eat properly, drink properly, sleep properly, or do anything properly. His health wasn't going to last indefinitely; he was already cheating the percentages, he suspected.

But using his body carelessly wasn't suicide. He'd never even approached suicide. Why?

There seemed no answer. He wasn't resigned to anything, he hadn't accepted or adjusted to the life he'd been forced into. Yet here he was, eight months after the plague's last victim, nine since he'd spoken to another human being, ten since Virginia had died. Here he was with no future and a virtually hopeless present. Still plodding on.

Instinct? Or was he just stupid? Too unimaginative to destroy himself? Why hadn't he done it in the beginning, when he was in the very depths? What had impelled him to enclose the house, install a freezer, a generator, an electric stove, a water tank, build a hothouse, a workbench, burn down the houses on each side of his, collect records and books and mountains of canned supplies, even—it was fantastic when you thought about it—even put a fancy mural on the wall?

Was the life force something more than words, a tangible, mind-controlling potency? Was nature somehow, in him, maintaining its spark against its own encroachments?

He closed his eyes. Why think, why reason? There was no answer. His continuance was an accident and an attendant bovinity. He was just too dumb to end it all, and that was about the size of it.

Later he glued up the sliced mural and put it back into place. The slits didn't show too badly unless he stood very close to the paper.

He tried briefly to get back to the problem of the bacilli, but he realized that he couldn't concentrate on anything except the dog. To his complete astonishment, he later found himself offering up a stumbling prayer that the dog would be protected. It was a moment in which he felt a desperate need to believe in a God that shepherded his own creations. But, even praying, he felt a twinge of self-reproach, and knew he might start mocking his own prayer at any second.

Somehow, though, he managed to ignore his iconoclastic self and went on praying anyway. Because he wanted the dog, because he needed the dog.

CHAPTER THIRTEEN

In the morning when he went outside he found that the milk and hamburger were gone.

His eyes rushed over the lawn. There were two women crumpled on the grass but the dog wasn't there. A breath of relief passed his lips. Thank God for that, he thought. Then he grinned to himself. If I were religious now, he thought, I'd find in this a vindication of my prayer.

Immediately afterward he began berating himself for not being awake when the dog had come. It must have been after dawn, when the streets were safe. The dog must have evolved a system to have lived so long. But he should have been awake to watch.

He consoled himself with the hope that he was winning the dog over, if only with food. He was briefly worried by the idea that the vampires had taken the food, and not the dog. But a quick check ended that fear. The hamburger had not been lifted over the garlic ring, but dragged through it along the cement of the porch. And all around the bowl were tiny milk splashes, still moist, that could have been made only by a dog's lapping tongue.

Before he had breakfast he put out more milk and more hamburger, placing them in the shade so the milk wouldn't get too warm. After a moment's deliberation he also put out a bowl of cold water.

Then, after eating, he took the two women to the fire and, returning, stopped at a market and picked up two dozen cans of the best dog food as well as boxes of dog biscuit, dog candy, dog soap, flea powder, and a wire brush.

Lord, you'd think I was having a baby or something, he thought as he struggled back to the car with his arms full. A grin faltered on his lips. Why pretend? he thought. I'm more excited than I've been in a year. The eagerness he'd felt upon seeing the germ in his microscope was nothing compared with what he felt about the dog.

He drove home at eighty miles an hour, and he couldn't help a groan of disappointment when he saw that the meat and drink were untouched. Well, what the hell do you expect? he asked himself sarcastically. The dog can't eat every hour on the hour.

Putting down the dog food and equipment on the kitchen table, he looked at his watch. Ten-fifteen. The dog would be back when it got hungry again. Patience, he told himself. Get yourself at least *one* virtue, anyway.

He put away the cans and boxes. Then he checked the outside of the house and the hothouse. There was a loose board to fasten and a pane to repair on the hothouse roof.

While he collected garlic bulbs, he wondered once again why the vampires had never set fire to his house. It seemed such an obvious tactic. Was it possible they were afraid of matches? Or was it that they were just too stupid? After all, their brains could not be so fully operative as they had been before. The change from life to mobile death must have involved some tissue deterioration.

No, that theory wasn't any good, because there were living ones around his house at night too. Nothing was wrong with their brains, was there?

He skipped it. He was in no mood for problems. He spent the rest of the morning preparing and hanging garlic strands. Once he wondered about the fact that garlic bulbs worked. In legend it was always the blossoms of the garlic plant. He shrugged. What was the difference? The proof of the garlic was in its chasing ability. He imagined that the blossoms would work too.

After lunch he sat at the peephole looking out at the bowls and the plate. There was no sound anywhere except for the almost inaudible humming of the air-conditioning units in the bedroom, bathroom, and kitchen.

The dog came at four. Neville had almost fallen into a doze as he sat there before the peephole. Then his eyes blinked and focused as the dog came hobbling slowly across the street, looking at the house with white-rimmed, cautious eyes. He wondered what was wrong with the dog's paw. He wanted very much to fix it and get the dog's affection. Shades of Androcles, he thought in the gloom of his house.

He forced himself to sit still and watch. It was incredible, the feeling of warmth and normality it gave him to see the dog slurping up the milk and eating the hamburger, its jaws snapping and popping with relish. He sat there with a gentle smile on his face, a smile he wasn't conscious of. It was such a nice dog.

His throat swallowed convulsively as the dog finished eating and started away from the porch. Jumping up from the stool, he moved quickly for the front door.

Then he held himself back. No, that wasn't the way, he decided reluctantly. You'll just scare him if you go out. Let him go now, let him go.

He went back to the peephole and watched the dog wobbling across the street and moving in between those two houses again. He felt a tightness in his throat as he watched it leave. It's all right, he soothed himself, he'll be back.

He turned away from the peephole and made himself a mild drink. Sitting in the chair and sipping slowly, he wondered where the dog went at night. At first he'd been worried about not having it in the house with him. But then he'd realized that the dog must be a master at hiding itself to have lasted so long.

It was probably, he thought, one of those freak accidents that followed no percentage law. Somehow, by luck, by coincidence, maybe by a little skill, that one dog had survived the plague and the grisly victims of the plague.

That started him thinking. If a dog, with its limited intelligence, could manage to subsist through it all, wouldn't a person with a reasoning brain have that much more chance for survival?

He made himself think about something else. It was dangerous to hope. That was a truism he had long accepted.

The next morning the dog came again. This time Robert Neville opened the front door and went out. The dog immediately bolted away from the dish and bowls, right ear flattened back, legs scrambling frantically across the street.

Neville twitched with the repressed instinct to pursue. As casually as he could manage, he sat down on the edge of the porch.

Across the street the dog ran between the houses again and disappeared. After fifteen minutes of sitting, Neville went in again.

After a small breakfast he put out more food.

The dog came at four and Neville went out again, this time making sure that the dog was finished eating.

Once more the dog fled. But this time, seeing that it was not pursued, it stopped across the street and looked back for a moment.

"It's all right, boy," Neville called out, but at the sound of his voice the dog ran away again.

Neville sat on the porch stiffly, teeth gritted with impatience. Goddamn it, what's the matter with him? he thought. The damn *mutt!*

He forced himself to think of what the dog must have gone through. The endless nights of groveling in the blackness, hidden God knew where, its gaunt chest laboring in the night while all around its shivering form the vampires walked. The foraging for food and water, the struggle for life in a world without masters, housed in a body that man had made dependent on himself.

Poor little fella, he thought, I'll be good to you when you come and live with me.

Maybe, the thought came then, a dog had *more* chance of survival than a human. Dogs were smaller, they could hide in places the vampires couldn't go. They could probably sense the alien nature of those about them, probably *smell* it.

That didn't make him any happier. For always, in spite of reason, he had clung to the hope that someday he would find someone like himself—a man, a woman, a child, it didn't matter. Sex was fast losing its meaning without the endless prodding of mass hypnosis. Loneliness he still felt.

Sometimes he had indulged in daydreams about finding someone. More often, though, he had tried to adjust to what he sincerely believed was the inevitable—that he was actually the only one left in the world. At least in as much of the world as he could ever hope to know.

Thinking about it, he almost forgot that nightfall was approaching.

With a start he looked up and saw Ben Cortman running at him from across the street.

"Neville!"

He jumped up from the porch and ran into the house, locking and bolting the door behind him with shaking hands.

⧯

For a certain period he went out on the porch just as the dog had finished eating. Every time he went out the dog ran away, but as the days passed it ran with decreasing speed, and soon it was stopping halfway across the street to look back and bark at him. Neville never followed, but sat down on the porch and watched. It was a game they played.

Then one day Neville sat on the porch *before* the dog came. And, when it appeared across the street, he remained seated.

For about fifteen minutes the dog hovered near the curb suspiciously, unwilling to approach the food. Neville edged as far away from the food as he could in order to encourage the dog. Unthinking, he crossed his legs, and the dog shrank away at the unexpected motion. Neville held himself quietly then and the dog kept moving around restlessly in the street, its eyes moving from Neville to the food and back again.

"Come on, boy," Neville said to it. "Eat your food, that's a good dog."

Another ten minutes passed. The dog was now on the lawn, moving in concentric arcs that became shorter and shorter.

The dog stopped. Then slowly, very slowly, one paw at a time, it began moving up on the dish and bowls, its eyes never leaving Neville for a second.

"That's the boy," Neville said quietly.

This time the dog didn't flinch or back away at the sound of his voice. Still Neville made sure he sat motionless so that no abrupt movement would startle the dog.

The dog moved yet closer, stalking the plate, its body tense and waiting for the least motion from Neville.

"That's right," Neville told the dog.

Suddenly the dog darted in and grabbed the meat. Neville's pleased laughter followed its frantically erratic wobble across the street.

"You little son of a gun," he said appreciatively.

Then he sat and watched the dog as it ate. It crouched down on a yellow lawn across the street, its eyes on Neville while it wolfed down the hamburger. Enjoy it, he thought, watching the dog. From now on you get dog food. I can't afford to let you have any more fresh meat.

When the dog had finished it straightened up and came across the street again, a little less hesitantly. Neville still sat there, feeling his heart thud nervously. The dog was beginning to trust him, and somehow it made him tremble. He sat there, his eyes fastened on the dog.

"That's right, boy," he heard himself saying aloud. "Get your water now, that's a good dog."

A sudden smile of delight raised his lips as he saw the dog's good ear stand up. He's *listening*! he thought excitedly. He hears what I say, the little son of a gun!

"Come on, boy." He went on talking eagerly. "Get your water and your milk now, that's a good boy. I won't hurt you. Atta boy."

The dog went to the water and drank gingerly, its head lifting with sudden jerks to watch him, then dipping down again.

"I'm not doing anything," Neville told the dog.

He couldn't get over how odd his voice sounded. When a man didn't hear the sound of his own voice for almost a year, it sounded very strange to him. A year was a long time to live in silence. When you come live with me, he thought, I'll talk your ear off.

The dog finished the water.

"Come 'ere, boy," Neville said invitingly, patting his leg. "*Come* on."

The dog looked at him curiously, its good ear twitching again. Those eyes, Neville thought. What a world of feeling in those eyes! Distrust, fear, hope, loneliness— all etched in those big brown eyes. Poor little guy.

"Come on, boy, I won't hurt you," he said gently.

Then he stood up and the dog ran away. Neville stood there looking at the fleeing dog shaking his head slowly.

More days passed. Each day Neville sat on the porch while the dog ate, and before long the dog approached the dish and bowls without hesitation, almost boldly, with the assurance of the dog that knows its human conquest.

And all the time Neville would talk to it.

"That's a good boy. Eat up the food. That's *good* food, isn't it? Sure it is. I'm your friend. I gave you that food. Eat it up, boy, that's right. That's a *good* dog," endlessly cajoling, praising, pouring soft words into the dog's frightened mind as it ate.

And every day he sat a little bit closer to it, until the day came when he could have reached out and touched the dog if he'd stretched a little. He didn't, though. I'm not taking any chances, he told himself. I don't want to scare him.

But it was hard to keep his hands still. He could almost feel them twitching empathically with his strong desire to reach out and stroke the dog's head. He had such a terrible yearning to love something again, and the dog was such a beautifully ugly dog.

He kept talking to the dog until it became quite used to the sound of his voice. It hardly looked up now when he spoke. It came and went without trepidation, eating and barking its curt acknowledgment from across the street. Soon now, Neville told himself, I'll be able to pat his head. The days passed into pleasant weeks, each hour bringing him closer to a companion.

Then one day the dog didn't come.

Neville was frantic. He'd got so used to the dog's coming and going that it had become the fulcrum of his daily schedule, everything fitting around the dog's mealtimes, investigation forgotten, everything pushed aside but his desire to have the dog in his house.

He spent a nerve-racked afternoon searching the neighborhood, calling out in a loud voice for the dog. But no amount of searching helped, and he went home to a tasteless dinner. The dog didn't come for dinner that night or for breakfast the next morning. Again Neville searched, but with less hope. They've got him, he kept hearing the words in his mind, the dirty bastards have got him. But he couldn't really believe it. He wouldn't let himself believe it.

On the afternoon of the third day he was in the garage when he heard the sound of the metal bowl clinking outside. With a gasp he ran out into the daylight.

"You're *back*!" he cried.

The dog jerked away from the plate nervously, water dripping from its jaws.

Neville's heart leaped. The dog's eyes were glazed and it was panting for breath, its dark tongue hanging out.

"No," he said, his voice breaking. "Oh, *no*."

The dog still backed across the lawn on trembling stalks of legs.

Quickly Neville sat down on the porch steps and stayed there trembling. Oh, no, he thought in anguish, oh, God, *no.*

He sat there watching it tremble fitfully as it lapped up the water. No. No. It's not true.

"Not true," he murmured without realizing it.

Then, instinctively, he reached out his hand. The dog drew back a little, teeth bared in a throaty snarl.

"It's all right, boy," Neville said quietly. "I won't hurt you." He didn't even know what he was saying.

He couldn't stop the dog from leaving. He tried to follow it, but it was gone before he could discover where it hid. He'd decided it must be under a house somewhere, but that didn't do him any good.

He couldn't sleep that night. He paced restlessly, drinking pots of coffee and cursing the sluggishness of time. He had to get hold of the dog, he had to. And soon. He had to cure it.

But how? His throat moved. There had to be a way. Even with the little he knew there *must* be a way.

The next morning he sat right beside the bowl and he felt his lips shaking as the dog came limping slowly across the street. It didn't eat anything. Its eyes were more dull and listless than they'd been the day before. Neville wanted to jump at it and try to grab hold of it, take it in the house, nurse it.

But he knew that if he jumped and missed he might undo everything. The dog might never return.

All through the meal his hand kept twitching out to pat the dog's head. But every time it did, the dog cringed away with a snarl. He tried being forceful. "*Stop* that!" he said in a firm, angry tone, but that only frightened the dog more and it drew away farther from him. Neville had to talk to it for fifteen minutes, his voice a hoarse, trembling sound, before the dog would return to the water.

This time he managed to follow the slow-moving dog and saw which house it squirmed under. There was a little metal screen he could have put up over the opening, but he didn't. He didn't want to frighten the dog. And besides, there would be no way of getting the dog then except through the floor, and that would take too long. He had to get the dog fast.

When the dog didn't return that afternoon, he took a dish of milk and put it under the house where the dog was. The next morning the bowl was empty. He was going to put more milk in it when he realized that the dog might never leave his lair then. He put the bowl back in front of his house and prayed that the dog was strong enough to reach it. He was too worried even to criticize his inept prayer.

When the dog didn't come that afternoon he went back and looked in. He paced back and forth outside the opening and almost put milk there anyway. No, the dog would *never* leave then.

He went home and spent a sleepless night. The dog didn't come in the morning. Again he went to the house. He listened at the opening but couldn't hear any sound of breathing. Either it was too far back for him to hear or . . .

He went back to the house and sat on the porch. He didn't have breakfast or lunch. He just sat there.

That afternoon, late, the dog came limping out between the houses, moving slowly on its bony legs. Neville forced himself to sit there without moving until the dog had reached the food. Then, quickly, he reached down and picked up the dog.

Immediately it tried to snap at him, but he caught its jaws in his right hand and held them together. Its lean, almost hairless body squirmed feebly in his grasp and pitifully terrified whines pulsed in its throat.

"It's all right," he kept saying. "It's all right, boy."

Quickly he took it into his room and put it down on the little bed of blankets he'd arranged for the dog. As soon as he took his hand off its jaws the dog snapped at him and he jerked his hand back. The dog lunged over the linoleum with a violent scrabbling of paws, heading for the door. Neville jumped up and blocked its way. The dog's legs slipped on the smooth surface, then it got a little traction and disappeared under the bed.

Neville got on his knees and looked under the bed. In the gloom there he saw the two glowing coals of eyes and heard the fitful panting.

"*Come* on, boy," he pleaded unhappily. "I won't hurt you. You're *sick.* You need help."

The dog wouldn't budge. With a groan Neville got up finally and went out, closing the door behind him. He went and got the bowls and filled them with milk and water. He put them in the bedroom near the dog's bed.

He stood by his own bed a moment, listening to the panting dog, his face lined with pain.

"Oh," he muttered plaintively, "why don't you *trust* me?"

He was eating dinner when he heard the horrible crying and whining.

Heart pounding, he jumped up from the table and raced across the living room. He threw open the bedroom door and flicked on the light.

Over in the corner by the bench the dog was trying to dig a hole in the floor.

Terrified whines shook its body as its front paws clawed frenziedly at the linoleum, slipping futilely on the smoothness of it.

"Boy, it's all right!" Neville said quickly.

The dog jerked around and backed into the corner, hackles rising, jaws drawn back all the way from its yellowish-white teeth, a half-mad sound quivering in its throat.

Suddenly Neville knew what was wrong. It was nighttime and the terrified dog was trying to dig itself a hole to bury itself in.

He stood there helplessly, his brain refusing to work properly as the dog edged away from the corner, then scuttled underneath the workbench.

An idea finally came. Neville moved to his bed quickly and pulled off the top blanket. Returning to the bench, he crouched down and looked under it.

The dog was almost flattened against the wall, its body shaking violently, guttural snarls bubbling in its throat.

"All right, boy," he said. "All right."

The dog shrank back as Neville stuck the blanket underneath the bench and then stood up. Neville went over to the door and remained there a minute looking back. If only I could *do* something, he thought helplessly. But I can't even get close to him.

Well, he decided grimly, if the dog didn't accept him soon, he'd have to try a little chloroform. Then he could at least work on the dog, fix its paw and try somehow to cure it.

He went back to the kitchen but he couldn't eat. Finally he dumped the contents of his plate into the garbage disposal and poured the coffee back into the pot. In the living room he made himself a drink and downed it. It tasted flat and unappetizing. He put down the glass and went back to the bedroom with a somber face.

The dog had dug itself under the folds of the blanket and there it was still shaking, whining ceaselessly. No use trying to work on it now, he thought; it's too frightened.

He walked back to the bed and sat down. He ran his hands through his hair and then put them over his face. Cure it, cure it, he thought, and one of his hands bunched into a fist to strike feebly at the mattress.

Reaching out abruptly, he turned off the light and lay down fully clothed. Still lying down, he worked off his sandals and listened to them thump on the floor.

Silence. He lay there staring at the ceiling. Why don't I get up? he wondered. Why don't I try to *do* something?

He turned on his side. Get some sleep. The words came automatically. He knew he wasn't going to sleep, though. He lay in the darkness listening to the dog's whimpering. Die, it's going to die, he kept thinking, there's nothing in the world I can do.

At last, unable to bear the sound, he reached over and switched on the bedside lamp. As he moved across the room in his stocking feet, he heard the dog trying suddenly to jerk loose from the blanketing. But it got all tangled up in the folds and began yelping, terror-stricken, while its body flailed wildly under the wool.

Neville knelt beside it and put his hands on its body. He heard the choking snarl and the muffled click of its teeth as it snapped at him through the blanket.

"All right," he said. "Stop it now."

The dog kept struggling against him, its high-pitched whining never stopping, its gaunt body shaking without control. Neville kept his hands firmly on its body, pinning it down, talking to it quietly, gently.

"It's all right now, fella, *all* right. Nobody's going to hurt you. Take it easy, now. Come on, relax, now. Come on, boy. Take it easy. Relax. That's right, relax. That's it. Calm down. Nobody's going to hurt you. We'll take care of you."

He went on talking intermittently for almost an hour, his voice a low, hypnotic murmuring in the silence of the room. And slowly, hesitantly, the dog's trembling eased off. A smile faltered on Neville's lips as he went on talking, talking.

"That's right. Take it easy, now. We'll take care of you."

Soon the dog lay still beneath his strong hands, the only movement its harsh breathing. Neville began patting its head, began running his right hand over its body, stroking and soothing.

"That's a good dog," he said softly. "*Good* dog. I'll take care of you now. Nobody will hurt you. You understand, don't you, fella? Sure you do. Sure. You're *my* dog, aren't you?"

Carefully he sat down on the cool linoleum, still patting the dog.

"You're a good dog, a *good* dog."

His voice was calm, it was quiet with resignation.

After about an hour he picked up the dog. For a moment it struggled and started whining, but Neville talked to it again and it soon calmed down.

He sat down on his bed and held the blanket-covered dog in his lap. He sat there for hours holding the dog, patting and stroking and talking. The dog lay immobile in his lap, breathing easier.

It was about eleven that night when Neville slowly undid the blanket folds and exposed the dog's head.

For a few minutes it cringed away from his hand, snapping a little. But he kept talking to it quietly, and after a while his hand rested on the warm neck and he was moving his fingers gently, scratching and caressing.

He smiled down at the dog, his throat moving.

"You'll be all better soon," he whispered. "Real soon."

The dog looked up at him with its dulled, sick eyes and then its tongue faltered out and licked roughly and moistly across the palm of Neville's hand.

Something broke in Neville's throat. He sat there silently while tears ran slowly down his cheeks.

In a week the dog was dead.

CHAPTER FOURTEEN

There was no debauch of drinking. Far from it. He found that he actually drank less. Something had changed. Trying to analyze it, he came to the conclusion that his last drunk had put him on the bottom, at the very nadir of frustrated despair. Now, unless he put himself under the ground, the only way he could go was up.

After the first few weeks of building up intense hope about the dog, it had slowly dawned on him that intense hope was not the answer and never had been. In a world of monotonous horror there could be no salvation in wild dreaming. Horror he had adjusted to. But monotony was the greater obstacle, and he realized it now, understood it at long last. And understanding it seemed to give him a sort of quiet peace, a sense of having spread all the cards on his mental table, examined them, and settled conclusively on the desired hand.

Burying the dog had not been the agony he had supposed it would be. In a way, it was almost like burying threadbare hopes and false excitements. From that day on he learned to accept the dungeon he existed in, neither seeking to escape with sudden derring-do nor beating his pate bloody on its walls.

And, thus resigned, he returned to work.

It had happened almost a year before, several days after he had put Virginia to her second and final rest.

Hollow and bleak, a sense of absolute loss in him, he was walking the streets late one afternoon, hands listless at his sides, feet shuffling with the rhythm of despair. His face mirrored nothing of the helpless agony he felt. His face was a blank.

He had wandered through the streets for hours, neither knowing nor caring where he was going. All he knew was that he couldn't return to the empty rooms of the house, couldn't look at the things they had touched and held and known with him. He couldn't look at Kathy's empty bed, at her clothes hanging still and useless in the closet, couldn't look at the bed that he and Virginia had slept in, at Virginia's clothes, her jewelry, all her perfumes on the bureau. He couldn't go near the house.

And so he walked and wandered, and he didn't know where he was when the people started milling past him, when the man caught his arm and breathed garlic in his face.

"Come, brother, come," the man said, his voice a grating rasp. He saw the man's throat moving like clammy turkey skin, the red-splotched cheeks, the feverish eyes, the black suit, unpressed, unclean. "Come and be saved, brother, *saved*."

Robert Neville stared at the man. He didn't understand. The man pulled him on, his fingers like skeleton fingers on Neville's arm.

"It's never too late, brother," said the man. "Salvation comes to him who . . ."

The last of his words were lost now in the rising murmur of sound from the great tent they were approaching. It sounded like the sea imprisoned under canvas, roaring to escape. Robert Neville tried to loose his arm.

"I don't want to—"

The man didn't hear. He pulled Neville on with him and they walked toward the waterfall of crying and stamping. The man did not let go. Robert Neville felt as if he were being dragged into a tidal wave.

"But I don't—"

The tent had swallowed him then, the ocean of shouting, stamping, hand-clapping sound engulfed him. He flinched instinctively and felt his heart begin pumping heavily. He was surrounded now by people, hundreds of them, swelling and gushing around him like waters closing in. And yelling and clapping and crying out words Robert Neville couldn't understand.

Then the cries died down and he heard the voice that stabbed through the half-light like knifing doom, that crackled and bit shrilly over the loud-speaker system.

"Do you want to fear the holy cross of God? Do you want to look into the mirror and not see the face that Almighty God has given you? Do you want to come crawling back from the grave like a monster out of hell?"

The voice enjoined hoarsely, pulsing, driving.

"Do you want to be changed into a black unholy animal? Do you want to stain the evening sky with hell-born bat wings? I ask you—do you want to be turned into godless, night-cursed husks, into creatures of eternal damnation?"

"No!" the people erupted, terror-stricken. "No, *save* us!"

Robert Neville backed away, bumping into flailing-handed, white-jawed true believers screaming out for succor from the lowering skies.

"Well, I'm *telling* you! I'm *telling* you, so listen to the word of God! Behold, evil shall go forth from nation to nation and the slain of the Lord shall be at that day from one end of the earth even unto the other end of the earth! Is that a lie, is that a *lie*?"

"No! *No!*"

"I tell you that unless we become as little children, stainless and pure in the eyes of Our Lord—unless we stand up and shout out the glory of Almighty God and of His only begotten son, Jesus Christ, our Saviour—unless we fall on our *knees* and beg forgiveness for our grievous offenses—we are damned! I'll say it again, so *listen*! We are damned, we are damned, *we are damned*!"

"Amen!"

"Save us!"

The people twisted and moaned and smote their brows and shrieked in mortal terror and screamed out terrible hallelujahs.

Robert Neville was shoved about, stumbling and lost in a treadmill of hopes, in a crossfire of frenzied worship.

"God has punished us for our great transgressions! God has unleashed the terrible force of His almighty wrath! God has set loose the second deluge upon us—a deluge, a flood, a world-consuming torrent of creatures from *hell*! He has opened the grave, He has unsealed the crypt, He has turned the dead from their black tombs—*and set them upon us*! And death and hell delivered up the dead which were in them! That's the word of God! O God, You have punished us, O God, You have seen the terrible face of our transgressions, O God, You have struck us with the might of Your almighty wrath!"

Clapping hands like the spatter of irregular rifle fire, swaying bodies like stalks in a terrible wind, moans of the great potential dead, screams of the fighting living. Robert Neville strained through their violent ranks, face white, hands before him like those of a blind man seeking shelter.

He escaped, weak and trembling, stumbling away from them. Inside the tent the people screamed. But night had already fallen.

He thought about that now as he sat in the living room nursing a mild drink, a psychology text resting on his lap.

A quotation had started the train of thought, sending him back to that evening ten months before, when he'd been pulled into the wild revival meeting.

"This condition, known as hysterical blindness, may be partial or complete, including one, several, or all objects."

That was the quotation he'd read. It had started him working on the problem again.

A new approach now. Before, he had stubbornly persisted in attributing all vampire phenomena to the germ. If certain of these phenomena did not fit in with the bacilli, he felt inclined to judge their cause as superstition. True, he'd vaguely considered psychological explanations, but he'd never really given much credence to such a possibility. Now, released at last from unyielding preconceptions, he did.

There was no reason, he knew, why some of the phenomena could not be physically caused, the rest psychological. And, now that he accepted it, it seemed one of those patent answers that only a blind man would miss. Well, I always was the blind-man type, he thought in quiet amusement.

Consider, he thought then, the shock undergone by a victim of the plague.

Toward the end of the plague, yellow journalism had spread a cancerous dread of vampires to all corners of the nation. He could remember himself the rash of pseudo-scientific articles that veiled an out-and-out fright campaign designed to sell papers.

There was something grotesquely amusing in that; the frenetic attempt to sell papers while the world died. Not that all newspapers had done that. Those papers that had lived in honesty and integrity died the same way.

Yellow journalism, though, *had* been rampant in the final days. And, in addition, a great upsurge in revivalism had occurred. In a typical desperation for quick answers, easily understood, people had turned to primitive worship as the solution. With less than success. Not only had they died as quickly as the rest of the people, but they had died with terror in their hearts, with a mortal dread flowing in their very veins.

And then, Robert Neville thought, to have this hideous dread vindicated. To regain consciousness beneath hot, heavy soil and know that death had not brought rest. To find themselves clawing up through the earth, their bodies driven now by a strange, hideous need.

Such traumatic shocks could undo what mind was left. And such shocks could explain much.

The cross, first of all.

Once they were forced to accept vindication of the dread of being repelled by an object that had been a focal point of worship, their minds could have snapped. Dread of the cross sprang up. And, driven on despite already created dreads, the vampire could have acquired an intense mental loathing, and this self-hatred could have set up a block in their weakened minds causing them to be blind to their own abhorred image. It could make them lonely, soul-lost slaves of the night, afraid to approach anyone, living a solitary existence, often seeking solace in the soil of their native land, struggling to gain a sense of communion with something, with anything.

The water? That he *did* accept as superstition, a carryover of the traditional legend that witches were incapable of crossing running water, as written down in the story of Tam O'Shanter. Witches, vampires—in all these feared beings there was a sort of interwoven kinship. Legends and superstitions could overlap, and did.

And the living vampires? That was simple too now.

In life there were the deranged, the insane. What better hold than vampirism for these to catch on to? He was certain that all the living who came to his house at night were insane, thinking themselves true vampires although actually they were only demented sufferers. And that would explain the fact that they'd never taken the obvious step of burning his house. They simply could not think that logically.

He remembered the man who one night had climbed to the top of the light post in front of the house and, while Robert Neville had watched through the peephole, had leaped into space, waving his arms frantically. Neville hadn't been able to explain it at the time, but now the answer seemed obvious. The man had thought he was a bat.

Neville sat looking at the half-finished drink, a thin smile fastened to his lips.

So, he thought, slowly, surely, we find out about them. Find out that they are no invincible race. Far from it; they are a highly perishable race requiring the strictest of physical conditions for the furtherance of their Godforsaken existence.

He put the drink down on the table.

I don't need it, he thought. My emotions don't need feeding any more. I don't need liquor for forgetting or for escaping. I don't have to escape from anything. Not now.

For the first time since the dog had died he smiled and felt within himself a quiet, well-modulated satisfaction. There were still many things to learn, but not so many as before. Strangely, life was be-coming almost bearable. I don the robe of hermit without a cry, he thought.

On the phonograph, music played, quiet and unhurried.

Outside, the vampires waited.

PART THREE: June 1978

CHAPTER FIFTEEN

He was out hunting for Cortman. It had become a relaxing hobby, hunting for Cortman; one of the few diversions left to him. On those days when he didn't care to leave the neighborhood and there was no demanding work to be done on the house, he would search. Under cars, behind bushes, under houses, up fireplaces, in closets, under beds, in refrigerators; any place into which a moderately corpulent male body could conceivably be squeezed.

Ben Cortman could be in any one of those places at one time or another. He changed his hiding place constantly. Neville felt certain that Cortman knew he was singled out for capture. He felt, further, that Cortman relished the peril of it. If the phrase were not such an obvious anachronism, Neville would have said that Ben Cortman had a zest for life. Sometimes he thought Cortman was happier now than he ever had been before.

Neville ambled slowly up Compton Boulevard toward the next house he meant to search. An uneventful morning had passed. Cortman was not found, even though Neville knew he was somewhere in the neighborhood. He had to be, because he was always the first one at the house at night. The other ones were almost always strangers. Their turnover was great, because they invariably stayed in the neighborhood and Neville found them and destroyed them. Not Cortman.

As he strolled, Neville wondered again what he'd do if he found Cortman. True, his plan had always been the same: immediate disposal. But that was on the surface. He knew it wouldn't be that easy. Oh, it wasn't that he felt anything toward Cortman. It wasn't even that Cortman represented a part of the past. The past was dead and he knew it and accepted it.

No, it wasn't either of those things. What it probably was, Neville decided, was that he didn't want to cut off a recreational activity. The rest were such dull, robot-like creatures. Ben, at least, had some imagination. For some reason, his brain hadn't weakened like the others'. It could be, Neville often theorized, that Ben Cortman was born to be dead. Undead, that is, he thought, a wry smile playing on his full lips.

It no longer occurred to him that Cortman was out to kill him. That was a negligible menace.

Neville sank down on the next porch with a slow groan. Then, reaching lethargically into his pocket, he took out his pipe. With an idle thumb he tamped rough tobacco shreds down into the pipe bowl. In a few moments smoke swirls were floating lazily about his head in the warm, still air.

It was a bigger, more relaxed Neville that gazed out across the wide field on the other side of the boulevard. An evenly paced hermit life had increased his weight to 230 pounds. His face was full, his body broad and muscular underneath the loose-fitting denim he wore. He had long before given up shaving. Only rarely did he crop his thick blond beard, so that it remained two to three inches from his skin. His hair was thinning and was long and straggly. Set in the deep tan of his face, his blue eyes were calm and unexcitable.

He leaned back against the brick step, puffing out slow clouds of smoke. Far out across that field he knew there was still a depression in the ground where he had buried Virginia, where she had unburied herself. But knowing it brought no glimmer of reflective sorrow to his eyes. Rather than go on suffering, he had learned to stultify himself to introspection. Time had lost its multidimensional scope. There was only the present for Robert Neville; a present based on day-today survival marked by neither heights of joy nor depths of despair. I am predominantly vegetable, he often thought to himself. That was the way he wanted it.

Robert Neville sat gazing at the white spot out in the field for several minutes before he realized that it was moving.

His eyes blinked once and the skin tightened over his face. He made a slight sound in his throat, a sound of doubting question. Then, standing up, he raised his left hand to shade the sunlight from his eyes.

His teeth bit convulsively into the pipestem.

A woman.

He didn't even try to catch the pipe when it fell from his mouth as his jaw went slack. For a long, breathless moment, he stood there on the porch step, staring.

He closed his eyes, opened them. She was still there. Robert Neville felt the increasing thud in his chest as he watched the woman.

She didn't see him. Her head was down as she walked across the long field. He could see her reddish hair blowing in the breeze, her arms swinging loosely at her sides. His throat moved. It was such an incredible sight after three years that his mind could not assimilate it. He kept blinking and staring as he stood motionless in the shade of the house.

A woman. Alive. *In the daylight.*

He stood, mouth partly open, gaping at the woman. She was young, he could see now as she came closer; probably in her twenties. She wore a wrinkled and dirty white dress. She was very tan, her hair was red. In the dead silence of the afternoon Neville thought he heard the crunch of her shoes in the long grass.

I've gone mad. The words presented themselves abruptly. He felt less shock at that possibility than he did at the notion that she was real. He had, in fact, been vaguely preparing himself for just such a delusion. It seemed feasible. The man who died of thirst saw mirages of lakes. Why shouldn't a man who thirsted for companionship see a woman walking in the sun?

He started suddenly. No, it wasn't that. For, unless his delusion had sound as well as sight, he now heard her walking through the grass. He knew it was real. The movement of her hair, of her arms. She still looked at the ground. Who was she? Where was she going? Where had she been?

He didn't know what welled up in him. It was too quick to analyze, an instinct that broke through every barrier of time-erected reserve.

His left arm went up.

"Hi!" he cried. He jumped down to the sidewalk. "*Hi*, there!"

A moment of sudden, complete silence. Her head jerked up and they looked at each other. Alive, he thought. Alive!

He wanted to shout more, but he felt suddenly choked up. His tongue felt wooden, his brain refused to function. Alive. The word kept repeating itself in his mind, Alive, alive, alive. . . .

With a sudden twisting motion the young woman turned and began running wildly back across the field.

For a moment Neville stood there twitching, uncertain of what to do. Then his heart seemed to burst and he lunged across the sidewalk. His boots jolted down into the street and thudded across.

"Wait!" he heard himself cry.

The woman did not wait. He saw her bronze legs pumping as she fled across the uneven surface of the field. And suddenly he realized that words could not stop her. He thought of how shocked he had been at seeing her. How much more shocked she must have felt hearing a sudden shout end long silence and seeing a great, bearded man waving at her!

His legs drove him up over the other curb and into the field. His heart was pounding heavily now. She's alive! He couldn't stop thinking that. Alive. *A woman alive!*

She couldn't run as fast as he could. Almost immediately Neville began catching up with her. She glanced back over her shoulder with terrified eyes.

"I won't hurt you!" he cried, but she kept running.

Suddenly she tripped and went crashing down on one knee. Her face turned again and he saw the twisted fright on it.

"I won't *hurt* you!" he yelled again.

With a desperate lunge she regained her footing and ran on.

No sound now but the sound of her shoes and his boots thrashing through the heavy grass. He began jumping over the grass to avoid its impending height and gained more ground. The skirt of her dress whipped against the grass, holding her back.

"Stop!" he cried, again, but more from instinct than with any hope that she would stop.

She didn't. She ran still faster and, gritting his teeth, Neville put another burst of speed into his pursuit. He followed in a straight line as the girl weaved across the field, her light reddish hair billowing behind her.

Now he was so close he could hear her tortured breathing. He didn't like to frighten her, but he couldn't stop now. Everything else in the world seemed to have fallen from view but her. He had to catch her.

His long, powerful legs pistoned on, his boots thudded on the earth.

Another stretch of field. The two of them ran, panting. She glanced back at him again to see how close he was. He didn't realize how frightening he looked; six foot three in his boots, a gigantic bearded man with an intent look.

Now his hand lurched out and he caught her by the right shoulder.

With a gasping scream the young woman twisted away and stumbled to the side. Losing balance, she fell on one hip on the rocky ground. Neville jumped forward to help her up. She scuttled back over the ground and tried to get up, but she slipped and fell again, this time on her back. Her skirt jerked up over her knees. She shoved herself up with a breathless whimper, her dark eyes terrified.

"Here," he gasped, reaching out his hand.

She slapped it aside with a slight cry and struggled to her feet. He caught her by the arm and her free hand lashed out, raking jagged nails across his forehead and right temple. With a grunt he jerked back his arm and she whirled and began running again.

Neville jumped forward again and caught her by the shoulders. "What are you afraid—"

He couldn't finish. Her hand drove stingingly across his mouth. Then there was only the sound of gasping and struggling, of their feet scrabbling and slipping on the earth, crackling down the thick grass.

"Will you *stop*!" he cried, but she kept battling.

She jerked back and his taut fingers ripped away part of her dress. He let go and the material fluttered down to her waist. He saw her tanned shoulder and the white brassiere cup over her left breast.

She clawed out at him and he caught her wrists in an iron grip. Her right foot drove a bone-numbing kick to his shin.

"Damn it!"

With a snarl of rage he drove his right palm across her face. She staggered back, then looked at him dizzily. Abruptly she started crying helplessly. She sank to her knees before him, holding her arms over her head as if to ward off further blows.

Neville stood there gasping, looking down at her cringing form. He blinked, then took a deep breath.

"Get up," he said. "I'm not going to *hurt* you."

She didn't raise her head. He looked down confusedly at her. He didn't know what to say.

"I said I'm not going to hurt you," he told her again.

She looked up. But his face seemed to frighten her again, for she shrank back. She crouched there looking up at him fearfully.

"What are you afraid of?" he asked.

He didn't realize that his voice was devoid of warmth, that it was the harsh, sterile voice of a man who had lost all touch with humanity.

He took a step toward her and she drew back again with a frightened gasp. He extended his hand.

"Here," he said. "Stand up."

She got up slowly but without his help. Noticing suddenly her exposed breast, she reached down and held up the torn material of her dress.

They stood there breathing harshly and looking at each other. And, now that the first shock had passed, Neville didn't know what to say. He'd been dreaming of this moment for years. His dreams had never been like this.

"What . . . what's your name?" he asked.

She didn't answer. Her eyes stayed on his face, her lips kept trembling.

"Well?" he asked loudly, and she flinched.

"R-Ruth." Her voice faltered.

A shudder ran through Robert Neville's body. The sound of her voice seemed to loosen everything in him. Questions disappeared. He felt his heart beating heavily. He almost felt as if he were going to cry.

His hand moved out, almost unconsciously. Her shoulder trembled under his palm.

"Ruth," he said in a flat, lifeless voice.

His throat moved as he stared at her.

"Ruth," he said again.

The two of them, the man and the woman, stood facing each other in the great, hot field.

CHAPTER SIXTEEN

The woman lay motionless on his bed, sleeping. It was past four in the afternoon. At least twenty times Neville had stolen into the bedroom to look at her and see if she were awake. Now he sat in the kitchen drinking coffee and worrying.

What if she *is* infected, though? he argued with himself.

The worry had started a few hours before, while Ruth was sleeping. Now, he couldn't rid himself of the fear. No matter how he reasoned, it didn't help. All right, she was tanned from the sun, she had been walking in the daylight. The dog had been in the daylight too.

Neville's fingers tapped restlessly on the table.

Simplicity had departed; the dream had faded into disturbing complexity. There had been no wondrous embrace, no magic words spoken. Beyond her name he had got nothing from her. Getting her to the house had been a battle. Getting her to enter had been even worse. She had cried and begged him not to kill her. No matter what he said to her, she kept crying and begging. He had visualized something on the order of a Hollywood production; stars in their eyes, entering the house, arms about each other, fade-out. Instead he had been forced to tug and cajole and argue and scold while she held back. The entrance had been less than romantic. He had to drag her in.

Once in the house, she had been no less frightened. He'd tried to act comfortingly, but all she did was cower in one corner the way the dog had done. She wouldn't eat or drink anything he gave her. Finally he'd been compelled to take her in the bedroom and lock her in. Now she was asleep.

He sighed wearily and fingered the handle of his cup.

All these years, he thought, dreaming about a companion. Now I meet one and the first thing I do is distrust her, treat her crudely and impatiently.

And yet there was really nothing else he could do. He had accepted too long the proposition that he was the only normal person left. It didn't matter that she looked normal. He'd seen too many of them lying in their coma that looked as healthy as she. They weren't, though, and he knew it. The simple fact that she had been walking in the sunlight wasn't enough to tip the scales on the side of trusting acceptance. He had doubted too long. His concept of the society had become ironbound. It was almost impossible for him to believe that there were others like him. And, after the first shock had diminished, all the dogma of his long years alone had asserted itself.

With a heavy breath he rose and went back to the bedroom. She was still in the same position. Maybe, he thought, she's gone back into coma again.

He stood over the bed, staring down at her. Ruth. There was so much about her he wanted to know. And yet he was almost afraid to find out. Because if she were like the others, there was only one course open. And it was better not to know anything about the people you killed.

His hands twitched at his sides, his blue eyes gazed flatly at her. What if it had been a freak occurrence? What if she had snapped out of coma for a little while and gone wandering? It seemed possible. And yet, as far as he knew, daylight was the one thing the germ could not endure. Why wasn't that enough to convince him she was normal?

Well, there was only one way to make sure.

He bent over and put his hand on her shoulder.

"Wake up," he said.

She didn't stir. His mouth tightened and his fingers drew in on her soft shoulder.

Then he noticed the thin golden chain around her throat. Reaching in with rough fingers, he drew it out of the bosom of her dress.

He was looking at the tiny gold cross when she woke up and recoiled into the pillow. She's not in coma; that was all he thought.

"What are you d-doing?" she asked faintly.

It was harder to distrust her when she spoke. The sound of the human voice was so strange to him that it had a power over him it had never had before.

"I'm . . . nothing," he said.

Awkwardly he stepped back and leaned against the wall. He looked at her a moment longer. Then he asked, "Where are you from?"

She lay there looking blankly at him.

"I asked you where you were from," he said.

Again she said nothing. He pushed himself away from the wall with a tight look on his face.

"Ing-Inglewood," she said hastily.

He looked at her coldly for a moment, then leaned back against the wall.

"I see," he said. "Did . . . did you live alone?"

"I was married."

"Where is your husband?"

Her throat moved. "He's dead."

"For how long?"

"Last week."

"And what did you do after he died?"

"Ran." She bit into her lower lip. "I ran away."

"You mean you've been wandering all this time?"

"Y-yes."

He looked at her without a word. Then abruptly he turned and his boots thumped loudly as he walked into the kitchen. Pulling open a cabinet door, he drew down a handful of garlic cloves. He put them on a dish, tore them into pieces, and mashed them to a pulp. The acrid fumes assailed his nostrils.

She was propped up on one elbow when he came back. Without hesitation he pushed the dish almost to her face.

She turned her head away with a faint cry.

"What are you doing?" she asked, and coughed once.

"Why do you turn away?"

"Please . . ."

"Why do you turn away?"

"It *smells*!" Her voice broke into a sob. "Don't! You're making me sick!"

He pushed the plate still closer to her face. With a gagging sound she backed away and pressed against the wall, her legs drawn up on the bed.

"Stop it! *Please!*" she begged.

He drew back the dish and watched her body twitching as her stomach convulsed.

"You're one of them," he said to her, quietly venomous.

She sat up suddenly and ran past him into the bathroom. The door slammed behind her and he could hear the sound of her terrible retching.

Thin-lipped, he put the dish down on the bedside table. His throat moved as he swallowed.

Infected. It had been a clear sign. He had learned over a year before that garlic was an allergen to any system infected with the *vampiris* bacillus. When the system was exposed to garlic, the stimulated tissues sensitized the cells, causing an abnormal reaction to any further contact with garlic. That was why putting it into their veins had accomplished little. They had to be exposed to the odor.

He sank down on the bed. And the woman had reacted in the wrong way.

After a moment Robert Neville frowned. If what she had said was true, she'd been wandering around for a week. She would naturally be exhausted and weak, and under those conditions the smell of so much garlic *could* have made her retch.

His fists thudded down onto the mattress. He still didn't know, then, not for certain. And, objectively, he knew he had no right to decide on inadequate evidence. It was something he'd learned the hard way, something he knew and believed absolutely.

He was still sitting there when she unlocked the bathroom door and came out. She stood in the hall a moment looking at him, then went into the living room. He rose and followed. When he came into the living room she was sitting on the couch.

"Are you satisfied?" she asked.

"Never mind that," he said. "You're on trial, not me."

She looked up angrily as if she meant to say something. Then her body slumped and she shook her head. He felt a twinge of sympathy for a moment. She looked so helpless, her thin hands resting on her lap. She didn't seem to care any more about her torn dress. He looked at the slight swelling of her breast. Her figure was very slim, almost curveless. Not at all like the woman he'd used to envision. Never mind that, he told himself, that doesn't matter any more.

He sat down in the chair and looked across at her. She didn't return his gaze.

"Listen to me," he said then. "I have every reason to suspect you of being infected. Especially now that you've reacted in such a way to garlic."

She said nothing.

"Haven't you anything to say?" he asked.

She raised her eyes.

"You think I'm one of them," she said.

"I think you *might* be."

"And what about this?" she asked, holding up her cross.

"That means nothing," he said.

"I'm awake," she said. "I'm not in a coma."

He said nothing. It was something he couldn't argue with, even though it didn't assuage doubt.

"I've been in Inglewood many times," he said finally. "Why didn't you hear my car?"

"Inglewood is a big place," she said.

He looked at her carefully, his fingers tapping on the arm of the chair.

"I'd . . . like to believe you," he said.

"Would you?" she asked. Another stomach contraction hit her and she bent over with a gasp, teeth clenched. Robert Neville sat there wondering why he didn't feel more compassion for her. Emotion was a difficult thing to summon from the dead, though. He had spent it all and felt hollow now, without feeling.

After a moment she looked up. Her eyes were hard.

"I've had a weak stomach all my life," she said. "I saw my husband killed last week. Torn to pieces. Right in front of my eyes I saw it. I lost two children to the plague. And for the past week I've been wandering all over. Hiding at night, not eating more than a few scraps of food. Sick with fear, unable to sleep more than a couple of hours at a time. Then I hear someone shout at me. You chase me over a field, hit me, drag me to your house. Then when I get sick because you shove a plate of reeking garlic in my face, you tell me I'm infected!"

Her hands twitched in her lap.

"What do you *expect* to happen?" she said angrily.

She slumped back against the couch back and closed her eyes. Her hands picked nervously at her skirt. For a moment she tried to tuck in the torn piece, but it fell down again and she sobbed angrily.

He leaned forward in the chair. He was beginning to feel guilty now, in spite of suspicions and doubts. He couldn't help it. He had forgotten about sobbing women. He raised a hand slowly to his beard and plucked confusedly as he watched her.

"Would . . ." he started. He swallowed. "Would you let me take a sample of your blood?" he asked. "I could—"

She stood up suddenly and stumbled toward the door.

He got up quickly.

"What are you doing?" he asked.

She didn't answer. Her hands fumbled awkwardly with the lock.

"You can't go out there," he said, surprised. "The street will be full of them in a little while."

"I'm not staying here," she sobbed. "What's the difference if they kill me?"

His hands closed over her arm. She tried to pull away.

"Leave me alone!" she cried. "I didn't ask to come here. You dragged me here. Why don't you leave me alone?"

He stood by her awkwardly, not knowing what to say.

"You can't go out," he said again.

He led her back to the couch. Then he went and got her a small tumbler of whisky at the bar. Never mind whether she's infected or not, he thought, never mind.

He handed her the tumbler. She shook her head.

"Drink it," he said. "It'll calm you down."

She looked up angrily. "So you can shove more garlic in my face?"

He shook his head.

"Drink it now," he said.

After a few moments she took the glass and took a sip of the whisky. It made her cough. She put the tumbler on the arm of the couch and a deep breath shook her body.

"Why do you want me to stay?" she asked unhappily.

He looked at her without a definite answer in his mind. Then he said, "Even if you *are* infected, I can't let you go out there. You don't know what they'd do to you."

Her eyes closed. "I don't care," she said.

CHAPTER SEVENTEEN

"I don't understand it," he told her over supper.

"Almost three years now, and still there are some of them alive. Food supplies are being used up. As far as I know, they still lie in a coma during the day." He shook his head. "But they're not dead. Three years and they're not dead. What keeps them going?"

She was wearing his bathrobe. About five she had relented, taken a bath, and changed. Her slender body was shapeless in the voluminous terry-cloth folds. She'd borrowed his comb and drawn her hair back into a pony tail fastened with a piece of twine.

Ruth fingered her coffee cup.

"We used to see them sometimes," she said. "We were afraid to go near them, though. We didn't think we should touch them."

"Didn't you know they'd come back after they died?"

She shook her head. "No."

"Didn't you wonder about the people who attacked your house at night?"

"It never entered our minds that they were . . ." She shook her head slowly. "It's hard to believe something like that."

"I suppose," he said.

He glanced at her as they sat eating silently. It was hard too to believe that here was a normal woman. Hard to believe that, after all these years, a companion had come. It was more than just doubting her. It was doubting that anything so remarkable could happen in such a lost world.

"Tell me more about them," Ruth said.

He got up and took the coffeepot off the stove. He poured more into her cup, into his, then replaced the pot and sat down.

"How do you feel now?" he asked her.

"I feel better, thank you."

He nodded and spooned sugar into his coffee. He felt her eyes on him as he stirred. What's she thinking? he wondered. He took a deep breath, wondering why the tightness in him didn't break. For a while he'd thought that he trusted her. Now he wasn't sure.

"You still don't trust me," she said, seeming to read his mind.

He looked up quickly, then shrugged.

"It's . . . not that," he said.

"Of course it is," she said quietly. She sighed. "Oh, very well. If you have to check my blood, check it."

He looked at her suspiciously, his mind questioning: Is it a trick? He hid the movement of his throat in swallowing coffee. It was stupid, he thought, to be so suspicious.

He put down the cup.

"Good," he said. "Very good."

He looked at her as she stared into the coffee.

"If you *are* infected," he told her, "I'll do everything I can to cure you."

Her eyes met his. "And if you can't?" she said.

Silence a moment.

"Let's wait and see," he said then.

They both drank coffee. Then he asked, "Shall we do it now?"

"Please," she said, "in the morning. I . . . still feel a little ill."

"All right," he said, nodding. "In the morning."

They finished their meal in silence. Neville felt only a small satisfaction that she was going to let him check her blood. He was afraid he might discover that she *was* infected. In the meantime he had to pass an evening and a night with her, perhaps get to know her and be attracted to her. When in the morning he might have to . . .

Later, in the living room, they sat looking at the mural, sipping port, and listening to Schubert's Fourth Symphony.

"I wouldn't have believed it," she said, seeming to cheer up. "I never thought I'd be listening to music again. Drinking wine."

She looked around the room.

"You've certainly done a wonderful job," she said.

"What about *your* house?" he asked.

"It was nothing like this," she said. "We didn't have a—"

"How did you protect your house?" he interrupted.

"Oh.—" She thought a moment. "We had it boarded up, of course. And we used crosses."

"They don't always work," he said quietly, after a moment of looking at her.

She looked blank. "They don't?"

"Why should a Jew fear the cross?" he said. "Why should a vampire who had been a Jew fear it? Most people were afraid of becoming vampires. Most of them suffer from hysterical blindness before mirrors. But as far as the cross goes—well, neither a Jew nor a Hindu nor a Mohammedan nor an atheist, for that matter, would fear the cross."

She sat holding her wineglass and looking at him with expressionless eyes.

"That's why the cross doesn't always work," he said.

"You didn't let me finish," she said. "We used garlic too."

"I thought it made you sick."

"I was already sick. I used to weigh a hundred and twenty. I weigh ninety-eight pounds now."

He nodded. But as he went into the kitchen to get another bottle of wine, he thought, She would have adjusted to it by now. After three years.

Then again, she might not have. What was the point in doubting her now? She was going to let him check her blood. What else could she do? It's me, he thought. I've been by myself too long. I won't believe anything unless I see it in a microscope. Heredity triumphs again. I'm my father's son, damn his moldering bones.

Standing in the dark kitchen, digging his blunt nail under the wrapping around the neck of the bottle, Robert Neville looked into the living room at Ruth.

His eyes ran over the robe, resting a moment on the slight promi-
nence of her breasts, dropping then to the bronzed calves and ankles,
up to the smooth kneecaps. She had a body like a young girl's. She
certainly didn't look like the mother of two.

The most unusual feature of the entire affair, he thought, was that
he felt no physical desire for her.

If she had come two years before, maybe even later, he might have
violated her. There had been some terrible moments in those days,
moments when the most terrible of solutions to his need were considered, were often dwelt upon until they drove him half mad.

But then the experiments had begun. Smoking had tapered off,
drinking lost its compulsive nature. Deliberately and with surprising
success, he had submerged himself in investigation.

His sex drive had diminished, had virtually disappeared. Salvation
of the monk, he thought. The drive had to go sooner or later, or no
normal man could dedicate himself to any life that excluded sex.

Now, happily, he felt almost nothing; perhaps a hardly discernible
stirring far beneath the rocky strata of abstinence. He was content to
leave it at that. Especially since there was no certainty that Ruth
was the companion he had waited for. Or even the certainty that he
could allow her to live beyond tomorrow. *Cure* her?

Curing was unlikely.

He went back into the living room with the opened bottle. She
smiled at him briefly as he poured more wine for her.

"I've been admiring your mural," she said. "It almost makes you
believe you're in the woods."

He grunted.

"It must have taken a lot of work to get your house like this," she
said.

"You should know," he said. "You went through the same thing."

"We had nothing like this," she said. "Our house was small. Our
food locker was half the size of yours."

"You must have run out of food," he said, looking at her carefully.

"Frozen food," she said. "We were living out of cans."

He nodded. Logical, his mind had to admit. But he still didn't like it. It was all intuition, he knew, but he didn't like it.

"What about water?" he asked then.

She looked at him silently for a moment.

"You don't believe a word I've said, do you?" she said.

"It's not that," he said. "I'm just curious how you lived."

"You can't hide it from your voice," she said. "You've been alone too long. You've lost the talent for deceit."

He grunted, getting the uncomfortable feeling that she was playing with him. That's ridiculous, he argued. She's just a woman. She was probably right. He probably *was* a gruff and graceless hermit. What did it matter?

"Tell me about your husband," he said abruptly.

Something flitted over her face, a shade of memory. She lifted the glass of dark wine to her lips.

"Not now," she said. "Please."

He slumped back on the couch, unable to analyze the formless dissatisfaction he felt. Everything she said and did could be a result of what she'd been through. It could also be a lie.

Why should she lie? he asked himself. In the morning he would check her blood. What could lying tonight profit her when, in a matter of hours, he'd know the truth?

"You know," he said, trying to ease the moment, "I've been thinking. If three people could survive the plague, why not more?"

"Do you think that's possible?" she asked.

"Why not? There must have been others who were immune for one reason or another."

"Tell me more about the germ," she said.

He hesitated a moment, then put down his wineglass. What if he told her everything? What if she escaped and came back after death with all the knowledge that *he* had?

"There's an awful lot of detail," he said.

"You were saying something about the cross before," she said. "How do you know it's true?"

"You remember what I said about Ben Cortman?" he said, glad to restate something she already knew rather than go into fresh material.

"You mean that man you—"

He nodded. "Yes. Come here," he said, standing. "I'll show him to you."

As he stood behind her looking out the peephole, he smelled the odor of her hair and skin. It made him draw back a little. Isn't that remarkable? he thought. I don't like the smell. Like Gulliver returning from the logical horses, I find the human smell offensive.

"He's the one by the lamppost," he said.

She made a slight sound of acknowledgment. Then she said, "There are so few. Where are they?"

"I've killed off most of them," he said, "but they manage to keep a few ahead of me."

"How come the lamp is on out there?" she said. "I thought they destroyed the electrical system."

"I connected it with my generator," he said, "so I could watch them."

"Don't they break the bulb?"

"I have a very strong globe over the bulb."

"Don't they climb up and try to break it?"

"I have garlic all over the post."

She shook her head. "You've thought of everything."

Stepping back, he looked at her a moment. How can she look at them so calmly, he wondered, ask me questions, make comments, when only a week ago she saw their kind tear her husband to pieces? Doubts again, he thought. Won't they ever stop?

He knew they wouldn't until he knew about her for sure.

She turned away from the window then.

"Will you excuse me a moment?" she said.

He watched her walk into the bathroom and heard her lock the door behind her. Then he went back to the couch after closing the peephole door. A wry smile played on his lips. He looked down into the tawny wine depths and tugged abstractedly at his beard.

"Will you excuse me a moment?"

For some reason the words seemed grotesquely amusing, the carry-over from a lost age. Emily Post mincing through the grave-yard. Etiquette for Young Vampires.

The smile was gone.

And what now? What did the future hold for him? In a week would she still be here with him, or crumpled in the never cooling fire?

He knew that, if she were infected, he'd have to try to cure her whether it worked or not. But what if she were free of the bacillus? In a way, that was a more nerve-racking possibility. The other way he would merely go on as before, breaking neither schedule nor standards. But if she stayed, if they had to establish a relationship, perhaps become husband and wife, have children . . .

Yes, that was more terrifying.

He suddenly realized that he had become an ill-tempered and inveterate bachelor again. He no longer thought about his wife, his child, his past life. The present was enough. And he was afraid of the possible demand that he make sacrifices and accept responsibility again. He was afraid of giving out his heart, of removing the chains he had forged around it to keep emotion prisoner. He was afraid of loving again.

When she came out of the bathroom he was still sitting there, thinking. The record player, unnoticed by him, let out only a thin scratching sound.

Ruth lifted the record from the turntable and turned it. The third movement of the symphony began.

"Well, what about Cortman?" she asked, sitting down.

He looked at her blankly. "Cortman?"

"You were going to tell me something about him and the cross."

"Oh. Well, one night I got him in here and showed him the cross."

"What happened?"

Shall I kill her now? Shall I not even investigate, but kill her and burn her?

His throat moved. Such thoughts were a hideous testimony to the world he had accepted; a world in which murder was easier than hope.

Well, he wasn't that far gone yet, he thought. I'm a man, not a destroyer.

"What's wrong?" she said nervously.

"What?"

"You're staring at me."

"I'm sorry," he said coldly. "I . . . I'm just thinking."

She didn't say any more. She drank her wine and he saw her hand shake as she held the glass. He forced down all introspection. He didn't want her to know what he felt.

"When I showed him the cross," he said, "he laughed in my face."

She nodded once.

"But when I held a torah before his eyes, I got the reaction I wanted."

"A what?"

"A torah. Tablet of law, I believe it is."

"And that . . . got a reaction?"

"Yes. I had him tied up, but when he saw the torah he broke loose and attacked me."

"What happened?" She seemed to have lost her fright again.

"He struck me on the head with something. I don't remember what. I was almost knocked out. But, using the torah, I backed him to the door and got rid of him."

"Oh."

"So you see, the cross hasn't the power the legend says it has. My theory is that, since the legend came into its own in Europe, a continent predominantly Catholic, the cross would naturally become the symbol of defense against powers of darkness."

"Couldn't you use your gun on Cortman?" she asked.

"How do you know I had a gun?"

"I . . . assumed as much," she said. "*We* had guns."

"Then you must know bullets have no effect on vampires."

"We were . . . never sure," she said, then went on quickly: "Do you know why that's so? Why don't bullets affect them?"

He shook his head. "I don't know," he said.

They sat in silence listening to the music.

He did know, but, doubting again, he didn't want to tell her.

Through experiments on the dead vampires he had discovered that the bacilli effected the creation of a powerful body glue that sealed bullet openings as soon as they were made. Bullets were enclosed almost immediately, and since the system was activated by germs, a bullet couldn't hurt it. The system could, in fact, contain almost an indefinite amount of bullets, since the body glue prevented a penetration of more than a few fractions of an inch. Shooting vampires was like throwing pebbles into tar.

As he sat looking at her, she arranged the folds of the robe around her legs and he got a momentary glimpse of brown thigh. Far from being attracted, he felt irritated. It was a typical feminine gesture, he thought, an artificial movement.

As the moments passed he could almost sense himself drifting farther and farther from her. In a way he almost regretted having found her at all. Through the years he had achieved a certain degree of peace. He had accepted solitude, found it not half bad. Now this . . . ending it all.

In order to fill the emptiness of the moment, he reached for his pipe and pouch. He stuffed tobacco into the bowl and lit it. For a second he wondered if he should ask if she minded. He didn't ask.

The music ended. She got up and he watched her while she looked through his records. She seemed like a young girl, she was so slender. Who is she? he thought. Who is she really?

"May I play this?" she asked, holding up an album.

He didn't even look at it. "If you like," he said.

She sat down as Rachmaninoff's Second Piano Concerto began. Her taste isn't remarkably advanced, he thought, looking at her without expression.

"Tell me about yourself," she said.

Another typical feminine question, he thought. Then he berated himself for being so critical. What was the point in irritating himself by doubting her?

"Nothing to tell," he said.

She was smiling again. *Was* she laughing at him?

"You scared the life out of me this afternoon," she said. "You and your bristly beard. And those wild eyes."

He blew out smoke. Wild eyes? That was ridiculous. What was she trying to do? Break down his reserve with cuteness?

"What do you look like under all those whiskers?" she asked.

He tried to smile at her but he couldn't.

"Nothing," he said. "Just an ordinary face."

"How old are you, Robert?"

His throat moved. It was the first time she'd spoken his name. It gave him a strange, restless feeling to hear a woman speak his name after so long. Don't call me that, he almost said to her. He didn't want to lose the distance between them. If she were infected and he couldn't cure her, he wanted it to be a stranger that he put away.

She turned her head away.

"You don't have to talk to me if you don't want to," she said quietly. "I won't bother you. I'll go tomorrow."

His chest muscles tightened.

"But . . ." he said.

"I don't want to spoil your life," she said. "You don't have to feel any obligation to me just because . . . we're the only ones left."

His eyes were bleak as he looked at her, and he felt a brief stirring of guilt at her words. Why should I doubt her? he told himself. If she's infected, she'll never get away alive. What's there to fear?

"I'm sorry," he said. "I . . . I *have* been alone a long time."

She didn't look up.

"If you'd like to talk," he said, "I'll be glad to . . . tell you anything I can."

She hesitated a moment. Then she looked at him, her eyes not committing themselves at all.

"I *would* like to know about the disease," she said. "I lost my two girls because of it. And it caused my husband's death."

He looked at her and then spoke.

"It's a bacillus," he said, "a cylindrical bacterium. It creates an iso-tonic solution in the blood, circulates the blood slower than normal, activates all bodily functions, lives on fresh blood, and provides energy. Deprived of blood, it makes self-killing bacteriophages or else sporulates."

She looked blank. He realized then that she couldn't have understood. Terms so common to him now were completely foreign to her.

"Well," he said, "most of those things aren't so important. To sporulate is to create an oval body that has all the basic ingredients of the vegetative bacterium. The germ does that when it gets no fresh blood. Then, when the vampire host decomposes, these spores go flying out and seek new hosts. They find one, germinate—and one more system is infected."

She shook her head incredulously.

"Bacteriophages are inanimate proteins that are also created when the system gets no blood. Unlike the spores, though, in this case ab-normal metabolism destroys the cells."

Quickly he told her about the imperfect waste disposal of the lymphatic system, the garlic as allergen causing anaphylaxis, the various vectors of the disease.

"Then why are we immune?" she asked.

For a long moment he looked at her, withholding any answer. Then, with a shrug, he said, "I don't know about you. As for me, while I was stationed in Panama during the war I was bitten by a vampire bat. And, though I can't prove it, my theory is that the bat had previously encountered a true vampire and acquired the *vampiris* germ. The germ caused the bat to seek human rather than animal blood. But, by the time the germ had passed into my system, it had been weakened in some way by the bat's system. It made me terribly ill, of course, but it didn't kill me, and as a result, my body built up an immunity to it. That's my theory, anyway. I can't find any better reason."

"But . . . didn't the same thing happen to others down there?"

"I don't know," he said quietly. "I killed the bat." He shrugged. "Maybe I was the first human it had attacked."

She looked at him without a word, her surveillance making Neville feel restive. He went on talking even though he didn't really want to.

Briefly he told her about the major obstacle in his study of the vampires.

"At first I thought the stake had to hit their hearts," he said. "I believed the legend. I found out that wasn't so. I put stakes in all parts of their bodies and they died. That made me think it was hemorrhage. But then one day . . ."

And he told her about the woman who had decomposed before his eyes.

"I knew then it couldn't be hemorrhage," he went on, feeling a sort of pleasure in reciting his discoveries. "I didn't know what to do. Then one day it came to me."

"What?" she asked.

"I took a dead vampire. I put his arm into an artificial vacuum. I punctured his arm inside that vacuum. Blood spurted out." He paused. "But that's all."

She stared at him.

"You don't see," he said.

"I. . . . No," she admitted.

"When I let air back into the tank, the arm decomposed," he said. She still stared.

"You see," he said, "the bacillus is a facultative saprophyte. It lives with or without oxygen; but with a difference. Inside the system, it is anaerobic and sets up a symbiosis with the system. The vampire feeds it fresh blood, the bacteria provides the energy so the vampire can get more fresh blood. The germ also causes, I might add, the growth of the canine teeth."

"Yes?" she said.

"When air enters," he said, "the situation changes instantaneously. The germ becomes aerobic and, instead of being symbiotic, it becomes virulently parasitic." He paused. "It eats the host," he said.

"Then the stake . . ." she started.

"Lets air in. Of course. Lets it in and keeps the flesh open so that the body glue can't function. So the heart has nothing to do with it. What I do now is cut the wrists deep enough so that the body glue can't work." He smiled a little. "When I think of all the time I used to spend making stakes!"

She nodded and, noticing the wineglass in her hand, put it down.

"That's why the woman I told you about broke down so rapidly," he said. "She'd been dead so long that as soon as air struck her system the germs caused spontaneous dissolution."

Her throat moved and a shudder ran down through her.

"It's horrible," she said.

He looked at her in surprise. Horrible? Wasn't that odd? He hadn't thought that for years. For him the word "horror" had become obsolete. A surfeiting of terror soon made terror a cliché. To Robert Neville the situation merely existed as natural fact. It had no adjectives.

"And what about the . . . the ones who are still alive?" she asked.

"Well," he said, "when you cut their wrists the germ naturally becomes parasitic. But mostly they die from simple hemorrhage."

"Simple—"

She turned away quickly and her lips were pressed into a tight, thin line.

"What's the matter?" he asked.

"N-nothing. Nothing," she said.

He smiled. "One gets used to these things," he said. "One has to."

Again she shuddered, the smooth column of her throat contracting.

"You can't abide by Robert's Rules of Order in the jungle," he said. "Believe me, it's the only thing I can do. Is it better to let them die of the disease and return—in a far more terrible way?"

She pressed her hands together.

"But you said a lot of them are—are still living," she said nervously. "How do you know they're not going to *stay* alive?"

"I know," he said. "I know the germ, know how it multiplies. No matter how long their systems fight it, in the end the germ will win. I've made antibiotics, injected dozens of them. But it doesn't work, it can't work. You can't make vaccines work when they're already deep in the disease. Their bodies can't fight germs and make antibodies at the same time. It can't be done, believe me. It's a trap. If I didn't kill them, sooner or later they'd die and come after me. I have no choice; no choice at all."

They were silent then and the only sound in the room was the rasping of the needle on the inner grooves of the record. She wouldn't look at him, but kept staring at the floor with bleak eyes. It was strange, he thought, to find himself vaguely on the defensive for what yesterday was accepted necessity. In the years that had passed he had never once considered the possibility that he was wrong. It took her presence to bring about such thoughts. And they were strange, alien thoughts.

"Do you actually think I'm wrong?" he asked in an incredulous voice.

She bit into her lower lip.

"Ruth," he said.

"It's not for me to say," she answered.

CHAPTER EIGHTEEN

"Virge!"

The dark form recoiled against the wall as Robert Neville's hoarse cry ripped open the silent blackness.

He jerked his body up from the couch and stared with sleep-clouded eyes across the room, his chest pulsing with heartbeats like maniac fists on a dungeon wall.

He lurched up to his feet, brain still foggy with sleep, unable to define time or place.

"Virge?" he said again, weakly, shakily. "Virge?"

"It—it's me," the faltering voice said in the darkness.

He took a trembling step toward the thin stream of light spearing through the open peephole. He blinked dully at the light.

She gasped as he put his hand out and clutched her shoulder.

"It's Ruth. *Ruth,*" she said in a terrified whisper.

He stood there rocking slowly in the darkness, eyes gazing without comprehension at the dark form before him.

"It's Ruth," she said again, more loudly.

Waking came like a hose blast of numbing shock. Something twisted cold knots into his chest and stomach. It wasn't Virge. He shook his head suddenly, rubbed shaking fingers across his eyes.

Then he stood there staring, weighted beneath a sudden depression.

"Oh," he muttered faintly. "Oh, I . . ."

He remained there, feeling his body weaving slowly in the dark as the mists cleared from his brain.

He looked at the open peephole, then back at her.

"What are you doing?" he asked, voice still thick with sleep.

"Nothing," she said nervously. "I . . . couldn't sleep."

He blinked his eyes suddenly at the flaring lamplight. Then his hands dropped down from the lamp switch and he turned around. She was against the wall still, blinking at the light, her hands at her sides drawn into tight fists.

"Why are you dressed?" he asked in a surprised voice.

Her throat moved and she stared at him. He rubbed his eyes again and pushed back the long hair from his temples.

"I was . . . just looking out," she said.

"But why are you dressed?"

"I couldn't sleep."

He stood looking at her, still a little groggy, feeling his heartbeat slowly diminish. Through the open peephole he heard them yelling outside, and he heard Cortman shout, "Come out, Neville!" Moving to the peephole, he pushed the small wooden door shut and turned to her.

"I want to know why you're dressed," he said again.

"No reason," she said.

"Were you going to leave while I was asleep?"

"No, I . . ."

"*Were* you?"

She gasped as he grabbed her wrist.

"No, no," she said quickly. "How could I, with them out there?"

He stood breathing heavily, looking at her frightened face. His throat moved slowly as he remembered the shock of waking up and thinking that she was Virge.

Abruptly he dropped her arm and turned away. And he'd thought the past was dead. How long did it take for a past to die?

She said nothing as he poured a tumblerful of whisky and swallowed it convulsively. Virge, Virge, he thought miserably, still with me. He closed his eyes and jammed his teeth together.

"Was that her name?" he heard Ruth ask.

His muscles tightened, then went slack.

"It's all right," he said in a dead voice. "Go to bed."

She drew back a little. "I'm sorry," she said. "I didn't mean . . ."

Suddenly he knew he didn't want her to go to bed. He wanted her to stay with him. He didn't know why, he just didn't want to be alone.

"I thought you were my wife," he heard himself saying. "I woke up and I thought—"

He drank a mouthful of whisky, coughing as part of it went down the wrong way. Ruth stayed in the shadows, listening.

"She came back, you see," he said. "I buried her, but one night she came back. She looked like—like you did. An outline, a shadow. *Dead.* But she came back. I tried to keep her with me. I tried, but she wasn't the same any more . . . you see. All she wanted was—"

He forced down the sob in his throat.

"My own wife," he said in a trembling voice, "coming back to drink my blood!"

He jammed down the glass on the bar top. Turning away, he paced restlessly to the peephole, turned, and went back and stood again before the bar. Ruth said nothing; she just stood in the darkness, listening.

"I put her away again," he said. "I had to do the same thing to her I'd done to the others. My own wife." There was a clicking in his throat. "A stake," he said in a terrible voice. "I had to put a stake in her. It was the only thing I knew to do. I—"

He couldn't finish. He stood there a long time, shivering helplessly, his eyes tightly shut.

Then he spoke again.

"Almost three years ago I did that. And I still remember it, it's still with me. What can you do? What can you *do*?" He drove a fist down on the bar top as the anguish of memory swept over him again. "No matter how you try, you can't forget or—or adjust or—*ever* get away from it!"

He ran shaking fingers through his hair.

"I know what you feel, I know. I didn't at first, I didn't trust you. I was safe, secure in my little shell. Now . . ." He shook his head slowly, defeatedly. "In a second, it's all gone. Adjustment, security, peace—all gone."

"Robert."

Her voice was as broken and lost as his.

"Why were we punished like this?" she asked.

He drew in a shuddering breath.

"I don't know," he answered bitterly. "There's no answer, no reason. It just is."

She was close to him now. And suddenly, without hesitation or drawing back, he drew her against him, and they were two people holding each other tightly in the lost measure of night.

"Robert, *Robert*."

Her hands rubbed over his back, stroking and clutching, while his arms held her firmly and he pressed his eyes shut against her warm, soft hair.

Their mouths held together for a long time and her arms gripped with desperate tightness around his neck.

Then they were sitting in the darkness, pressing close together, as if all the heat in the world were in their bodies and they would share the warmth between them. He felt the shuddering rise and fall of her breasts as she held close to him, her arms tight around his body, her face against his neck. His big hands moved roughly through her hair, stroking and feeling the silky strands.

"I'm sorry, Ruth."

"Sorry?"

"For being so cruel to you, for not trusting you."

She was silent, holding tight.

"Oh, Robert," she said then, "it's so unfair. So *unfair*. Why are we still alive? Why aren't we all dead? It would be better if we were all dead."

"Shhh, shhh," he said, feeling emotion for her like a released current pouring from his heart and mind. "It'll be all right."

He felt her shaking her head slowly against him.

"It will, it will," he said.

"How can it?"

"It *will*," he said, even though he knew he really couldn't believe it, even though he knew it was only released tension forming words in his mind.

"No," she said. "No."

"Yes, it will. It will, Ruth."

He didn't know how long it was they sat there holding each other close. He forgot everything, time and place; it was just the two of them together, needing each other, survivors of a black terror embracing because they had found each other.

But then he wanted to do something for her, to help her.

"Come," he said. "We'll check you."

She stiffened in his arms.

"No, no," he said quickly. "Don't be afraid. I'm sure we won't find anything. But if we do, I'll cure you. I swear I'll cure you, Ruth."

She was looking at him in the darkness, not saying a word. He stood and pulled her up with him, trembling with an excitement he hadn't felt in endless years. He wanted to cure her, to help her.

"Let me," he said. "I won't hurt you. I promise I won't. Let's *know*. Let's find out for sure. Then we can plan and work. I'll save you, Ruth. I will. Or I'll die myself."

She was still tense, holding back.

"Come with me, Ruth."

Now that the strength of his reserve had gone, there was nothing left to brace himself on, and he was shaking like a palsied man.

He led her into the bedroom. And when he saw in the lamplight how frightened she was, he pulled her close and stroked her hair.

"It's all right," he said. "All right, Ruth. No matter what we find, it'll be all right. Don't you understand?"

He sat her down on the stool and her face was completely blank, her body shuddering as he heated the needle over a Bunsen flame.

He bent over and kissed her on the cheek.

"It's all right now," he said gently. "It's all right."

She closed her eyes as he jabbed in the needle. He could feel the pain in his own finger as he pressed out blood and rubbed it on the slide.

"There. There," he said anxiously, pressing a little cotton to the nick on her finger. He felt himself trembling helplessly. No matter how he tried to control it, he couldn't. His fingers were almost incapable of making the slide, and he kept looking at Ruth and smiling at her, trying to take the look of taut fright from her features.

"Don't be afraid," he said. "Please don't. I'll cure you if you're infected. I will, Ruth, I will."

She sat without a word, looking at him with listless eyes as he worked. Her hands kept stirring restlessly in her lap.

"What will you do if—if I *am*," she said then.

"I'm not sure," he said. "Not yet. But there are a lot of things we can do."

"What?"

"Vaccines, for one."

"You said vaccines didn't work," she said, her voice shaking a little.

"Yes, but . . ." He broke off as he slid the glass slide onto the microscope.

"Robert, what could you do?"

She slid off the stool as he bent over the microscope.

"Robert, don't look!" she begged suddenly, her voice pleading.

But he'd already seen.

He didn't realize that his breath had stopped. His blank eyes met hers.

"Ruth," he whispered in a shocked voice.

The wooden mallet crashed down on his forehead.

A burst of pain filled Robert Neville's head and he felt one leg give way. As he fell to one side he knocked over the microscope. His right knee hit the floor and he looked up in dazed bewilderment at her fright-twisted face. The mallet came down again and he cried out in pain. He fell to both knees and his palms struck the floor as he toppled forward. A hundred miles away he heard her gasping sob.

"Ruth," he mumbled.

"I *told* you not to!" she cried.

He clutched out at her legs and she drove the mallet down a third time, this time on the back of his skull.

"Ruth!"

Robert Neville's hands went limp and slid off her calves, rubbing away part of the tan. He fell on his face and his fingers drew in convulsively as night filled his brain.

CHAPTER NINETEEN

When he opened his eyes there was no sound in the house.

He lay there a moment looking confusedly at the floor. Then, with a startled grunt, he sat up. A package of needles exploded in his head and he slumped down on the cold floor, hands pressed to his throbbing skull. A clicking sound filled his throat as he lay there.

After a few minutes he pulled himself up slowly by gripping the edge of the bench. The floor undulated beneath him as he held on tightly, eyes closed, legs wavering.

A minute later he managed to stumble into the bathroom. There he threw cold water in his face and sat on the bathtub edge pressing a cold, wet cloth to his forehead.

What had happened? He kept blinking and staring at the white-tiled floor.

He stood up and walked slowly into the living room. It was empty. The front door stood half open in the gray of early morning. She was gone.

Then he remembered. He struggled back to the bedroom, using the walls to guide him.

The note was on the bench next to the overturned microscope. He picked up the paper with numbed fingers and carried it to the bed. Sinking down with a groan, he held the letter before his eyes. But the letters blurred and ran. He shook his head and pressed his eyes shut. After a little while he read:

Robert:

Now you know. Know that I was spying on you, know that almost everything I told you was a lie.

I'm writing this note, though, because I want to save you if I can.

When I was first given the job of spying on you, I had no feelings about your life. Because I *did* have a husband, Robert. You killed him.

But now it's different. I know now that you were just as much forced into your situation as we were forced into ours. We *are* infected. But you already know that. What you don't understand yet is that we're going to stay alive. We've found a way to do that and we're going to set up society again slowly but surely. We're going to do away with all those wretched creatures whom death has cheated. And, even though I pray otherwise, we may decide to kill you and those like you.

Those like me? he thought with a start. But he kept reading.

I'll try to save you. I'll tell them you're too well armed for us to attack now. Use the time I'm giving you, Robert! Get away from your house, go into the mountains and save yourself. There are only a handful of us now. But sooner or later we'll be too well organized, and nothing I say will stop the rest from destroying you. For God's sake, Robert, go now, while you can!

I know you may not believe this. You may not believe that we can live in the sun for short periods now. You may not believe that my tan was only make-up. You may not believe that we can live with the germ now.

That's why I'm leaving one of my pills.

I took them all the time I was here. I kept them in a belt around my waist. You'll discover that they're a combination of defebrinated blood and a drug. I don't know myself just what it is. The blood feeds the germs, the drug prevents its multiplication. It was the discovery of this pill that saved us from dying, that is helping to set up society again slowly.

Believe me, it's true. And escape!

Forgive me, too. I didn't mean to hit you, it nearly killed me to do it. But I was so terribly frightened of what you'd do when you found out.

Forgive me for having to lie to you about so many things. But please believe this: When we were together in the darkness, close to each other, I wasn't spying on you. I was loving you.

Ruth

He read the letter again. Then his hands fell forward and he sat there staring with empty eyes at the floor. He couldn't believe it. He shook his head slowly and tried to understand, but adjustment eluded him.

He walked unsteadily to the bench. He picked up the small amber pill and held it in his palm, smelled it, tasted it. He felt as if all the security of reason were ebbing away from him. The framework of his life was collapsing and it frightened him.

Yet how did he refute the evidence? The pill, the tan coming off her leg, her walking in the sun, her reaction to garlic.

He sank down on the stool and looked at the mallet lying on the floor. Slowly, ploddingly, his mind went over the evidence.

When he'd first seen her she'd run from him. Had it been a ruse? No, she'd been genuinely frightened. She must have been startled by his cry, then, even though she'd been expecting it, and forgotten all about her job. Then later, when she'd calmed down, she'd talked him into thinking that her reaction to garlic was the reaction of a sick stomach. And she had lied and smiled and feigned hopeless acceptance and carefully got all the information she'd been sent after. And, when she'd wanted to leave, she couldn't because of Cortman and the others. He had awakened then. They had embraced, they had . . .

His white-knuckled fist jolted down on the bench. "I was loving you." Lie. Lie! His fingers crumpled up the letter and flung it away bitterly.

Rage made the pain in his head flare hotly and he pressed both hands against it and closed his eyes with a groan.

Then he looked up. Slowly he slid off the stool and placed the microscope back on its base.

The rest of her letter wasn't a lie, he knew that. Without the pill, without any evidence of word or memory, he knew. He knew what even Ruth and her people didn't seem to know.

He looked into the eyepiece for a long time. Yes, he knew. And the admission of what he saw changed his entire world. How stupid and ineffective he felt for never having foreseen it! Especially after reading the phrase a hundred, a thousand times. But then he'd never really appreciated it. Such a short phrase it was, but meaning so much.

Bacteria can mutate.

PART FOUR: January 1979

❦❦❦

CHAPTER TWENTY

They came by night. Came in their dark cars with their spotlights and their guns and their axes and pikes. Came from the blackness with a great sound of motors, the long white arms of their spotlights snapping around the boulevard corner and clutching out at Cimarron Street.

Robert Neville was sitting at the peephole when they came. He had put down a book and was sitting there watching idly when the beams splashed white across the bloodless vampire faces and they whirled with a gasp, their dark animal eyes staring at the blinding lights.

Neville jumped back from the peephole, his heart thudding with the abrupt shock. For a moment he stood there trembling in the dark room, unable to decide what to do. His throat contracted and he heard the roar of the car motors even through the soundproofing on his house. He thought of the pistols in his bureau, the submachine gun on his workbench, thought of defending his house against them.

Then he pressed his fingers in until the nails dug at his palms. No, he'd made his decision, he'd worked it out carefully through the past months. He would not fight.

With a heavy, sinking sensation in the pit of his stomach he stepped back to the peephole and looked out.

The street was a scene of rushing, violent action illuminated by the bald glare of the spotlights. Men rushed at men, the sound of running boots covered the pavement. Then a shot rang out, echoing hollowly; more shots.

Two male vampires went thrashing down onto their sides. Four men grabbed them by the arms and jerked them up while two other men drove the glittering lance points of their pikes into the vampires' chests. Neville's face twitched as screams filled the night. He felt his chest shuddering with labored breath as he watched from his house.

The dark-suited men knew exactly what they were doing. There were about seven vampires visible, six men and a woman. The men surrounded the seven, held their flailing arms, and drove razor-tipped pikes deep into their bodies. Blood spouted out on the dark pavement and the vampires perished one by one. Neville felt himself shivering more and more. Is this the new society? The words flashed across his mind. He tried to believe that the men were forced into what they were doing, but shock brought terrible doubt. Did they have to do it like this, with such a black and brutal slaughtering? Why did they slay with alarum by night, when by day the vampires could be dispatched in peace?

Robert Neville felt tight fists shaking at his sides. He didn't like the looks of them, he didn't like the methodical butchery. They were more like gangsters than men forced into a situation. There were looks of vicious triumph on their faces, white and stark in the spotlights. Their faces were cruel and emotionless.

Suddenly Neville felt himself shudder violently, remembering. Where was Ben Cortman?

His eyes fled over the street but he couldn't see Cortman. He pressed against the peephole and looked up and down the street. He didn't want them to get Cortman, he realized, didn't want them to destroy Cortman like that. With a sense of inward shock he could not analyze in the rush of the moment, he realized that he felt more deeply toward the vampires than he did toward their executioners.

Now the seven vampires lay crumpled and still in their pools of stolen blood. The spotlights were moving around the street, flaying open the night. Neville turned his head away as the brilliant glare blazed across the front of his house. Then the spotlight had turned about and he looked again.

A shout. Neville's eyes jumped toward the focus of the spotlights. He stiffened.

Cortman was on the roof of the house across the street. He was pulling himself up toward the chimney, body flattened on the shingles.

Abruptly it came to Neville that it was in that chimney that Ben Cortman had hidden most of the time, and he felt a wrench of despair at the knowledge. His lips pressed together tightly. Why hadn't he looked more carefully? He couldn't fight the sick apprehension he felt at the thought of Cortman's being killed by these brutal strangers. Objectively, it was pointless, but he could not repress the feeling. Cortman was not theirs to put to rest.

But there was nothing he could do.

With bleak, tortured eyes he watched the spotlights cluster on Cortman's wriggling body. He watched the white hands reaching out slowly for handholds on the roof. Slowly, slowly, as if Cortman had all the time in the world. Hurry up! Neville felt himself twitch with the unspoken words as he watched. He felt himself straining with Cortman's agonizingly slow movements.

The men did not shout, they did not command. They raised their rifles now and the night was torn open again with their exploding fire.

Neville almost felt the bullets in his own flesh. His body jerked with convulsive shudders as he watched Cortman's body jerk under the impact of the bullets.

Still Cortman kept crawling, and Neville saw his white face, his teeth gritted together. The end of Oliver Hardy, he thought, the death of all comedy and all laughter. He didn't hear the continuous fusillade of shots. He didn't even feel the tears running down his cheeks. His eyes were riveted on the ungainly form of his old friend inching up the brightly lit roof.

Now Cortman rose up on his knees and clutched at the chimney edge with spasmodic fingers. His body lurched as more bullets struck. His dark eyes glared into the blinding spotlights, his lips were drawn back in a soundless snarl.

Then he was standing up beside the chimney and Neville's face was white and taut as he watched Cortman start to raise his right leg.

And then the hammering machine gun splattered Cortman's flesh with lead. For a moment Cortman stood erect in the hot blast, palsied hands raised high over his head, a look of berserk defiance twisting his white features.

"Ben," Neville muttered in a croaking whisper.

Ben Cortman's body folded, slumped forward, fell. It slid and rolled slowly down the shingled incline, then dropped into space. In the sudden silence Neville heard the thump of it from across the street. Sick-eyed, he watched the men rush at the writhing body with their pikes.

Then Neville closed his eyes and his nails dug furrows in the flesh of his palms.

A clumping of boots. Neville jerked back into the darkness. He stood in the middle of the room, waiting for them to call to him and tell him to come out. He held himself rigidly. I'm not going to fight, he told himself strongly. Even though he wanted to fight, even though he already hated the dark men with their guns and their bloodstained pikes.

But he wasn't going to fight. He had worked out his decision very carefully. They were doing what they had to do, albeit with unnecessary violence and seeming relish. He had killed their people and they had to capture him and save themselves. He would not fight. He'd throw himself upon the justice of their new society. When they called to him he would go out and surrender; it was his decision.

But they didn't call. Neville lurched back with a gasp as the ax blade bit deeply into the front door. He stood trembling in the dark living room. What were they doing? Why didn't they call on him to surrender? He wasn't a vampire, he was a man like them. What were they doing?

He whirled and stared at the kitchen. They were chopping at the boarded-up back door too. He took a nervous step toward the hallway. His frightened eyes rushed from the back to the front door. He felt his heart pumping. He didn't understand, he didn't understand!

With a grunt of shocked surprise he jumped into the hall as the enclosed house rang with the gun explosion. The men were shooting away the lock on the front door. Another reverberating shot made his ears ring.

And, suddenly, he knew. They weren't going to take him to their courts, to their justice. They were going to exterminate him.

With a frightened murmur he ran into the bedroom. His hands fumbled in the bureau drawer.

He straightened up on trembling legs, the guns in his hands. But what if they *were* going to take him prisoner? He'd only judged by the fact that they hadn't called on him to come out. There were no lights in the house; maybe they thought he was already gone.

He stood shivering in the darkness of the bedroom, not knowing what to do, mutters of terror filling his throat. Why hadn't he left! Why hadn't he listened to her and left? Fool!

One of his guns fell from nerveless fingers as the front door was crushed in. Heavy feet thudded into the living room and Robert Neville shuffled back across the floor, his remaining pistol held out with rigid, blood-drained fingers. They weren't going to kill him without a fight!

He gasped as he collided with the bench. He stood there tautly. In the front room a man said something he couldn't understand, then flashlight beams shone into the hall. Neville caught his breath. He felt the room spinning around him. So this is the end. It was the only thing he could think. So this is the end.

Heavy shoes thumped in the hall. Neville's fingers tightened still more on the pistol and his eyes stared with wild fright at the doorway.

Two men came in.

Their white beams played around the room, struck his face. The two men recoiled abruptly.

"He's got a gun!" one of them cried, and fired his pistol.

Neville heard the bullet smash into the wall over his head. Then the pistol was jolting in his hand, splashing his face with bursts of light. He didn't fire at any one of them; he just kept pulling the trigger automatically. One of the men cried out in pain.

Then Neville felt a violent club blow across his chest. He staggered back, and jagged, burning pain exploded in his body. He fired once more, then crashed to his knees, the pistol slipping from his fingers.

"You got him!" he heard someone cry as he fell on his face. He tried to reach out for the pistol but a dark boot stamped on his hand and broke it. Neville drew in his hand with a rattling gasp and stared through pain-glazed eyes at the floor.

Rough hands slid under his armpits and pulled him up. He kept wondering when they would shoot him again. Virge, he thought, Virge, I'm coming with you now. The pain in his chest was like molten lead poured over him from a great height. He felt and heard his boot tips scraping over the floor and waited for death. I want to die in my own house, he thought. He struggled feebly but they didn't stop. Hot pain raked saw-toothed nails through his chest as they dragged him through the front room.

"No," he groaned. "No!"

Then pain surged up from his chest and drove a barbed club into his brain. Everything began spinning away into blackness.

"Virge," he muttered in a hoarse whisper.

And the dark men dragged his lifeless body from the house. Into the night. Into the world that was theirs and no longer his.

CHAPTER TWENTY-ONE

Sound; a murmured rustle in the air. Robert Neville coughed weakly, then grimaced as the pain filled his chest. A bubbling groan passed his lips and his head rolled slightly on the flat pillow. The sound grew stronger, it became a rumbling mixture of noises. His hands drew in slowly at his sides. Why didn't they take the fire off his chest? He could feel hot coals dropping through openings in his flesh. Another groan, agonized and breathless, twitched his graying lips. Then his eyes fluttered open.

He stared at the rough plaster ceiling for a full minute without blinking. Pain ebbed and swelled in his chest with an endless, nerve-clutching throb. His face remained a taut, lined mask of resistance to the pain. If he relaxed for a second, it enveloped him completely; he had to fight it. For the first few minutes he could only struggle with the pain, suffering beneath its hot stabbing. Then, after a while, his brain began to function; slowly, like a machine faltering, starting and stopping, turning and jamming gears.

Where am I? It was his first thought. The pain was awful. He looked down at his chest and saw that it was bound with a wide bandage, a great, moist spot of red rising and falling jerkily in the middle of it. He closed his eyes and swallowed. I'm hurt, he thought. I'm hurt badly. His mouth and throat felt powdery dry. Where am I, what am I . . .

Then he remembered; the dark men and the attack on his house. And he knew where he was even before he turned his head slowly, achingly, and saw the barred windows across the tiny cubicle. He looked at the windows for a long time, face tight, teeth clenched together. The sound was outside; the rushing, confused sound.

He let his head roll back on the pillow and lay staring at the ceiling. It was hard to understand the moment on its own terms. Hard to believe it wasn't all a nightmare. Over three years alone in his house. Now this.

But he couldn't doubt the sharp, shifting pain in his chest and he couldn't doubt the way the moist, red spot kept getting bigger and bigger. He closed his eyes. I'm going to die, he thought.

He tried to understand that. But that didn't work either. In spite of having lived with death all these years, in spite of having walked a tightrope of bare existence across an endless maw of death—in spite of that he couldn't understand it. Personal death still was a thing beyond comprehension.

He was still on his back when the door behind him opened.

He couldn't turn; it hurt too much. He lay there and listened to footsteps approach the bed, then stop. He looked up but the person hadn't come into view yet. My executioner, he thought, the justice of this new society. He closed his eyes and waited.

The shoes moved again until he knew the person was by the cot. He tried to swallow but his throat was too dry. He ran his tongue over his lips.

"Are you thirsty?"

He looked up with dulled eyes at her and suddenly his heart began throbbing. The increased blood flow made the pain billow up and swallow him for a moment. He couldn't cut off the groan of agony. He twisted his head on the pillow, biting his lips and clutching at the blanket feverishly. The red spot grew bigger.

She was on her knees now, patting perspiration from his brow, touching his lips with a cool, wet cloth. The pain began to subside slowly and her face came into gradual focus. Neville lay motionless, staring at her with pain-filled eyes.

"So," he finally said.

She didn't answer. She got up and sat on the edge of the bed. She patted his brow again. Then she reached over his head and he heard her pouring water into a glass.

The pain dug razors into him as she lifted his head a little so he could drink. This is what they must have felt when the pikes went into them, he thought. This cutting, biting agony, the escape of life's blood.

His head fell back on the pillow.

"Thank you," he murmured.

She sat looking down at him, a strange mixture of sympathy and detachment on her face. Her reddish hair was drawn back into a tight cluster behind her head and clipped there. She looked very clean-cut and self-possessed.

"You wouldn't believe me, would you?" she said.

A little cough puffed out his cheeks. His mouth opened and he sucked in some of the damp morning air.

"I . . . believed you," he said.

"Then why didn't you go?"

He tried to speak but the words jumbled together. His throat moved and he drew in another faltering breath.

"I . . . couldn't," he muttered. "I almost went several times. Once I even packed and . . . started out. But I couldn't, I couldn't . . . go. I was too used to the . . . the house. It was a habit, just . . . just like the habit of living. I got . . . used to it."

Her eyes ran over his sweat-greased face and she pressed her lips together as she patted his forehead again.

"It's too late now," she said then. "You know that, don't you?"

Something clicked in his throat as he swallowed.

"I know," he said.

He tried to smile but his lips only twitched.

"Why did you fight them?" she said. "They had orders to bring you in unharmed. If you hadn't fired at them they wouldn't have harmed you."

His throat contracted.

"What difference . . ." he gasped.

His eyes closed and he gritted his teeth tightly to force back the pain.

When he opened them again she was still there. The expression on her face had not changed.

His smile was weak and tortured.

"Your . . . your society is . . . certainly a fine one," he gasped. "Who are those . . . those gangsters who came to get me? The . . . the council of justice?"

Her look was dispassionate. She's changed, he thought suddenly.

"New societies are always primitive," she answered. "You should know that. In a way we're like a revolutionary group—repossessing society by violence. It's inevitable. Violence is no stranger to you. You've killed. Many times."

"Only to . . . to survive."

"That's exactly why we're killing," she said calmly. "To survive. We can't allow the dead to exist beside the living. Their brains are impaired, they exist for only one purpose. They *have* to be destroyed. As one who killed the dead *and* the living, you know that."

The deep breath he took made the pain wrench at his insides. His eyes were stark with pain as he shuddered. It's got to end soon, he thought. I can't stand much more of this. No, death did not frighten him. He didn't understand it, but he didn't fear it either.

The swelling pain sank down and the clouds passed from his eyes. He looked up at her calm face.

"I hope so," he said. "But . . . but did you see their faces when they . . . they killed?" His throat moved convulsively. "Joy," he mumbled. "Pure joy."

Her smile was thin and withdrawn. She *has* changed, he thought, entirely.

"Did you ever see *your* face," she asked, "when you killed?" She patted his brow with the cloth. "I saw it—remember? It was frightening. And you weren't even killing then, you were just chasing me."

He closed his eyes. Why am I listening to her? he thought. She's become a brainless convert to this new violence.

"Maybe you did see joy on their faces," she said. "It's not surprising. They're young. And they *are* killers—assigned killers, legal killers. They're respected for their killing, admired for it. What can you expect from them? They're only fallible men. And men can learn to enjoy killing. That's an old story, Neville. You know that."

He looked up at her. Her smile was the tight, forced smile of a woman who was trying to forgo being a woman in favor of her dedication.

"Robert Neville," she said, "the last of the old race."

His face tightened.

"Last?" he muttered, feeling the heavy sinking of utter loneliness in him.

"As far as we know," she said casually. "You're quite unique, you know. When you're gone, there won't be anyone else like you within our particular society."

He looked toward the window.

"Those are . . . people . . . outside," he said.

She nodded. "They're waiting."

"For my death?"

"For your execution," she said.

He felt himself tighten as he looked up at her.

"You'd better hurry," he said, without fear, with a sudden defiance in his hoarse voice.

They looked at each other for a long moment. Then something seemed to give in her. Her face grew blank.

"I knew it," she said softly. "I knew you wouldn't be afraid."

Impulsively she put her hand over his.

"When I first heard that they were ordered to your house, I was going to go there and warn you. But then I knew that if you were still there, nothing would make you go. Then I was going to try to help you escape after they brought you in. But they told me you'd been shot and I knew that escape was impossible too."

A smile flitted over her lips.

"I'm glad you're not afraid," she said. "You're very brave." Her voice grew soft. "Robert."

They were silent and he felt her hand tighten on his.

"How is it you can . . . come in here?" he asked then.

"I'm a ranking officer in the new society," she said.

His hand stirred under hers.

"Don't . . . let it get . . ." He coughed up blood. "Don't let it get . . . too brutal. Too heartless."

"What can I—" she started, then stopped. She smiled at him. "I'll try," she said.

He couldn't go on. The pain was getting worse. It twisted and turned like a clutching animal in his body.

Ruth leaned over him.

"Robert," she said, "listen to me. They mean to execute you. Even though you're wounded. They have to. The people have been out there all night, waiting. They're terrified of you, Robert, they hate you. And they want your life."

She reached up quickly and unbuttoned her blouse. Reaching under her brassiere, she took out a tiny packet and pressed it into his right palm.

"It's all I can do, Robert," she whispered, "to make it easier. I warned you, I *told* you to go." Her voice broke a little. "You just can't fight so many, Robert."

"I know." The words were gagging sounds in his throat.

For a moment she stood over his bed, a look of natural compassion on her face. It was all a pose, he thought, her coming in and being so official. She was afraid to be herself. I can understand that.

Ruth bent over him and her cool lips pressed on his.

"You'll be with her soon," she murmured hastily.

Then she straightened up, her lips pressed together tightly. She buttoned the two top buttons of her blouse. A moment longer she looked down at him. Then her eyes glanced at his right hand.

"Take them soon," she murmured, and turned away quickly.

He heard her footsteps moving across the floor. Then the door was shutting and he heard the sound of it being locked. He closed his eyes and felt warm tears pushing out from beneath the lids. Good-by, Ruth.

Good-by, everything.

Then, suddenly, he drew in a quick breath. Bracing himself, he pushed himself up to a sitting position. He refused to let himself collapse at the burning pain that exploded in his chest. Teeth grating together, he stood up on his feet. For a moment he almost fell, but, catching his balance, he stumbled across the floor on vibrating legs he could hardly feel.

He fell against the window and looked out.

The street was filled with people. They milled and stirred in the gray light of morning, the sound of their talking like the buzzing of a million insects.

He looked out over the people, his left hand gripping the bars with bloodless fingers, his eyes fever-lit.

Then someone saw him.

For a moment there was an increased babbling of voices, a few startled cries.

Then sudden silence, as though a heavy blanket had fallen over their heads. They all stood looking up at him with their white faces. He stared back. And suddenly he thought, I'm the abnormal one now. Normalcy was a majority concept, the standard of many and not the standard of just one man.

Abruptly that realization joined with what he saw on their faces— awe, fear, shrinking horror—and he knew that they *were* afraid of him. To them he was some terrible scourge they had never seen, a scourge even worse than the disease they had come to live with. He was an invisible specter who had left for evidence of his existence the bloodless bodies of their loved ones. And he understood what they felt and did not hate them. His right hand tightened on the tiny envelope of pills. So long as the end did not come with violence, so long as it did not have to be a butchery before their eyes . . .

Robert Neville looked out over the new people of the earth. He knew he did not belong to them; he knew that, like the vampires, he was anathema and black terror to be destroyed. And, abruptly, the concept came, amusing to him even in his pain.

A coughing chuckle filled his throat. He turned and leaned against the wall while he swallowed the pills. Full circle, he thought while the final lethargy crept into his limbs. Full circle. A new terror born in death, a new superstition entering the unassailable fortress of forever.

I am legend.

BURIED TALENTS

A man in a wrinkled, black suit entered the fairgrounds. He was tall and lean, his skin the color of drying leather. He wore a faded sport shirt underneath his suit coat, white with yellow stripes. His hair was black and greasy, parted in the middle and brushed back flat on each side. His eyes were pale blue. There was no expression on his face. It was a hundred and two degrees in the sun but he was not perspiring.

He walked to one of the booths and stood there watching people try to toss ping-pong balls into dozens of little fish bowls on a table. A fat man wearing a straw hat and waving a bamboo cane in his right hand kept telling everyone how easy it was. "Try your luck!" he told them. "Win a prize! There's nothing to it!" He had an unlit, half-smoked cigar between his lips which he shifted from side to side as he spoke.

For awhile, the tall man in the wrinkled, black suit stood watching. Not one person managed a ping-pong ball into a fish bowl. Some of them tried to throw the balls in. Others tried to bounce them off the table. None of them had any luck.

At the end of seven minutes, the man in the black suit pushed between the people until he was standing by the booth. He took a quarter from his right hand trouser pocket and laid it on the counter. "Yes, sir!" said the fat man. "Try your luck!" He tossed the quarter into a metal box beneath the counter. Reaching down, he picked three grimy ping-pong balls from a basket. He clapped them on the counter and the tall man picked them up.

"Toss a ball in the fish bowl!" said the fat man. "Win a prize! There's nothing to it!" Sweat was trickling down his florid face. He took a quarter from a teenage boy and set three ping-pong balls in front of him.

The man in the black suit looked at the three ping-pong balls on his left palm. He hefted them, his face immobile. The man in the straw hat turned away. He tapped at the fish bowls with his cane. He shifted the stump of cigar in his mouth. "Toss a ball in the fish bowl!" he said. "A prize for everybody! Nothing to it!"

Behind him, a ping-pong ball clinked into one of the bowls. He turned and looked at the bowl. He looked at the man in the black suit. "There you are!" he said. "See that? Nothing to it! Easiest game on the fairgrounds!"

The tall man threw another ping-pong ball. It arced across the booth and landed in the same bowl. All the other people trying missed.

"Yes, sir!" the fat man said. "A prize for everybody! Nothing to it!" He picked up two quarters and set six ping-pong balls before a man and wife.

He turned and saw the third ping-pong ball dropping into the fish bowl. It didn't touch the neck of the bowl. It didn't bounce. It landed on the other two balls and lay there.

"See?" the man in the straw hat said. "A prize on his very first turn! Easiest game on the fairgrounds!" Reaching over to a set of wooden shelves, he picked up an ashtray and set it on the counter. "Yes, sir! Nothing to it!" he said. He took a quarter from a man in overalls and set three ping-pong balls in front of him.

The man in the black suit pushed away the ashtray. He laid another quarter on the counter. "Three more ping-pong balls," he said.

The fat man grinned. "Three more ping-pong balls it is!" he said.

He reached below the counter, picked up three more balls and set them on the counter in front of the man. "Step right up!" he said. He caught a ping-pong ball which someone had bounced off the table. He kept an eye on the tall man while he stooped to retrieve some ping-pong balls on the ground.

The man in the black suit raised his right hand, holding one of the ping-pong balls. He threw it overhand, his face expressionless. The ball curved through the air and fell into the fish bowl with the other three balls. It didn't bounce.

The man in the straw hat stood with a grunt. He dumped a handful of ping-pong balls into the basket underneath the counter. "Try your luck and win a prize!" he said. "Easy as pie!" He set three ping-pong balls in front of a boy and took his quarter. His eyes grew narrow as he watched the tall man raise his hand to throw the second ball. "No leaning in," he told the man.

The man in the black suit glanced at him. "I'm not," he said.

The fat man nodded. "Go ahead," he said.

The tall man threw the second ping-pong ball. It seemed to float across the booth. It fell through the neck of the bowl and landed on top of the other four balls.

"Wait a second," said the fat man, holding up his hand.

The other people who were throwing stopped. The fat man leaned across the table. Sweat was running down beneath the collar of his long-sleeved shirt. He shifted the soggy cigar in his mouth as he scooped the five balls from the bowl. He straightened up and looked at them. He hooked the bamboo cane over his left forearm and rolled the balls between his palms.

"Okay, folks!" he said. He cleared his throat. "Keep throwing! Win a prize!" He dropped the balls into the basket underneath the counter. Taking another quarter from the man in overalls, he set three ping-pong balls in front of him.

The man in the black suit raised his hand and threw the sixth ball. The fat man watched it arc through the air. It fell into the bowl he'd emptied. It didn't roll around inside. It landed on the bottom, bounced once, straight up, then lay motionless.

The fat man grabbed the ashtray, stuck it on the shelf and picked up a fish bowl like the ones on the table. It was filled with pink colored water and had a goldfish fluttering around in it. "There you go!" he said. He turned away and tapped on the empty fish bowls with his cane. "Step right up!" he said. "Toss a ball in the fish bowl! Win a prize! There's nothing to it!"

Turning back, he saw the man in the wrinkled suit had pushed away the goldfish in the bowl and placed another quarter on the counter. "Three more ping-pong balls," he said.

The fat man looked at him. He shifted the damp cigar in his mouth.

"Three more ping-pong balls," the tall man said.

The man in the straw hat hesitated. Suddenly, he noticed people looking at him and, without a word, he took the quarter and set three ping-pong balls on the counter. He turned around and tapped the fish bowls with his cane. "Step right up and try your luck!" he said. "Easiest game on the fairgrounds!" He removed his straw hat and rubbed the left sleeve of his shirt across his forehead. He was almost bald. The small amount of hair on his head was plastered to his scalp by sweat. He put his straw hat back on and set three ping-pong balls in front of a boy. He put the quarter in the metal box underneath the counter.

A number of people were watching the tall man now. When he threw the first of the three ping-pong balls into the fish bowl some of them applauded and a small boy cheered. The fat man watched suspiciously. His small eyes shifted as the man in the black suit threw his second ping-pong ball into the fish bowl with the other two balls. He scowled and seemed about to speak. The scatter of applause appeared to irritate him.

The man in the wrinkled suit tossed the third ping-pong ball. It landed on top of the other three. Several people cheered and all of them clapped.

The fat man's cheeks were redder now. He put the fish bowl with the goldfish back on its shelf. He gestured toward a higher shelf. "What'll it be?" he asked.

The tall man put a quarter on the counter. "Three more ping-pong balls," he said in a brisk voice. He picked up three more ping-pong balls from the basket and rolled them between his palms.

"Don't give him the bad ones now," someone said in a mocking voice.

"No bad ones!" the fat man said. "They're all the same!" He set the balls on the counter and picked up the quarter. He tossed it into the metal box underneath the counter. The man in the black suit raised his hand.

"Wait a second," the fat man said. He turned and reached across the table. Picking up the fish bowl, he turned it over and dumped the four ping-pong balls into the basket. He seemed to hesitate before he put the empty fish bowl back in place.

Nobody else was throwing now. They watched the tall man curiously as he raised his hand and threw the first of his three ping-pong balls. It curved through the air and landed in the same fish bowl, dropping straight down through the neck. It bounced once, then was still. The people cheered and applauded. The fat man rubbed his left hand across his eyebrows and flicked the sweat from his fingertips with an angry gesture.

The man in the black suit threw his second ping-pong ball. It landed on the same fish bowl.

"*Hold* it," said the fat man.

The tall man looked at him.

"What are you doing?" the fat man asked.

"Throwing ping-pong balls," the tall man answered. Everybody laughed. The fat man's face got redder. "I know that!" he said.

"It's done with mirrors," someone said and everybody laughed again.

"Funny," said the fat man. He shifted the wet cigar in his mouth and gestured curtly. "Go on," he said.

The tall man in the black suit raised his hand and threw the third ping-pong ball. It arced across the booth as though it were being carried by an invisible hand. It landed in the fish bowl on top of the other two balls. Everybody cheered and clapped their hands.

The fat man in the straw hat grabbed a casserole dish and dumped it on the counter. The man in the black suit didn't look at it. He put another quarter down. "Three more ping-pong balls," he said.

The fat man turned away from him. "Step right up and win a prize!" he called. "Toss a ping-pong ball—!"

The noise of disapproval everybody made drowned him out. He turned back, bristling. "Four rounds to a customer!" he shouted.

"Where does it say that?" someone asked.

"That's the rule!" the fat man said. He turned his back on the man and tapped the fish bowls with his cane. "Step right up and win a prize!" he said.

"I came here yesterday and played *five* rounds!" a man said loudly.

"That's because you didn't win!" a teenage boy replied. Most of the people laughed and clapped but some of them booed. "Let him play!" a man's voice ordered. Everybody took it up immediately. "Let him play!" they demanded.

The man in the straw hat swallowed nervously. He looked around, a truculent expression on his face. Suddenly, he threw his hands up. "All right!" he said. "Don't get so excited!" He glared at the tall man as he picked up the quarter. Bending over, he grabbed three ping-pong balls and slammed them on the counter. He leaned in close to the man and muttered, "If you're pulling something fast, you'd better cut it out. This is an honest game."

The tall man stared at him. His face was blank. His eyes looked very pale in the leathery tan of his face. "What do you mean?" he asked.

"No one can throw that many balls in succession into those bowls," the fat man said.

The man in the black suit looked at him without expression. "*I* can," he said.

The fat man felt a coldness on his body. Stepping back, he watched the tall man throw the ping-pong balls. As each of them landed in the same fish bowl, the people cheered and clapped their hands.

The fat man took a set of steak knives from the top prize shelf and set it on the counter. He turned away quickly. "Step right up!" he said. "Toss a ball in the fish bowl! Win a prize!" His voice was trembling.

"He wants to play again," somebody said.

The man in the straw hat turned around. He saw the quarter on the counter in front of the tall man. "No more prizes," he said.

The man in the black suit pointed at the items on top of the wooden shelves—a four-slice electric toaster, a short wave radio, a drill set and a portable typewriter. "What about them?" he asked.

The fat man cleared his throat. "They're only for display," he said. He looked around for help.

"Where does it say *that?*" someone demanded.

"That's what they are, so just take my word for it!" the man in the straw hat said. His face was dripping with sweat.

"I'll play for them," the tall man said.

"Now *look!*" The fat man's face was very red. "They're only for display, I said! Now get the hell—!"

He broke off with a wheezing gasp and staggered back against the table, dropping his cane. The faces of the people swam before his eyes. He heard their angry voices as though from a distance. He saw the blurred figure of the man in the black suit turn away and push through the crowd. He straightened up and blinked his eyes. The steak knives were gone.

Almost everybody left the booth. A few of them remained. The fat man tried to ignore their threatening grumbles. He picked a quarter off the counter and set three ping-pong balls in front of a boy. "Try your luck," he said. His voice was faint. He tossed the quarter into the metal box underneath the counter. He leaned against a corner post and pressed both hands against his stomach. The cigar fell out of his mouth. "God," he said.

It felt as though he was bleeding inside.

THE NEAR DEPARTED

The small man opened the door and stepped in out of the glaring sunlight. He was in his early fifties, a spindly, plain looking man with receding gray hair. He closed the door without a sound, then stood in the shadowy foyer, waiting for his eyes to adjust to the change in light. He was wearing a black suit, white shirt, and black tie. His face was pale and dry-skinned despite the heat of the day.

When his eyes had refocused themselves, he removed his Panama hat and moved along the hallway to the office, his black shoes soundless on the carpeting.

The mortician looked up from his desk. "Good afternoon," he said.

"Good afternoon." The small man's voice was soft.

"Can I help you?"

"Yes, you can," the small man said.

The mortician gestured to the arm chair on the other side of his desk. "Please."

The small man perched on the edge of the chair and set the Panama hat on his lap. He watched the mortician open a drawer and remove a printed form.

"Now," the mortician said. He withdrew a black pen from its onyx holder. "Who is the deceased?" he asked gently.

"My wife," the small man said.

The mortician made a sympathetic noise. "I'm sorry," he said.

"Yes." The small man gazed at him blankly.

"What is her name?" the mortician asked.

"Marie," the small man answered quietly. "Arnold."

The mortician wrote the name. "Address?" he asked.

The small man told him.

"Is she there now?" the mortician asked.

"She's there," the small man said.

The mortician nodded.

"I want everything perfect," the small man said. "I want the best you have."

"Of course," the mortician said. "Of course."

"Cost is unimportant," said the small man. His throat moved as he swallowed dryly. "Everything is unimportant now. Except for this."

"I understand."

"She always had the best. I saw to it."

"Of course."

"There'll be many people," said the small man. "Everybody loved her. She's so beautiful. So young. She has to have the very best. You understand?"

"Absolutely," the mortician reassured him. "You'll be more than satisfied, I guarantee you."

"She's so beautiful," the small man said. "So young."

"I'm sure," the mortician said.

The small man sat without moving as the mortician asked him questions. His voice did not vary in tone as he spoke. His eyes blinked so infrequently the mortician never saw them doing it.

When the form was completed, the small man signed and stood. The mortician stood and walked around the desk. "I guarantee you you'll be satisfied," he said, his hand extended.

The small man took his hand and gripped it momentarily. His palm was dry and cool.

"We'll be over at your house within the hour," the mortician told him.

"Fine," the small man said.

The mortician walked beside him down the hallway.

"I want everything perfect for her," the small man said. "Nothing but the very best."

"Everything will be exactly as you wish."

"She deserves the best." The small man stared ahead. "She's so beautiful," he said. "Everybody loved her. Everybody. She's so young and beautiful."

"When did she die?" the mortician asked.

The small man didn't seem to hear. He opened the door and stepped into the sunlight, putting on his Panama hat. He was halfway to his car when he replied, a faint smile on his lips, "As soon as I get home."

PREY

Amelia arrived at her apartment at six-fourteen. Hanging her coat in the hall closet, she carried the small package into the living room and sat on the sofa. She nudged off her shoes while she unwrapped the package on her lap. The wooden box resembled a casket. Amelia raised its lid and smiled. It was the ugliest doll she'd ever seen. Seven inches long and carved from wood, it had a skeletal body and an oversized head. Its expression was maniacally fierce, its pointed teeth completely bared, its glaring eyes protuberant. It clutched an eight-inch spear in its right hand. A length of fine, gold chain was wrapped around its body from the shoulders to the knees. A tiny scroll was wedged between the doll and the inside wall of its box. Amelia picked it up and unrolled it. There was handwriting on it. *This is He Who Kills,* it began. *He is a deadly hunter.* Amelia smiled as she read the rest of the words. Arthur would be pleased.

The thought of Arthur made her turn to look at the telephone on the table beside her. After a while, she sighed and set the wooden box on the sofa. Lifting the telephone to her lap, she picked up the receiver and dialed a number.

Her mother answered.

"Hello, Mom," Amelia said.

"Haven't you left yet?" her mother asked.

Amelia steeled herself. "Mom, I know it's Friday night—" she started.

She couldn't finish. There was silence on the line. Amelia closed her eyes. Mom, please, she thought. She swallowed. "There's this man," she said. "His name is Arthur Breslow. He's a high-school teacher."

"You aren't coming," her mother said.

Amelia shivered. "It's his birthday," she said. She opened her eyes and looked at the doll. "I sort of promised him we'd . . . spend the evening together."

Her mother was silent. There aren't any good movies playing tonight, anyway, Amelia's mind continued. "We could go tomorrow night," she said.

Her mother was silent.

"Mom?"

"Now even Friday night's too much for you."

"Mom, I see you two, three nights a week."

"To *visit*," said her mother. "When you have your own room here."

"Mom, *let's not start on that again*," Amelia said. I'm not a child, she thought. Stop treating me as though I were a child!

"How long have you been seeing him?" her mother asked.

"A month or so."

"Without telling me," her mother said.

"I had every intention of telling you." Amelia's head was starting to throb. I will *not* get a headache, she told herself. She looked at the doll. It seemed to be glaring at her. "He's a nice man, Mom," she said.

Her mother didn't speak. Amelia felt her stomach muscles drawing taut. I won't be able to eat tonight, she thought.

She was conscious suddenly of huddling over the telephone. She forced herself to sit erect. *I'm thirty-three years old*, she thought. Reaching out, she lifted the doll from its box. "You should see what I'm giving him for his birthday," she said. "I found it in a curio shop on Third Avenue. It's a genuine Zuni fetish doll, extremely rare. Arthur is a buff on anthropology. That's why I got it for him."

There was silence on the line. All right, *don't talk*, Amelia thought.

"It's a hunting fetish," she continued, trying hard to sound untroubled. "It's supposed to have the spirit of a Zuni hunter trapped inside it. There's a golden chain around it to prevent the spirit from—" She couldn't think of the word; ran a shaking finger over the chain. "—escaping, I guess," she said. "His name is He Who Kills. You should see his face." She felt warm tears trickling down her cheeks.

"Have a good time," said her mother, hanging up.

Amelia stared at the receiver, listening to the dial tone. Why is it always like this? she thought. She dropped the receiver onto its cradle and set aside the telephone. The darkening room looked blurred to her. She stood the doll on the coffee-table edge and pushed to her feet. I'll take my bath now, she told herself. I'll meet him and we'll have a lovely time. She walked across the living room. A lovely time, her mind repeated emptily. She knew it wasn't possible. Oh, *Mom*! she thought. She clenched her fists in helpless fury as she went into the bedroom.

In the living room, the doll fell off the table edge. It landed head down and the spear point, sticking into the carpet, braced the doll's legs in the air.

The fine, gold chain began to slither downward.

⊏◊⊐

It was almost dark when Amelia came back into the living room. She had taken off her clothes and was wearing her terrycloth robe. In the bathroom, water was running into the tub.

She sat on the sofa and placed the telephone on her lap. For several minutes, she stared at it. At last, with a heavy sigh, she lifted the receiver and dialed a number.

"Arthur?" she said when he answered.

"Yes?" Amelia knew the tone—pleasant but suspecting. She couldn't speak.

"Your mother," Arthur finally said.

That cold, heavy sinking in her stomach. "It's our night together," she explained. "Every Friday—" She stopped and waited. Arthur didn't speak. "I've mentioned it before," she said.

"I know you've mentioned it," he said.

Amelia rubbed at her temple.

"She's still running your life, isn't she?" he said.

Amelia tensed. "I just don't want to hurt her feelings anymore," she said. "My moving out was hard enough on her."

"I don't want to hurt her feelings either," Arthur said. "But how many birthdays a year do I have? We *planned* on this."

"I know." She felt her stomach muscles tightening again.

"Are you really going to let her do this to you?" Arthur asked. "One Friday night out of the whole year?"

Amelia closed her eyes. Her lips moved soundlessly. I just can't hurt her feelings anymore, she thought. She swallowed. "She's my mother," she said.

"Very well," he said. "I'm sorry. I was looking forward to it, but—" He paused. "I'm sorry," he said. He hung up quietly.

Amelia sat in silence for a long time, listening to the dial tone. She started when the recorded voice said loudly, "Please hang up." Putting the receiver down, she replaced the telephone on its table. So much for my birthday present, she thought. It would be pointless to give it to Arthur now. She reached out, switching on the table lamp. She'd take the doll back tomorrow.

The doll was not on the coffee table. Looking down, Amelia saw the gold chain lying on the carpet. She eased off the sofa edge onto her knees and picked it up, dropping it into the wooden box. The doll was not beneath the coffee table. Bending over, Amelia felt around underneath the sofa.

She cried out, jerking back her hand. Straightening up, she turned to the lamp and looked at her hand. There was something wedged beneath the index fingernail. She shivered as she plucked it out. It was the head of the doll's spear. She dropped it into the box and put the finger in her mouth. Bending over again, she felt around more cautiously beneath the sofa.

She couldn't find the doll. Standing with a weary groan, she started pulling one end of the sofa from the wall. It was terribly heavy. She recalled the night that she and her mother had shopped for the furniture. She'd wanted to furnish the apartment in Danish modern. Mother had insisted on this heavy, maple sofa; it had been on sale. Amelia grunted as she dragged it from the wall. She was conscious of the water running in the bathroom. She'd better turn it off soon.

She looked at the section of carpet she'd cleared, catching sight of the spear shaft. The doll was not beside it. Amelia picked it up and set it on the coffee table. The doll was caught beneath the sofa, she decided; when she'd moved the sofa, she had moved the doll as well.

She thought she heard a sound behind her—fragile, skittering. Amelia turned. The sound had stopped. She felt a chill move up the backs of her legs. "It's He Who Kills," she said with a smile. "He's taken off his chain and gone—"

She broke off suddenly. There had definitely been a noise inside the kitchen; a metallic, rasping sound. Amelia swallowed nervously. What's going on? she thought. She walked across the living room and reached into the kitchen, switching on the light. She peered inside. Everything looked normal. Her gaze moved falteringly across the stove, the pan of water on it, the table and chair, the drawers and cabinet doors all shut, the electric clock, the small refrigerator with the cookbook lying on top of it, the picture on the wall, the knife rack fastened to the cabinet side—

—its small knife missing.

Amelia stared at the knife rack. Don't be silly, she told herself. She'd put the knife in the drawer, that's all. Stepping into the kitchen, she pulled out the silverware drawer. The knife was not inside it.

Another sound made her look down quickly at the floor. She

gasped in shock. For several moments, she could not react; then, stepping to the doorway, she looked into the living room, her heartbeat thudding. Had it been imagination? She was sure she'd seen a movement.

"Oh, come on," she said. She made a disparaging sound. She hadn't seen a thing.

Across the room, the lamp went out.

Amelia jumped so startledly, she rammed her right elbow against the doorjamb. Crying out, she clutched the elbow with her left hand, eyes closed momentarily, her face a mask of pain.

She opened her eyes and looked into the darkened living room. "Come on," she told herself in aggravation. Three sounds plus a burned-out bulb did not add up to anything as idiotic as—

She willed away the thought. She had to turn the water off. Leaving the kitchen, she started for the hall. She rubbed her elbow, grimacing.

There was another sound. Amelia froze. Something was coming across the carpet toward her. She looked down dumbly. No, she thought.

She saw it then—a rapid movement near the floor. There was a glint of metal, instantly, a stabbing pain in her right calf. Amelia gasped. She kicked out blindly. Pain again. She felt warm blood running down her skin. She turned and lunged into the hall. The throw rug slipped beneath her and she fell against the wall, hot pain lancing through her right ankle. She clutched at the wall to keep from falling, then went sprawling on her side. She thrashed around with a sob of fear.

More movement, dark on dark. Pain in her left calf, then her right again. Amelia cried out. Something brushed along her thigh. She scrabbled back, then lurched up blindly, almost falling again. She fought for balance, reaching out convulsively. The heel of her left hand rammed against the wall, supporting her. She twisted around and rushed into the darkened bedroom. Slamming the door, she fell against it, panting. Something banged against it on the other side, something small and near the floor.

Amelia listened, trying not to breathe so loudly. She pulled carefully at the knob to make sure the latch had caught. When there were no further sounds outside the door, she backed toward the bed. She started as she bumped against the mattress edge. Slumping down, she grabbed at the extension phone and pulled it to her lap. Whom could she call? The police? They'd think her mad. Mother? She was too far off.

She was dialing Arthur's number by the light from the bathroom when the doorknob started turning. Suddenly, her fingers couldn't move. She stared across the darkened room. The door latch clicked. The telephone slipped off her lap. She heard it thudding onto the carpet as the door swung open. Something dropped from the outside knob.

Amelia jerked back, pulling up her legs. A shadowy form was scurrying across the carpet toward the bed. She gaped at it. It isn't true, she thought. She stiffened at the tugging on her bedspread. *It was climbing up to get her.* No, she thought; *it isn't true.* She couldn't move. She stared at the edge of the mattress.

Something that looked like a tiny head appeared. Amelia twisted around with a cry of shock, flung herself across the bed and jumped to the floor. Plunging into the bathroom, she sprung around and slammed the door, gasping at the pain in her ankle. She had barely thumbed in the button on the doorknob when something banged against the bottom of the door. Amelia heard a noise like the scratching of a rat. Then it was still.

She turned and leaned across the tub. The level of the water was almost to the overflow drain. As she twisted shut the faucets, she saw drops of blood falling into the water. Straightening up, she turned to the medicine-cabinet mirror above the sink.

She caught her breath in horror as she saw the gash across her neck. She pressed a shaking hand against it. Abruptly, she became aware of pain in her legs and looked down. She'd been slashed along the calves of both legs. Blood was running down her ankles, dripping off the edges of her feet. Amelia started crying. Blood ran between the fingers of the hand against her neck. It trickled down her wrist. She looked at her reflection through a glaze of tears.

Something in her aroused her, a wretchedness, a look of terrified surrender. *No,* she thought. She reached out for the medicine-cabinet door. Opening it, she pulled out iodine, gauze and tape. She dropped the cover of the toilet seat and sank down gingerly. It was a struggle to remove the stopper of the iodine bottle. She had to rap it hard against the sink three times before it opened.

The burning of the antiseptic on her calves made her gasp. Amelia clenched her teeth as she wrapped gauze around her right leg.

A sound made her twist toward the door. She saw the knife blade being jabbed beneath it. It's trying to stab my feet, she thought; it thinks I'm standing there. She felt unreal to be considering its thoughts. *This is He Who Kills*; the scroll flashed suddenly across her mind. *He is a deadly hunter*. Amelia stared at the poking knife blade. God, she thought.

Hastily, she bandaged both her legs, then stood and, looking into the mirror, cleaned the blood from her neck with a washrag. She swabbed some iodine along the edges of the gash, hissing at the fiery pain.

She whirled at the new sound, heartbeat leaping. Stepping to the door, she leaned down, listening hard. There was a faint metallic noise inside the knob.

The doll was trying to unlock it.

Amelia backed off slowly, staring at the knob. She tried to visualize the doll. Was it hanging from the knob by one arm, using the other to probe inside the knob lock with the knife? The vision was insane. She felt an icy prickling on the back of her neck. *I mustn't let it in,* she thought.

A hoarse cry pulled her lips back as the doorknob button popped out. Reaching out impulsively, she dragged a bath towel off its rack. The doorknob turned, the latch clicked free. The door began to open.

Suddenly the doll came darting in. It moved so quickly that its figure blurred before Amelia's eyes. She swung the towel down hard, as though it were a huge bug rushing at her. The doll was knocked against the wall. Amelia heaved the towel on top of it and lurched across the floor, gasping at the pain in her ankle. Flinging open the door, she lunged into the bedroom.

She was almost to the hall door when her ankle gave. She pitched across the carpet with a cry of shock. There was a noise behind her. Twisting around, she saw the doll come through the bathroom doorway like a jumping spider. She saw the knife blade glinting in the light. Then the doll was in the shadows, coming at her fast. Amelia scrabbled back. She glanced over her shoulder, saw the closet and backed into its darkness, clawing for the doorknob.

Pain again, an icy slashing at her foot. Amelia screamed and heaved back. Reaching up, she yanked a topcoat down. It fell across the doll. She jerked down everything in reach. The doll was buried underneath a mound of blouses, skirts and dresses. Amelia pitched across the moving pile of clothes. She forced herself to stand and limped into the hall as quickly as she could. The sound of thrashing underneath the clothes faded from her hearing. She hobbled to the door. Unlocking it, she pulled the knob.

The door was held. Amelia reached up quickly to the bolt. It had been shot. She tried to pull it free. It wouldn't budge. She clawed at it with sudden terror. It was twisted out of shape. "No," she muttered. *She was trapped.* "Oh, God." She started pounding on the door. "Please help me! *Help* me!"

Sound in the bedroom. Amelia whirled and lurched across the living room. She dropped to her knees beside the sofa, feeling for the telephone, but her fingers trembled so much that she couldn't dial the numbers. She began to sob, then twisted around with a strangled cry. The doll was rushing at her from the hallway.

Amelia grabbed an ashtray from the coffee table and hurled it at the doll. She threw a vase, a wooden box, a figurine. She couldn't hit the doll. It reached her, started jabbing at her legs. Amelia reared up blindly and fell across the coffee table. Rolling to her knees, she stood again. She staggered toward the hall, shoving over furniture to stop the doll. She toppled a chair, a table. Picking up a lamp, she hurled it at the floor. She backed into the hall and, spinning, rushed into the closet, slammed the door shut.

She held the knob with rigid fingers. Waves of hot breath pulsed against her face. She cried out as the knife was jabbed beneath the door, its sharp point sticking into one of her toes. She shuffled back, shifting her grip on the knob. Her robe hung open. She could feel a trickle of blood between her breasts. Her legs felt numb with pain. She closed her eyes. Please, someone help, she thought.

She stiffened as the doorknob started turning in her grasp. Her flesh went cold. It couldn't be stronger than she: it *couldn't* be. Amelia tightened her grip. *Please,* she thought. The side of her head bumped against the front edge of her suitcase on the shelf.

The thought exploded in her mind. Holding the knob with her right hand, she reached up, fumbling, with her left. The suitcase clasps were open. With a sudden wrench, she turned the doorknob, shoving at the door as hard as possible. It rushed away from her. She heard it bang against the wall. The doll thumped down.

Amelia reached up, hauling down her suitcase. Yanking open the lid, she fell to her knees in the closet doorway, holding the suitcase like an open book. She braced herself, eyes wide, teeth clenched together. She felt the doll's weight as it banged against the suitcase bottom. Instantly, she slammed the lid and threw the suitcase flat. Falling across it, she held it shut until her shaking hands could fasten the clasps. The sound of them clicking into place made her sob with relief. She shoved away the suitcase. It slid across the hall and bumped against the wall. Amelia struggled to her feet, trying not to listen to the frenzied kicking and scratching inside the suitcase.

She switched on the hall light and tried to open the bolt. It was hopelessly wedged. She turned and limped across the living room, glancing at her legs. The bandages were hanging loose. Both legs were streaked with caking blood, some of the gashes still bleeding. She felt at her throat. The cut was still wet. Amelia pressed her shaking lips together. She'd get to a doctor soon now.

Removing the ice pick from its kitchen drawer, she returned to the hall. A cutting sound made her look toward the suitcase. She caught her breath. The knife blade was protruding from the suitcase wall, moving up and down with a sawing motion. Amelia stared at it. She felt as though her body had been turned to stone.

She limped to the suitcase and knelt beside it, looking with revulsion at the sawing blade. It was smeared with blood. She tried to pinch it with the fingers of her left hand, pull it out. The blade was twisted, jerked down, and she cried out, snatching back her hand. There was a deep slice in her thumb. Blood ran down across her palm. Amelia pressed the finger to her robe. She felt as though her mind was going blank.

Pushing to her feet, she limped back to the door and started prying at the bolt. She couldn't get it loose. Her thumb began to ache. She pushed the ice pick underneath the bolt socket and tried to force it off the wall. The ice pick point broke off. Amelia slipped and almost fell. She pushed up, whimpering. There was no time, no time. She looked around in desperation.

The window! She could throw the suitcase out! She visualized it tumbling through the darkness. Hastily, she dropped the ice pick, turning toward the suitcase.

She froze. The doll had forced its head and shoulders through the rent in the suitcase wall. Amelia watched it struggling to get out. She felt paralyzed. The twisting doll was staring at her. No, she thought, it isn't true. The doll jerked free its legs and jumped to the floor.

Amelia jerked around and ran into the living room. Her right foot landed on a shard of broken crockery. She felt it cutting deep into her heel and lost her balance. Landing on her side, she thrashed around. The doll came leaping at her. She could see the knife blade glint. She kicked out wildly, knocking back the doll. Lunging to her feet, she reeled into the kitchen, whirled, and started pushing shut the door.

Something kept it from closing. Amelia thought she heard a screaming in her mind. Looking down, she saw the knife and a tiny wooden hand. The doll's arm was wedged between the door and the jamb! Amelia shoved against the door with all her might, aghast at the strength with which the door was pushed the other way. There was a cracking noise. A fierce smile pulled her lips back and she pushed berserkly at the door. The screaming in her mind grew louder, drowning out the sound of splintering wood.

The knife blade sagged. Amelia dropped to her knees and tugged at it. She pulled the knife into the kitchen, seeing the wooden hand and wrist fall from the handle of the knife. With a gagging noise, she struggled to her feet and dropped the knife into the sink. The door slammed hard against her side; the doll rushed in.

Amelia jerked away from it. Picking up the chair, she slung it toward the doll. It jumped aside, then ran around the fallen chair. Amelia snatched the pan of water off the stove and hurled it down. The pan clanged loudly off the floor, spraying water on the doll.

She stared at the doll. It wasn't coming after her. It was trying to climb the sink, leaping up and clutching at the counter side with one hand. It wants the knife, she thought. It has to have its weapon.

She knew abruptly what to do. Stepping over to the stove, she pulled down the broiler door and twisted the knob on all the way. She heard the puffing detonation of the gas as she turned to grab the doll.

She cried out as the doll began to kick and twist, its maddened thrashing flinging her from one side of the kitchen to the other. The screaming filled her mind again and suddenly she knew it was the spirit in the doll that screamed. She slid and crashed against the table, wrenched herself around and, dropping to her knees before the stove, flung the doll inside. She slammed the door and fell against it.

The door was almost driven out. Amelia pressed her shoulder, then her back against it, turning to brace her legs against the wall. She tried to ignore the pounding scrabble of the doll inside the broiler. She watched the red blood pulsing from her heel. The smell of burning wood began to reach her and she closed her eyes. The door was getting hot. She shifted carefully. The kicking and pounding filled her ears. The screaming flooded through her mind. She knew her back would get burned, but she didn't dare to move. The smell of burning wood grew worse. Her foot ached terribly.

Amelia looked up at the electric clock on the wall. It was four minutes to seven. She watched the red second hand revolving slowly. A minute passed. The screaming in her mind was fading now. She shifted uncomfortably, gritting her teeth against the burning heat on her back.

Another minute passed. The kicking and the pounding stopped. The screaming faded more and more. The smell of burning wood had filled the kitchen. There was a pall of gray smoke in the air. That they'll see, Amelia thought. Now that it's over, they'll come and help. That's the way it always is.

She started to ease herself away from the broiler door, ready to throw her weight back against it if she had to. She turned around and got on her knees. The reek of charred wood made her nauseated. She had to know, though. Reaching out, she pulled down the door.

Something dark and stifling rushed across her and she heard the screaming in her mind once more as hotness flooded over her and into her. It was a scream of victory now.

Amelia stood and turned off the broiler. She took a pair of ice tongs from its drawer and lifted out the blackened twist of wood. She dropped it into the sink and ran water over it until the smoke had stopped. Then she went into the bedroom, picked up the telephone and depressed its cradle. After a moment, she released the cradle and dialed her mother's number.

"This is Amelia, Mom," she said. "I'm sorry I acted the way I did. I want us to spend the evening together. It's a little late, though. Can you come by my place and we'll go from here?" She listened. "Good," she said. "I'll wait for you."

Hanging up, she walked into the kitchen, where she slid the longest carving knife from its place in the rack. She went to the front door and pushed back its bolt, which now moved freely. She carried the knife into the living room, took off her bathrobe and danced a dance of hunting, of the joy of hunting, of the joy of the impending kill.

Then she sat down, cross-legged, in the corner. He Who Kills sat, cross-legged, in the corner, in the darkness, waiting for the prey to come.

WITCH WAR

Seven pretty little girls sitting in a row. Outside, night, pouring rain—war weather. Inside, toasty warm. Seven overalled little girls chatting. Plaque on the wall saying: P.G. CENTER.

Sky clearing its throat with thunder, picking and dropping lint lightning from immeasurable shoulders. Rain hushing the world, bowing the trees, pocking earth. Square building, low, with one wall plastic.

Inside, the buzzing talk of seven pretty little girls.

"So I say to him—'Don't give me *that*, Mr. High and Mighty.' So he says, 'Oh yeah?' And I say, 'Yeah!' "

"Honest, will I ever be glad when this thing's over. I saw the cutest hat on my last furlough. Oh, *what* I wouldn't give to wear it!"

"You too? Don't I *know* it! You just can't get your hair right. Not in *this* weather. Why don't they let us get rid of it?"

"*Men!* They make me sick."

Seven gestures, seven postures, seven laughters ringing thin beneath thunder. Teeth showing in girl giggles. Hands tireless, painting pictures in the air.

P.G. Center. Girls. Seven of them. Pretty. Not one over sixteen. Curls. Pigtails. Bangs. Pouting little lips—smiling, frowning, shaping emotion on emotion. Sparkling young eyes—glittering, twinkling, narrowing, cold or warm.

Seven healthy young bodies restive on wooden chairs. Smooth adolescent limbs. Girls—pretty girls—seven of them.

◆

An army of ugly shapeless men, stumbling in mud, struggling along the pitchblack muddy road.

Rain a torrent. Buckets of it thrown on each exhausted man. Sucking sound of great boots sinking into oozy yellow-brown mud, pulling loose. Mud dripping from heels and soles.

Plodding men—hundreds of them—soaked, miserable, depleted. Young men bent over like old men. Jaws hanging loosely, mouth gasping at black wet air, tongues lolling, sunken eyes looking at nothing, betraying nothing.

Rest.

Men sink down in the mud, fall on their packs. Heads thrown back, mouths open, rain splashing on yellow teeth. Hands immobile—scrawny heaps of flesh and bone. Legs without motion— khaki lengths of worm-eaten wood. Hundreds of useless limbs fixed to hundreds of useless trunks.

In back, ahead, beside, rumble trucks and tanks and tiny cars. Thick tires splattering mud. Fat treads sinking, tearing at mucky slime. Rain drumming wet fingers on metal and canvas.

Lightning flashbulbs without pictures. Momentary burst of light. The face of war seen for a second—made of rusty guns and turning wheels and faces staring.

Blackness. A night hand blotting out the brief storm glow. Windblown rain flitting over fields and roads, drenching trees and trucks. Rivulets of bubbly rain tearing scars from the earth. Thunder, lightning.

A whistle. Dead men resurrected. Boots in sucking mud again— deeper, closer, nearer. Approach to a city that bars the way to a city that bars the way to a . . .

An officer sat in the communication room of the P.G. Center. He peered at the operator, who sat hunched over the control board, phones over his ears, writing down a message.

The officer watched the operator. They are coming, he thought. Cold, wet and afraid they are marching at us. He shivered and shut his eyes.

He opened them quickly. Visions fill his darkened pupils—of curling smoke, flaming men, unimaginable horrors that shape themselves without words or pictures.

"Sir," said the operator, "from advance observation post. Enemy forces sighted."

The officer got up, walked over to the operator and took the message. He read it, face blank, mouth parenthesized. "Yes," he said.

He turned on his heel and went to the door. He opened it and went into the next room. The seven girls stopped talking. Silence breathed on the walls.

The officer stood with his back to the plastic window. "Enemies," he said, "two miles away. Right in front of you."

He turned and pointed out the window. "Right out there. Two miles away. Any questions?"

A girl giggled.

"Any vehicles?" another asked.

"Yes. Five trucks, five small command cars, two tanks."

"That's too easy," laughed the girl, slender fingers fussing with her hair.

"That's all," said the officer. He started from the room. "Go to it," he added and, under his breath, "Monsters!"

He left.

"Oh, me," sighed one of the girls, "here we go again."

"What a bore," said another. She opened her delicate mouth and plucked out chewing gum. She put it under her chair seat.

"At least it stopped raining," said a redhead, tying her shoelaces.

The seven girls looked around at each other. *Are you ready?* said their eyes. *I'm ready, I suppose.* They adjusted themselves on the chairs with girlish grunts and sighs. They hooked their feet around the legs of their chairs. All gum was placed in storage. Mouths were tightened into prudish fixity. The pretty little girls made ready for the game.

Finally they were silent on their chairs. One of them took a deep breath. So did another. They all tensed their milky flesh and clasped fragile fingers together. One quickly scratched her head to get it over with. Another sneezed prettily.

"Now," said a girl on the right end of the row.

Seven pairs of beady eyes shut. Seven innocent little minds began to picture, to visualize, to transport.

Lips rolled into thin gashes, faces drained of color, bodies shivered passionately. Their fingers twitching with concentration, seven pretty little girls fought a war.

<hr />

The men were coming over the rise of a hill when the attack came. The leading men, feet poised for the next step, burst into flame.

There was no time to scream. Their rifles slapped down into the muck, their eyes were lost in fire. They stumbled a few steps and fell, hissing and charred, into the soft mud.

Men yelled. The ranks broke. They began to throw up their weapons and fire at the night. More troops puffed incandescently, flared up, were dead.

"Spread out!" screamed an officer as his gesturing fingers sprouted flame and his face went up in licking yellow heat.

The men looked everywhere. Their dumb terrified eyes searched for an enemy. They fired into the fields and woods. They shot each other. They broke into flopping runs over the mud.

A truck was enveloped in fire. Its driver leaped out, a two-legged torch. The truck went bumping over the road, turned, wove crazily over the field, crashed into a tree, exploded and was eaten up in blazing light. Black shadows flitted in and out of the aura of light around the flames. Screams rent the night.

Man after man burst into flame, fell crashing on his face in the mud. Spots of searing light lashed the wet darkness—screams—running coals, sputtering, glowing, dying—incendiary ranks—trucks cremated—tanks blowing up.

A little blonde, her body tense with repressed excitement. Her lips twitch, a giggle hovers in her throat. Her nostrils dilate. She shudders in giddy fright. She imagines, imagines. . . .

A soldier runs headlong across a field, screaming, his eyes insane with horror. A gigantic boulder rushes at him from the black sky.

His body is driven into the earth, mangled. From the rock edge, fingertips protrude.

The boulder lifts from the ground, crashes down again, a shapeless trip hammer. A flaming truck is flattened. The boulder flies again to the black sky.

A pretty brunette, her face a feverish mask. Wild thoughts tumble through her virginal brain. Her scalp grows taut with ecstatic fear. Her lips draw back from clenching teeth. A gasp of terror hisses from her lips. She imagines, imagines. . . .

A soldier falls to his knees. His head jerks back. In the light of burning comrades, he stares dumbly at the white-foamed wave that towers over him.

It crashes down, sweeps his body over the muddy earth, fills his lungs with salt water. The tidal wave roars over the field, drowns a hundred flaming men, tosses their corpses in the air with thundering whitecaps.

Suddenly the water stops, flies into a million pieces and disintegrates.

A lovely little redhead, hands drawn under her chin in tight bloodless fists. Her lips tremble, a throb of delight expands her chest. Her white

*throat contracts, she gulps in a breath of air. Her nose wrinkles with
dreadful joy. She imagines, imagines. . . .*

A running soldier collides with a lion. He cannot see in the darkness. His hands strike wildly at the shaggy mane. He clubs with his rifle butt.

A scream. His face is torn off with one blow of thick claws. A jungle roar billows in the night.

A red-eyed elephant tramples wildly through the mud, picking up men in its thick trunk, hurling them through the air, mashing them under driving black columns.

Wolves bound from the darkness, spring, tear at throats. Gorillas scream and bounce in the mud, leap at falling soldiers.

A rhinoceros, leather skin glowing in the light of living torches, crashes into a burning tank, wheels, thunders into blackness, is gone.

Fangs—claws—ripping teeth—shrieks—trumpeting—roars. The sky rains snakes.

※

Silence. Vast brooding silence. Not a breeze, not a drop of rain, not a grumble of distant thunder. The battle is ended.

Gray morning mist rolls over the burned, the torn, the drowned, the crushed, the poisoned, the sprawling dead.

Motionless trucks—silent tanks, wisps of oily smoke still rising from their shattered hulks. Great death covering the field. Another battle in another war.

Victory—everyone is dead.

※

The girls stretched languidly. They extended their arms and rotated their round shoulders. Pink lips grew wide in pretty little yawns. They looked at each other and tittered in embarrassment. Some of them blushed. A few looked guilty.

Then they all laughed out loud. They opened more gumpacks,

drew compacts from pockets, spoke intimately with schoolgirl whispers, with late-night dormitory whispers.

Muted giggles rose up fluttering in the warm room.

"Aren't we awful?" one of them said, powdering her pert nose.

Later they all went downstairs and had breakfast.

DANCE OF THE DEAD

❖❖❖

I wanna RIDE!
with my Rota-Mota honey
by my SIDE!
As we whiz along the highway
We will HUG and SNUGGLE
And we'll have a
little STRUGGLE!

STRUGGLE (strug´´l), n., act of promiscuous loveplay; usage evolved during WW III.

Double beams spread buttery lamplight on the highway. Rotor-Motors Convertible, Model C, 1997, rushed after it. Light spurted ahead, yellow glowing. The car pursued with a twelve-cylindered snarling pursuit. Night blotted in behind, jet and still. The car sped on. ST. LOUIS—10.

"I wanna FLY!" they sang, "with the Rota-Mota apple of my EYE!" they sang. "It's the only way of living. . . ."

The quartet singing:

Len, 23.

Bud, 24.

Barbara, 20.

Peggy, 18.

Len with Barbara, Bud with Peggy.

Bud at the wheel, snapping around tilted curves, roaring up black-shouldered hills, shooting the car across silent flatlands. At the top of three lungs (the fourth gentler), competing with wind that buffeted their heads, that whipped their hair to lashing threads—singing:

"You can have your walkin' under MOONLIGHT BEAMS! At a hundred miles an hour let me DREAM my DREAMS!"

Needle quivering at 130, two 5-mph notches from gauge's end. *A sudden dip!* Their young frames jolted and the thrown-up laughter of three was windswept into night. Around a curve, darting up and down a hill, flashing across a leveled plain—an ebony bullet skimming earth.

"In my *ROTORY, MOTORY, FLOATERY*, drivin' machi-i-i-ine!"

"YOU'LL BE A FLOATER IN YOUR ROTOR-MOTOR."

In the back seat:
"Have a jab, Bab."
"Thanks, I had one after supper" (pushing away needle fixed to eye-dropper).
In the front seat:
"You meana tell me this is the first time you ever been t'Saint Loo!"
"But I just started school in September."
"Hey, you're a *frosh*!"
Back seat joining front seat:
"Hey, *frosh*, have a mussle-tussle."
(Needle passed forward, eye bulb quivering amber juice.)
"*Live* it, girl!"

MUSSLE-TUSSLE (mus´ ´l-tus´ ´l), n., slang for the result of inject-
ing a drug into a muscle; usage evolved during WW III.

Peggy's lips failed at smiling. Her fingers twitched.

"No, thanks, I'm not . . ."

"Come *on*, frosh!" Len leaning hard over the seat, white-browed
under black blowing hair. Pushing the needle at her face. "Live it,
girl! Grab a li'l mussle-tussle!"

"I'd rather not," said Peggy. "If you don't—"

"What's *'at*, frosh?" yelled Len and pressed his leg against the
pressing leg of Barbara.

Peggy shook her head and golden hair flew across her cheeks and
eyes. Underneath her yellow dress, underneath her white brassiere,
underneath her young breast—a heart throbbed heavily. *Watch your
step, darling, that's all we ask. Remember, you're all we have in the world
now.* Mother words drumming at her; the needle making her draw
back into the seat.

"*Come* on, frosh!"

The car groaned its shifting weight around a curve and centrifu-
gal force pressed Peggy into Bud's lean hip. His hand dropped down
and fingered at her leg. Underneath her yellow dress, underneath
her sheer stocking—flesh crawled. Lips failed again; the smile was
a twitch of red.

"Frosh, live it up!"

"Lay off, Len, jab your own dates."

"But we gotta teach frosh how to mussle-tussle!"

"Lay off, I said! She's my date!"

The black car roaring, chasing its own light. Peggy anchored down
the feeling hand with hers. The wind whistled over them and
grabbed down chilly fingers at their hair. She didn't want his hand
there but she felt grateful to him.

Her vaguely frightened eyes watched the road lurch beneath the wheels. In back, a silent struggle began, taut hands rubbing, parted mouths clinging. Search for the sweet elusive at 120 miles-per-hour.

"Rota-Mota honey," Len moaned the moan between salivary kisses. In the front seat a young girl's heart beat unsteadily. ST. LOUIS—6.

"No kiddin', you never been to Saint Loo?"

"No, I . . ."

"Then you never saw the loopy's dance?"

Throat contracting suddenly. "No, I . . . is that what . . . we're going to—"

"Hey, frosh never saw the loopy's dance!" Bud yelled back.

Lips parted, slurping; skirt was adjusted with blasé aplomb. "No kiddin'!" Len fired up the words. "Girl, you haven't *lived*!"

"Oh, she's *got* to see *that*," said Barbara, buttoning a button.

"Let's go there then!" yelled Len. "Let's give frosh a thrill!"

"Good enough," said Bud and squeezed her leg. "Good enough up here, right, Peg?"

Peggy's throat moved in the dark and the wind clutched harshly at her hair. She'd heard of it, she'd read of it but never had she thought she'd—

Choose your school friends carefully, darling. Be very careful.

But when no one spoke to you for two whole months? When you were lonely and wanted to talk and laugh and be alive? And someone spoke to you finally and asked you to go out with them?

"I yam Popeye, the sailor man!" Bud sang.

In back, they crowed artificial delight. Bud was taking a course in Pre-War Comics and Cartoons—2. This week the class was studying Popeye. Bud had fallen in love with the one-eyed seaman and told Len and Barbara all about him; taught them dialogue and song.

"I yam Popeye, the sailor man! I like to go swimmin' with bow-legged women! I yam Popeye, the sailor man!"

Laughter. Peggy smiled falteringly. The hand left her leg as the car screeched around a curve and she was thrown against the door. Wind dashed blunt coldness in her eyes and forced her back, blinking. 110—115—120 miles-per-hour. ST. LOUIS—3. *Be very careful, dear.*

Popeye cocked wicked eye.

"O, Olive Oyl, you is my sweet patootie."

Elbow nudging Peggy. "You be Olive Oyl—*you.*"

Peggy smiled nervously. "I can't."

"Sure!"

In the back seat, Wimpy came up for air to announce, "I will gladly pay you Tuesday for a hamburger today."

Three fierce voices and a faint fourth raged against the howl of wind. "I fights to the *fin*-ish 'cause I eats my *spin*-ach! I yam Popeye, the sailor man! *Toot! Toot!*"

"I yam what I yam," reiterated Popeye gravelly and put his hand on the yellow-skirted leg of Olive Oyl. In the back, two members of the quartet returned to feeling struggle.

ST. LOUIS—1. The black car roared through the darkened suburbs. "On with the noises!" Bud sang out. They all took out their plasticate nose-and-mouth pieces and adjusted them.

ANCE IN YOUR PANTS WOULD BE A PITY!
WEAR YOUR NOSIES IN THE CITY!!

ANCE (anse), n., slang for anticivilian germs; usage evolved during WW III.

"You'll like the loopy's dance!" Bud shouted to her over the shriek of wind. "It's sen-*saysh!*"

Peggy felt a cold that wasn't of the night or of the wind. *Remember, darling, there are terrible things in the world today. Things you must avoid.*

"Couldn't we go somewhere else?" Peggy said but her voice was inaudible. She heard Bud singing, "I like to go swimmin' with bow-legged women!" She felt his hand on her leg again while, in the back, was the silence of grinding passion without kisses.

Dance of the dead. The words trickled ice across Peggy's brain.

ST. LOUIS.

The black car sped into the ruins.

⊰✦⊱

It was a place of smoke and blatant joys. Air resounded with the bleating of revelers and there was a noise of sounding brass spinning out a cloud of music—1997 music, a frenzy of twisted dissonances. Dancers, shoe-horned into the tiny square of open floor, ground pulsing bodies together. A network of bursting sounds lanced through the mass of them; dancers singing:

> *"Hurt me! Bruise me! Squeeze me TIGHT!*
> *Scorch my blood with hot DELIGHT!*
> *Please abuse me every NIGHT!*
> *LOVER, LOVER, LOVER, be a* beast-to-me!"

Elements of explosion restrained within the dancing bounds— instead of fragmenting, quivering. "Oh, be a beast, beast, beast, *Beast*, BEAST to me!"

"How is *this*, Olive old goil?" Popeye inquired of the light of his eye as they struggled after the waiter. "Nothin' like this in Sykesville, eh?"

Peggy smiled but her hand in Bud's felt numb. As they passed by a murky lighted table, a hand she didn't see felt at her leg. She twitched and bumped against a hard knee across the narrow aisle. As she stumbled and lurched through the hot and smoky, thick-aired room, she felt a dozen eyes disrobing her, abusing her. Bud jerked her along and she felt her lips trembling.

"Hey, how about that!" Bud exulted as they sat. "Right by the stage!"

From cigarette mists, the waiter plunged and hovered, pencil poised, beside their table.

"What'll it be!" His questioning shout cut through cacophony.

"Whiskey-water!" Bud and Len paralleled orders, then turned to their dates. "What'll it be!" the waiter's request echoed from their lips.

"*Green Swamp!*" Barbara said and, "*Green Swamp* here!" Len passed it along. Gin, Invasion Blood (1997 Rum), lime juice, sugar, mint spray, splintered ice—a popular college girl drink.

"What about you, honey?" Bud asked his date.

Peggy smiled. "Just some ginger ale," she said, her voice a fluttering frailty in the massive clash and fog of smoke.

"What?" asked Bud and, "What's that, didn't hear!" the waiter shouted.

"Ginger ale."

"*What?*"

"Ginger ale!"

"GINGER ALE!" Len screamed it out and the drummer, behind the raging curtain of noise that was the band's music, almost heard it. Len banged down his fist. *One—Two—Three!*

CHORUS: *Ginger Ale was only twelve years old!*
Went to church and was as good as gold.
Till that day when—

"Come *on*, come *on*!" the waiter squalled. "Let's have that order, kids! I'm busy!"

"Two whiskey-waters and two Green Swamps!" Len sang out and the waiter was gone into the swirling maniac mist.

Peggy felt her young heart flutter helplessly. *Above all, don't drink when you're out on a date. Promise us that, darling, you must promise us that.* She tried to push away instructions etched in brain.

"How you like this place, honey? *Loopy*, ain't it?" Bud fired the question at her; a red-faced, happy-faced Bud.

LOOPY (lōō´ pī), adj., common alter. of L.U.P.

She smiled at Bud, a smile of nervous politeness. Her eyes moved around, her face inclined and she was looking up at the stage. *Loopy*. The word scalpeled at her mind. *Loopy, loopy.*

The stage was five yards deep at the radius of its wooden semicircle. A waist-high rail girdled the circumference, two pale purple spotlights, unlit, hung at each rail end. Purple on white— the thought came. *Darling, isn't Sykesville Business College good enough? No! I don't want to take a business course, I want to major in art at the University!*

The drinks were brought and Peggy watched the disembodied waiter's arm thud down a high, green-looking glass before her. *Presto!*—the arm was gone. She looked into the murky green swamp depths and saw chipped ice bobbing.

"A toast! Pick up your glass, Peg!" Bud clarioned.

They all clinked glasses:

"To lust primordial!" Bud toasted.

"To beds intemperate!" Len added.

"To flesh insensate!" Barbara added a third link.

Their eyes zeroed in on Peggy's face, demanding. She didn't understand.

"Finish it!" Bud told her, plagued by freshman sluggishness.

"To . . . u-*us*," she faltered.

"How o-*ri*-ginal," stabbed Barbara and Peggy felt heat licking up her smooth cheeks. It passed unnoticed as three Youths of America with Whom the Future Rested gurgled down their liquor thirstily. Peggy fingered at her glass, a smile printed to lips that would not smile unaided.

"Come on, *drink*, girl!" Bud shouted to her across the vast distance of one foot. "Chuggalug!"

"Live it, girl," Len suggested abstractedly, fingers searching once more for soft leg. And finding, under the table, soft leg waiting.

Peggy didn't want to drink, she was afraid to drink. Mother words kept pounding—*never on a date, honey, never*. She raised the glass a little.

"Uncle Buddy will help, will help!"

Uncle Buddy leaning close, vapor of whiskey haloing his head. Uncle Buddy pushing cold glass to shaking young lips. "Come on, Olive Oyl, old goil! Down the hatch!"

Choking sprayed the bosom of her dress with green swamp droplets. Flaming liquid trickled into her stomach, sending offshoots of fire into her veins.

Bangity boom crash smash POW!! The drummer applied the *coup de grâce* to what had been, in ancient times, a lover's waltz. Lights dropped and Peggy sat coughing and tear-eyed in the smoky cellar club.

She felt Bud's hand clamp strongly on her shoulder and, in the murk, she felt herself pulled off balance and felt Bud's hot wet mouth pressing at her lips. She jerked away and then the purple spots went on and a mottle-faced Bud drew back, gurgling, "I fights to the finish," and reaching for his drink.

"Hey, the loopy now, the loopy!" Len said eagerly, releasing exploratory hands.

Peggy's heart jolted and she thought she was going to cry out and run thrashing through the dark, smoke-filled room. But a sophomore hand anchored her to the chair and she looked up in white-faced dread at the man who came out on the stage and faced the microphone which, like a metal spider, had swung down to meet him.

"May I have your attention, ladies and gentlemen," he said, a grimfaced, sepulchral-voiced man whose eyes moved out over them like flicks of doom. Peggy's breath was labored, she felt thin lines of green swamp water filtering hotly through her chest and stomach. It made her blink dizzily. *Mother.* The word escaped cells of the mind and trembled into conscious freedom. *Mother, take me home.*

"As you know, the act you are about to see is not for the faint of heart, the weak of will." The man plodded through the words like a cow enmired. "Let me caution those of you whose nerves are not what they ought to be—*leave now.* We make no guarantees of responsibility. We can't even afford to maintain a house doctor."

No laughter appreciative. "Cut the crap and get off stage," Len grumbled to himself. Peggy felt her fingers twitching.

"As you know," the man went on, his voice gilded with learned sonority, "this is not an offering of mere sensation but an honest scientific demonstration."

"Loophole for Loopy's!" Bud and Len heaved up the words with the thoughtless reaction of hungry dogs salivating at a bell.

It was, in 1997, a comeback so rigidly standard it had assumed the status of a catechism answer. A crenel in the postwar law allowed the LUP performance if it was orally prefaced as an exposition of science. Through this legal chink had poured so much abusing of the law that few cared any longer. A feeble government was grateful to contain infractions of the law at all.

When hoots and shoutings had evaporated in the smoke-clogged air, the man, his arms upraised in patient benediction, spoke again.

Peggy watched the studied movement of his lips, her heart swelling, then contracting in slow, spasmodic beats. An iciness was creeping up her legs. She felt it rising toward the threadlike fires in her body and her fingers twitched around the chilly moisture of the glass. *I want to go, please take me home*— Will-spent words were in her mind again.

"Ladies and gentlemen," the man concluded, "brace yourselves."

A gong sounded its hollow, shivering resonance, the man's voice thickened and slowed.

"The L. U. Phenomenon!"

The man was gone; the microphone had risen and was gone. Music began; a moaning brassiness, all muted. A jazzman's conception of *the palpable obscure*—mounted on a pulse of thumping drum. A dolor of saxophone, a menace of trombone, a harnessed bleating of trumpet—they raped the air with stridor.

Peggy felt a shudder plaiting down her back and her gaze dropped quickly to the murky whiteness of the table. Smoke and darkness, dissonance and heat surrounded her.

Without meaning to, but driven by an impulse of nervous fear, she raised the glass and drank. The glacial trickle in her throat sent another shudder rippling through her. Then further shoots of liquored heat budded in her veins and a numbness settled in her temples. Through parted lips, she forced out a shaking breath.

Now a restless, murmuring movement started through the room, the sound of it like willows in a soughing wind. Peggy dared not lift her gaze to the purpled silence of the stage. She stared down at the shifting glimmer of her drink, feeling muscle strands draw tightly in her stomach, feeling the hollow thumping of her heart. *I'd like to leave, please let's leave.*

The music labored toward a rasping dissonant climax, its brass components struggling, in vain, for unity.

A hand stroked once at Peggy's leg and it was the hand of Popeye, the sailor man, who muttered roupily, "Olive Oyl, you is my goil." She barely felt or heard. Automatonlike, she raised the cold and sweating glass again and felt the chilling in her throat and then the flaring network of warmth inside her.

SWISH!

The curtain swept open with such a rush, she almost dropped her glass. It thumped down heavily on the table, swamp water cascading up its sides and raining on her hand. The music exploded shrapnel of ear-cutting cacophony and her body jerked. On the tablecloth, her hands twitched white on white while claws of uncontrollable demand pulled up her frightened eyes.

The music fled, frothing behind a wake of swelling drum rolls. The nightclub was a wordless crypt, all breathing checked. Cobwebs of smoke drifted in the purple light across the stage. No sound except the muffled, rolling drum.

Peggy's body was a petrifaction in its chair, smitten to rock around her leaping heart, while, through the wavering haze of smoke and liquored dizziness, she looked up in horror to where it stood.

It had been a woman.

Her hair was black, a framing of snarled ebony for the tallow mask that was her face. Her shadow-rimmed eyes were closed behind lids as smooth and white as ivory. Her mouth, a lipless and unmoving line, stood like a clotted sword wound beneath her nose. Her throat, her shoulders and her arms were white, were motionless. At her sides, protruding from the sleeve ends of the green transparency she wore, hung alabaster hands.

Across this marble statue, the spotlights coated purple shimmer.

Still paralyzed, Peggy stared up at its motionless features, her fingers knitted in a bloodless tangle on her lap. The pulse of drumbeats in the air seemed to fill her body, its rhythm altering her heartbeat.

In the black emptiness behind her, she heard Len muttering, "I love my wife but, oh, you corpse," and heard the wheeze of helpless snickers that escaped from Bud and Barbara. The cold still rose in her, a silent tidal dread.

Somewhere in the smoke-fogged darkness, a man cleared viscid nervousness from his throat and a murmur of appreciative relief strained through the audience.

Still no motion on the stage, no sound but the sluggish cadence of the drum, thumping at the silence like someone seeking entrance at a far-off door. The thing that was a nameless victim of the plague stood palely rigid while the distillation sluiced through its blood-clogged veins.

Now the drum throbs hastened like the pulsebeat of a rising panic.

Peggy felt the chill begin to swallow her. Her throat started tightening, her breathing was a string of lip-parted gasps.

The loopy's eyelid twitched.

Abrupt, black, straining silence webbed the room. Even the breath choked off in Peggy's throat when she saw the pale eyes flutter open. Something creaked in the stillness; her body pressed back unconsciously against the chair. Her eyes were wide, unblinking circles that sucked into her brain the sight of the thing that had been a woman.

Music again; a brass-throated moaning from the dark, like some animal made of welded horns mewling its derangement in a midnight alley.

Suddenly, the right arm of the loopy jerked at its side, the tendons contracted. The left arm twitched alike, snapped out, then fell back and thudded in purple-white limpness against the thigh. The right arm out, the left arm out, the right, the left-right-left-right—like marionette arms twitching from an amateur's dangling strings.

The music caught the time, drum brushes scratching out a rhythm for the convulsions of the loopy's muscles. Peggy pressed back further, her body numbed and cold, her face a livid, staring mask in the fringes of the stage light.

The loopy's right foot moved now, jerking up inflexibly as the distillation constricted muscles in its leg. A second and a third contraction caused the leg to twitch, the left leg flung out in a violent spasm and then the woman's body lurched stiffly forward, filming the transparent silk to its light and shadow.

Peggy heard the sudden hiss of breath that passed the clenching teeth of Bud and Len and a wave of nausea sprayed foaming sickness up her stomach walls. Before her eyes, the stage abruptly undulated with a watery glitter and it seemed as if the flailing loopy was headed straight for her.

Gasping dizzily, she pressed back in horror, unable to take her eyes from its now agitated face.

She watched the mouth jerk to a gaping cavity, then a twisted scar that split into a wound again. She saw the dark nostrils twitching, saw writhing flesh beneath the ivory cheeks, saw furrows dug and undug in the purple whiteness of the forehead. She saw one lifeless eye wink monstrously and heard the gasp of startled laughter in the room.

While music blared into a fit of grating noise, the woman's arms and legs kept jerking with convulsive cramps that threw her body around the purpled stage like a full-sized rag doll given spastic life.

It was a nightmare in an endless sleep. Peggy shivered in helpless terror as she watched the loopy's twisting, leaping dance. The blood in her had turned to ice; there was no life in her but the endless, pounding stagger of her heart. Her eyes were frozen spheres staring at the woman's body writhing white and flaccid underneath the clinging silk.

Then, something went wrong.

Up till then, its muscular seizures had bound the loopy to an area of several yards before the amber flat which was the background for its paroxysmal dance. Now its erratic surging drove the loopy toward the stage-encircling rail.

Peggy heard the thump and creaking strain of wood as the loopy's hip collided with the rail. She cringed into a shuddering knot, her eyes still raised fixedly to the purple-splashed face whose every feature was deformed by throes of warping convulsion.

The loopy staggered back and Peggy saw and heard its leprous hands slapping with a fitful rhythm at its silk-scaled thighs.

Again it sprang forward like a maniac marionette and the woman's stomach thudded sickeningly into the railing wood. The dark mouth gaped, clamped shut and then the loopy twisted through a jerking revolution and crashed back against the rail again, almost above the table where Peggy sat.

Peggy couldn't breathe. She sat rooted to the chair, her lips a trembling circle of stricken dread, a pounding of blood at her temples as she watched the loopy spin again, its arms a blur of flailing white.

The lurid bleaching of its face dropped toward Peggy as the loopy crashed into the waist-high rail again and bent across its top. The mask of lavender-rained whiteness hung above her, dark eyes twitching open into a hideous stare.

Peggy felt the floor begin to move and the livid face was blurred with darkness, then reappeared in a burst of luminosity. Sound fled on brass-shoed feet, then plunged into her brain again—a smearing discord.

The loopy kept on jerking forward, driving itself against the rail as though it meant to scale it. With every spastic lurch, the diaphanous silk fluttered like a film about its body and every savage collision with the railing tautened the green transparency across its swollen flesh. Peggy looked up in rigid muteness at the loopy's fierce attack on the railing, her eyes unable to escape the wild distortion of the woman's face with its black frame of tangled, snapping hair.

What happened then happened in a blurring passage of seconds.

The grim-faced man came rushing across the purple-lighted stage; the thing that had been a woman went crashing, twitching, flailing at the rail, doubling over it, the spasmodic hitching flinging up its muscle-knotted legs.

A clawing fall.

Peggy lurched back in her chair and the scream that started in her throat was forced back into a strangled gag as the loopy came crashing down onto the table, its limbs a thrash of naked whiteness.

Barbara screamed, the audience gasped and Peggy saw, on the fringe of vision, Bud jumping up, his face a twist of stunned surprise.

The loopy flopped and twisted on the table like a new-caught fish. The music stopped, grinding into silence; a rush of agitated murmur filled the room and blackness swept in brain-submerging waves across Peggy's mind.

Then the cold white hand slapped across her mouth, the dark eyes stared at her in purple light and Peggy felt the darkness flooding.

The horror-smoked room went turning on its side.

⧯⧯⧯

Consciousness. It flickered in her brain like gauze-veiled candle-light. A murmuring of sound, a blur of shadow before her eyes.

Breath dripped like syrup from her mouth.

"Here, Peg."

She heard Bud's voice and felt the chilly metal of a flask neck pressed against lips. She swallowed, twisting slightly at the trickle of fire in her throat and stomach, then coughed and pushed away the flask with deadened fingers.

Behind her, a rustling movement. "Hey, she's *back*," Len said. "Ol' Olive Oyl is back."

"You feel all right?" asked Barbara.

She felt all right. Her heart was like a drum hanging from piano wire in her chest, slowly, slowly beaten. Her hands and feet were numb, not with cold but with a sultry torpor. Thoughts moved with a tranquil lethargy, her brain a leisurely machine imbedded in swaths of woolly packing.

She felt all right.

Peggy looked across the night with sleepy eyes. They were on a hilltop, the braked convertible crouching on a jutting edge. Far below, the country slept, a carpet of light and shadow beneath the chalky moon.

An arm snake moved around her waist. "Where are we?" she asked him in a languid voice.

"Few miles outside school," Bud said. "How d'ya feel, honey?"

She stretched, her body a delicious strain of muscles. She sagged back, limp, against his arm.

"Wonderful," she murmured with a dizzy smile and scratched the tiny itching bump on her left shoulder. Warmth radiated through

her flesh; the night was a sabled glow. There seemed—*somewhere*—to be a memory, but it crouched in secret behind folds of thick content.

"Woman, you were *out*," laughed Bud; and Barbara added and Len added, "*Were* you!" and "Olive Oyl went *plunko!*"

"Out?" Her casual murmur went unheard.

The flask went around and Peggy drank again, relaxing further as the liquor needled fire through her veins.

"Man, I never saw a loopy dance like that!" Len said.

A momentary chill across her back, then warmth again. "Oh," said Peggy, "that's right. I forgot."

She smiled.

"That was what I calls a grand finale!" Len said, dragging back his willing date, who murmured, "*Lenny* boy."

"LUP," Bud muttered, nuzzling at Peggy's hair. "Son of a gun." He reached out idly for the radio knob.

LUP (Lifeless Undead Phenomenon)—This freak of physiological abnormality was discovered during the war when, following certain germ-gas attacks, many of the dead troops were found erect and performing the spasmodic gyrations which, later, became known as the "loopy's" (LUP's) dance. The particular germ spray responsible was later distilled and is now used in carefully controlled experiments which are conducted only under the strictest of legal license and supervision.

Music surrounded them, its melancholy fingers touching at their hearts. Peggy leaned against her date and felt no need to curb exploring hands. Somewhere, deep within the jellied layers of her mind, there was something trying to escape. It fluttered like a frantic moth imprisoned in congealing wax, struggling wildly but only growing weaker in attempt as the chrysalis hardened.

Four voices sang softly in the night.

"If the world is here tomorrow
I'll be waiting, dear, for you
If the stars are there tomorrow
I'll be wishing on them too."

Four young voices singing, a murmur in immensity. Four bodies, two by two, slackly warm and drugged. A singing, an embracing— a wordless accepting.

"Star light, star bright
Let there be another night."

The singing ended but the song went on.
A young girl sighed.
"Isn't it romantic?" said Olive Oyl.

DRESS OF WHITE SILK

━◈━◈━◈━

Quiet is here and all in me.

Granma locked me in my room and wont let me out. Because its happened she says. I guess I was bad. Only it was the dress. Mommas dress I mean. She is gone away forever. Granma says your momma is in heaven. I dont know how. Can she go in heaven if shes dead?

Now I hear granma. She is in mommas room. She is putting mommas dress down the box. Why does she always? And locks it too. I wish she didnt. Its a pretty dress and smells sweet so. And warm. I love to touch it against my cheek. But I cant never again. I guess that is why granma is mad at me.

But I amnt sure. All day it was only like everyday. Mary Jane came over to my house. She lives across the street. Everyday she comes to my house and play. Today she was.

I have seven dolls and a fire truck. Today granma said play with your dolls and it. Dont you go inside your mommas room now she said. She always says it. She just means not mess up I think. Because she says it all the time. Dont go in your mommas room. Like that.

But its nice in mommas room. When it rains I go there. Or when granma is doing her nap I do. I dont make noise. I just sit on the bed and touch the white cover. Like when I was only small. The room smells like sweet.

I make believe momma is dressing and I am allowed in. I smell her white silk dress. Her going out for night dress. She called it that I dont remember when.

I hear it moving if I listen hard. I make believe to see her sitting at the dressing table. Like touching on perfume or something I mean. And see her dark eyes. I can remember.

Its so nice if it rains and I see eyes on the window. The rain sounds like a big giant outside. He says shushshush so every one will be quiet. I like to make believe that in mommas room.

What I like almost best is to sit at mommas dressing table. It is like pink and big and smells sweet too. The seat in front has a pillow sewed in it. There are bottles and bottles with bumps and have colored perfume in them. And you can see almost your whole self in the mirror.

When I sit there I make believe to be momma. I say be quiet mother I am going out and you can not stop me. It is something I say I dont know why like I hear it in me. And oh stop your sobbing mother they will not catch me I have my magic dress.

When I pretend I brush my hair long. But I only use my own brush from my room. I didnt never use mommas brush. I dont think granma is mad at me for that because I never use mommas brush. I wouldnt never.

Sometimes I did open the box up. Because I know where granma puts the key. I saw her once when she wouldnt know I saw her. She puts the key on the hook in mommas closet. Behind the door I mean.

I could open the box lots of times. Thats because I like to look at mommas dress. I like best to look at it. It is so pretty and feels soft and like silky. I could touch it for a million years.

I kneel on the rug with roses on it. I hold the dress in my arms and like breathe from it. I touch it against my cheek. I wish I could take it to sleep with me and hold it. I like to. Now I cant. Because granma says. And she says I should burn it up but I loved her so. And she cries about the dress.

I wasnt never bad with it. I put it back neat like it was never touched. Granma never knew. I laughed that she never knew before. But she knows now I did it I guess. And shell punish me. What did it hurt her? Wasnt it my mommas dress?

What I like real best in mommas room is look at the picture of momma. It has a gold thing around it. Frame is what granma says. It is on the wall on top the bureau.

Momma is pretty. Your momma was pretty granma says. Why does she? I see momma there smiling on me and she *is* pretty. For always.

Her hair is black. Like mine. Her eyes are even pretty like black. Her mouth is red so red. I like the dress and its the white one. It is all down on her shoulders. Her skin is white almost white like the dress. And so are her hands. She is so pretty. I love her even if she is gone away forever. I love her so much.

I guess I think thats what made me bad. I mean to Mary Jane.

Mary Jane came from lunch like she does. Granma went to do her nap. She said dont forget now no going to your mommas room. I told her no granma. And I was saying the truth but then Mary Jane and I was playing fire truck. Mary Jane said I bet you havent no mother I bet you made up it all she said.

I got mad at her. I have a momma I know. She made me mad at her to say I made up it all. She said Im a liar. I mean about the bed and the dressing table and the picture and the dress even and every thing.

I said well Ill show you smarty.

I looked into granmas room. She was doing her nap still. I went down and said Mary Jane to come on because granma wont know.

She wasnt so smart after then. She giggled like she does. Even she made a scaredy noise when she hit into the table in the hall upstairs. I said youre a scaredy cat to her. She said back well *my* house isnt so dark like this. Like that was so much.

We went in mommas room. It was more dark than you could see. I said this is my mommas room I suppose I made up it all.

She was by the door and she wasnt smart then either. She didnt say any word. She looked around the room. She jumped when I got her arm. Well come on I said.

I sat on the bed and said this is my mommas bed see how soft it is. She didnt say nothing. Scaredy cat I said. Am not she said like she does.

I said to sit down how can you tell if its soft if you dont sit down. She sat down by me. I said feel how soft it is. Smell how sweet it is.

I closed my eyes but funny it wasnt like always. Because Mary Jane was there. I told her to stop feeling the cover. You said to she said. Well stop it I said.

See I said and I pulled her up. Thats the dressing table. I took her and brought her there. She said let go. It was so quiet and like always. I started to feel bad. Because Mary Jane was there. Because it was in my mommas room and momma wouldnt like Mary Jane there.

But I had to show her the things because. I showed her the mirror. We looked at each other in it. She looked white. Mary Jane is a scaredy cat I said. Am not am not she said anyway nobodys house is so quiet and dark inside. Anyway she said it smells.

I got mad at her. No it doesnt smell I said. Does so she said you said it did. I got madder too. It smells like sugar she said. It smells like sick people in your mommas room.

Dont say my mommas room is like sick people I said to her.

Well you didnt show me no dress and youre lying she said there isnt no dress. I felt all warm inside so I pulled her hair. Ill show you I said youre going to see my mommas dress and youll better not call me a liar.

I made her stand still and I got the key off the hook. I kneeled down. I opened the box with the key.

Mary Jane said pew that smells like garbage.

I put my nails in her and she pulled away and got mad. Dont you pinch me she said and she was all red. Im telling my mother on you she said. And anyway its not a white dress its dirty and ugly she said.

Its not dirty I said. I said it so loud I wonder why granma didnt hear. I pulled out the dress from the box. I held it up to show her how its white. It fell open like the rain whispering and the bottom touched on the rug.

It is too white I said all white and clean and silky.

No she said she was so mad and red it has a hole in it. I got more madder. If my momma was here shed show you I said. You got no momma she said all ugly. I hate her.

I have. I said it way loud. I pointed my finger to mommas picture. Well who can see in this stupid dark room she said. I pushed her hard and she hit against the bureau. See then I said mean look at the picture. Thats my momma and shes the most beautiful lady in the world.

Shes ugly she has funny hands Mary Jane said. She hasnt I said shes the most beautiful lady in the world!

Not not she said *she has buck teeth.*

I dont remember then. I think the dress moved in my arms. Mary Jane screamed. I dont remember what. It got dark and the curtains were closed I think. I couldnt see anyway. I couldnt hear nothing except buck teeth funny hands buck teeth funny hands even when no one was saying it.

There was something else because I think I heard some one call *dont let her say that!* I couldnt hold to the dress. And I had it on me I cant remember. Because I was grown up strong. But I was a little girl still I think. I mean outside.

I think I was terrible bad then.

Granma took me away from there I guess. I dont know. She was screaming god help us its happened its happened. Over and over. I dont know why. She pulled me all the way here to my room and locked me in. She wont let me out. Well Im not so scared. Who cares if she locks me in a million billion years? She doesn't have to even give me supper. Im not hungry anyway.

Im full.

MAD HOUSE

He sits down at his desk. He picks up a long, yellow pencil and starts to write on a pad. The lead point breaks.

The ends of his lips turn down. The eye pupils grow small in the hard mask of his face. Quietly, mouth pressed into an ugly, lipless gash, he picks up the pencil sharpener.

He grinds off the shavings and tosses the sharpener back in the drawer. Once more he starts to write. As he does so, the point snaps again and the lead rolls across the paper.

Suddenly his face becomes livid. Wild rage clamps the muscles of his body. He yells at the pencil, curses it with a stream of outrage. He glares at it with actual hate. He breaks it in two with a brutal snap and flings it into the wastebasket with a triumphant, "There! See how you like it in *there*!"

He sits tensely on the chair, his eyes wide, his lips trembling. He shakes with a frenzied wrath; it sprays his insides with acid.

The pencil lies in the wastebasket, broken and still. It is wood, lead, metal, rubber; all dead, without appreciation of the burning fury it has caused.

And yet . . .

He is quietly standing by the window, peering out at the street. He is letting the tightness sough away. He does not hear the rustle in the wastebasket which ceases immediately.

Soon his body is normal again. He sits down. He uses a fountain pen.

❖

He sits down before his typewriter.

He inserts a sheet of paper and begins tapping on the keys.

His fingers are large. He hits two keys at once. The two strikers are jammed together. They stand in the air, hovering impotently over the black ribbon.

He reaches over in disgust and slaps them back. They separate, flap back into their separate berths. He starts typing again.

He hits a wrong key. The start of a curse falls from his lips, unfinished. He snatches up the round eraser and rubs the unwanted letter from the sheet of paper.

He drops the eraser and starts to type again. The paper has shifted on the roller. The next sentences are on a level slightly above the original. He clenches a fist, ignores the mistake.

The machine sticks. His shoulders twitch, he slams a fist on the space bar with a loud curse. The carriage jumps, the bell tinkles. He shoves the carriage over and it crashes to a halt.

He types faster. Three keys stick together. He clenches his teeth and whines in helpless fury. He smacks the type arms. They will not come apart. He forces them to separate with bent, shaking fingers. They fall away. He sees that his fingers are smudged with ink. He curses out loud, trying to outrage the very air for revenge on the stupid machine.

Now he hits the keys brutally, fingers falling like the stiff claws of a derrick. Another mistake, he erases savagely. He types still faster. Four keys stick together.

He screams.

He slams his fist on the machine. He clutches at the paper and rips it from the machine in jagged pieces. He welds the fragments in his fist and hurls the crumpled ball across the room. He beats the carriage over and slams the cover down on the machine.

He jumps up and glares down.

"You fool!" he shouts with a bitter, revolted voice. "You stupid, idiotic, asinine *fool*!"

Scorn drips from his voice. He keeps talking, he drives himself into a craze.

"You're no damn good. You're no damn good at all. I'm going to break you in pieces. I'm going to crack you into splinters, melt you, *kill* you! You stupid, moronic, lousy goddamn machine!"

He quivers as he yells. And he wonders, deep in the self-isolated recesses of his mind whether he is killing himself with anger, whether he is destroying his system with fury.

He turns and stalks away. He is too outraged to notice the cover of the machine slip down and hear the slight whirring of metal such as he might hear if the keys trembled in their slots.

❖

He is shaving. The razor will not cut. Or the razor is too sharp and cuts too much.

Both times a muffled curse billows through his lips. He hurls the razor on the floor and kicks it against the wall.

He is cleaning his teeth. He draws the fine silk floss between his teeth. It shreds off. A fuzzy bit remains in the gap. He tries to press another piece down to get that bit out. He cannot force the white thread down. It snaps in his fingers.

He screams. He screams at the man in the mirror and draws back his hand, throws the floss away violently. It hits the wall. It hangs there and waves in the rush of angry breeze from the man.

He has torn another piece of floss from the container. He is giving the dental floss another chance. He is holding back his fury. If the floss knows what is good for it, it will plunge down between the teeth and draw out the shredded bit immediately.

It does. The man is mollified. The systematic juices leave off bubbling, the fires sink, the coals are scattered.

But the anger is still there, apart. Energy is never lost; a primal law.

He is eating.

His wife places a steak before him. He picks up the knife and fork and slices. The meat is tough, the blade is dull.

A spot of red puffs up in the flesh of his cheeks. His eyes narrow. He draws the knife through the meat. The blade will not sever the browned flesh.

His eyes widen. Withheld tempest tightens and shakes him. He saws at the meat as though to give it one last opportunity to yield.

The meat will not yield.

He howls. *"God damn it!"* White teeth jam together. The knife is hurled across the room.

The woman appears, alarm etching transient scars on her forehead. Her husband is beyond himself. Her husband is shooting poison through his arteries. Her husband is releasing another cloud of animal temper. It is mist that clings. It hangs over the furniture, drips from the walls.

It is alive.

So through the days and nights. His anger falling like frenzied axe blows in his house, on everything he owns. Sprays of teeth-grinding hysteria clouding his windows and falling to his floors. Oceans of wild, uncontrolled hate flooding through every room of his house; filling each iota of space with a shifting, throbbing life.

He lay on his back and stared at the sun-mottled ceiling.

The last day, he told himself. The phrase had been creeping in and out of his brain since he'd awakened.

In the bathroom he could hear the water running. He could hear the medicine cabinet being opened and then closed again. He could hear the sound of her slippers shuffling on the tile floor.

Sally, he thought, don't leave me.

"I'll take it easy if you stay," he promised the air in a whisper.

But he knew he couldn't take it easy. That was too hard. It was easier to fly off the handle, easier to scream and rant and attack.

He turned on his side and stared out into the hall at the bathroom door. He could see the line of light under the door. Sally is in there, he thought. Sally, my wife, whom I married many years ago when I was young and full of hope.

He closed his eyes suddenly and clenched his fists. It came on him again. The sickness that prevailed with more violence every time he contracted it. The sickness of despair, of lost ambition. It ruined everything. It cast a vapor of bitterness over all his comings and goings. It jaded appetite, ruined sleep, destroyed affection.

"Perhaps if we'd had children," he muttered and knew before he said it that it wasn't the answer.

Children. How happy they would be watching their wretched father sinking deeper into his pit of introspective fever each day.

All right, tortured his mind, let's have the facts. He gritted his teeth and tried to make his mind a blank. But, like a dull-eyed idiot, his mind repeated the words that he muttered often in his sleep through restless, tossing nights.

I'm forty years old. I teach English at Fort College. Once I had hoped to be a writer. I thought this would be a fine place to write. I would teach class part of the day and write with the rest of my time. I met Sally at school and married her. I thought everything would be just fine. I thought success was inevitable. Eighteen years ago.

Eighteen years.

How, he thought, did you mark the passing of almost two decades? The time seemed a shapeless lump of failing efforts, of nights spent in anguish; of the secret, the answer, the revelation always being withheld from him. Dangled overhead like cheese swinging in a maddening arc over the head of a berserk rat.

And resentment creeping. Days spent watching Sally buy food and clothing and pay rent with his meager salary. Watching her buy new curtains or new chair covers and feeling a stab of pain every time because he was that much farther removed from the point where he could devote his time to writing. Every penny she spent he felt like a blow at his aspirations.

He forced himself to think that way. He forced himself to believe that it was only the time he needed to do good writing.

But once a furious student had yelled at him, "You're just a third-rate talent hiding behind a desk!"

He remembered that. Oh, God, how he remembered that moment. Remembered the cold sickness that had convulsed him when those words hit his brain. Recalled the trembling and the shaky unreason of his voice.

He had failed the student for the semester despite good marks. There had been a great to-do about it. The student's father had come to the school. They had all gone before Dr. Ramsay, the head of the English Department.

He remembered that too; the scene could crowd out all other memories. Him, sitting on one side of the conference table, facing the irate father and son. Dr. Ramsay stroking his beard until he thought he'd hurl something at him. Dr. Ramsay had said—well let's see if we can't straighten out this matter.

They had consulted the record book and found the student was right. Dr. Ramsay had looked up at him in great surprise. Well, I can't see what . . . he had said and let his syrupy voice break off and looked probingly at him, waiting for an explanation.

And the explanation had been hopeless, a jumbled and pointless affair. Irresponsible attitude, he had said, flaunting of unpardonable behavior; morally a failure. And Dr. Ramsay, his thick neck getting red, telling him in no uncertain terms that morals were not subject to the grading system at Fort College.

There was more but he'd forgotten it. He'd made an effort to forget it. But he couldn't forget that it would be years before he made a professorship. Ramsay would hold it back. And his salary would go on being insufficient and bills would mount and he would never get his writing done.

He regained the present to find himself clutching the sheets with taut fingers. He found himself glaring in hate at the bathroom door. Go on!—his mind snapped vindictively—Go home to your precious mother. See if I care. Why just a trial separation? Make it permanent. Give me some peace. Maybe I can do some writing then.

Maybe I can do some writing then.

The phrase made him sick. It had no meaning anymore. Like a word that is repeated until it becomes gibberish that sentence, for him, had been used to extinction. It sounded silly; like some bit of cliché from a soap opera. Hero saying in dramatic tones—Now, by God, maybe I can do some writing. Senseless.

For a moment, though, he wondered if it was true. Now that she was leaving could he forget about her and really get some work done? Quit his job? Go somewhere and hole up in a cheap furnished room and write?

You have $123.89 in the bank, his mind informed him. He pretended it was the only thing that kept him from it. But, far back in his mind, he wondered if he could write anywhere. Often the question threw itself at him when he was least expecting it. You have four hours every morning, the statement would rise like a menacing wraith. You have time to write many thousands of words. Why don't you?

And the answer was always lost in a tangle of becauses and wells and endless reasons that he clung to like a drowning man at straws.

The bathroom door opened and she came out, dressed in her good red suit.

For no reason at all, it seemed, he suddenly realized that she'd been wearing that same outfit for more than three years and never a new one. The realization angered him even more. He closed his eyes and hoped she wasn't looking at him. I hate her, he thought. I hate her because she has destroyed my life.

He heard the rustle of her skirt as she sat at the dressing table and pulled out a drawer. He kept his eyes shut and listened to the venetian blinds tap lightly against the window frame as morning breeze touched them. He could smell her perfume floating lightly on the air.

And he tried to think of the house empty all the time. He tried to think of coming home from class and not finding Sally there waiting for him. The idea seemed, somehow, impossible. And that angered him. Yes, he thought, she's gotten to me. She's worked on me until I am so dependent of her for really unessential things that I suffer under the delusion that I cannot do without her.

He turned suddenly on the mattress and looked at her.

"So, you're really going," he said in a cold voice.

She turned briefly and looked at him. There was no anger on her face. She looked tired.

"Yes," she said. "I'm going."

Good riddance. The words tried to pass his lips. He cut them off.

"I suppose you have your reasons," he said.

Her shoulders twitched a moment in what he took for a shrug of weary amusement.

"I have no intention of arguing with you," he said. "Your life is your own."

"Thank you," she murmured.

She's waiting for apologies, he thought. Waiting to be told that he didn't hate her as he'd said. That he hadn't struck *her* but all his twisted and shattered hopes; the mocking spectacle of his own lost faith.

"And just how long is this *trial* separation going to last?" he said, his voice acidulous.

She shook her head.

"I don't know, Chris," she said quietly. "It's up to you."

"Up to me," he said. "It's always up to me, isn't it?"

"Oh, please darl—Chris. I don't want to argue anymore. I'm too tired to argue."

"It's easier to just pack and run away."

She turned and looked at him. Her eyes were very dark and unhappy.

"Run away?" she said. "After eighteen years you accuse me of that? Eighteen years of watching you destroy yourself. And me along with you. Oh, don't look surprised. I'm sure you know you've driven me half insane too."

She turned away and he saw her shoulders twitch. She brushed some tears from her eyes.

"It's n-not just because you hit me," she said. "You kept saying that last night when I said I was leaving. Do you think it would matter if . . ." She took a deep breath. "If it meant you were angry with *me*? If it was that I could be hit every day. But you didn't hit me. I'm nothing to you. I'm not wanted."

"Oh, stop being so . . ."

"No," she broke in. "That's why I'm going. Because I can't bear to watch you hate me more every day for something that . . . that isn't my fault."

"I suppose you . . ."

"Oh, don't say anymore," she said, getting up. She hurried out of the room and he heard her walk into the living room. He stared at the dressing table.

Don't say anymore?—his mind asked as though she were still there. Well, there's more to say; lots more. You don't seem to realize what I've lost. You don't seem to understand. I had hopes, oh God, what hopes I had. I was going to write prose to make the people sit up and gasp. I was going to tell them things they needed badly to know. I was going to tell them in so entertaining a way that they would never realize that the truth was getting to them. I was going to create immortal works.

Now when I die, I shall only be dead. I am trapped in this depressing village, entombed in a college of science where men gape at dust and do not even know that there are stars above their heads. And what can I do, what can . . . ?

The thoughts broke off. He looked miserably at her perfume bottles, at the powder box that tinkled "Always" when the cover was lifted off.

I'll remember you. Always.

With a heart that's true. Always.

The words are childish and comical, he thought. But his throat contracted and he felt himself shudder.

"Sally," he said. So quietly that he could hardly hear it himself.

After a while he got up and dressed.

While he was putting on his trousers a rug slid from under him and he had to grab the dresser for support. He glared down, heart pounding in the total fury he had learned to summon in the space of seconds.

"Damn you," he muttered.

He forgot Sally. He forgot everything. He just wanted to get even with the rug. He kicked it violently under the bed. The anger plunged down and disappeared. He shook his head. I'm sick, he thought. He thought of going in to her and telling her he was sick.

His mouth tightened as he went into the bathroom. I'm not sick, he thought. Not in body anyway. It's my mind that's ill and she only makes it worse.

The bathroom was still damply warm from her use of it. He opened the window a trifle and got a splinter in his finger. He cursed the window in a muffled voice. He looked up. Why so quiet? he asked. So *she* won't hear me?

"Damn you!" he snarled loudly at the window. And he picked at his finger until he had pulled out the sliver of wood.

He jerked at the cabinet door. It stuck. His face reddened. He pulled harder and the door flew open and cracked him on the wrist. He spun about and grabbed his wrist, threw back his head with a whining gasp.

He stood there, eyes clouded with pain, staring at the ceiling. He looked at the crack that ran in a crazy meandering line across the ceiling. Then he closed his eyes.

And began to sense something. Intangible. A sense of menace. He wondered about it. Why it's myself, of course, he answered then. It is the moral decrepitude of my own subconscious. It is bawling out to me, saying: You are to be punished for driving your poor wife away to her mother's arms. You are not a man. You are a—

"Oh, shut up," he said.

He washed his hands and face. He ran an inspecting finger over his chin. He needed a shave. He opened the cabinet door gingerly and took out his straight razor. He held it up and looked at it.

The handle has expanded. He told himself that quickly as the blade appeared to fall out of the handle willfully. It made him shiver to see it flop out like that and glitter in the light from the cabinet light fixture.

He stared in repelled fascination at the bright steel. He touched the blade edge. So sharp, he thought. The slightest touch would sever flesh. What a hideous thing it was.

"It's my hand."

He said it involuntarily and shut the razor suddenly. It *was* his hand, it had to be. It couldn't have been the razor moving by itself. That was sick imagination.

But he didn't shave. He put the razor back in the cabinet with a vague sense of forestalling doom.

Don't care if we *are* expected to shave every day, he muttered. I'm not taking a chance on my hand slipping. I'd better get a safety razor anyway. This kind isn't for me, I'm too nervous.

Suddenly, impelled by those words, the picture of him eighteen years before flew into his brain.

He remembered a date he'd had with Sally. He remembered telling her he was so calm it was akin to being dead. Nothing bothers me, he'd said. And it was true, at the time. He remembered too telling her he didn't like coffee, that one cup kept him awake at night. That he didn't smoke, didn't like the taste or smell. I like to stay healthy, he'd said. He remembered the exact words.

"And now," he muttered at his lean and worn reflection.

Now he drank gallons of coffee a day. Until it sloshed like a black pool in his stomach and he couldn't sleep any more than he could fly. Now he smoked endless strings of finger-yellowing cigarettes until his throat felt raw and clogged, until he couldn't write in pencil because his hand shook so much.

But all that stimulation didn't help his writing any. Paper still remained blank in the typewriter. Words never came, plots died on him. Characters eluded him, mocking him with laughter from behind the veil of their non-creation.

And time passed. It flew by faster and faster, seeming to single him out for highest punishment. He—a man who had begun to value time so neurotically that it overbalanced his life and made him sick to think of its passing.

As he brushed his teeth he tried to recall when this irrational temper had first begun to control him. But there was no way of tracing its course. Somewhere in mists that could not be pierced, it had started. With a word of petulance, an angry contraction of muscles. With a glare of unrecallable animosity.

And from there, like a swelling amoeba, it had gone its own perverted and downward course of evolution, reaching its present nadir in him; a taut embittered man who found his only solace in hating.

He spit out white froth and rinsed his mouth. As he put down the glass, it cracked and a barb of glass drove into his hand.

"Damn!" he yelled.

He spun on his heel and clenched his fist. It sprang open instantly as the sliver sank into his palm. He stood with tears on his cheeks, breathing heavily. He thought of Sally listening to him, hearing once more the audible evidence of his snapping nerves.

Stop it!—he ordered himself. You can never do anything until you rid yourself of this enervating temper.

He closed his eyes. For a moment he wondered why it seemed that everything was happening to him lately. As if some revenging power had taken roost in the house, pouring a savage life into inanimate things. Threatening him. But the thought was just a faceless, passing figure in the crushing horde of thoughts that mobbed past his mind's eye; seen but not appreciated.

He drew the glass sliver from his palm. He put on his dark tie.

Then he went into the dining room, consulting his watch. It was ten thirty already. More than half the morning was gone. More than half the time for sitting and trying to write the prose that would make people sit up and gasp.

It happened that way more often now than he would even admit to himself. Sleeping late, making up errands, doing anything to forestall the terrible moment when he must sit down before his typewriter and try to wrench some harvest from the growing desert of his mind.

It was harder every time. And he grew more angry every time; and hated more. And never noticed until now, when it was too late, that Sally had grown desperate and could no longer stand his temper or his hate.

She was sitting at the kitchen table drinking dark coffee. She too drank more than she once had. Like him, she drank it black, without sugar. It jangled her nerves too. And she smoked now although she'd never smoked until a year before. She got no pleasure from it.

She drew the fumes deep down into her lungs and then blew them out quickly. And her hands shook almost as badly as his did.

He poured himself a cup of coffee and sat down across from her. She started to get up.

"What's the matter? Can't you stand the sight of me?"

She sat back and took a deep pull on the cigarette in her hand. Then she stamped it out on the saucer.

He felt sick. He wanted to get out of the house suddenly. It felt alien and strange to him. He had the feeling that she had renounced all claim to it, that she had retreated from it. The touch of her fingers and the loving indulgences she had bestowed on every room; all these things were taken back. They had lost tangibility because she was leaving. She was deserting it and it was not their home anymore. He felt it strongly.

Sinking back against the chair he pushed away his cup and stared at the yellow oilcloth on the table. He felt as if he and Sally were frozen in time; that seconds were drawn out like some fantastic taffy until each one seemed an eternity. The clock ticked slower. And the house was a different house.

"What train are you getting?" he asked, knowing before he spoke that there was only one morning train.

"Eleven forty-seven," she said.

When she said it, he felt as if his stomach were pulled back hard against his backbone. He gasped, so actual was the physical pain. She glanced up at him.

"Burned myself," he said hastily, and she got up and put her cup and saucer in the sink.

Why did I say that?—he thought. Why couldn't I say that I gasped because I was filled with terror at the thought of her leaving me? Why do I always say the things I don't mean to say? I'm not bad. But every time I speak I build higher the walls of hatred and bitterness around me until I cannot escape from them.

With words I have knit my shroud and will bury myself therein.

He looked at her back and a sad smile raised his lips. I can think of words when my wife is leaving me. It is very sad.

Sally had walked out of the kitchen. His mind reverted to its sullen attitude. This is a game we're playing. Follow the leader. You walk in one room, head high, the justified spouse, the injured party. I am supposed to follow, slope shouldered and contrite, pouring out apologetic hecatombs.

Once more conscious of himself, he sat tensely at the table, rage making his body tremble. Consciously he relaxed and pressed his left hand over his eyes. He sat there trying to lose his misery in silence and blackness.

It wouldn't work.

And then his cigarette really burned him and he sat erect. The cigarette hit the floor scattering ashes. He bent over and picked it up. He threw it at the wastecan and missed. To hell with it, he thought. He got up and dumped his cup and saucer in the sink. The saucer broke in half and nicked his right thumb. He let it bleed. He didn't care.

She was in the extra room finishing her packing.

The extra room. The words tortured him now. When had they stopped calling it "the nursery"? When had it begun to eat her insides out because she was so full of love and wanted children badly? When had he begun to replace this loss with nothing better than volcanic temper and days and nights of sheath-scraped nerves?

He stood in the doorway and watched her. He wanted to get out the typewriter and sit down and write reams of words. He wanted to glory in his coming freedom. Think of all the money he could save. Think of how soon he could go away and write all the things he'd always meant to write.

He stood in the doorway, sick.

Is all this possible?—his mind asked, incredulous. Possible that she was leaving? But she and he were man and wife. They had lived and loved in this house for more than eighteen years. Now she was leaving. Putting articles of clothing in her old black suitcase and leaving. He couldn't reconcile himself to that. He couldn't understand it or ally it with the functions of the day. Where did it fit into the pattern?—the pattern that was Sally right there cleaning and cooking and trying to make their home happy and warm.

He shivered and, turning abruptly, went back into the bedroom.

He slumped on the bed and stared at the delicately whirring electric clock on their bedside table.

Past eleven, he saw. In less than an hour I have to hold class for a group of idiot freshmen. And, on the desk in the living room, is a mountain of mid-term examinations with essays that I must suffer through, feeling my stomach turn at their paucity of intelligence, their adolescent phraseology.

And all that tripe, all those miles of hideous prose, had been wound into an eternal skein in his head. And there it sat unraveling into his own writing until he wondered if he could stand the thought of living anymore. I have digested the worst, he thought. Is it any wonder that I exude it piecemeal?

Temper began again, a low banking fire in him, gradually fanned by further thinking. I've done no writing this morning. Like every morning after every other morning as time passes. I do less and less. I write nothing. Or I write worthless material. I could write better when I was twenty than I can now.

I'll *never* write anything good!

He jolted to his feet and his head snapped around as he looked for something to strike at, something to break, something to hate with such hate that it would wither in the blast.

It seemed as though the room clouded. He felt a throbbing. His left leg banged against a corner of the bed.

He gasped in fury. He wept. Tears of hate and repentance and self commiseration. I'm lost, he thought. Lost. There is nothing.

He became very calm, icy calm. Drained of pity, of emotion. He put on his suit coat. He put on his hat and got his briefcase off the dresser.

He stopped before the door to the room where she still fussed with her bag. So she will have something to occupy herself with now, he thought, so she won't have to look at me. He felt his heart thudding like a heavy drum beat.

"Have a nice time at your mother's," he said dispassionately.

She looked up and saw the expression on his face. She turned away and put a hand to her eyes. He felt a sudden need to run to her and beg her forgiveness. Make everything right again.

Then he thought again of papers and years of writing undone. He turned away and walked across the living room. The small rug slipped a little and it helped to focus the strength of anger he needed. He kicked it aside and it fluttered against the wall in a rumpled heap.

He slammed the door behind him.

His mind gibbered. Now, soap opera like, she has thrown herself on the coverlet and is weeping tears of martyr-tinged sorrow. Now she is digging nails into the pillow and moaning my name and wishing she were dead.

His shoes clicked rapidly on the sidewalk. God help me, he thought. God help all us poor wretches who would create and find that we must lose our hearts for it because we cannot afford to spend our time at it.

It was a beautiful day. His eyes saw that but his mind would not attest to it. The trees were thick with green and the air warm and fresh. Spring breezes flooded down the streets. He felt them brush over him as he walked down the block, crossed Main Street to the bus stop.

He stood there on the corner looking back at the house.

She is in there, his mind persisted in analysis. In there, the house in which we've lived for more than eight years. She is packing or crying or doing something. And soon she will call the Campus Cab Company. A cab will come driving out. The driver will honk the horn, Sally will put on her light spring coat and take her suitcase out on the porch. She will lock the door behind her for the last time.

"No—"

He couldn't keep the word from strangling in his throat. He kept staring at the house. His head ached. He saw everything weaving. I'm sick, he thought.

"I'm *sick!*"

He shouted it. There was no one around to hear. He stood gazing at the house. She is going away forever, said his mind.

Very well then! I'll write, write, write. He let the words soak into his mind and displace all else.

A man had a choice, after all. He devoted his life to his work or to his wife and children and home. It could not be combined; not in this day and age. In this insane world where God was second to income and goodness to wealth.

He glanced aside as the green-striped bus topped the distant hill and approached. He put the briefcase under his arm and reached into his coat pocket for a token. There was a hole in the pocket. Sally had been meaning to sew it. Well, she would never sew it now. What did it matter anyway?

I would rather have my soul intact than the suit of clothes I wear.

Words, words, he thought, as the bus stopped before him. They flood through me now that she is leaving. Is that evidence that it is her presence that clogs the channels of thought?

He dropped the token in the coin box and weaved down the length of the bus. He passed a professor he knew and nodded to him distractedly. He slumped down on the back seat and stared at the grimy, rubberized floor boards.

This is a great life, his mind ranted. I am so pleased with this, my life and these, my great and noble accomplishments.

He opened the briefcase a moment and looked in at the thick prospectus he had outlined with the aid of Dr. Ramsay.

First week—1. *Everyman*. Discussion of. Reading of selections from *Classic Readings For College Freshmen*. *2. Beowulf*. Reading of. Class discussion. Twenty minute quotation quiz.

He shoved the sheaf of papers back into the briefcase. It sickens me, he thought. I hate these things. The classics have become anathema to me. I begin to loathe the very mention of them. Chaucer, the Elizabethan poets, Dryden, Pope, Shakespeare. What higher insult to a man than to grow to hate these names because he must share them by part with unappreciative clods? Because he must strain them thin and make them palatable for the dullards who should better be digging ditches.

He got off the bus downtown and started down the long slope of Ninth Street.

Walking, he felt as though he were a ship with its hawser cut, prey to a twisted network of currents. He felt apart from the city, the country, the world. If someone told me I were a ghost, he thought, I would be inclined to believe.

What is she doing now?

He wondered about it as the buildings floated past him. What is she thinking as I stand here and the town of Fort drifts by me like vaporous stage flats? What are her hands holding? What expression has she on her lovely face?

She is alone in the house, our house. What might have been our *home*. Now it is only a shell, a hollow box with sticks of wood and metal for furnishings. Nothing but inanimate dead matter.

No matter what John Morton said.

Him with his gold leaves parting and his test tubes and his God of the microscope. For all his erudite talk and his papers of slide-ruled figures; despite all that—it was simple witchcraft he professed. It was idiocy. The idiocy that prompted that ass Charles Fort to burden the world with his nebulous fancies. The idiocy that made that fool of a millionaire endow this place and from the arid soil erect these huge stone structures and house within a zoo of wild-eyed scientists always searching for some fashion of elixir while the rest of the clowns blew the world out from under them.

No, there is nothing right with the world, he thought as he plodded under the arch and onto the wide, green campus.

He looked across at the huge Physical Sciences Center, its granite face beaming in the late morning sun.

Now she is calling the cab. He consulted his watch. No. She is in the cab already. Riding through the silent streets. Past the houses and down into the shopping district. Past the red brick buildings spewing out yokels and students. Through the town that was a potpourri of the sophisticated and the rustic.

Now the cab was turning left on Tenth Street. Now it was pulling up the hill, topping it. Gliding down toward the railroad station. Now . . .

"Chris!"

His head snapped around and his body twitched in surprise. He looked toward the wide-doored entrance to the Mental Sciences Building. Dr. Morton was coming out.

We attended school together eighteen years ago, he thought. But I took only a small interest in science. I preferred wasting my time on the culture of the centuries. That's why I'm an associate and he's a doctor and the head of his department.

All this fled like racing winds through his mind as Dr. Morton approached, smiling. He clapped Chris on the shoulder.

"Hello there," he said. "How are things?"

"How are they ever?"

Dr. Morton's smile faded.

"What is it, Chris?" he asked.

I won't tell you about Sally, Chris thought. Not if I die first. You'll never know it from me.

"The usual," he said.

"Still on the outs with Ramsay?"

Chris shrugged. Morton looked over at the large clock on the face of the Mental Sciences Building.

"Say, look," he said. "Why are we standing here? Your class isn't for a half hour yet, is it?"

Chris didn't answer. He's going to invite me for coffee, he thought. He's going to regale me with more of his inane theories. He's going to use me as whipping boy for his mental merry-go-round.

"Let's get some coffee," Morton said, taking Chris's arm. They walked along in silence for a few steps.

"How's Sally?" Morton asked then.

"She's fine," he answered in an even voice.

"Good. Oh, incidentally. I'll probably drop by tomorrow or the next day for that book I left there last Thursday night."

"All right."

"What were you saying about Ramsay now?"

"I wasn't."

Morton skipped that. "Been thinking anymore about what I told you?" he asked.

"If you're referring to your fairy tale about my house—no. I haven't been giving it any more thought than it deserves—which is none."

They turned the corner of the building and walked toward Ninth Street.

"Chris, that's an indefensible attitude," Morton said. "You have no right to doubt when you don't know."

Chris felt like pulling his arm away, turning and leaving Morton standing there. He was sick of words and words and words. He wanted to be alone. He almost felt as if he could put a pistol to his head now, get it over with. Yes, I could—he thought. If someone handed it to me now it would be done in a moment.

They went up the stone steps to the sidewalk and crossed over to the Campus Cafe. Morton opened the door and ushered Chris in. Chris went in back and slid into a wooden booth.

Morton brought two coffees and sat across from him.

"Now listen," he said, stirring in sugar, "I'm your best friend. At least I regard myself as such. And I'm damned if I'll sit by like a mute and watch you kill yourself."

Chris felt his heart jump. He swallowed. He got rid of the thoughts as though they were visible to Morton.

"Forget it," he said. "I don't care what proofs you have. I don't believe any of it."

"What'll it take to convince you, damn it?" Morton said. "Do you have to lose your life first?"

"Look," Chris said pettishly. "I don't believe it. That's *it*. Forget it now, let it go."

"Listen, Chris, I can show you . . ."

"You can show me nothing!" Chris cut in.

Morton was patient. "It's a recognized phenomenon," he said.

Chris looked at him in disgust and shook his head.

"What dreams you white-frocked kiddies have in the sanctified cloister of your laboratories. You can make yourself believe anything after a while. As long as you can make up a measurement for it."

"Will you listen to me, Chris? How many times have you complained to me about splinters, about closet doors flying open, about rugs slipping? How many times?"

"Oh, for God's sake, don't start *that* again. I'll get up and walk out of here. I'm in no mood for your lectures. Save them for those poor idiots who pay tuition to hear them."

Morton looked at him with a shake of his head.

"I wish I could get to you," he said.

"Forget it."

"Forget it?" Morton squirmed. "Can't you see that you're in danger because of your temper?"

"I'm telling you, John . . ."

"Where do you think that temper of yours goes? Do you think it disappears? No. It doesn't. It goes into your rooms and into your furniture and into the air. It goes into Sally. It makes everything sick; including you. It crowds you out. It welds a link between animate and inanimate. *Psychobolie.* Oh, don't look so petulant; like a child who can't stand to hear the word *spinach.* Sit down, for God's sake. You're an adult; listen like one."

Chris lit a cigarette. He let Morton's voice drift into a non-intelligent hum. He glanced at the wall clock. Quarter to twelve. In two minutes, if the schedule was adhered to, she would be going. The train would move and the town of Fort would pass away from her.

"I've told you any number of times," Morton was saying. "No one knows what matter is made of. Atoms, electrons, pure energy—all words. Who knows where it will end? We guess, we theorize, we make up means of measurement. But we don't know.

"And that's for matter. Think of the human brain and its still unknown capacities. It's an uncharted continent, Chris. It may stay that way for a long time. And all that time the suspected powers will still be affecting us and, maybe, affecting matter; even if we *can't* measure it on a gauge.

"And I say you're poisoning your house. I say your temper has become ingrained in the structure, in every article you touch. All of them influenced by you and your ungovernable rages. And I think too that if it weren't for Sally's presence acting as an abortive factor, well . . . you might actually be attacked by . . ."

Chris heard the last few sentences.

"Oh, stop this gibberish!" he snapped angrily. "You're talking like a juvenile after his first Tom Swift novel."

Morton sighed. He ran his fingers over the cup edge and shook his head sadly.

"Well," he said, "all I can do is hope that nothing breaks down. It's obvious to me that you're not going to listen."

"Congratulations on one statement I can agree with," said Chris. He looked at his watch. "And now if you'll excuse me I'll go and listen to saddle-shoed cretins stumble over passages they haven't the slightest ability to assimilate."

They got up.

"I'll take it," said Morton but Chris slapped a coin on the counter and walked out. Morton followed, putting his change into his pocket slowly.

In the street he patted Chris on the shoulder.

"Try to take it easy," he said. "Look, why don't you and Sally come out to the house tonight? We could have a few rounds of bridge."

"That's impossible," Chris said.

The students were reading a selection from *King Lear*. Their heads were bent over the books. He stared at them without seeing them.

I've got to resign myself to it, he told himself. I've got to forget her, that's all. She's gone. I'm not going to bewail the fact. I'm not going to hope against hope that she'll return. I don't *want* her back. I'm better off without her. Free and unfettered now.

His thoughts drained off. He felt empty and helpless. He felt as though he could never write another word for the rest of his life. Maybe, he thought, sullenly displeased with the idea, maybe it was only the upset of her leaving that enabled my brain to find words. For, after all, the words I thought of, the ideas that flourished, though briefly, were all to do with her—her going and my wretchedness because of it.

He caught himself short. No!—he cried in silent battle. I will not let it be that way. I'm strong. This feeling is only temporary, I'll very soon have learned to do without her. And then I'll do work. Such work as I have only dreamed of doing. After all, haven't I lived eighteen years more? Haven't those years filled me to overflowing with sights and sounds, ideals, impressions, interpretations?

He trembled with excitement.

Someone was waving a hand in his face. He focused his eyes and looked coldly at the girl.

"Well?" he said.

"Could you tell us when you're going to give back our mid-term papers, Professor Neal?" she asked.

He stared at her, his right cheek twitching. He felt about to hurl every invective at his command into her face. His fists closed.

"You'll get them back when they're marked," he said tensely.

"Yes, but . . ."

"You heard me," he said.

His voice rose at the end of the sentence. The girl sat down. As he lowered his head he noticed that she looked at the boy next to her and shrugged her shoulders, a look of disgust on her face.

"Miss . . ."

He fumbled with his record book and found her name.

"Miss Forbes!"

She looked up, her features drained of color, her red lips standing out sharply against her white skin. Painted alabaster idiot. The words clawed at him.

"You may get out of this room," he ordered sharply.

Confusion filled her face.

"Why?" she asked in a thin, plaintive voice.

"Perhaps you didn't hear me," he said, the fury rising. "I said get out of this room!"

"But . . ."

"Do you hear me!" he shouted.

Hurriedly she collected her books, her hands shaking, her face burning with embarrassment. She kept her eyes on the floor and her throat moved convulsively as she edged along the aisle and went out the doorway.

The door closed behind her. He sank back. He felt a terrible sickness in himself. Now, he thought, they will all turn against me in defense of an addle-witted little girl. Dr. Ramsay would have more fuel for his simple little fire.

And they were right.

He couldn't keep his mind from it. They *were* right. He knew it. In that far recess of mind which he could not cow with thoughtless passion, he knew he was a stupid fool. I have no right to teach others. I cannot even teach myself to be a human being. He wanted to cry out the words and weep confessions and throw himself from one of the open windows.

"The whispering will stop!" he demanded fiercely.

The room was quiet. He sat tensely, waiting for any signs of militance. I am your teacher, he told himself, I am to be obeyed, I am . . .

The concept died. He drifted away again. What were students or a girl asking about mid-term papers? What was anything?

He glanced at his watch. In a few minutes the train would pull into Centralia. She would change to the main line express to Indianapolis. Then up to Detroit and her mother. Gone.

Gone. He tried to visualize the word, put it into living terms. But the thought of the house without her was almost beyond his means. Because it wasn't the house without her; it was something else.

He began to think of what John had said.

Was it possible? He was in a mood to accept the incredible. It was incredible that she had left him. Why not extend the impossibilities that were happening to him?

All right then, he thought angrily. The house is alive. I've given it this life with deadly outpourings of wrath. I hope to God that when I get back there and enter the door, the roof collapses. I hope the walls buckle and I'm crushed to pulp by the crushing weight of plaster and wood and brick. That's what I want. Some agency to do away with me. I cannot drive myself to it. If only a gun would commit my suicide for me. Or gas blow its deadly fumes at me for the asking or a razor slice my flesh upon request.

The door opened. He glanced up. Dr. Ramsay stood there, face drawn into a mask of indignation. Behind him in the hall Chris could see the girl, her face streaked with tears.

"A moment, Neal," Ramsay said sharply and stepped back into the hall again.

Chris sat at the desk staring at the door. He felt suddenly very tired, exhausted. He felt as if getting up and moving into the hall was more than he could possibly manage. He glanced at the class. A few of them were trying to repress smiles.

"For tomorrow you will finish the reading of *King Lear*," he said. Some of them groaned.

Ramsay appeared in the doorway again, his cheeks pink.

"Are you coming, Neal?" he asked loudly.

Chris felt himself tighten with anger as he walked across the room and out into the hall. The girl lowered her eyes. She stood beside Dr. Ramsay's portly frame.

"What's this I hear, Neal?" Ramsay asked.

That's right, Chris thought. Don't ever call me professor. I'll never be one, will I? You'll see to that, you bastard.

"I don't understand," he said, as coolly as possible.

"Miss Forbes here claims you ejected her from class for no reason at all."

"Then Miss Forbes is lying quite stupidly," he said. Let me hold this anger, he thought. Don't let it flood loose. He shook with holding it back.

The girl gasped and took out her handkerchief again. Ramsay turned and patted her shoulder.

"Go in my office, child. Wait for me."

She turned away slowly. Politician!—cried Neal's mind. How easy it is for you to be popular with them. You don't have to deal with their bungling minds.

Miss Forbes turned the corner and Ramsay looked back.

"Your explanation had better be good," he said. "I'm getting a little weary, Neal, of your behavior."

Chris didn't speak. Why am I standing here?—he suddenly wondered. Why, in all the world, am I standing in this dimlit hall and, voluntarily, listening to this pompous boor berate me?

"I'm waiting, Neal."

Chris tightened. "I told you she was lying," he said quietly.

"I choose to believe otherwise," said Dr. Ramsay, his voice trembling.

A shudder ran through Chris. His head moved forward and he spoke slowly, teeth clenched.

"You can believe anything you damn well please."

Ramsay's mouth twitched.

"I think it's time you appeared before the board," he muttered.

"Fine!" said Chris loudly. Ramsay made a move to close the classroom door. Chris gave it a kick and it banged against the wall. A girl gasped.

"What's the matter?" Chris yelled. "Don't you want your students to hear me tell you off? Don't you even want them to suspect that you're a dolt, a windbag, an ass!"

Ramsay raised shaking fists before his chest. His lips trembled violently.

"This will do, Neal!" he cried.

Chris reached out and shoved the heavy man aside, snarling, "Oh, *get* out of my way!"

He started away. The hall fled past him. He heard the bell ring. It sounded as though it rang in another existence. The building throbbed with life; students poured from classrooms.

"Neal!" called Dr. Ramsay.

He kept walking. Oh, God, let me out of here, I'm suffocating, he thought. My hat, my briefcase. Leave them. Get out of here. Dizzily he descended the stairs surrounded by milling students. They swirled about him like an unidentifiable tide. His brain was far from them.

⟡

Staring ahead dully he walked along the first floor hall. He turned and went out the door and down the porch steps to the campus sidewalk. He paid no attention to the students who stared at his ruffled blond hair, his mussed clothes. He kept walking. I've done it, he thought belligerently. I've made the break. I'm *free*!

I'm sick.

All the way down to Main Street and out on the bus he kept renewing his stores of anger. He went over those few moments in the hallway again and again. He summoned up the vision of Ramsay's stolid face, repeated his words. He kept himself taut and furious. I'm glad, he told himself forcibly. Everything is solved. Sally has left me. Good. My job is done. Good. Now I'm free to do as I like. A strained and angry joy pounded through him. He felt alone, a stranger in the world and glad of it.

At his stop, he got off the bus and walked determinedly toward the house pretending to ignore the pain he felt at approaching it. It's just an empty house, he thought. Nothing more. Despite all puerile theories, it is nothing but a house.

Then, when he went in, he found her sitting on the couch.

He almost staggered as if someone had struck him. He stood dumbly, staring at her. She had her hands tightly clasped. She was looking at him.

He swallowed.

"Well," he managed to say.

"I . . ." Her throat contracted. "Well . . ."

"Well *what*!" he said quickly and loudly to hide the shaking in his voice.

She stood up. "Chris, please. Won't you . . . ask me to stay?" She looked at him like a little girl, pleading.

The look enraged him. All his day dreams shattered; he saw the growing thing of new ideas ground under foot.

"Ask you to stay!" he yelled at her. "By God, I'll ask you nothing!"

"Chris! Don't!"

She's buckling, cried his mind. She's cracking. Get her now. Get her out of here. Drive her from these walls!

"Chris," she sobbed, "be kind. Please be kind."

"Kind!"

He almost choked on the word. He felt a wild heat coursing his body.

"Have *you* been kind? Driving me crazy, into a pit of despair. I can't get out. Do you understand? Never. Never! Do you understand that! I'll never write. I *can't* write! You drained it out of me! You killed it! Understand *that*? *Killed* it!"

She backed away toward the dining room. He followed her, hands shaking at his sides, feeling that she had driven him to this confession and hating her the more for it.

"Chris," she murmured in fright.

It seemed as if his rage grew cell-like, swelling him with fury until he was nothing of bone and blood but a hating accusation made flesh.

"I don't want you!" he yelled. "You're right, I don't want you! Get out of here!"

Her eyes were wide, her mouth an open wound. Suddenly she ran past him, eyes glistening with tears. She fled through the front doorway.

He went to the window and watched her running down the block, her dark brown hair streaming behind her.

Dizzy suddenly, he sank down on the couch and closed his eyes. He dug his nails into his palms. Oh God, I *am* sick, his mind churned.

He twitched and looked around stupidly. What was it? This feeling that he was sinking into the couch, into the floorboards, dissolving in the air, joining the molecules of the house. He whimpered softly, looking around. His head ached; he pressed a palm against his forehead.

"What?" he muttered. "What?"

He stood up. As though there were fumes he tried to smell them. As though it were a sound he tried to hear it. He turned around to see it. As though there were something with depth and length and width; something menacing.

He wavered, fell back on the couch. He stared around. There was nothing; all intangible. It might only be in the mind. The furniture lay as it did before. The sunlight filtered through the windows, piercing the gauzelike curtains, making gold patterns on the inlaid wooden floor. The walls were still creamy, the ceiling was as it was before. Yet there was this darkening, darkening . . .

What?

He pushed up and walked dizzily around the room. He forgot about Sally. He was in the dining room. He touched the table, he stared at the dark oak. He went into the kitchen. He stood by the sink and looked out the window.

Far up the block, he saw her walking, stumbling. She must have been waiting for the bus. Now she couldn't wait any longer and she was walking away from the house, away from him.

"I'll go after her," he muttered.

No, he thought. No, I won't go after her like a . . .

He forgot like what. He stared down at the sink. He felt drunk. Everything was fuzzy on the edges.

She's washed the cups. The broken saucer was thrown away. He looked at the nick on his thumb. It was dried. He'd forgotten about it.

He looked around suddenly as if someone had sneaked behind him. He stared at the wall. Something was rising. He felt it. It's not me. But it had to be; it had to be imagination.

Imagination!

He slammed a fist on the sink. I'll write. Write, *write*. Sit down and drain it all away in words; this feeling of anguish and terror and loneliness. Write it out of my system.

He cried, "Yes!"

He ran from the kitchen. He refused to accept the instinctive fear in himself. He ignored the menace that seemed to thicken the very air.

A rug slipped. He kicked it aside. He sat down. The air hummed. He tore off the cover on the typewriter. He sat nervously, staring at the keyboard. The moment before attack. It was in the air. But it's *my* attack!—he thought triumphantly, my attack on stupidity and fear.

He rolled a sheet into the typewriter. He tried to collect his throbbing thoughts. Write, the word called in his mind. Write—*now*.

"Now!" he cried.

He felt the desk lurch against his shins.

The flaring pain knifed open his senses. He kicked the desk in automatic frenzy. More pain. He kicked again. The desk flung back at him. He screamed.

He'd seen it move.

⊏✪⊐

He tried to back off, the anger torn from him. The typewriter keys moved under his hands. His eyes swept down. He couldn't tell whether he was moving the keys or whether they moved by themselves. He pulled hysterically, trying to dislodge his fingers but he couldn't. The keys were moving faster than his eye could see. They were a blur of motion. He felt them shredding his skin, peeling his fingers. They were raw. Blood started to ooze out.

He cried out and pulled. He managed to jerk away his fingers and jump back in the chair.

His belt buckle caught, the desk drawer came flying out. It

slammed into his stomach. He yelled again. The pain was a black cloud pouring over his head.

He threw down a hand to shove in the drawer. He saw the yellow pencils lying there. They glared. His hand slipped, it banged into the drawer.

One of the pencils jabbed at him.

He always kept the points sharp. It was like the bite of a snake. He snapped back his hand with a gasp of pain. The point was jammed under a nail. It was imbedded in raw, tender flesh. He cried out in fury and pain. He pulled at the pencil with his other hand. The point flew out and jabbed into his palm. He couldn't get rid of the pencil, it kept dragging over his hand. He pulled at it and it made black, jagged lines on his skin. It tore the skin open.

He heaved the pencil across the room. It bounced on the wall. It seemed to jump as it fell on the eraser. It rolled over and was still.

He lost his balance. The chair fell back with a rush. His head banged sharply against the floorboards. His outclutched hand grabbed at the window sill. Tiny splinters flashed into his skin like invisible needles. He howled in deathly fear. He kicked his legs. The mid-term papers showered down over him like the beating wings of insane bird flocks.

The chair snapped up again on its springs. The heavy wheels rolled over his raw, bloody hands. He drew them back with a shriek. He reared a leg and kicked the chair over violently. It crashed on the side against the mantelpiece. The wheels spun and chattered like a swarm of furious insects.

He jumped up. He lost his balance and fell again, crashing against the window sill. The curtains fell on him like a python. The rods snapped. They flew down and struck him across the scalp. He felt warm blood trickle across his forehead. He thrashed about on the floor. The curtains seemed to writhe around him like serpents. He screamed again. He tore at them wildly. His eyes were terror-stricken.

He threw them off and lurched up suddenly, staggering around for balance. The pain in his hands assailed him. He looked at them. They were like raw butcher meat, skin hanging down in shreds. He had to bandage them. He turned toward the bathroom.

At his first step the rug slid from under him, the rug he had kicked aside. He felt himself rush through the air. He reached down his hands instinctively to block the fall.

The white pain made his body leap. One finger snapped. Splinters shot into his raw fingers, he felt a burning pain in one ankle.

He tried to scramble up but the floor was like ice under him. He was deadly silent. His heart thudded in his chest. He tried to rise again. He fell, hissing with pain.

The bookshelf loomed over him. He cried out and flung up an arm. The case came crashing down on him. The top shelf drove into his skull. Black waves dashed over him, a sharp blade of pain drove into his head. Books showered over him. He rolled on his side with a groan. He tried to crawl out from underneath. He shoved the books aside weakly and they fell open. He felt the page edges slicing into his fingers like razor blades.

The pain cleared his head. He sat up and hurled the books aside. He kicked the bookcase back against the wall. The back fell off it and it crashed down.

He rose up, the room spinning before his eyes. He staggered into the wall, tried to hold on. The wall shifted under his hands it seemed. He couldn't hold on. He slipped to his knees, pushed up again.

"Bandage myself," he muttered hoarsely.

The words filled his brain. He staggered up through the quivering dining room, into the bathroom.

He stopped. No! Get out of the house! He knew it was not his will that brought him in there.

He tried to turn but he slipped on the tiles and cracked his elbow against the edge of the bathtub. A shooting pain barbed into his upper arm. The arm went numb. He sprawled on the floor, writhing in pain. The walls clouded; they welled around him like a blank shroud.

He sat up, breath tearing at his throat. He pushed himself up with a gasp. His arm shot out, he pulled open the cabinet door. It flew open against his cheek, tearing a jagged rip in the soft flesh.

His head snapped back. The crack in the ceiling looked like a wide idiot smile on a blank, white face. He lowered his head, whimpering in fright. He tried to back away.

His hand reached out. For iodine, for gauze!—his mind cried.

His hand came out with the razor.

It flopped in his hand like a new caught fish. His other hand reached in. For iodine, for gauze!—shrieked his mind.

His hand came out with dental floss. It flooded out of the tube like an endless white worm. It coiled around his throat and shoulders. It choked him.

The long shiny blade slipped from its sheath.

He could not stop his hand. It drew the razor heavily across his chest. It slit open the shirt. It sliced a valley through his chest. Blood spurted out.

He tried to hurl away the razor. It stuck to his hand. It slashed at him, at his arms and hands and legs and body.

At his throat.

A scream of utter horror flooded from his lips. He ran from the bathroom, staggering wildly into the living room.

"Sally!" he screamed, "Sally, Sally, Sally . . ."

The razor touched his throat. The room went black. Pain. Life ebbing away into the night. Silence over all the world.

The next day Dr. Morton came. He called the police. And later the coroner wrote in his report:

Died of self-inflicted wounds.

THE FUNERAL

Morton Silkline was in his office musing over floral arrangements for the Fenton obsequies when the chiming strains of "I am Crossing o'er the Bar to Join the Choir Invisible" announced an entrant into Clooney's Cut-Rate Catafalque.

Blinking meditation from his liver-colored eyes, Silkline knit his fingers to a placid clasp, then settled back against the sable leather of his chair, a smile of funereal welcome on his lips. Out in the stillness of the hallway, footsteps sounded on the muffling carpet, moving with a leisured pace and, just before the tall man entered, the desk clock buzzed a curt acknowledgment to 7:30.

Rising as if caught in the midst of a *tête-à-tête* with death's bright angel, Morton Silkline circled the glossy desk on whispering feet and extended one flaccid-fingered hand.

"Ah, good evening, sir," he dulceted, his smile a precise compendium of sympathy and welcome, his voice a calculated drip of obeisance.

The man's handshake was cool and bone-cracking but Silkline managed to repress reaction to a momentary flicker of agony in his cinnamon eyes.

"Won't you be seated?" he murmured, fluttering his bruised hand toward The Grieved One's chair.

"Thank you," said the man, his voice a baritoned politeness as he seated himself, unbuttoning the front of his velvet-collared overcoat and placing his dark homburg on the glass top of the desk.

"My name is Morton Silkline," Silkline offered as he recircled to his chair, settling on the cushion like a diffident butterfly.

"Asper," said the man.

"May I say that I am proud to meet you, Mister Asper?" Silkline purred.

"Thank you," said the man.

"Well, now," Silkline said, getting down to the business of bereavement, "what can Clooney's do to ease your sorrow?"

The man crossed his dark-trousered legs. "I should like," he said, "to make arrangements for a funeral service."

Silkline nodded once with an I-am-here-to-succor smile.

"Of course," he said, "you've come to the right place, sir." His gaze elevated a few inches beyond the pale. *"When loved ones lie upon that lonely couch of everlasting sleep,"* he recited, *"let Clooney draw the coverlet."*

His gaze returned and he smiled with a modest subservience. "Mrs. Clooney," he said, "made that up. We like to pass it along to those who come to us for comfort."

"Very nice," the man said. "Extremely poetic. But to details: I'd like to engage your largest parlor."

"I see," Silkline answered, restraining himself, only with effort, from the rubbing together of hands. "That would be our Eternal Rest Room."

The man nodded affably. "Fine. And I would also like to buy your most expensive casket."

Silkline could barely restrain a boyish grin. His cardiac muscle flexing vigorously, he forced back folds of sorrowful solicitude across his face.

"I'm sure," he said, "that can be effected."

"With gold trimmings?" the man said.

"Why . . . yes," said Director Silkline, clicking audibly as he swallowed. "I'm certain that Clooney's can satisfy your every need in this time of grievous loss. Naturally—" His voice slipped a jot from the condoling to the fiduciary "—it will entail a bit more expenditure than might, otherwise, be—"

"The cost is of no importance," said the man, waving it away. "I want only the best of everything."

"It will be so, sir, it *will* be so," declared a fervent Morton Silkline.

"Capital," said the man.

"Now," Silkline went on, briskly, "will you be wishing our Mr. Mossmound to deliver his sermon *On Crossing The Great Divide* or have you a denominational ceremony in mind?"

"I think not," said the man, shaking his head, thoughtfully. "A friend of mine will speak at the services."

"Ah," said Silkline, nodding, "I see."

Reaching forward, he plucked the gold pen from its onyx holder, then with two fingers of his left hand, drew out an application form from the ivory box on his desk top. He looked up with the accredited expression for the Asking of Painful Questions.

"And," he said, "what is the name of the deceased, may I ask?"

"Asper," said the man.

Silkline glanced up, smiling politely. "A relative?" he inquired.

"Me," said the man.

Silkline's laugh was a faint coughing.

"I beg your pardon?" he said. "I thought you said—"

"*Me*," the man repeated.

"But, I don't—"

"You see," the man explained, "I never had a proper going off. It was catch-as-catch-can, you might say; all improvised. Nothing—how shall I put it?—*tasty*." The man shrugged his wide shoulders. "I always regretted that," he said. "I always intended to make up for it."

Morton Silkline had returned the pen to its holder with a decisive jabbing of the hand and was on his feet, pulsing with a harsh distemper.

"Indeed, sir," he commented. "In*deed*."

The man looked surprised at the vexation of Morton Silkline.

"I—" he began.

"I am as fully prepared as the next fellow for a trifling badinage," Silkline interrupted, "but *not* during work hours. I think you fail to realize, sir, just where you are. This is Clooney's, a much respected ossuary; not a place for trivial joking or—"

He shrank back and stared, open-mouthed, at the black-garbed man who was suddenly on his feet, eyes glittering with a light most unseemly.

"This," the man said, balefully, "is not a joke."

"Is not—" Silkline could manage no more.

"I came here," said the man, "with a most serious purpose in mind." His eyes glowed now like cherry-bright coals. "And I expect this purpose to be gratified," he said. "Do you understand?"

"I—"

"On Tuesday next," the man continued, "at 8:30 p.m., my friends and I will arrive here for the service. You will have everything prepared by then. Full payments will be made directly following the exequies. Are there any questions?"

"I—"

"I need hardly remind you," said the man, picking up his homburg, "that this affair is of the utmost importance to me." He paused potently before allowing his voice to sink to a forbidding basso profundo. "I expect all to go well."

Bowing a modicum from the waist, the man turned and moved in two regal strides across the office, pausing a moment at the door.

"Uh . . . one additional item," he said. "That mirror in the foyer . . . *remove it*. And, I might add, any others that my friends and I might chance upon during our stay in your parlors."

The man raised one gray-gloved hand. "And now good night."

When Morton Silkline reached the hall, his customer was just flapping out a small window. Quite suddenly, Morton Silkline found the floor.

━◇━

They arrived at 8:30, conversing as they entered the foyer of Clooney's to be met by a tremble-legged Morton Silkline about whose eyes hung the raccoon circles of sleepless nights.

"Good evening," greeted the tall man, noting, with a pleased nod, the absence of the wall mirror.

"Good—" was the total of Silkline's wordage.

His vocal cords went slack and his eyes, embossed with daze, moved from figure to figure in the tall man's coterie—the gnarl-faced hunchback whom Silkline heard addressed as Ygor; the peak-hatted crone upon whose ceremented shoulder a black cat crouched; the hulking hairy-handed man who clicked yellow teeth together and regarded Silkline with markedly more than casual eyes; the waxen-featured little man who licked his lips and smiled at Silkline as though he possessed some inner satisfaction; the half-dozen men and women in evening dress, all cherry-eyed and -lipped and—Silkline cringed—superbly toothed.

Silkline hung against the wall, mouth a circular entrance way, hands twitching feebly at his sides as the chatting assemblage passed him by, headed for the Eternal Rest Room.

"Join us," the tall man said.

Silkline stirred fitfully from the wall and stumble-wove an erratic path down the hallway, eyes still saucer-round with stupor.

"I trust," the man said pleasantly, "everything is well prepared."

"Oh," Silkline squeaked. "Oh—oh, yes."

"Sterling," said the man.

When the two of them entered the room, the others were grouped in an admiring semicircle about the casket.

"Is good," the hunchback was muttering to himself. "Is good box."

"Aye, be that a casket or be that a casket, Delphinia?" cackled the ancient crone and Delphinia replied, "Mrrrrow."

While the others nodded, smiling felicitous smiles and murmuring, "Ah. Ah."

Then one of the evening-dressed women said, "Let Ludwig see," and the semicircle split open so the tall man could pass.

He ran his long fingers over the gold work on the sides and top of the casket, nodding appreciatively. "Splendid," he murmured, voice husky with emotion. "Quite splendid. Just what I always wanted."

"You picked a beauty, lad," said a tall white-haired gentleman.

"Well, try it on fer size!" the chuckling crone declared.

Smiling boyishly, Ludwig climbed into the casket and wriggled into place. "A perfect fit," he said, contentedly.

"Master look good," mumbled Ygor, nodding crookedly. "Look good in box."

Then the hairy-handed man demanded they begin because he had an appointment at 9:15, and everyone hurried to their chairs.

"Come, duck," said the crone, waving a scrawny hand at the ossified Silkline. "Sit by my side. I likes the pretty boys, I do, eh, Delphinia?" Delphinia said, "Mrrrrow."

"Please, Jenny," Ludwig Asper asked her, opening his eyes a moment. "I'm serious. You know what this means to me."

The crone shrugged. "Aye. Aye," she muttered, then pulled off her peaky hat and fluffed at dank curls as the zombie-stiff Silkline quivered into place beside her, aided by the guiding hand of the little waxen-faced man.

"Hello, pretty boy," the crone whispered, leaning over and jabbing a spear-point elbow into Silkline's ribs.

Then the tall white-haired gentleman from the Carpathian zone rose and the service began.

"Good friends," said the gentleman, "we have gathered ourselves within these bud-wreathed walls to pay homage to our comrade, Ludwig Asper, whom the pious and unyielding fates have chosen to pluck from existence and place within that bleak sarcophagus of all eternity."

"*Ci–git*," someone murmured; "*Chant du cygne*," another. Ygor wept and the waxen-featured little man, sitting on the other side of Morton Silkline, leaned over to murmur, "*Tasty*," but Silkline wasn't sure it was in reference to the funeral address.

"And thus," the gentleman from Carpathia went on, "we collect our bitter selves about this, our comrade's bier; about this litter of sorrow, this cairn, this cromlech, this unhappy tumulus—"

"*Clearer, clearer*," demanded Jenny, stamping one pointy-toed and petulant shoe. "Mrrrro*w*," said Delphinia and the crone winked one blood-laced eye at Silkline who shrank away only to brush against the little man who gazed at him with berry eyes and murmured once again, "*Tasty*."

The white-haired gentleman paused long enough to gaze down his royal nose at the crone. Then he continued, "—this mastaba, this sorrowing tope, this ghat, this dread dokhma—"

"What did he say?" asked Ygor, pausing in mid-sob. "What, what?"

"This ain't no declamation tourney, lad," the crone declared. "Keep it crisp, I say."

Ludwig raised his head again, a look of pained embarrassment on his face. "Jenny," he said. "*Please*."

"Aaaah . . . *toad's teeth*!" snapped the crone jadedly, and Delphinia moaned.

"*Requiescas in pace*, dear brother," the Count went on, testily. "The memory of you shall not perish with your untimely sepulture. You are, dear friend, not so much out of the game as playing on another field."

At which the hairy-handed man rose and hulked from the room with the guttural announcement, "*Go*," and Silkline felt himself rendered an icicle as he heard a sudden padding of clawed feet on the hallway rug and a baying which echoed back along the walls.

"Ullgate says he has a dinner appointment," the little man asided with a bright-eyed smile. Silkline's chair creaked with shuddering.

The white-haired gentleman stood tall and silent, his red eyes shut, his mouth tight-lipped with aristocratic pique.

"Count," pleaded Ludwig. "Please."

"Am I to endure these vulgar calumnies?" asked the Count. "These—"

"Well, *la-de-da*," crooned Jenny to her cat.

"Silence, woman!" roared the Count, his head disappearing momentarily in a white, trailing vapor, then reappearing as he gained control.

Ludwig sat up, face a twist of aggravation. "Jenny," he declared, "I think you'd better leave."

"You think to throw old Jenny of Boston out?" the crone challenged. "Well, you got a think that's coming then!"

And, as a shriveling Silkline watched, the crone slapped on her pointed hat and sprouted minor lightning at the fingertips. A snail-backed Delphinia bristled ebony hairs as the Count stepped forward, hand outstretched, to clamp onto the crone's shoulder, then stiffened in mid-stride as sizzling fire ringed him.

"Haa!" crowed Jenny while a horror-stricken Silkline gagged, "My *rug!*"

"Jen-*ny!*" Ludwig cried, clambering out. The crone gestured and all the flowers in the room began exploding like popcorn.

"No-o," moaned Silkline as the curtains flared and split. Chairs were overthrown. The Count bicarbonated to a hissing stream of white which flew at Jenny—who flung up her arms and vanished, cat and all, in an orange spume as the air grew thick with squeaks and rib-winged flapping.

Just before the bulbous-eyed Morton Silkline toppled forward, the waxen-faced man leaned over, smiling toothfully, squeezed the Director's numbed arm and murmured, *"Tasty."*

Then Silkline was at one with the rug.

Morton Silkline slumped in his sable-leathered chair, still twitching slightly even though a week had passed since the nerve-splitting event. On his desk lay the note that Ludwig Asper had left pinned to his unconscious chest.

Sir, it read. *Accept, in addition to this bag of gold (which I trust will cover all costs) my regrets that full decorum was not effected by the guests at my funeral. For, save for that, the entire preparation was most satisfactory to me.*

Silkline put down the note and grazed a loving touch across the hill of glinting coins on his desk. Through judicious inquiry, he had gleaned the information that a connection in Mexico (namely, a cosmetician nephew in Carillo's Cut-Rate Catacomb) could safely dispose of the gold at mutual profit. All things considered, the affair had not been really as bad as all—

Morton Silkline looked up as something entered his office.

He would have chosen to leap back screaming and vanish in the flowered pattern of the wallpaper but he was too petrified. Once more gape-mouthed he stared at the huge, tentacled, ocher-dripping shapelessness that weaved and swayed before him.

"A friend," it said politely, "recommended you to me."

Silkline sat bug-eyed for a lengthy moment but then his twitching hand accidentally touched the gold again. And he found strength.

"You've come," he said, breathing through his mouth, "to the right place—uh . . . *sir. Pomps*—" He swallowed mightily and braced himself "—*for all circumstances.*"

He reached for his pen, blowing away the yellow-green smoke which was beginning to obscure the office.

"Name of the deceased?" he asked, businesslike.

FROM SHADOWED PLACES

Dr. Jennings hooked in toward the curb, the tires of his Jaguar spewing out a froth of slush. Braking hard, he jerked the key loose with his left hand while his right clutched for the satchel at his side. In a moment, he was on the street, waiting for a breach in traffic.

His gaze leaped upward to the windows of Peter Lang's apartment. Was Patricia all right? She'd sounded awful on the phone—tremulous, near to panic. Jennings lowered his eyes and frowned uneasily at the line of passing cars. Then, as an opening appeared in the procession, he lunged forward.

The glass door swung pneumatically shut behind him as he strode across the lobby. *Father, hurry! Please! I don't know what to do with him!* Patricia's stricken voice re-echoed in his mind. He stepped into the elevator and pressed the tenth-floor button. *I can't tell you on the phone! You've got to come!* Jennings stared ahead with sightless eyes, unconscious of the whispering closure of the doors.

Patricia's three-month engagement to Lang had certainly been a troubled one. Even so, he wouldn't feel justified in telling her to break it off. Lang could hardly be classified as one of the idle rich. True, he'd never had to face a job of work in his entire twenty-seven years. Still, he wasn't indolent or helpless. One of the world's ranking hunter-sportsmen, he handled himself and his chosen world with graceful authority. There was a readily mined vein of humor in him and a sense of basic justice despite his air of swagger. Most of all, he seemed to love Patricia very much.

Still, all this trouble—

Jennings twitched, blinking his eyes into focus. The elevator doors were open. Realizing that the tenth floor had been reached, he lurched into the corridor, shoe heels squeaking on the polished tile. Without thinking, he thrust the satchel underneath his arm and began pulling off his gloves. Before he'd reached the apartment, they were in his pocket and his coat had been unbuttoned.

A pencilled note was tacked unevenly to the door. *Come in.* Jennings felt a tremor at the sight of Pat's misshapen scrawl. Bracing himself, he turned the knob and went inside.

He froze in unexpected shock. The living room was a shambles, chairs and tables overturned, lamps broken, a clutter of books hurled across the floor, and, scattered everywhere, a debris of splintered glasses, matches, cigarette butts. Dozens of liquor stains islanded the white carpeting. On the bar, an upset bottle trickled Scotch across the counter edge while, from the giant wall speakers, a steady rasping flooded the room. Jennings stared, aghast. *Peter must have gone insane.*

Thrusting his bag onto the hall table, he shed his hat and coat, then grabbed his bag again, and hastened down the steps into the living room. Crossing to the built-in sound system, he switched it off.

"*Father?*"

"Yes." Jennings heard his daughter sob with relief and hurried towards the bedroom.

They were on the floor beneath the picture window. Pat was on her knees embracing Peter who had drawn his naked body into a heap, arms pressed across his face. As Jennings knelt beside them, Patricia looked at him with terror-haunted eyes.

"He tried to jump," she said. "He tried to kill himself." Her voice was fitful, hoarse.

"All right." Jennings drew away the rigid quiver of her arms and tried to raise Lang's head. Peter gasped, recoiling from his touch, and bound himself again into a ball of limbs and torso. Jennings stared at his constricted form. Almost in horror, he watched the crawl of muscles in Peter's back and shoulders. Snakes seemed to writhe beneath the sun-darkened skin.

"How long has he been like this?" he asked.

"I don't know." Her face was a mask of anguish. "I don't know."

"Go in the living room and pour yourself a drink," her father ordered, "I'll take care of him."

"He tried to jump right through the window."

"Patricia."

She began to cry and Jennings turned away; tears were what she needed. Once again, he tried to uncurl the inflexible knot of Peter's body. Once again, the young man gasped and shrank away from him.

"Try to relax," said Jennings, "I want to get you on your bed."

"No!" said Peter, his voice a pain-thickened whisper.

"I can't help you, boy, unless—"

Jennings stopped, his face gone blank. In an instant, Lang's body had lost its rigidity. His legs were straightening out, his arms were slipping from their tense position at his face. A stridulous breath swelled out his lungs.

Peter raised his head.

The sight made Jennings gasp. If ever a face could be described as tortured, it was Lang's. Darkly bearded, bloodless, stark-eyed, it was the face of a man enduring inexplicable torment.

"What *is* it?" Jennings asked, appalled.

Peter grinned; it was the final, hideous touch that made the doctor shudder. "Hasn't Patty told you?" Peter answered.

"Told me what?"

Peter hissed, apparently amused. "I'm being hexed," he said. "Some scrawny—"

"Darling, *don't*," begged Pat.

"What are you talking about?" demanded Jennings.

"Drink?" asked Peter. "Darling?"

Patricia pushed unsteadily to her feet and started for the living room. Jennings helped Lang to his bed.

"What's this all about?" he asked.

Lang fell back heavily on his pillow. "What I said," he answered. "Hexed. Cursed. Witch doctor." He snickered feebly. "Bastard's killing me. Been three months now—almost since Patty and I met."

"Are you—?" Jennings started.

"Codeine ineffectual," said Lang. "Even morphine—got some. Nothing." He sucked in at the air. "No fever, no chills. No symptoms for the AMA. Just—someone killing me." He peered up through slitted eyes. "Funny?"

"Are you serious?"

Peter snorted. "Who the hell knows?" he said. "Maybe it's delirium tremens. God knows I've drunk enough today to—" The tangle of his dark hair rustled on the pillow as he looked towards the window. "Hell, it's night," he said. He turned back quickly. "Time?" he asked.

"After ten," said Jennings. "What about—?"

"Thursday, isn't it?" asked Lang.

Jennings stared at him.

"No, I see it isn't." Lang started coughing dryly. "Drink!" he called. As his gaze jumped towards the doorway, Jennings glanced across his shoulder. Patricia was back.

"It's all spilled," she said, her voice like that of a frightened child.

"All right, don't worry," muttered Lang. "Don't need it. I'll be dead soon anyway."

"Don't talk like that!"

"Honey, I'd be glad to die right now," said Peter, staring at the ceiling. His broad chest hitched unevenly as he breathed. "Sorry, darling, I don't mean it. Uh-oh, here we go again." He spoke so mildly that his seizure caught them by surprise.

Abruptly, he was floundering on the bed, his muscle-knotted legs kicking like pistons, his arms clamped down across the drumhide tautness of his face. A noise like the shrilling of a violin wavered in his throat, and Jennings saw saliva running from the corners of his mouth. Turning suddenly, the doctor lurched across the room for his bag.

Before he'd reached it, Peter's thrashing body had fallen from the bed. The young man reared up, screaming, on his face the wide-mouthed, slavering frenzy of an animal. Patricia tried to hold him back but, with a snarl, he shoved her brutally aside and staggered for the window.

Jennings met him with the hypodermic. For several moments, they were locked in reeling struggle, Peter's distended, teeth-bared face inches from the doctor's, his vein-corded hands scrabbling for Jennings's throat. He cried out hoarsely as the needle pierced his skin and, springing backwards, lost his balance, fell. He tried to stand, his crazed eyes looking towards the window. Then the drug was in his blood and he was sitting with the flaccid posture of a rag doll. Torpor glazed his eyes. "Bastard's killing me," he muttered.

They laid him on the bed and covered up the sluggish twitching of his body.

"Killing me," said Lang. "Black bastard."

"Does he really *believe* this?" Jennings asked.

"Father, *look* at him," she answered.

"You believe it too?"

"*I* don't know." She shook her head impotently. "All I know is that I've seen him change from what he was to—*this*. He isn't sick, father. There's nothing wrong with him." She shuddered. "Yet he's dying."

"Why didn't you call me sooner?"

"I couldn't," she said. "I was afraid to leave him for a second."

Jennings drew his fingers from the young man's fluttering pulse. "Has he been examined at all?"

She nodded tiredly. "Yes," she answered, "when it started getting

worse, he went to see a specialist. He thought, perhaps his brain—"
She shook her head. "There's nothing wrong with him."

"But why does he say he's being—?" Jennings found himself unable to speak the word.

"*I don't know,*" she said. "Sometimes, he seems to believe it. Mostly he jokes about it."

"But on what grounds—?"

"Some incident on his last safari," said Patricia. "I don't really know what happened. Some—Zulu native threatened him; said he was a witch doctor and was going to—" Her voice broke into a wracking sob. "Oh, God, how can such a thing be true? How can it *happen?*"

"The point, I think, is whether Peter, actually, believes it's happening," said Jennings. He turned to Lang. "And, from the look of him—"

"Father, I've been wondering if—" Patricia swallowed. "If maybe Dr. Howell could help him."

Jennings stared at her for a moment. Then he said, "You *do* believe it, don't you?"

"Father, *try to understand.*" There was a trembling undertone of panic in her voice, "You've only seen Peter now and then. I've watched it happening to him almost day by day. Something is destroying him! I don't know what it is, but I'll try anything to stop it. *Anything.*"

"All right." He pressed a reassuring hand against her back. "Go phone while I examine him."

After she'd gone into the living room—the telephone connected in the bedroom had been ripped from the wall—Jennings drew the covers down and looked at Peter's bronzed and muscular body. It was trembling with minute vibrations—as if, within the chemical imprisoning of the drug, each separate nerve still pulsed and throbbed.

Jennings clenched his teeth in vague distress. Somewhere, at the core of his perception, where the rationale of science had yet to filter, he sensed that medical inquiry would be pointless. Still, he felt distaste for what Patricia might be setting up. It went against the grain of learned acceptance. It offended mentality.

It, also, frightened him.

The drug's effect was almost gone now, Jennings saw. Ordinarily, it would have rendered Lang unconscious for six to eight hours. Now—in *forty minutes*—he was in the living room with them, lying on the sofa in his bathrobe, saying, "Patty, it's ridiculous. What good's another doctor going to do?"

"All right then, it's ridiculous!" she said. "What would you *like* for us to do—just stand around and watch you—?" She couldn't finish.

"Shhh." Lang stroked her hair with trembling fingers. "Patty, Patty. Hang on, darling. Maybe I can beat it."

"You're *going* to beat it." Patricia kissed his hand. "It's both of us, Peter. I won't go on without you."

"Don't *you* talk like that." Lang twisted on the sofa. "Oh, Christ, it's starting up again." He forced a smile. "No, I'm all right," he told her, "just—crawly, sort of." His smile flared into a sudden grimace of pain. "So this Dr. Howell is going to solve my problem, is he? How?"

Jennings saw Patricia bite her lip. "It's a—*her*, darling," she told Lang.

"Great," he said. He twitched convulsively. "That's what we need. What is she, a chiropractor?"

"She's an anthropologist."

"*Dandy*. What's she going to do, explain the ethnic origins of superstition to me?" Lang spoke rapidly as if trying to outdistance pain with words.

"She's been to Africa," said Pat. "She—"

"So have I," said Peter. "Great place to visit. Just don't screw around with witch doctors." His laughter withered to a gasping cry. "Oh, God, you scrawny, black bastard, if I had you here!" His hands clawed out as if to throttle some invisible assailant.

"I beg your pardon—"

They turned in surprise. A young black woman was looking down at them from the entrance hall.

"There was a card on the door," she said.

"Of course; we'd forgotten." Jennings was on his feet now. He heard Patricia whispering to Lang, "I *meant* to tell you. Please don't be biased." Peter looked at her sharply, his expression even more surprised now. *"Biased*?" he said.

Jennings and his daughter moved across the room.

"Thank you for coming." Patricia pressed her cheek to Dr. Howell's.

"It's nice to see you, Pat," said Dr. Howell. She smiled across Patricia's shoulder at the doctor.

"Had you any trouble getting here?" he asked.

"No, no, the subway never fails me." Lurice Howell unbuttoned her coat and turned as Jennings reached to help her. Pat looked at the overnight bag that Lurice had set on the floor, then glanced at Peter.

Lang did not take his eyes from Lurice Howell as she approached him, flanked by Pat and Jennings.

"Peter, this is Dr. Howell," said Pat. "She and I went to Columbia together. She teaches anthropology at City College."

Lurice smiled. "Good evening," she said.

"Not so very," Peter answered. From the corners of his eyes Jennings saw the way Patricia stiffened.

Dr. Howell's expression did not alter. Her voice remained the same. "And who's the scrawny, black bastard you wish you had here?" she asked.

Peter's face went momentarily blank. Then, his teeth clenched against the pain, he answered, "What's that supposed to mean?"

"A question," said Lurice.

"If you're planning to conduct a seminar on race relations, skip it," muttered Lang, "I'm not in the mood."

"*Peter.*"

He looked at Pat through pain-filmed eyes. "What do you want?" he demanded. "You're already convinced I'm prejudiced, so—" He dropped his head back on the sofa arm and jammed his eyes shut. "Jesus, stick a *knife* in me," he rasped.

The straining smile had gone from Dr. Howell's lips. She glanced at Jennings gravely as he spoke. "I've examined him," he told her. "There's not a sign of physical impairment, not a hint of brain injury."

"How should there be?" she answered, quietly. "It's not disease. It's juju."

Jennings stared at her. "You—"

"*There* we go," said Peter, hoarsely. "Now we've got it." He was sitting up again, whitened fingers digging at the cushions. "That's the answer. *Juju.*"

"Do you doubt it?" asked Lurice.

"I *doubt* it."

"The way you doubt your prejudice?"

"Oh, Jesus. *God.*" Lang filled his lungs with a guttural, sucking noise. "I was hurting and I wanted something to hate so I picked on that lousy savage to—" He fell back heavily. "The hell with it. Think what you like." He clamped a palsied hand across his eyes. "Just let me die. Oh, Jesus, Jesus God, sweet Jesus, *let me die.*" Suddenly, he looked at Jennings. "Another shot?" he begged.

"Peter, your heart can't—"

"*Damn* my heart!" Peter's head was rocking back and forth now. "*Half* strength then! You can't refuse a dying man!"

Pat jammed the edge of a shaking fist against her lips, trying not to cry.

"*Please!*" said Peter.

After the injection had taken effect, Lang slumped back, his face and neck soaked with perspiration. "Thanks," he gasped. His pale lips twitched into a smile as Patricia knelt beside him and began to dry his face with a towel. "Greetings, love," he muttered. She couldn't speak.

Peter's hooded eyes turned to Dr. Howell. "All right, I'm sorry, I apologize," he told her curtly. "I thank you for coming, but I don't believe it."

"Then why is it working?" asked Lurice.

"I don't even know what's happening!" snapped Lang.

"I think you do," said Dr. Howell, an urgency rising in her voice, "and *I* know, Mr. Lang. Juju is the most fearsome pagan sorcery in the world. Centuries of mass belief alone would be enough to give it terrifying power. It *has* that power, Mr. Lang. You know it does."

"And how do *you* know, Dr. Howell?" he countered.

"When I was twenty-two," she said, "I spent a year in a Zulu village doing field work for my Ph.D. While I was there, the *ngombo* took a fancy to me and taught me almost everything she knew."

"*Ngombo?*" asked Patricia.

"*Witch doctor,*" said Peter, in disgust.

"I thought witch doctors were men," said Jennings.

"No, most of them are women," said Lurice. "Shrewd, observant women who work very hard at their profession."

"*Frauds,*" said Peter.

Lurice smiled at him. "Yes," she said, "they are. Frauds. Parasites. Loafers. Scaremongers. Still—" Her smile grew hard. "—what do you suppose is making you feel as though a thousand spiders were crawling all over you?"

For the first time since he'd entered the apartment, Jennings saw a look of fear on Peter's face. "*You know that?*" Peter asked her.

"I know everything you're going through," said Dr. Howell. "I've been through it myself."

"*When?*" demanded Lang. There was no derogation in his voice now.

"During that year," said Dr. Howell, "a witch doctor from a nearby village put a death curse on me. Kuringa saved me from it."

"Tell me," said Peter, breaking in on her. Jennings noticed that the young man's breath was quickening. It appalled him to realize that the second injection was already beginning to lose its effect.

"Tell you what?" said Lurice. "About the long-nailed fingers scraping at your insides? About the feeling that you have to pull yourself into a ball in order to crush the snake uncoiling in your belly?"

Peter gaped at her.

"The feeling that your blood has turned to acid?" said Lurice. "That, if you move, you'll crumble because your bones have all been sucked hollow?"

Peter's lips began to shake.

"The feeling that your brain is being eaten by a pack of furry rats? That your eyes are just about to melt and dribble down your cheeks like jelly? That—?"

"That's enough." Lang's body seemed to jolt, he shuddered so spasmodically.

"I only said these things to convince you that I know," said Lurice. "I remember my own pain as if I'd suffered it this morning instead of seven years ago. I can help you if you'll let me, Mr. Lang. Put aside your skepticism. You *do* believe it or it couldn't hurt you, don't you see that?"

"Darling, *please*," said Patricia.

Peter looked at her. Then his gaze moved back to Dr. Howell.

"We mustn't wait much longer, Mr. Lang," she warned.

"All *right*!" He closed his eyes. "All right then, *try*. I sure as hell can't get any worse."

"*Quickly*," begged Patricia.

"Yes." Lurice Howell turned and walked across the room to get her overnight bag.

It was as she picked it up that Jennings saw the look cross her face—as if some formidable complication had just occurred to her. She glanced at them. "Pat," she said.

"*Yes.*"

"Come here a moment."

Patricia pushed up hurriedly and moved to her side. Jennings watched them for a moment before his eyes shifted to Lang. The young man was starting to twitch again. It's *coming*, Jennings thought. *Juju is the most fearsome pagan sorcery in the world—*

"What?"

Jennings glanced at the women. Pat was staring at Dr. Howell in shock.

"I'm sorry," said Lurice, "I should have told you from the start, but there wasn't any opportunity."

Pat hesitated. "It has to be that way?" she asked.

"Yes. It does."

Patricia looked at Peter with a questioning apprehension in her eyes. Abruptly, then, she nodded. "All right," she said, "but *hurry.*"

Without another word, Lurice Howell went into the bedroom. Jennings watched his daughter as she looked intently at the door behind which the black woman had closeted herself. He could not fathom the meaning of her look. For now the fear in Pat's expression was of a different sort.

The bedroom door opened and Dr. Howell came out. Jennings, turning from the sofa, caught his breath. Lurice was naked to the waist and garbed below with a skirt composed of several colored handkerchiefs knotted together. Her legs and feet were bare. Jennings gaped at her. The blouse and skirt she'd worn had revealed nothing of her voluptuous breasts, the sinuous abundance of her hips. Suddenly conscious of his blatant observation, Jennings turned his eyes towards Pat. Her expression, as she stared at Dr. Howell, was unmistakable now.

Jennings looked back at Peter. Due to its masking of pain, the young man's face was more difficult to read.

"Please understand, I've never done this before," said Lurice, embarrassed by their staring silence.

"We understand," said Jennings, once more unable to take his eyes from her.

A bright red spot was painted on each of her tawny cheeks and, over her twisted, twine-held hair, she wore a helmet-like plume of feathers, each of a chestnut hue with a vivid white eye at the tip. Her breasts thrust out from a tangle of necklaces made of animals teeth, skeins of brightly colored yarn, beads, and strips of snake skin. On her left arm—banded at the biceps with a strip of angora fleece—was slung a small shield of dappled oxhide.

The contrast between the bag and her outfit was marked enough. The effect of her appearance in the Manhattan duplex created a ripple of indefinable dread in Jennings as she moved towards them with a shy, almost childlike defiance—as if her shame were balanced by a knowledge of her physical wealth. Jennings was startled to see that her stomach was tattooed, hundreds of tiny welts forming a design of concentric circles around her navel.

"Kuringa insisted on it," said Lurice as if he'd asked. "It was her price for teaching me her secrets." She smiled fleetingly. "I managed to dissuade her from filing my teeth to a point."

Jennings sensed that she was talking to hide her embarrassment and he felt a surge of empathy for her as she set her bag down, opened it and started to remove its contents.

"The welts are raised by making small incisions in the flesh," she said, "and pressing into each incision a dab of paste." She put, on the coffee table, a vial of grumous liquid, a handful of small, polished bones. "The paste I had to make myself. I had to catch a land crab with my bare hands and tear off one of its claws. I had to tear the skin from a living frog and the jaw from a monkey." She put on the table a bundle of what looked like tiny lances. "The claws, the skin, and the jaw, together with some plant ingredients, I pounded into the paste."

Jennings looked surprised as she withdrew an LP from the bag and set it on the turntable.

"When I say *'Now,'* Doctor," she asked, "will you put on the turntable arm?"

Jennings nodded mutely, watching her with what was close to fascination. She seemed to know exactly what she was doing. Ignoring the slit-eyed stare of Lang, the uncertain surveillance of Patricia, Lurice set the various objects on the floor. As she squatted, Pat could not restrain a gasp. Underneath the skirt of handkerchiefs, Lurice's loins were uncovered.

"Well, I may not live," said Peter—his face was almost white now—"but it looks as if I'm going to have a fascinating death."

Lurice interrupted him. "If the three of you will sit in a circle," she said. The prim refinement of her voice coming from the lips of what seemed a pagan goddess struck Jennings forcibly as he moved to assist Lang.

The seizure came as Peter tried to stand. In an instant, he was in the throes of it, groveling on the floor, his body doubled, his knees and elbows thumping at the rug. Abruptly, he flopped over, forcing back his head, the muscles of his spine tensed so acutely that his back arched upward from the floor. Pale foam ribboned from the slash of his mouth, his staring eyes seemed frozen in their sockets.

"Lurice!" screamed Pat.

"There's nothing we can do until it passes," said Lurice. She stared at Lang with sickened eyes. Then, as his bathrobe came undone and he was thrashing naked on the rug, she turned away, her face tightening with a look that Jennings, glancing at her, saw, to his added disquietude, was a look of fear. Then he and Pat were bent across Lang's afflicted body, trying to hold him in check.

"Let him go," said Lurice. "There's nothing you can do."

Patricia glared at her in frightened animosity. As Peter's body finally shuddered into immobility, she drew the edges of his robe together and refastened the sash.

"*Now*. Into the circle, quickly," said Lurice, clearly forcing herself against some inner dread. "No, he has to sit alone," she said, as Patricia braced herself beside him, supporting his back.

"He'll *fall*," said Pat, an undercurrent of resentment in her voice.

"Patricia, if you want my help—!"

Uncertainly, her eyes drifting from Peter's pain-wasted features to the harried expression on Lurice's face, Patricia edged away and settled herself.

"Cross-legged, please," said Lurice. "Mr. Lang?"

Peter grunted, eyes half-closed.

"During the ceremony, I'll ask you for a token of payment. Some unimportant personal item will suffice."

Peter nodded. "All right; let's *go*," he said, "I can't take much more."

Lurice's breasts rose, quivering, as she drew in breath. "No talking now," she murmured. Nervously, she sat across from Peter and bowed her head. Except for Lang's stentorian breathing, the room grew deathly still. Jennings could hear, faintly, in the distance, the sounds of traffic. It seemed impossible to adjust his mind to what was about to happen; an attempted ritual of jungle sorcery—in a New York City apartment.

He tried, in vain, to clear his mind of misgivings. He didn't believe in this. Yet here he sat, his crossed legs already beginning to cramp. Here sat Peter Lang, obviously close to death with not a symptom to explain it. Here sat his daughter, terrified, struggling mentally against that which she herself had initiated. And there most bizarre of all, sat—not Dr. Howell, an intelligent professor of anthropology, a cultured, civilized woman—but a near-naked African witch doctor with her implements of barbarous magic.

There was a rattling noise. Jennings blinked his eyes and looked at Lurice. In her left hand, she was clutching the sheaf of what looked like miniature lances. With her right, she was picking up the cluster of tiny, polished bones. She shook them in her palm like dice and tossed them onto the rug, her gaze intent on their fall.

She stared at their pattern on the carpeting, then picked them up again. Across from her, Peter's breath was growing tortured. What if he suffered another attack? Jennings wondered. Would the ceremony have to be restarted?

He twitched as Lurice broke the silence.

"Why do you come here?" she asked. She looked at Peter coldly, almost glaring at him. "Why do you consult me? Is it because you have no success with women?"

"What?" Peter stared at her bewilderedly.

"Is someone in your house sick? Is that why you come to me?" asked Lurice, her voice imperious. Jennings realized abruptly that she was—completely now—a witch doctor questioning her male client, arrogantly contemptuous of his inferior status.

"Are *you* sick?" She almost spat the words, her shoulders jerking back so that her breasts hitched upwards. Jennings glanced involuntarily at his daughter. Pat was sitting like a statue, cheeks pale, lips a narrow, bloodless line.

"Speak up, man!" ordered Lurice—ordered the scowling *ngombo*.

"Yes! I'm sick!" Peter's chest lurched with breath. "I'm *sick*."

"Then speak of it," said Lurice. "Tell me how this sickness came upon you."

Either Peter was in such pain now that any notion of resistance was destroyed—or else he had been captured by the fascination of Lurice's presence. Probably it was a combination of the two, thought Jennings as he watched Lang begin to speak, his voice compelled, his eyes held by Lurice's burning stare.

"One night, this man came sneaking into camp," he said. "He tried to steal some food. When I chased him, he got furious and threatened me. He said he'd kill me." Jennings wondered if Lurice had hypnotized Peter, the young man's voice was so mechanical.

"And he carried, in a sack at his side—" Lurice's voice seemed to prompt like a hypnotist's.

"He carried a doll," said Peter. His throat contracted as he swallowed. "It spoke to me," he said.

"The fetish spoke to you," said Lurice. "What did the fetish say?"

"It said that I would die. It said that, when the moon was like a bow, I would die."

Abruptly, Peter shivered and closed his eyes. Lurice threw down the bones again and stared at them. Abruptly, she flung down the tiny lances.

"It is not Mbwiri nor Hebiezo," she said. "It is not Atando nor Fuofuo nor Sovi. It is not Kundi or Sogbla. It is not a demon of the forest that devours you. It is an evil spirit that belongs to a *ngombo* who has been offended. The *ngombo* has brought evil to your house. The evil spirit of the *ngombo* has fastened itself upon you in revenge for your offense against its master. Do you understand?"

Peter was barely able to speak. He nodded jerkily. "Yes."

"Say—*Yes, I understand.*"

"Yes." He shuddered. "Yes. I understand."

"You will pay me now," she told him.

Peter stared at her for several moments before lowering his eyes. His twitching fingers reached into the pockets of his robe and came out empty. Suddenly, he gasped, his shoulders hitching forward as a spasm of pain rushed through him. He reached into his pockets a second time as if he weren't sure that they were empty. Then, frantically, he wrenched the ring from the third finger of his left hand and held it out. Jennings's gaze darted to his daughter. Her face was like stone as she watched Peter handing over the ring she'd given him.

"*Now,*" said Lurice.

Jennings pushed to his feet and, stumbling because of the numbness in his legs, he moved to the turntable and lowered the stylus in place. Before he'd settled back into the circle, the record started playing.

In a moment, the room was filled with drumbeats, with a chanting of voices and a slow, uneven clapping of hands. His gaze intent on Lurice, Jennings had the impression that everything was fading at the edges of his vision, that Lurice, alone, was visible, standing in a dimly nebulous light.

She had left her oxhide shield on the floor and was holding the bottle in her hand. As Jennings watched, she pulled the stopper loose and drank the contents with a single swallow. Vaguely, through the daze of fascination that gripped his mind, Jennings wondered what it was she'd drunk.

The bottle thudded on the floor.

Lurice began to dance.

She started languidly. Only her arms and shoulders moved at first, their restless sinuating timed to the cadence of the drumbeats. Jennings stared at her, imagining that his heart had altered its rhythm to that of the drums. He watched the writhing of her shoulders, the serpentine gestures she was making with her arms and hands. He heard the rustling of her necklaces. Time and place were gone for him. He might have been sitting in a jungle glade, watching the somnolent twisting of her dance.

"Clap hands," said the *ngombo*.

Without hesitation, Jennings started clapping in time with the drums. He glanced at Patricia. She was doing the same, her eyes still fixed on Lurice. Only Peter sat motionless, looking straight ahead, the muscles of his jaw quivering as he ground his teeth together. For a fleeting moment, Jennings was a doctor once again, looking at his patient in concern. Then turning back, he was redrawn into the mindless captivation of Lurice's dance.

The drumbeats were accelerating now, becoming louder. Lurice began to move within the circle, turning slowly, arms and shoulders still in undulant motion. No matter where she moved, her eyes remained on Peter, and Jennings realized that her gesturing was exclusively for Lang—drawing, gathering gestures as if she sought to lure him to her side.

Suddenly, she bent over, her breasts dropping heavily, then jerking upward as their muscles caught. She shook herself with feverish abandon, swinging her breasts from side to side and rattling her necklaces, her wild face hovering inches over Peter's. Jennings felt his stomach muscles pulling in as Lurice drew her talon-shaped fingers over Peter's cheeks, then straightened up and pivoted, her shoulders thrust back carelessly, her teeth bared in a grimace of savage zeal. In a moment, she had spun around to face her client again.

A second time she bent herself, this time stalking back and forth in front of Peter with a catlike gait, a rabid crooning in her throat. From the corners of his eyes, Jennings saw his daughter straining forward and he glanced at her. The expression on her face was terrible.

Suddenly, Patricia's lips flared back as in a soundless cry and Jennings looked back quickly at Lurice. His breath choked off. Leaning over, she had clutched her breasts with digging fingers and was thrusting them at Peter's face. Peter stared at her, his body trembling. Crooning again, Lurice drew back. She lowered her hands and Jennings tightened as he saw that she was pulling at the skirt of handkerchiefs. In a moment, it had fluttered to the carpeting and she was back at Peter. It was then that Jennings knew exactly what she'd drunk.

"*No.*" Patricia's vemon-thickened voice made him twist around, his heartbeat lurching. She was starting to her feet.

"*Pat!*" he whispered.

She looked at him and, for a moment, they were staring at each other. Then, with a violent shudder, she sank to the floor again and Jennings turned away from her.

Lurice was on her knees in front of Peter now, rocking back and forth and rubbing at her thighs with flattened hands. She couldn't seem to breathe. Her open mouth kept sucking at the air with wheezing noises. Jennings saw perspiration trickling down her cheeks; he saw it glistening on her back and shoulders. No, he thought. The word came automatically, the voicing of some alien dread that seemed to rise up, choking, in him. No. He watched Lurice's hand clutch upwards at her breasts again, proferring them to Peter. No. The word was lurking terror in his mind. He kept on staring at Lurice, fearing what was going to happen, fascinated at its possibility. Drumbeats throbbed and billowed in his ears. His heartbeat pounded.

No!

Lurice's hands had clawed out suddenly and torn apart the edges of Lang's robe. Patricia's gasp was hoarse, astounded. Jennings only caught a glimpse of her distorted face before his gaze was drawn back to Lurice. Swallowed by the frenzied thundering of the drums, the howl of chanting voices, the explosive clapping, he felt as if his head were going numb, as if the room were tilting. In a dreamlike haze, he saw Lurice's hands begin to rub at Peter's flesh. He saw a look of nightmare on the young man's face as torment closed a vise around him—torment that was just as much carnality as agony. Lurice moved closer to him. Closer. Now her writhing, sweat-laved body pendulated inches from his own, her hands caressing wantonly.

"Come into me." Her voice was bestial, gluttonous. "Come into me."

"Get away from him." Patricia's guttural warning tore Jennings from entrancement. Jerking around, he saw her reaching for Lurice—who, in that instant, clamped herself on Peter's body.

Jennings lunged at Pat, not understanding why he should restrain her, only sensing that he must. She twisted wildly in his grip, her hot breath spilling on his cheeks, her body violent in rage.

"Get away from him!" she screamed at Lurice. *"Get your hands away from him!"*

"Patricia!"

"Let me *go!*"

Lurice's scream of anguish paralyzed them. Stunned, they watched her flinging back from Peter and collapsing on her back, her legs jerked in, arms flung across her face. Jennings felt a burst of horror in himself. His gaze leaped up to Peter's face. The look of pain had vanished from it. Only stunned bewilderment remained.

"What *is* it?" gasped Patricia.

Jennings's voice was hollow, awed. *"She's taken it away from him,"* he said.

"Oh, my God—" Aghast, Patricia watched her friend.

The feeling that you have to pull yourself into a ball in order to crush the snake uncoiling in your belly. The words assaulted Jennings's mind. He watched the rippling crawl of muscles underneath Lurice's flesh, the spastic twitching of her legs. Across the room, the record stopped and, in the sudden stillness, he could hear a shrill whine quavering in Lurice's throat. *The feeling that your blood has turned to acid, that, if you move, you'll crumble because your bones have all been sucked hollow.* Eyes haunted, Jennings watched her suffering Peter's agony. *The feeling that your brain is being eaten by a pack of furry rats, that your eyes are just about to melt and dribble down your cheeks like jelly.* Lurice's legs kicked out. She twisted onto her back and started rolling on her shoulders. Her legs jerked in until her feet were resting on the carpet. Convulsively, she reared her hips. Her stomach heaved with tortured breath, her swollen breasts lolled from side to side.

"Peter!"

Patricia's horrified whisper made Jennings's head snap up. Peter's eyes were glittering as he watched Lurice's thrashing body. He had started pushing to his knees, a look not human drawn across his features. Now his hands were reaching for Lurice. Jennings caught him by the shoulders, but Peter didn't seem to notice. He kept reaching for Lurice.

"Peter."

Lang tried to shove him aside but Jennings tightened his grip. *"For God's sake*—Peter!"

The noise Lang uttered made Jennings's skin crawl. He clamped his fingers brutally in Peter's hair and jerked him around so that they faced each other.

"Use your mind, man!" Jennings ordered. "Your *mind!*"

Peter blinked. He stared at Jennings with the eyes of a newly awakened man. Jennings pulled his hands away and turned back quickly.

Lurice was lying motionless on her back, her dark eyes staring at the ceiling. With a gasp, Jennings leaned over and pressed a finger underneath her left breast. Her heartbeat was nearly imperceptible. He looked at her eyes again. They had the glassy stare of a corpse. He gaped at them in disbelief. Suddenly, they closed and a protracted, body-wracking shudder passed through Lurice. Jennings watched her, open-mouthed, unable to move. No, he thought. It was impossible. She couldn't be—

"Lurice!" he cried.

She opened her eyes and looked at him. After several moments, her lips stirred feebly as she tried to smile.

"It's over now," she whispered.

The car moved along Seventh Avenue, its tires hissing on the slush. Across the seat from Jennings, Dr. Howell slumped, motionless, in her exhaustion. A shamed, remorseful Pat had bathed and dressed her, after which Jennings had helped her to his car. Just before they'd left the apartment, Peter had attempted to thank her, then, unable to find the words, had kissed her hand and turned away in silence.

Jennings glanced at her. "You know," he said, "if I hadn't actually seen what happened tonight, I wouldn't believe it for a moment. I'm still not sure that I do."

"It isn't easy to accept," she said.

Jennings drove in silence for a while before he spoke again. "Dr. Howell?"

"Yes?"

He hesitated. Then he asked, "Why did you do it?"

"If I hadn't," said Lurice, "your future son-in-law would have died before the night was over. You have no idea how close he came."

"Granting that," said Jennings, "what I mean is—why did you deliberately subject yourself to such—abasement?"

"There was no alternative," she answered. "Mr. Lang couldn't possibly have coped with what was happening to him. I could. It was as simple as that. Everything else was—unfortunate necessity."

"And something of a Pandora's box as well," he said.

"I know," she said, "I was afraid of it but there was nothing I could do."

"You told Patricia what was going to happen?"

"No," said Lurice, "I couldn't tell her everything. I tried to brace her for the shock of what was coming but, of course, I had to withhold some of it. Otherwise she might have refused my help—and her fiancé would have died."

"It was an aphrodisiac in that bottle, wasn't it?"

"Yes," she answered, "I had to lose myself. If I hadn't, personal inhibitions would have kept me from doing what was necessary."

"What happened just before the end of it—" Jennings began.

"Mr. Lang's apparent lust for me?" said Lurice. "It was only a derangement of the moment. The sudden extraction of the pain left him, for a period of seconds, without conscious volition. Without, if you will, civilized restraint. It was an animal who wanted me, not a man. You saw that, when you ordered him to use his mind, the lust was controlled."

"But the animal was there," said Jennings, grimly.

"It's always there," she answered. "The trouble is that people forget it."

Minutes later, Jennings parked in front of Dr. Howell's apartment house and turned to her.

"I think we both know how much sickness you exposed—and cured tonight," he said.

"I hope so," said Lurice. "Not for myself but—" She smiled a little. *"Not for myself I make this prayer,"* she recited. "Are you familiar with that?"

"I'm afraid I'm not."

He listened quietly as Dr. Howell recited again. Then, as he started to get out of the car, she held him back. "Please don't," she said, "I'm fine now." Pushing open the door, she stood on the sidewalk. For several moments, they looked at each other. Then Jennings reached over and squeezed her hand.

"Good night, my dear," he said.

Lurice Howell returned his smile. "Good night, Doctor." She closed the door and turned away.

Jennings watched her walk across the sidewalk and enter her apartment house. Then, drawing his car into the street again, he made a U-turn and started back towards Seventh Avenue. As he drove, he began remembering the Countee Cullen poem that Lurice had spoken for him.

Not for myself I make this prayer
But for this race of mine
That stretches forth from shadowed places
Dark hands for bread and wine.

Jennings's fingers tightened on the wheel.

"Use your mind, man," he said. "Your *mind.*"

PERSON TO PERSON

The ringing telephone stirred Millman from his sleep. His eyelids fluttered as he drifted up toward consciousness. The telephone kept ringing and he groaned. "All right, all right."

Sliding his left arm from beneath the covers, he reached to the bedside table, feeling for the handset. His fingers closed around it and he carried the receiver to his ear. "Yes?" he mumbled.

He listened to the dial tone for a few seconds before grimacing irritably and reaching out to thump the handset back on its cradle.

His eyes opened wide as he looked toward the bedside table.

The telephone was still ringing.

He stretched out his arm and fumbled for the lamp switch. Twisting it, he averted his face from the glare, then picked up the handset again and pressed the receiver to his ear.

There was only the dial tone.

Millman stared, bewildered, at the handset. He could still hear the sound of a telephone ringing.

Several moments passed before it came to him that the ringing was inside his head.

"I have the test results," Dr. Vance told him.

Millman waited anxiously. "My immediate assumption was that it was *tinnitus*," Dr. Vance continued. "There's no sign of middle-ear infection, though, no symptoms such as earache, fever, a sensation of pressure in your ears."

"What *is* it then?" Millman asked.

"You know for a fact it doesn't ring all the time."

"Only at night," Millman answered. "It wakes me up."

"That wouldn't be the case if it was *tinnitus*," Dr. Vance said. "The ringing would be constant."

Millman looked at him in worried silence.

"Don't tell anyone I said this," Dr. Vance went on, "but you might try getting a chiropractic adjustment on your neck. I had a friend who suffered from what appeared to be *tinnitus*. After he got a neck adjustment, it went away."

"And if that doesn't work?" Millman asked.

"Try it first," the doctor said.

❧

Millman twisted on the bed with an angry groan.

The telephone was ringing again.

He reached out quickly with his left hand and grabbed the handset, carrying the earpiece to his head.

Then he slammed the handset down on its cradle. "Damn!" he cried.

He lay on his back, a look of apprehension on his face as he listened to the sound of the ringing telephone inside his head.

❧

"Everything's been tried?" Dr. Palmer asked.

"*Yes,*" Millman said despairingly. "There's no sign of a fracture or a concussion. Nothing wrong with my spine. No sign of any foreign body. No growths, no tumors, *nothing*. I even had a neck adjustment. It made no difference."

"The ringing happens every night?" Dr. Palmer asked.

"Yes."

"At the same time?"

"Three in morning," Millman answered. "I can't sleep any more. I just lie in bed waiting for it to start."

"And you're positive it sounds like a telephone ringing."

"It *is* a telephone ringing," Millman said impatiently.

"Try answering it then," suggested Dr. Palmer.

⚬

Millman lay on his back in the darkness, listening to the ringing sound inside his head. He wanted desperately to make it stop. But Dr. Palmer's suggestion disturbed him. It seemed a bizarre thing for a therapist to say.

Still. . . .

The telephone kept ringing. Millman's left hand twitched as though about to reach for the telephone on the bedside table. But he knew that wasn't where the ringing was coming from.

Impulsively, he visualized a telephone inside his head. He visualized his left hand picking up the handset. "Hel-*lo*," he said aloud.

"Well, finally," said the voice.

⚬

Millman felt himself recoil into the mattress, heartbeat pounding suddenly. *"My God,"* he said.

"Take it easy now," the voice responded, that of a man. "Don't get yourself in an uproar. There's a simple explanation."

Millman couldn't seem to breathe.

"Still there?" the man's voice asked.

Millman swallowed. He sucked in a wheezing breath and muttered, "Yes."

The voice said, "Good."

Millman had to ask, although he knew it was insane.

"Who *is* this?" he said.

"The name's not important," the man's voice replied. "I'm not allowed to tell you anyway."

"What are you talking about?" Millman's voice strained.

"Take it *easy*," the man's voice said. "You're getting yourself upset for nothing. I told you there's a simple explanation."

"What?" demanded Millman.

"Okay," the man's voice answered. "Here's what's going on. It's a government project; a *secret* project, it goes without saying. You'll have to keep it quiet. It's a matter of national security."

Millman's mouth slipped open. *National security?*

"I won't go into background," the man's voice continued. "You know the situation in the world. Our government maintains a constant policy of espionage. We have to know what's happening on the other side."

"But—" Millman started.

"Just listen," the man's voice interrupted. "We have agents all around the globe, sending us information. The transmission of their messages has always been a risk. Any device they use can be detected sooner or later. Which is why we're experimenting with inner-brain communication."

"Inner-brain—?"

"Yes." The man's voice cut Millman off. "A method by which agents can transmit information with no risk whatever of being intercepted. I don't mean telepathy or anything like that. I'm talking about a microscopic insert."

Millman tightened. *"What?"*

"Relax," the man's voice told him. "If it's so minute it never even showed up on your medical tests, it's certainly too small to bother you."

Millman tried to speak but couldn't.

"You're probably wondering why you were chosen for this experiment," the man's voice continued. "Actually, you're not the only one.

I can't tell you how many there are, but the number is considerable. As to *how* you were chosen, it was mathematical; a random generator."

"I don't understand," Millman said.

"To be perfectly candid," the man's voice went on, "only a few of you have reached the stage of answering our call. The rest are still fixated at the point of thinking it's a physical affliction, making endless rounds of doctor visits. Congratulations on being imaginative enough to answer the ringing—it *is* that of an actual telephone, by the way."

Millman braced himself. "But—" he began.

"—we never asked," the man's voice finished Millman's thought. "True. And we're sorry it disturbed you. Still—under the circumstances, we couldn't very well have asked for your permission.

"At any rate," he added, "we won't be bothering you as much now. The connection's been made."

"For how long?" Millman asked.

"I'm sorry," the man's voice responded. "That's not my decision to make."

Inside his head, Millman heard the distinct sound of a telephone handset being placed on its cradle.

He fell back on the pillow; he'd been unaware that he was leaning on his right elbow throughout his conversation with the man. In spite of his distress, he felt relieved that the ringing noise had stopped.

In seconds, he was heavily asleep.

The ringing of the telephone inside his head jarred Millman awake. His eyes sprang open and he twitched on the mattress. *"No,"* he said. It had been five days since he'd spoken with the man. He'd begun to hope it was over; that either the calls would not continue or that he'd imagined everything.

Grimacing, he snatched up the unseen handset. *"Yes,"* he said.

The ringing continued.

Millman looked confused. He visualized the telephone as clearly as he could, lifted the handset and brought it to his ear. "Hel-*lo*," he said.

The telephone kept ringing. Was it because he hadn't heard it for the past five nights that it sounded so painfully shrill to him?

In his mind, he visualized his hand grabbing at the handset. "Hello!" he said.

The ringing didn't stop. Millman made a pained noise. The sound seemed to pulse in stabbing waves against the tissues of his brain. He clenched his teeth, face contorted.

The telephone kept ringing. Millman kept snatching up the handset in his imagination, crying out, "Hel-*lo*!"

Abruptly, then, the man's voice answered. "You don't have to *shout*."

"For God's sake!" Millman cried.

"Take it *easy*," the man's voice told him.

"*Easy*?" Millman said. "The phone's been ringing in my head for ten minutes straight!"

"Five," the man corrected.

"Well, *why*?" demanded Millman.

"I've been *busy*." The man's voice had an edge to it. "You're not the only line I have to deal with, you know."

"I'm *sorry*," Millman said in a shaking voice. "But you—" He broke off, frowning. "Why did you keep *ringing* me then?"

"Oh, was I ringing you? I didn't realize," the man's voice said.

Millman looked astonished as he heard a handset click down in his head, breaking the connection.

Seconds later, the telephone began to ring again.

No matter how often he answered it, there was no response.

The ringing continued almost until dawn, Millman lying wide-eyed on his bed, teeth clenched, hands like talons clutching at the sheets.

❖

"I was wondering what happened to you," Dr. Palmer said.

Millman drew in labored breath. "I thought I knew what it was," he said. "I thought I had to keep it quiet."

"Keep what quiet?" Dr. Palmer asked.

When Millman had finished telling him what happened, Dr. Palmer gazed at him without acknowledgment.

Millman swallowed nervously. "I'm still not sure I'm not making a mistake in telling you," he said, unable to endure the silence. "But he's driving me crazy, ringing me every night from three a.m. to six and never answering."

Dr. Palmer began to speak, hesitated, then finally said, "You believe this?"

Millman regarded him blankly.

"You believe it's a secret government project?" the therapist asked.

"Well—" Millman broke off in confusion. "That's what he *said*. He—"

The expression on Dr. Palmer's face stopped him.

"David," the therapist said. "Does it really make sense to you?"

Millman struggled for an answer. "I—" He stopped; braced himself. "I *hear* the telephone ringing," he said. "I *answer* it. The man's voice *speaks* to me. I'm not imagining it."

Dr. Palmer sighed. "David, think about it," he said. "A secret government project? Citizens picked at random? Microscopic telephones implanted in their brains without them knowing it? Espionage agents of the United States government transmitting information this way?" He looked at Millman challengingly.

Millman stared back, feeling a heavy weight on his back. Dear God, he thought.

He fought against the feeling. "But I *hear* the ringing," he insisted. "I *hear* the man's voice."

"David, not to alarm you," Dr. Palmer replied, "but hearing voices in one's head has been in the symptomatology tradition for a long time."

❧

Millman drank black coffee with supper that evening. He wanted to remain alert.

Lying on his bed in the dark, propped on pillows leaned against the headboard, he waited for the ringing of the telephone to start.

And thought about what Dr. Palmer had said.

He'd gotten angry at the therapist's remark about hearing voices in one's head. Was Dr. Palmer implying that he'd gone insane?

"Not at all," the therapist had reassured him. "What I'm saying is that you're undergoing some kind of mental constraint. That your mind is seeking out a method of redressing it."

"By dreaming up a phone call from some secret government project?" Millman had responded tensely.

"The means by which the human mind attempts to deal with hidden problems can be infinite," Dr. Palmer had told him.

The room was still. Millman heard the whirring of the electric alarm clock on the bedside table.

Was Palmer right? he wondered.

True, it did seem awfully farfetched that the national government would go to such lengths to conduct a project so outlandish.

Still, the alternative. . . .

Millman bared his teeth in anger. It was all irrelevant anyway. If the man's voice didn't answer any more— and it hadn't in a week— what difference did it make? Palmer might be convinced that presently the voice would speak to him again because it needed to, but he was certainly not—

Millman caught his breath, jerking back against the headboard as the telephone began to ring. His gaze jumped to the clock. It was three.

He let the ringing go on for thirty seconds before mentally picking up the handset and saying, "Yes?"

"We're very displeased with you," the man's voice said; Millman tensed at the tone of it. "You were asked not to say anything about the project, weren't you?"

Millman swallowed nervously.

"Weren't you?" the man's voice snapped.

"Yes, but—"

"You were told it was a matter of national security," the man's voice cut him off. "Yet still you told your therapist."

Millman couldn't seem to fill his lungs with air. He made a wheezing sound. "How do you know?" he asked, his voice frail and breathless.

"Figure it out," the man's voice said. "If we can hear your voice when you speak to *us*. . . ."

He didn't finish. Millman shuddered. *Every word?* he thought in dismay. *Every single word I say?*

He struggled to resist. "You know what he told me then," he said. "You know what he thinks you are."

"Sure," the man's voice answered scornfully. "I'm not Agent 25409-J. I'm not William J. Lonsdale. I'm not married with three children. I don't work for the C.I.A. I'm your goddamn subconscious mind. Jesus, Millman. What the hell's the matter with you?"

Millman had no answer. He lay immobile, staring up into the darkness. He thought he heard the breathing of the man on the other end of the line.

"All right, listen to me," the man's voice said then. "We're going to try to cut you off the circuit. We *have* been trying for a week now; that's why we haven't spoken to you. I'll put it on priority now that you've blabbed to your therapist about us. Jesus, Millman!"

Millman heard the sound of a handset being set down.

Hard.

"But don't you *see?*" Palmer said with a smile. "Your subconscious mind was reacting angrily to having its ruse exposed. A step forward, David."

"He said he was going to cut me off the circuit."

Dr. Palmer shook his head, still smiling. "He won't cut you off," he said. "He has things to say."

"What if I don't want to listen to him anymore?" Millman said.

"David," Dr. Palmer said. "*David.* Con*sider.* You're being given an invaluable opportunity: to engage in dialogue with your own subconscious mind."

"What if the voice keeps picking on me?" Millman asked.

The therapist's gesture was casual.

"Hang up on him," he said.

✦

When the telephone began to ring in his head, Millman was loathe to answer it. The resonating jangle of the bell set his teeth on edge. Even so, it was preferable to the man's potentially abusive voice.

He remained immobile on the bed, a flinching expression on his face.

Could he hang up on the man?

Further, could he snatch up the invisible handset after the connection had been broken, making it impossible for the man to call him anymore? He imagined hearing a dial tone in his head, then an operator's voice, breaking in to tell him he should hang up if he wanted to make a call.

Millman scowled. Now he really *was* beginning to think like a man who was losing his mind.

Abruptly, he picked up the imaginary handset and said, "Hello."

"Thank you for answering," the man's voice said.

Millman tightened. *Now what?*" he thought.

"I apologize for speaking out of turn during our last conversation," the man's voice said. "It was uncalled for."

"Yes, it was," Millman said impulsively.

"I'm sorry," the man replied. Before Millman could respond, he continued. "Listen," he said, "I'm going to level with you."

Millman's eyes narrowed. *Now* what? he wondered.

"This government project thing," the voice went on. "It's all a lie."

Without thinking, Millman drew his left hand near his face to stare at it as though he actually held a handset in his grip.

"There's no such thing," the man confessed. "Your Dr. Palmer was correct. It *doesn't* make sense. Microscopic telephones implanted secretly in people's brains? I can't believe you bought it."

Millman made a sound of spluttering exasperation.

"I'll tell you what it is," the man's voice said. "I won't give you my name because I'm afraid you might report me to the police. They'd lock me up and throw the key away if they found out what I'm doing."

"What are you talking about *now?*" Millman demanded furiously.

"I'm an inventor," the man's voice said. "I've developed an apparatus which radiates short-wave energy that penetrates the mind of anyone the beamer is directed at, enabling two-way conversation with them. You're the first."

Millman couldn't tell if he felt horrified or enraged. The clashing emotions kept him speechless.

"I know this is as hard to believe as the government project idea," the man's voice continued. "The government would love to get their hands on this, I guarantee you. I'd destroy it first though. It gives me the creeps thinking what our government would do with this device. I'd never—"

Millman broke in fiercely. *"Why are you doing this to me?"* he demanded.

"As I said," the man's voice answered patiently, "I chose you as my first subject. I didn't have the nerve to tell you what was really going on so I made up the story about a government project when all the time—"

It all burst out explosively from Millman. *"Bullshit!"* he snarled. "I don't believe this story any more than I believe the other! You're no inventor! My therapist's been right all the time! You're my own—"

"You *fool!*" the man's voice cut him off. "You goddamned fool!"

Millman tried to answer but the words choked in his throat.

"You just can't leave well enough alone, can you?" the man's voice criticized him. "Just can't let me do this my own way. No! Not you! You're too goddamned smart for that!"

The animal-like sound the man made drowned out Millman's faint reply. "Well, you're *not* smart! Not at all!" the man's voice cried. "You're *dumb!* You always *have* been dumb! A dumb boy and a stupid man! Davie, you're an *idiot!*"

Millman lurched in shock as the handset crashed down in his head.

He lay in silence, struggling for breath.

He knew the voice.

❄️

Dr. Palmer gazed at him without a word.

Millman drew in a laboring breath. "I have to tell you something about my family," he said. "Something I never told you before."

"Yes?" asked Dr. Palmer.

"My mother suffered from dissociated consciousness," Millman said. "I mean, she was psychic. I won't go into details but she proved it many times."

"Yes?" Dr. Palmer's tone was still noncommittal.

"I think I inherited her ability," Millman told him.

The therapist had difficulty repressing a look of aggravation. "You're suggesting—" he began.

"I'm *telling*," Millman broke in irritably. "You were *right*. It's not a secret government project and it's certainly not what the man's voice told me last night."

"Instead—" Dr. Palmer prodded.

"It's my father," Millman answered.

The therapist didn't reply. He rubbed his lowered eyelids with the thumb and forefinger of his left hand. Millman felt a tightening of resentment in his body.

Dr. Palmer opened his eyes. "You believe that he's communicating with you from 'the other side' as it were?" he asked.

Millman nodded, features hardening. "I *do*."

The therapist sighed.

"Very well," he said. "Let's talk about it."

✦

The instant the telephone rang in his head, Millman snatched up the imagined handset. "I'm here," he said.

"That was prompt," the man's voice replied.

"I know who you are," Millman told him.

"You do." Millman had a fleeting impression of his father's face, a smile of faint amusement on it.

"Yes, I do," Millman answered. "Father."

The man chuckled. "So you've caught me," he said.

Millman was unable to control a throat-catching sob. *"Why are you doing this?"* he asked.

"Why?" the voice responded incredulously. "Why do I want to speak to my only begotten son? You ask such a question, *Davie*? Is it so difficult to comprehend?"

Millman was crying now. Tears ran off the sides of his face, soaking into the pillow case. *"Pop,"* he murmured.

"I want you to listen to me now," his father's voice continued.

Millman's chest hitched as he sobbed.

"Are you listening?" his father's voice inquired.

"Yes." Millman rubbed the trembling fingertips of his right hand over his eyes.

"The reason I'm calling you," his father's voice went on, "is that I feel you should be cognizant of certain things."

"What things?" Millman asked.

"You don't know?" his father's voice responded.

"No," Millman sniffled, rubbing a finger underneath his dripping nostrils.

His father's sigh was deep. "I'll have to tell you then," he said.

Millman waited.

"You're a loser," his father's voice told him.

"What?" asked Millman.

"I have to *explain?*" said his father's voice. "You leave me *nothing?* All right; I'll lay it on the line then. You married a bitch. You let her bleed you dry in every way. You let her poison the minds of your two sons against you. You let her divorce proceeding take you to the cleaners. You let her rip away your *manhood.*

"On top of that, you're a loser at your job. You let that moron boss of yours kick you around like a ball. You scrape to him and let him treat you like a piece of dog shit. *Dog shit,* Davie! Don't bother to deny! You know it's true! You're a loser in every department of life and you *know* it!"

Millman felt as though paralysis had gripped him, body and mind.

"Can you deny a single word I've spoken?" his father's voice challenged.

Millman sobbed. "Pop," he murmured pleadingly.

"Don't Pop me, you goddamn loser!" his father's voice lashed back. "I'm ashamed to call you my son! Thank God I'm dead and don't have to see you getting kicked around day after day!"

Millman cried out, agonized. "Pop, *don't!*"

Dr. Palmer rose from his chair and walked to the window. He had never done that before and Millman watched him uneasily, dabbing at his reddened eyes with a tear-clotted handkerchief. The therapist stood with his back to Millman, looking out at the street.

After a while, he returned to his chair and sat down with a tired grunt. He gazed at Millman silently. What kind of gaze was it? Millman wondered. Compassionate?

Or fed up?

"I don't do this ordinarily," Dr. Palmer began. "You know my method: to let you find the answers yourself. However—"

He exhaled heavily and clasped his hands beneath his chin. "I feel as though I simply can't allow this to proceed the way it's going," he continued. "I have to say something to you. I have to say—" he winced "—*enough*, David."

Millman stared at the therapist.

"I do not believe—any more than I believe it was a secret government project or an isolated inventor—that your father is communicating with you from beyond the grave. I believe, as I have from the start, that your subconscious mind has, somehow, found a way to speak to you *audibly*. Trying to establish some kind of resolution to your mental problems."

"But it's *his voice*," Millman insisted.

"David," Dr. Palmer's voice was firm now. "You believed it was the voice of Secret Agent 25409-J. You then believed, albeit briefly, that it was the voice of some inventor. Can't you see that this subconscious voice of yours *can make itself sound like anyone it chooses*?"

David felt helpless. He knew he couldn't bear any more of the abuse his father's voice had heaped on him. At the same time, he felt sick about the possibility of losing touch with his father.

"What should I do?" he asked in a feeble voice.

"*Confront it,*" Dr. Palmer urged. "Stop just listening and suffering and *talk back*. Start *retaliating*. Demand answers; explanations. Speak *up* for yourself. It's *your* subconscious, David. Hear it out but don't permit it to harass you mercilessly. *Take control.*"

Millman felt exhausted. "If only I could sleep," he murmured.

"That I can give you something for," the therapist said.

⊷

He couldn't confront the voice that night. He did as Dr. Palmer prescribed and took two capsules, sleeping deeply and without remembrance. If the telephone rang in his head, he didn't hear it.

It relaxed him enough to enjoy a good night's rest. At work the following day, he even found Mr. Fitch endurable. Once, he almost spoke back to him but managed to repress the impulse. There was no point in losing his job on top of everything else.

During the evening, Millman thought about Elaine and the boys.

Had the voice—whoever it belonged to—spoken the truth? *Was* Elaine a bitch who'd poisoned the minds of his sons against him? Was that why their behavior, when they saw him, was so remote? He'd told himself it was because they got together so infrequently; that he was virtually a stranger to them.

What if it was more than that?

It *was* true that the divorce settlement had left him very little. Still, it had been *his* choice. He didn't have to give her so much.

Thinking of it all made Millman tense and edgy, ready to confront the voice.

At three a.m., when the ringing in his head began, he grabbed the unseen handset and yanked it to his head. "I'm here," he said.

"*Are* you, Davie?" his father's voice responded scornfully.

"You can cut it out now," Millman answered.

"Cut what out, little boy?" his father's voice inquired mockingly.

Millman braced himself. It took all the will he had to resist that voice which had intimidated him throughout his childhood and adolescence.

"You're not my father," he said.

Silence.

Then his father's voice said, "I'm not?"

"No, you're not," Millman said, trying to keep his voice strong.

"Who *am* I then?" his father's voice asked. "The King of Siam?"

Millman shuddered with uncertain anger. *"I don't know,"* he admitted. "I only know you're not my father."

"You're a stupid boy," his father's voice responded. "You've always been a stupid boy."

"I defy you!" Millman cut him off. *"You're not my father!"*

"Who *am* I then?" the voice demanded.

"Me!" cried Millman. "My subconscious mind!"

"Your *subconscious mind?*" The voice broke into sudden laughter; totally insane, the laughter of a maniac.

"Stop it," Millman said.

The laughing continued, uncontrolled, deranged. Millman visualized a face behind it—white and twisted, staring, wild-eyed.

"Stop it," he ordered.

The laughter rose in pitch and volume. It began to echo in his head.

He had to mentally slam down the handset three times before the laughter cut off.

His hands almost vibrating they shook so badly, he washed down a pair of capsules.

When the telephone began to ring inside his head again, he tried to ignore it, waiting tensely for the drug to lower him into a heavy, deafened sleep.

The tiny, black-haired woman opened the door to her apartment and looked at Millman questioningly. She didn't look as old as he knew her to be.

"I spoke to you on the telephone this afternoon," he said. "I'm Myra Millman's son."

"Ah, yes." Mrs. Danning's false teeth showed in a smile as she stepped back to admit him.

There was a smell of burning incense in the dimly lit living room. Millman noticed crosses and religious paintings on the walls while he moved to the chair the tiny woman pointed at. He sat down, hoping that he wasn't making a mistake. Momentarily, he imagined Dr. Palmer's reaction to this. The idea made his throat feel dry.

Mrs. Danning perched on a chair across from him and asked him to repeat his story.

Millman told her everything from its beginning to the manic laughter. Mrs. Danning nodded when he spoke about the laughter. "That may well provide the clue," she declared. He wondered what she meant by that.

He watched in anxious silence as she closed her eyes and began to draw in deep, laboring breaths, both hands on her lap, palms facing upward.

Several minutes later, her features hardened with a look of disdain. "So," she said. "Now you see a psychic." Mrs. Danning bared her teeth so much that Millman saw her pale gums. "You just won't listen, will you?" she said. "You have to keep investigating. *Asshole!*"

Millman twitched on his chair, eyes fixed on the psychic. She had begun to rock back and forth, a humming in her throat. "Oh, yes," she said after a while. "Oh, yes." She repeated the words so many times that Millman lost count of them.

After ten minutes, she opened her eyes and looked at Millman. He began to speak but she raised her right hand to prevent it. He waited as she picked up a glass of water from the table beside her chair and gulped down every drop of it. She sighed.

"I think we have it now," she said.

"For God's sake, David!" Dr. Palmer cried. Millman had never heard such disapproval in the therapist's voice.

"I wasn't going to come back," he said defensively. "Wasn't going to tell you. But I thought you might be sympathetic."

"To what this woman told you?" Dr. Palmer asked, appalled. "That you're being possessed by some— some—?" He gestured angrily.

"Earthbound spirit," Millman said, willfully. "A disincarnate soul held prisoner by the magnetism of the living, doing everything he can to—"

"David, David." Dr. Palmer looked exasperated and despairing at the same time. "We're losing ground. Every time we get together, we seem to fall back a little more."

"The spirit is not at peace." Millman's voice was stubbornly insistent. "It wants to experience life again. So it invades my mind—"

"David—!" the therapist cut him off. *"Please!"*

Millman pushed up from his chair. "Oh, what's the use?" he muttered.

"Sit down," Dr. Palmer told him. Millman stood before the chair, unable to decide.

"Please sit down," the therapist requested quietly.

Millman didn't move at first. Then he sat back down, a look of sullen accusation on his face. "I don't think you appreciate—" he began.

"I appreciate that you are going through one hell of an ordeal," Dr. Palmer broke in.

"But you don't believe a word I've said."

"David, use your head," the therapist replied. *"Did you really think I would?"*

Millman blew out tired breath.

"I suppose not," he conceded.

He had never in his life felt so divided in his mind—so torn between desire and dread.

On the one hand, he wanted the telephone to ring in his head so he could resolve this madness.

On the other hand, he was terror-stricken by what might happen if he answered it.

Easy enough for Palmer to repeat his conviction that it was his subconscious mind.

What if he was wrong?

Millman was thinking that for what might well have been the hundredth time when the telephone began to ring in his head.

He drew in a long, slow, chest-expanding breath of air, then let it out until his lungs felt empty. All right, he told himself.

The time had come.

He saw the handset in his mind. Saw his left hand pick it up. Almost felt the earpiece press against his head. *"Yes,"* he said aloud.

"This is your father," the voice replied.

Millman answered, "No."

"What did you say?" The image of his father's face appeared in Millman's mind: thin-lipped, critical.

"You're not my father," he said.

"Who am I then?"

"I don't know," Millman answered desolately. "I just know you're not my father." Amazingly, he *did* know it now.

"You're right," the man's voice told him.

Millman started. *Was this the beginning of some new ploy?* he wondered. "Who *are* you then?" he demanded.

"This is a secret government project and I'm Agent 25409-J—" the man's voice started.

"Stop it," Millman said through clenched teeth. "Don't start that again. I won't have it."

"I'm an inventor," said the voice. "I've created a device that—"

"*Stop* it," Millman cut him off.

"Right," the man's voice said. "This is your father."

"*Stop* it, damn it!" Millman cried.

"Correct," the man's voice said. "I'm an earthbound spirit possessing you."

"God damn it, that's enough!" Millman shouted. He felt his heartbeat pound.

"*Right,*" the man's voice said. "This is Krol. I'm speaking to you from the planet Mars."

"I'm hanging up," Millman said.

He imagined doing it.

"You can't hang up," the voice informed him. "It's too late for that."

Millman stiffened. "Yes, I can," he said. He tried again to put the handset down.

"I'm *telling* you," the voice said coldly. "You can't *do* it anymore."

Millman made a frightened sound and tried again.

"You *should* be frightened," said the voice. "I'm going to kill you now."

Millman's body spasmed with a shudder. He slammed the handset down on its invisible cradle.

"I'm going to kill you now," the voice repeated.

"Get away from me," said Millman.

"Not so." The man's voice was one of cruel amusement. "You're mine now, little porker. Don't you know who this really is?"

"*Get away from me.*" Millman's voice was trembling now.

"All right, I'll tell you who I am," the man's voice said. "I have many names. One of them is Prince of Liars. Isn't that a gas?"

Millman shook his head, teeth gritted hard. Again and again, he slammed down the unseen handset.

"You're wasting time, little porker," said the man's voice. "I'm in charge now. Want to hear some other names? Lord of Vermin. Prince of Sinners. Serpent. Goat. Old Nick. Old *Davy*! Isn't *that* a gas?!"

"Get away from me!" cried Millman. "I won't listen to you anymore!"

"Yes you will!" the voice cried back. "You're mine now and I'm going to kill you!" The maniacal laughter began again.

Millman reached for the vial of capsules.

"That won't do you any good," the man's voice told him gleefully. "You can't escape me now."

Millman didn't try to answer. Shaking uncontrollably, he picked the cap off, shaking two capsules onto his palm.

"*Two*?" the man's voice asked. "Not half enough, old man. You'll never get away from me. You're mine, I'm going to kill you dead."

The laughter started in again, booming in some cavern in his mind.

Millman washed a pair of capsules down his throat, water spilling across his chin.

"Not half enough!" the man's voice cried, exultantly. He continued laughing with demented joy.

Millman pressed another capsule in his mouth, another, washed them down.

"*Not half enough*!" the man's voice yelled at him. "*You've let me in too long!*"

Millman's palsied hand shoved capsules in his mouth. He washed them down. The glass was empty now. He gulped down capsules dry, his face a mask of terror.

"Secret government project!" howled the voice. "Inventor! Father! Earthbound spirit! Krol from Mars! The Devil! Take another capsule, David!"

Millman lay on his right side on the bed, legs drawn up, twitching. *God, please take me out of here!* he kept begging, sobbing helplessly.

"*Your wish is my command,*" the voice said finally.

Inside his head, the telephone began to ring.

He lay in his bed, hands clasped behind his head, grinning at the sound.

Then he chuckled, picking up the handset in his mind. *"Ye*-es," he said musically.

"Please," the man's voice said.

"Please?" he said as though he didn't understand. "Please what?"

"Please let me back."

"Oh, no," he chided. "After all the trouble I went to? Keeping you so occupied you never dreamed what was coming? After all that work, you want me to let you *back*?"

His face became a mask of feral animosity.

"*Never*, asshole," he said. "You are out of here for good."

"No!" the man's voice cried.

He snickered. "Gotta go now, babe," he said.

He put the handset down, giggling as he visualized the look of shock on Davie's face. The little shit would try again of course, he knew.

While he waited for the ringing to begin, he made his plans for to-morrow.

First, a call to Elaine. Not another fucking nickel, bitch. And tell that pair of cretins you dropped not to bother me again.

As for Fitch—his eyes lit up—what sheer delight it was going to be to smash that ugly bastard in the mouth and stalk out on that nowhere job.

Then off to enjoy himself. Travel. Women. Fun. Women.

He'd worry about money when he ran out of it.

As for Palmer—he laughed aloud—the clever son of a bitch had it right all the time.

Now let him try to collect his bill!

He was cackling at the idea when the telephone began to ring in his head.

With a hissing smirk, he reached into his mind and yanked out all the wires. The ringing stopped abruptly. There, he thought.

He wouldn't need that line any more.